His hand moved, hot and slightly rough, against the bare skin of her upper arm. She shivered as he gripped her naked shoulder. He caressed her, his expression one of mystification. His thumb glided along the shaft of her collarbone, and back again, robbing the breath from her lungs. She felt dizzy, and as he swayed slightly, so did she.

She saw his throat move as he swallowed. He sighed and closed his eyes, his hands urging her toward him until she was crushed against him. She thought she heard him murmur her name....

She should return to her own chamber....

Just a few more moments. She closed her eyes and settled against him, feeling the heat from his half-naked body through the thin silk of her gown....

HEAVEN'S FIRE

by

Patricia Ryan

A TOPAZ BOOK

TOPAZ
Published by the Penguin Group
Penguin Books USA Inc., 375 Hudson Street,
New York, New York 10014, U.S.A.
Penguin Books Ltd, 27 Wrights Lane,
London W8 5TZ, England
Penguin Books Australia Ltd, Ringwood,
Victoria, Australia
Penguin Books Canada Ltd, 10 Alcorn Avenue,
Toronto, Ontario, Canada M4V 3B2
Penguin Books (N.Z.) Ltd, 182–190 Wairau Road,
Auckland 10, New Zealand

Penguin Books Ltd Registered Offices:
Harmondsworth, Middlesex, England

Published by Topaz, an imprint of Dutton Signet,
a division of Penguin Books USA Inc.

First Printing, October, 1996
10 9 8 7 6 5 4 3 2

 REGISTERED TRADEMARK—MARCA REGISTRADA

.Printed in Canada

In loving memory of my father,
Dan Lacy Burford,
an enlightened man of learning
who would have felt right at home
in medieval Oxford

ACKNOWLEDGMENTS

Heartfelt thanks to Kelly Cannizzaro for being such a good friend and sharing so generously of her medical expertise.

Thanks also to Dr. Joan Chisolm for her very creative help with some of the medical aspects of this story.

As always, I owe a debt of gratitude to my critique partners, Kathy Schaefer and Rina Najman; and to my twin sister, best friend, and most ruthless editor, Pamela Burford Loeser.

Finally, thank you, Leah Bassoff and Audrey LaFehr, for your vision and enthusiasm.

For thee the fates, severely kind, ordain
A cool suspense from pleasure and from pain;
Thy life a long, dead calm of fix'd repose;
No pulse that riots, and no blood that glows.
Still as the sea, 'ere winds were taught to blow,
Or moving spirit bade the waters flow;
Soft as the slumbers of a saint forgiv'n,
And mild as opening gleams of promis'd heav'n.
  Come Abelard! for what hast thou to dread?
The torch of Venus burns not for the dead;
Nature stands check'd; Religion disapproves;
Ev'n thou art cold—yet Eloisa loves.

From "Eloisa to Abelard,"
by Alexander Pope

Prologue

"Why'd you have to die, Sully?" Constance whispered to her husband as she bent her head to the task of sewing him into his shroud. "You weren't all *that* old."

Old enough, though. Close to sixty, if she had to guess, which made him old enough to be her grandfather. Nevertheless, it had been something of a cruel surprise to wake up that morning and discover his lifeless body in bed next to her. She couldn't begin to guess what malady had claimed him during the night. The world harbored countless mysterious ills. No one could be expected to comprehend all of them.

Constance didn't understand, but she did grieve—not only for Sully, but for herself. As she patiently worked the needle in and out of the heavy linen, she pondered the matter of her uncertain fate. What would become of her, now that Sully was gone? Pausing in her labor, she stretched her back and gazed around at the interior of the humble cottage in which she had spent the past two of her eighteen years, wedded to the village smithy.

The deerskin tacked over the doorway flew open, and Constance blinked at the stout figure silhouetted against the afternoon sun. It was the reeve's wife, an amiable woman of middle years. Her breath came in harsh gasps, and her face was bright red. "Constance! Run!"

"Ella, what are you—?"

"Now!" Ella yanked Constance from her stool and pushed her toward the doorway. "Sir Roger's coming for you!"

"Dear God." The young widow crossed herself. "Already? Sully's not even in his grave."

"The old swine's not wasting any time. He told Hugh he let you slip through his fingers once, and he don't mean to let it happen again."

"Is he on foot or horseback?" Constance asked, her heart tripping in her chest.

"Horseback," said Ella, "with rope to tie you up if you resist him. Go! If you follow the stream and run north through the woods, toward Oxford—"

"It won't work, Ella. You know that. Even if I could make it as far as Oxford, he'll have me found and brought back. You've seen what happens to the ones who've tried to escape. You've seen what they look like when they come back."

Ella shivered and looked away. Runaways were always returned in the dead of night, and always mutilated to one degree or another—especially the women.

"I'm quite fond of my eyes and my tongue," Constance said. "I've no desire to lose them."

"You always said you'd die rather than be Sir Roger's whore," Ella said. "You don't mean to . . . you're not going to . . ."

"Kill myself? Nay, 'twould bring too much satisfaction to Sir Roger."

"Satisfaction? He wants to lie with you, not bury you."

"Aye, but the priests say you're damned to hell if you take your own life, and Sir Roger thinks every word out of a priest's mouth is the voice of God Himself."

Ella nodded. "True enough. From the way he acts

with Father Osred, I'd say he's scared to death of the old hen."

Constance pondered that for a moment, and an idea began to take shape in her mind.

"Please, Constance," Ella urged, "will you *please* leave here before Sir Roger comes?"

"Aye." She took her friend's hands and nodded toward her late husband, laid out on the bed in his half-sewn shroud. "If you'll stay and tend to Sully."

"Of course. Just go!"

Constance kissed Ella on the cheek, then left the cottage and began walking purposefully to the south.

"Not that way!" Ella shouted from the doorway. "North, through the woods. Hurry!"

Constance did hurry—she ran, in fact—but not to the north. She raced on quaking legs to the rectory, praying that Father Osred would be home when she got there.

From the moment Constance had blossomed into womanhood at the advanced age of sixteen, Sir Roger Foliot had made no secret of his intention to bed her. The fat petty knight saw his villeins as naught but chattel, the males to be worked to early graves, the females—if they were comely—to amuse him in his bed and bear his bastards, be they willing or not. Moreover, it was whispered that he took pleasure from giving pain, and considering the bruised faces and vacant stares of the women he used, Constance had little doubt that this was true.

It was to escape Sir Roger's attentions that she had married Sully Smith, at the insistence of her father as he lay on his deathbed with a fever of the chest.

"Sir Roger's a loathsome creature, but he respects marriage," her father had counseled. "He fears the Church and reveres its sacraments. Marry Sully, and Sir Roger will leave you be."

And it had worked. But now Sully was dead, and Roger Foliot was coming for her.

As she approached the rectory, a thatched stone dwelling behind the church, she became aware of distant hoofbeats. Turning, she saw Sir Roger, mounted on his big black gelding, following her at a gallop.

"Father Osred!" she screamed, beating on the door with her fists. "Father Osred, let me in!"

The door swung open and she fell, gasping for air, into the arms of the elderly rector. "Constance! Easy, child."

"Father! He's coming for me!"

"Who?"

"Sir Roger!" She slammed the door closed and shoved the bolt across with trembling hands. "He couldn't even wait till Sully was in the ground."

The priest's expression went from puzzled to knowing. "Ah. Yes. Sir Roger ..."

She grabbed fistfuls of his black robe and drilled her gaze into his. "Help me, Father. Please. Don't let him take me."

The old man shook his head and tried to pry Constance's fingers loose, but she was too strong, and held on.

"Child, please," he implored. "I don't have as much influence with Sir Roger as people think. Even if I could send him away now, he'd come for you tonight—"

"Then let me stay here with you."

He blinked. "Stay here?"

"He wouldn't take me from under your very roof— I'm sure of it. I could keep house for you, like Maida did." Father Osred's housekeeper had died on All Saints' Day of a tiny scratch on her foot that had festered and poisoned her blood.

"Child, I—"

A furious pounding shook the front door. "Let me in!" bellowed Sir Roger from the other side—in French, of course. To Constance's knowledge, he'd never

learned a word of his villeins' language. "Come now,
Constance. Don't make me tie you up."

"Father, *please!*"

The priest backed up, but Constance didn't let go.
" 'Twould anger Sir Roger something fierce," he said.
"He'd know I was taking you in just to protect you
from him."

More thunderous battering on the door; the old
man flinched.

"What of it?" Constance challenged. "He's afraid
of you."

Father Osred shook his head. "He's afraid of Hell,
my dear. I must tread cautiously with Roger Foliot.
The day I push him too far is the day he demands a
more compliant parish priest. I'm an old man. What
would become of me if I had to leave Cuxham?"

"Constance!" screamed Sir Roger. "Don't make me
break this door down and take you by force!"

"Please, Father," she begged. "Let me stay. I'll
serve you well. I swear it. I'll do everything Maida
used to do."

The old priest looked down at her, his eyes lighting
with sudden interest. "Everything?"

"Yes, of course. Everything. Can I stay?"

He held her at arm's length and inspected her
slowly, head to toe. She wished she had bothered to
comb and braid her hair that morning. Hanging to her
knees in an inky black tangle, it gave her an unkempt
air, hardly what a respected rector would seek in a
housekeeper. Worse yet, she still had on the ragged
old kirtle in which she had washed Sully's body and
prepared it for burial. Her heart sank as she noticed
his attention linger wherever the damp wool clung to
her slender frame.

He met her gaze again, his eyes glittering darkly.
For a moment she was confused, but when he nodded
and said, "Yes—you may stay," she grabbed his hands
and kissed them.

"Thank you, Father. Thank you!"

"Open up, Father!" demanded Sir Roger. "Hand over the girl, and I'll be on my way."

The priest motioned for her to stand behind him, and then unbolted and opened the door. Constance peeked over his shoulder to see Roger Foliot's obese, brocade-clad form filling the doorway. He stood with hands on hips, a coil of rope looped around one wrist, glowering like an enraged bear. "Give her over, Father."

The rector's back stiffened. He made his reply in stony French, which Constance could follow passably well. "I'm sorry I can't oblige you, Sir Roger. Perhaps you weren't aware, but young Constance has consented to take over my cooking and cleaning, now that Maida has departed from this world." He somberly crossed himself.

Sir Roger frowned, his mouth agape. As ever, Constance was struck by how very much his face resembled a pan of bread dough, fully risen and waiting to be punched down. His dark little eyes narrowed until they were barely visible within the surrounding pink flesh. "What wicked scheme is this, Father? I claimed her first, and by God's Eyes I mean to—"

"Do you take the name of our Lord in vain even while you seek to make this girl your unwilling mistress? Do you?"

This forceful speech surprised Constance, and Sir Roger as well, judging from his perplexed expression and hasty sign of the cross. "I ... it's just not right, Father. She's to be mine now."

"She's to serve the Church now," the priest corrected, "by serving me. She will keep the rectory tidy and prepare my meals and tend to my needs."

The petty knight nodded slowly, a salacious grin curling his fleshy lips. "Your needs, eh?" A flutter of apprehension tickled Constance's scalp.

Father Osred took a step toward Sir Roger, who,

to Constance's astonishment, took a step back. "Such speculation is unseemly. As I said, young Constance is to serve the Church. And I daresay there must be a special place in Hell for one who would force a girl to commit sins of the flesh rather than serve as housekeeper to a harmless old priest."

A flood of red stained Sir Roger's corpulent face. Constance swore she saw a flicker of fear in his eyes before he composed his features. But by the time he met her gaze, all she detected was a cold rage that made her tremble. "You win," he said softly. "For now."

Emboldened, Constance stepped out from behind Father Osred. "For always," she declared in her awkward, heavily accented French. "I'll never be your whore, Roger Foliot. The very thought sickens me."

Sir Roger arched an eyebrow. " 'Never' is a terribly long time, is it not? Especially when one insists on seeking the protection of such very old men. Old men, you see, tend to die. Someday our dear Father Osred"—he nodded in the priest's direction—"will leave you to join his Maker, and then, rest assured that you will be mine."

Constance lifted her chin. "If you think for a moment I'd ever give myself to you . . ."

The fat knight chuckled. "Give yourself to me? Whatever makes you think I'd want you to? Aye, there are some men who like their pleasure handed to them like a tray of sweets. But I find there is greater pleasure to be gained by taking that which is not so freely offered—and I've the scratch marks to prove it. So don't comfort yourself with the naive notion that your resistance will deter me. And don't think for a moment that we're through with each other. You've outwitted me twice, but I'll be damned if I'll let it happen a third time."

He glanced again at the priest before adding, in measured tones, "If I were you, dear Constance, I'd make it a point to pray that the good Father Osred lives a long and healthy life. For when he is taken, I swear that nothing will keep you from me."

Turning, he heaved himself with a grunt into his saddle.

Constance shut the door, leaned back against it, and closed her eyes. "Thank God," she whispered.

When she opened her eyes, she saw Father Osred looking at her strangely. He cleared his throat. "Come."

Constance followed him into the other room, a small chamber as bare and gloomy as the rest of the house. She saw a large crucifix next to a window, and below it, a washbasin on a stand. Robes and vestments hung from hooks on the walls, against which stood several large wooden chests, and a bed. Father Osred swept aside the bed curtains, pulled down the quilt, and pressed a bony hand into the mattress. "Feathers," he said with a smile. He beckoned her over. "I don't imagine you've ever lain on a feather mattress."

"Nay, Father." Constance began to feel curiously chilly all over. This was the only bed in the two-room rectory.

The priest nodded cheerfully and began untying his robe. "You'll find this bed to your liking, I wager. Maida said she could never go back to a straw pallet after sleeping here."

Stunned, Constance crossed to the window and stared out at the churchyard as Father Osred continued to disrobe. "Father, I ..." *I what? Be careful what you say or you may find yourself turned away from here, and easy pickings for Sir Roger.*

She'd heard the whispers about Father Osred and Maida, but had paid them no heed. Now that marriage was forbidden to priests, many kept mistresses instead, a practice merely winked at by parishioners and church officials alike. But Father Osred was so old, and Maida, although much younger, had been plain and pious. But it appeared the whispers had been true. Constance had been such a fool. . . .

I'll do everything Maida used to do. And now he was taking her at her word.

"Constance?" She looked back over her shoulder to find him wearing naught but a long shirt, and pointing to an empty hook. "You can hang your things up here."

Dismayed at the bargain she had unwittingly struck, Constance considered her options. If she were to flee, Sir Roger would have her found and brought back. From among the many headstones in the churchyard, her eyes sought out that of young Hildreth, who had run away from Roger Foliot last summer and been returned in pitiful condition. Her body had been discovered that day, facedown in the river. Although the death had been judged accidental, Constance suspected she had taken her own life rather than spend the rest of her days freakishly disfigured.

She felt Father Osred unlacing the back of her kirtle. His touch, like Sully's, was ice-cold, but the resemblance ended there. The smithy's hands had been huge and work-roughened, the priest's were as soft and delicate as a gentlewoman's.

All her life she'd dreamed of freedom—freedom from Sir Roger, from Cuxham, from the servitude demanded by her poverty and her sex. But it was a dream that would have to wait—for now. She must be patient. She must bide her time, but keep her eyes and ears open, alert to any opportunity to get away without drawing attention to herself. It might take years; she only hoped Father Osred lived that long.

Father Osred tugged the kirtle over her head and hung it up. But when he reached for her linen shift, she pushed his hands away. "Nay, let me keep this. It's chilly."

He nodded understandingly. "Of course." Taking her by the hand, he led her to the bed and urged her to lie down. "Are you cold? Do you want the quilt?"

"Yes. Please."

He's not really such a bad sort, she thought as he covered them both and fumbled with her shift. Since he was a much smaller man than Sully, there was considerably less discomfort when he got on top of her. The act itself was over scarcely before it had begun, for which she was grateful. Her husband used to take forever, leaving her painfully raw.

He rolled off her, and presently she heard a high-pitched, whistling snore from his side of the bed. She felt drowsy herself, remarkable given the day's turbulent events. *Must be the feathers,* she thought, snuggling into the fluffy mattress. No wonder Maida had liked this bed so much.

Just before she drifted off, a thought occurred to her. Taking pains to be quiet, she rose and knelt in the rushes at the side of the bed. And then she prayed with all her heart that Father Osred would live a long and healthy life.

Chapter 1

A thousand years have passed since the beginnings of a city rose above the water-meadows where the Cherwell meets the Thames. The low slope, climbing up from the two rivers to the crossing of the four ways at the top, gave its shape to the narrow rectangle of the town. Saxons, Danes and Normans built upon it, crowned it with churches, encompassed it with walls. Monks set up in the fields around it altars and cloisters for pilgrimage and prayer. The Middle Ages took possession of it, and filled it with their genius and their dreams, their high-wrought, restless enterprise, their vain debates. And, as superstition widened into study, and the demand for knowledge refused to be repressed, teachers and scholars gradually made the place their own. . . .

—From *A History of the University of Oxford, Volume I*, by Charles Edward Mallet

March 1161, Oxford

"Duck, Father!"

Rainulf of Rouen, also known as Rainulf Fairfax—Doctor of Logic and Theology, Magister Scholarum of Oxford, and ordained priest—lowered his head just in time to avoid being struck by a flying tankard of ale.

"What the—?"

"It's Victor, Father," said Thomas. The young, sandy-haired scholar pointed to the rear of the alehouse, where Victor of Asekirche was climbing on top of a table, cheered on by his rowdy friends. "He wasn't aiming for you," Thomas explained. "He's got a quarrel with Burnell."

Rainulf turned to see the tavern keeper—a huge, barrel-chested brute in a greasy apron—reach beneath the counter from which he dispensed his ale and meat pies.

"Uh-oh . . ." Rainulf swiftly drained his tankard and stood as Burnell produced a huge oaken club. He didn't particularly want to involve himself in this altercation, and he wouldn't, were it not for Burnell's reputation for viciousness. He'd savagely beaten more than one scholar since they began flocking to Oxford just a few short years ago. It was even rumored he'd been responsible for a young man found bludgeoned to death last August in an alley off Fish Street. Victor, despite his many faults, did not deserve such a fate.

"Put it down, Burnell," Rainulf said quietly.

"This is none of your affair, priest," Burnell growled in anglicized French. He hefted the club in a beefy hand as he muscled his way through the boisterous assemblage of half-drunk students. "I told that one not to come in here no more, but he don't listen too good." Gripping the club with both hands, he swung it back and forth through the dark, stale air of the tavern, sending his young patrons scattering. "He'll mind me now, I wager."

"He's afraid to have me come in here!" Victor declared to the black-robed scholars crowded around the table on which he stood, hands on hips. "And do you know why?"

Rainulf ran a weary hand through his short hair. Victor, with his dark, striking looks and firebrand temperament, exercised tremendous influence over his fellow scholars. Were he of a mind to, he could use that influence to help dampen the spark of discord between the students of Oxford and the city's businessmen. Instead, he chose to fan it into flames of rage.

Burnell advanced a step, shaking his weapon in the air. "*I'll* tell you why I don't want you here! 'Cause you're a troublemaker, plain and simple. You don't know when to shut up."

Victor crossed his arms over his chest and adopted a careless, hip-shot stance. "Oh, I know when to shut up, all right, and I will. *After* I've told everybody about the sewage-tainted water you brew your ale with."

Burnell's face darkened with fury. "What? You've got no proof—"

"And God knows what's in those meat pies."

Burnell raised the club. "You little—"

"If you charged a fair price, I might not mind so much," Victor said. "But on top of it all, you're a thief!"

"That's it! Come down here and fight me like a man!" Victor withdrew something from beneath his black robe. Rainulf saw the flash of steel and cursed under his breath. The bastard son of a priest, young Victor had spent two years as a mercenary soldier before coming to Oxford, where he'd put considerably more energy into picking fights than studying. It was almost as if he *wanted* to end up dead in an alley some night.

Victor jumped down from the table and sliced the dagger through the air.

"Victor!" Rainulf stepped between the two men. "Both of you. Let's go outside and talk about—"

"No more talk, Father," Victor spat out. "It's time for action." He raised his voice and looked around at his inebriated audience. "It's time to let the brewers and innkeepers and landlords of Oxford know that those of us who've come here to study will not lie down for this kind of treatment anymore! It's time to demand decent food and drink and clean, safe rooms for our money!"

Cries of "Hear, hear!" filled the tavern.

Rainulf gestured toward the blade in Victor's hand. "And you think that's the way?"

"It's the only way his kind"—he nodded grimly toward Burnell—"understands."

Burnell took a step toward Victor. "What's that supposed to mean?"

Victor stepped forward as well. "Let me state it simply, so you'll grasp my meaning. If I have a dog and it does something wrong, do I try to reason with it? Nay, 'twould be a waste of breath. I beat it, because that's all it understands. 'Tis the same with those men who are little more than beasts themselves—"

Burnell brandished the club. "Get out of my way, Father."

"Nay." Rainulf reached for the club. "Hand it over."

Burnell yanked it away and stepped around him, raising the weapon high as Victor turned toward him. In the space of a heartbeat, Rainulf seized a small bench off the floor and brought it swiftly upward. It shattered on impact with the club, but succeeded in halting its downward progress. The priest wrested the weapon from Burnell and hurled it into the sawdust that covered the floor.

Grabbing the plank that had formed the bench's seat, Rainulf wheeled to face Victor as he thrust his dagger toward the dazed tavern keeper. Throwing himself between the two, he slammed the plank into Victor's midsection. For a moment the hotheaded scholar froze, looking slightly confused. Then he sank to his knees in the sawdust, the dagger slipping out of his fingers. Rainulf kicked it away and tossed aside the plank.

Raking both hands through his hair, Rainulf addressed the wide-eyed onlookers. "It's over. Go back to your ale." As the crowd dispersed, Burnell's wife guided her husband into the back room. Rainulf hauled Victor to his feet and aimed him toward the door. "I won't always be around to protect you from your own foolishness, Victor. Take my advice and keep clear of Burnell." He gave a not-so-gentle shove, and the young man lurched out into the bright noon sunshine and stumbled away.

Thomas stared at him. "You handle yourself well, Father. Did you learn to fight like that in the Holy Land?"

"Nay—at the University of Paris. I didn't fight like that in the Holy Land."

Thomas frowned. "But surely, on Crusade, you fought—"

"To kill," Rainulf finished shortly. "That's a different kind of fighting."

Thomas seemed to digest that for a moment, and then he nodded toward the front door. "Do you know that fellow?"

The man standing in the doorway had hair the color of polished copper and a milk-white face showered with hundreds of freckles. He wore a plain, clean tunic and clutched a leather bag.

Rainulf shook his head. "I would have remembered those freckles."

The stranger scanned the room, stilling when his gaze lit on Rainulf. This interest did not surprise Rainulf in the least. His height alone often drew attention, and in this dank little student tavern, he would have seemed sorely out of place, being the only master present and—at six-and-thirty years—by far the oldest man.

"Are you the one they call Rainulf Fairfax?" the stranger asked, his gaze resting on the priest's flaxen hair—the feature that had earned him the surname from his students.

"Aye."

He looked down at Rainulf's black robe—not a clerical robe, as was usually worn, but the cappa of a secular master, the open front of which revealed an ordinary brown tunic and chausses beneath. "They told me you were a priest."

Someone in the crowd harrumphed; someone else chuckled.

"They were right—more or less," Rainulf answered. A few of the scholars laughed good-naturedly, but Rainulf maintained his neutral expression.

"Are you or aren't you?"

"Why is it so important?" Rainulf demanded.

"I need a priest who's had smallpox," said the red-haired man. "They told me you fit that description."

"They?"

The man shrugged. "A couple of the other masters. If they were mistaken, kindly tell me and I'll trouble you no further."

"They weren't mistaken. But what's this about the pox?"

"There's been a lot of it in the village of Cuxham the past few weeks. I need you to perform Last Rites."

"I'm a teaching priest," Rainulf said. "I haven't performed the offices of the Church in years. There must be a parish priest in Cuxham. Can't he do it?"

"He's *been* doing it," said the stranger. "Only now he's come down with it himself. A bad case, too, but hopefully one of the last ones—I think this outbreak has run its course. Anyway, Father Osred is dying, most likely, and I promised Sir Roger Foliot I'd bring back a priest to give him Last Rites. Only, I've got to find one who's already had the pox, so as not to spread the contagion."

The man sounded quite knowledgeable, so Rainulf asked, "Are you a physician?"

"A traveling surgeon. My name's Will Geary. So, will you go?"

Rainulf tried to summon up a good reason for refusing, but, failing to do so, he sighed heavily and nodded. "I'll go."

*   *   *

Rainulf stopped at his St. John Street town house in order to change into sturdy traveling clothes and pack the things he'd need in his saddlebag. As an afterthought, he searched for and found a tiny silver reliquary containing a lock of hair of St. Nicaise, and slipped it in among the vestments and vials.

It was unusually warm for March, and despite his grim mission, Rainulf found the journey to Cuxham a pleasant one. Keeping to the route suggested by Will Geary, he rode twelve miles to the southeast until he reached the mill that marked the northern boundary of Cuxham. From there, he followed the stream south through woods and farmland until, presently, he came upon the small stone and thatch parish church. Behind it stood the rectory, and he would have ridden directly to it had his eye not been drawn to a figure digging a grave in the churchyard. He drew up his mount and watched from a distance, strangely captivated by the sight.

It was a woman—her age indeterminate, for she faced away from him—dressed in a homespun kirtle, her black hair plaited in two long braids tied together in back. Next to her on the ground, shaded from the midafternoon sun by a yew tree, lay a corpse beneath a blanket.

Dismounting, Rainulf hobbled his bay stallion by the stream and approached the woman, who still seemed unaware of his presence. As he got closer, he saw not one, but two empty graves dug into the earth. One appeared to be finished, given the sizable mound of dirt next to it. The other was still but a shallow trench. It was this second, fresh grave on which the woman labored so industriously, yet hampered by fatigue, if the slowness of her movements was any indication.

Rainulf looked around for a second corpse, but could see none. He did notice, scattered among the weathered headstones in the churchyard, several fresh graves—victims of the pox, no doubt.

He paused about ten feet from the woman and cleared his throat. She gasped and spun around, holding the shovel as if to swing it. Her face bore a bright red flush, and her hands shook. Rainulf saw fear in her wide brown eyes, then confusion. "You're not . . ." she began in the old Anglo-Saxon tongue. "I thought perhaps you were Sir . . ." She took a deep breath, as if relieved, and lowered the shovel. "Who are you?"

Rainulf took a step toward her, but she raised the shovel again, and he stopped in his tracks.

"Don't come any closer," she said. She had an odd, husky voice, unexpected in a woman of such slight build.

Rainulf held both hands up, palms out. "Easy," he said in English. "I'm Rainulf Fairfax. *Father* Rainulf Fairfax, from Oxford."

Her gaze took in his short, tousled hair, over which he wore no skullcap, and his rough traveling costume. "You don't look like much of a priest."

"I'm not," he agreed dryly.

A spark of amusement flashed in her eyes. Taking this as encouragement, Rainulf stepped forward again, but she thrust the shovel at him. "Get back!"

"I won't hurt you," he said reassuringly.

She smiled somewhat wryly. "I didn't think you would. It's just that I've got the yellow plague, and I wouldn't want you to catch it."

Rainulf's gaze narrowed on her reddened face. What he'd thought at first to be a flush of fear had not subsided, nor had the trembling of her hands. He suspected that, were she to let him touch her, her skin would be burning hot. This was how this awful disease began, he knew—with fever and chills and that strange scarlet tinge to the face and body. The pox themselves would appear later.

"Rest your mind, then," he said. "I've had this affliction already. I can't catch it again."

Her eyes searched his face. "You've had this?"

"I had several interesting diseases while a guest of the Turks some years back. Smallpox—what you call the yellow plague—was one of them." He tilted his head, pointing to the two minuscule indentations on the side of his jaw.

Lowering the shovel, the woman approached him slowly, her gaze riveted on the scars. "That's all the pockmarks you've got?" she asked incredulously. "Just those?"

"I was lucky."

"*I'll* say." She inclined her head toward the corpse under the yew. "Father Osred didn't get off so easily."

Rainulf walked over to the body and squatted down. He reached for the edge of the blanket to uncover the face, but hesitated, smelling, in addition to the stench of death, the distinctive, sickening odor of the final stages of smallpox. It was an odor that conjured up vivid memories. Closing his eyes, he found himself transported back to the Levant, to that foul underground cell in which he and two dozen other young soldiers endured a year of hellish suffering, all in the name of Christ. Their torment found new depths when the pox swept through their stinking hole, claiming one out of every four men, and leaving most of the rest wishing they'd been taken.

Peeling back the blanket, Rainulf sucked in a breath and executed a hasty sign of the cross. The face on which he gazed was so densely covered with yellowish pustules as to completely mask its features. The poor creature's thin white hair was the only indication of age. Had Rainulf not known the body to be that of the rector, he might even have thought it to be female.

"It's best this way," the woman said. Rainulf turned to find her standing right behind him, leaning on the

shovel and staring thoughtfully at the dead priest. "He
went blind in the end. Some of them do, you know."

"I know." He swallowed hard. She looked at him
inquiringly, and he met her eyes, drawn to something
in them that surprised and touched him. Compassion.
She felt compassion . . . for him! Here she was, suffering from this appalling malady that killed and blinded
and disfigured; yet, sensing his own grief, his own
nightmare, she had it within her to feel sympathy for
him.

A most strange woman, he thought, holding her
gaze. In the warm depths of her eyes he saw curiosity
and humor, and something else . . . wisdom.

"How old are you?" he asked.

She laughed, displaying teeth so straight and white
as to be the envy of the noblest lady. Her smile was
delightful, and infectious. Rainulf was actually tempted
to laugh himself—odd, given that he hadn't laughed
in a very long time, and somewhat inappropriate
under the circumstances. Instead, he marshaled his expression and asked, "What's so funny?"

"You," she said. "You're rather an odd person,
that's all."

"Me?" He pulled the blanket back over the body
and stood. "What's odd about *me*?"

She shook her head, grinning. "Asking my age like
that, out of the blue, and before you've even asked
my name. That's the kind of thing *I* do."

"What?"

"Ask the wrong questions at the wrong time." He
noticed a shiver course through her. She shook it off
and smiled gamely. "Or so Father Osred used to say.
He said I was like a little child, always asking questions."

"I'm very much the same, but then, I'm a teacher.
It's in my nature to ask questions—and, of course, to
question the answers."

She nodded knowingly. "*Disputatio.*"

Rainulf was taken by surprise that this obviously lowborn woman knew the Latin term for academic debate. She was remarkably well spoken for a woman in her circumstances, in addition to being well informed about things no Oxfordshire peasant had any business knowing. Rainulf wondered where she had learned so much.

She studied him for a moment. "I'm three-and-twenty years of age. And I know French as well as English and Latin, although I prefer speaking English. And my name, if it's of any interest to you, is Constance."

"Constance," he repeated. "A very pretty name. From the Latin. It means unchanging."

"I know."

Of course, thought Rainulf with amusement.

She screwed up her face. "I hate it. Why should one want to be *constant,* as if change were some great evil? If it weren't for change, everything would stagnate, would it not? And that which stagnates tends to putrefy, like a river that ceases to flow. What good can there be in that?"

Rainulf stared in awe at this fragile, exhausted young woman, her eyes glazed with fever, discoursing on the nature of change. She was right, of course; change was the very fabric of life itself. And death.

"My father wanted to name me Corliss," she continued, "but my mother wouldn't let him, worse luck."

"Corliss. Isn't that a man's name?"

She frowned indignantly, an expression that, coming from her, was surprisingly charming. "It's for a man *or* a woman! And it's much more suited to me than Constance!"

"Perhaps you're right," he conceded with a little bow. He nodded toward Father Osred's corpse. "I came to give him Last Rites."

"It's too late now," she said sadly as she rubbed her back.

"Too late for a proper job of it," he agreed, "but I can still perform the sacrament. There are those who believe it's useful, even when one has died unshriven."

She nodded. "Go ahead, then." Turning toward the half-dug grave, she added, "I'll finish here."

"Hold on there," he said. "You shouldn't be digging graves. You're ill, and ... well, isn't there someone ... your husband, perhaps—"

"I'm widowed."

"Ah. I'm sorry. Was it the pox?"

"Nay, it happened five years ago. There's no one but me to bury him, Father. The men who haven't gotten sick yet won't bury the dead for fear of catching their disease. And the ones who *have* gotten sick are still too weak. I wouldn't want to trouble them."

"I'll bury Father Osred," Rainulf said. "And I'll finish this second grave, if you'll tell me whom it's for."

"I thought you knew," she said, grinning as if at a slow-witted child. "It's for me."

The tall priest stared at Constance as if live eels had just sprouted from her head. "You're digging your own grave?"

"There's no one else to do it," she pointed out. "My friend Ella Hest has promised to come by in the morning and check on me. If I'm dead, she'll put me in the grave and fill it in, but she's getting on in years, so I didn't want her to have to actually dig it."

He frowned, clearly nonplussed. "You think you're going to die between now and tomorrow morning?"

"I may. Others have died this early, before the pox set in. The fever gets bad, and they lose their senses. Sometimes they have fits—"

"I know." He ran his long fingers distractedly through his close-cropped hair. It was the pale, glossy blond of a very young child. By contrast, his eyebrows and the hint of beard that darkened his strong jaw were black. His most distinctive feature, however, was his eyes—pale green lightly veiled with brown. Looking into them was like peering into the water at the edge of a lake, where it meets the shore and mixes with the earth. She saw intelligence in them, and kindness as well, which surprised her, since it was not a characteristic she normally associated with those of noble birth. This priest, despite his somewhat disreputable appearance, was clearly a highborn Norman—a fact evident in his manner, his educated speech, and the pronounced accent with which he spoke her native tongue.

His jaw clenched. Was he remembering the time when he himself had had the yellow plague? Judging from his reaction, he knew more than he cared to of this particular pestilence.

She gestured with the shovel toward the grave. "So you understand, then, why I need to finish this—"

"Nay!" He grabbed the shovel out of her hand. "I have no intention of letting you do this kind of labor while you're so gravely ill. And you mustn't worry so about dying."

"I'm not worrying about it," she corrected. "I'm preparing for it—while I'm still able to." She reached for the shovel, but he jerked it away from her, and she lost her balance. Things began to spin, and she felt her legs crumple beneath her.

"Constance?" His voice sounded as if he were speaking from a great distance. A fierce pain commenced behind her eyes, and she buried her head in her hands. She felt him grip her shoulders. "Constance?"

"I'm all right," she rasped, and struggled to rise. "I'll be fine."

Abruptly she felt weightless, and realized he'd lifted her in his arms. "Where do you live?" he asked.

"Nay," she protested, pushing against his broad shoulders. Quite useless, of course. She was weakened from illness, and he was clearly a strong man. He'd scooped her up as if she were but a child, and she could feel the solid muscles beneath the rough wool of his tunic.

"Where do you live?" he repeated patiently.

"Please ... my grave," she managed, as the pain in her head became blinding. "You don't understand. I promised Ella it would be ready."

"I'll dig it," he said.

"You will?"

"Of course, if it will ease your mind. Now, tell me where you live."

She pointed.

He frowned in evident puzzlement. "The rectory?"

Constance nodded. "I'm ... I *was* Father Osred's housekeeper."

She closed her eyes and felt the steady rhythm of his lengthy strides as he carried her across the churchyard and through the front door of the stone cottage.

"Where's your bed?"

"I sleep in there."

He brought her into the bedchamber and hesitated. She opened her eyes and saw him looking at the big featherbed, the vestments hanging on the hooks, the crucifix ... and then back at the bed. She saw comprehension dawn on him, but his expression betrayed no outward sign of shock or disapproval.

He sat her on the edge of the bed and glanced down at her kirtle, filthy from gravedigging. "You'll want to get out of that. Have you got a sleeping shift?"

She pointed to one hanging on the wall, and he brought it to her.

"Can you manage by yourself?" he asked. "I mean, if you need help, I can ..." He shrugged self-consciously, and Constance noted with amusement that his ears were bright pink.

She smiled. "Nay, I can manage. Thank you."

He nodded and left. Constance exchanged her dirt-smeared kirtle for the clean, long-sleeved linen shift and lay down on the bed. Every time she blinked, the ceiling beams appeared to shift and then slowly swim back into place. She waited until this strange dance had ceased, then sat up in bed and looked out through the little window at the churchyard.

She saw Father Rainulf unbuckle his belt and toss it aside, then whip his tunic off and throw it over a branch of the yew tree. Beneath it he wore a white linen shirt; chausses and leathern leggings bound with crisscrossed cords encased his long legs. He rolled up his shirtsleeves, revealing muscular forearms, then took the shovel and went to work on Constance's grave.

He worked quickly, digging with powerful, efficient movements and making swift progress. Constance watched with frank interest. Despite his intellectuality and aristocratic bearing, he struck her as remarkably virile—especially for a priest. She couldn't help wondering if he kept to his vow of chastity or, like many men of the cloth, had a mistress tucked conveniently away somewhere.

When the throbbing in her head and back became too much to bear, Constance closed her eyes and lay back down, hoping the pain would go away if she only kept still.

Upon awakening later in the afternoon, however, she found it undiminished. Moreover, on sitting up, she became aware of a vexatious burning sensation, as if her entire body had been scalded in boiling water. It was also clear that her fever had worsened considerably. Wrapping a throw around herself, she got out of bed and crossed unsteadily to the window.

Father Rainulf had climbed down into the grave, and only his head was visible as he dug. She watched him until, having completed his task, he set the shovel on the ground, braced his hands on the rim of the deep hole, and leapt out with one swift, agile motion.

He had removed his shirt and leathern leggings. Ex-

ertion had caused his chausses to slip a bit; the wool-
len hose hung low on his lean hips. Even from this
distance, she could see the sheen of perspiration on
his face and torso. His upper chest was densely furred
with black hair, which tapered off as she lowered her
eyes, disappearing beneath the low-slung chausses.
Wide-shouldered and long-limbed, he moved with an
easy grace that made it hard for her to tear her gaze
away.

He untied the waistcord of the chausses, and she
caught a fleeting glimpse of a patch of darkness low
on his flat belly before he yanked the hose up and
retied them. Lifting his shirt from the ground, he
shook it out and scrubbed it over his damp skin. Then
he put it back on, along with his tunic and belt, and
strode out of sight.

When he came back into view a short time later, he
had his saddlebag with him. Squatting on the ground
and unlatching it, he withdrew another white garment.
Constance thought perhaps it was a clean shirt, but
when he unfolded it and donned it over his tunic, she
discovered it to be a surplice. Next came a black skullcap, and then the stole, which he kissed and draped
over his shoulders.

"So, Rainulf Fairfax," Constance whispered as he
uncovered Father Osred's body and uncorked a small
vial, "it would appear that you're a priest, after all."

She wished she'd had enough linen—and enough
time—to sew the old rector into a suitable shroud. All
in all, it hadn't been so bad living with Father Osred.
In truth, he'd been good to her, even generous, and
she'd actually grown to feel a certain grudging affection for him. It had pained her to see him die so
horribly, and despite her fear of losing his protection
from Roger Foliot, she had prayed ceaselessly that
God would take him into His arms and bring him
peace.

As Constance watched Father Rainulf kneeling in

prayer, his image began to drift and fade. A chill swept through her, like the icy breeze from an open door in the dead of winter. She held on tight to the windowsill as the frigid pressure squeezed the thoughts from her mind and robbed her eyes of the power of sight.

God, please don't let me go blind, she begged silently as she felt her body hit the floor.

Chapter 2

"Constance!" Rainulf knelt beside the woman's limp form and pressed his fingertips to her throat. She blazed with fever, but she had a pulse. Carrying her back to bed, he covered her with the quilt and watched uneasily as she tossed her head back and forth on the pillow, murmuring incoherently.

She *was* a strange woman—most decidedly strange. For one thing, she said exactly what was on her mind, without mincing words. Rainulf, accustomed to the complex and obtuse verbal machinations of the academic community, found her candidness both disconcerting and refreshing.

She struck him as amazingly full of life—even in the throes of this horrid disease. Everything seemed to interest and amuse her. Most remarkable was her matter-of-fact acknowledgment of the possibility of her own death—of her place in the cycle of nature. For years Rainulf had engaged in ceaseless and often tiresome debates on the nature of death. He envied Constance her easy acceptance of it.

When she had quieted and seemed to be sleeping peacefully, Rainulf retired to the main room of the rectory—a sizable chamber, and very cheerful, thanks in large part to the colorfully decorated walls. The whitewashed stone had been painted all over with a variety of designs and patterns, often quite flowery and ornate.

Most of the windows were covered with parchment

on which an assortment of tiny creatures had been painted. Many were representations of the local fauna—leaping hares, mice stealing cheese, birds with worms in their beaks. Others were imaginary grotesques, such as a cross between a sheep and a stag, or a man with the head of a fish. There were many angels, all with hardy peasant faces and jolly smiles.

Rainulf's gaze was drawn to a writing desk near the largest window; such a desk was a rare sight outside the walls of a monastery or university. A sheet of parchment, neatly ruled in a double-page grid in preparation for writing, was tacked to its sloping surface. The upper left corners of each of the two pages featured sketches of elaborate capital letters embellished with haloed figures in flowing robes. An oxhorn filled with ink sat snugly in a hole in the desk's upper right corner; next to it lay several raven's quill pens, and a penknife. On a nearby table, he saw a large roll of parchment, and next to it, precisely arranged, a stylus, a stick of lead, a piece of pumice, some chunks of chalk, and a row of paint pots. Many priests made their own copies of borrowed books, but from all appearances, Father Osred had taken a rare pleasure in this work.

Rainulf opened a corner cupboard and discovered it filled with more books than he'd ever seen in such a humble place. Most were old and well worn—books of Gospel, lectionaries, a psalter, collections of model sermons, a handbook of parish duties, a manual of the sacraments, and several books of instruction in Latin. It was the handful of newer-looking volumes that most attracted him, though. He pulled one out and saw that it was a missal, flawlessly penned and illuminated. Turning to the last page, he found the scribe's signature enclosed in a wreath of twisting vines: *Constance me fecit.*

Rainulf blinked and read the words again, then whispered them out loud. "Constance made me ...

Constance?" He glanced toward the bedchamber's leather curtain, beyond which the ever-more-singular Constance lay in a fevered stupor.

"Nay ..." Replacing that volume, he slipped out another—a thick little breviary with minuscule writing on tissue-thin parchment—and flipped to the end. Shaking his head in disbelief, he read the words out loud: "Completed by Constance of Cuxham, 18 April 1159."

The largest of the newer books turned out to be the most unusual. Rather than leather, it was bound in wooden boards, which had been covered with fancifully embroidered linen, on which was stitched the title *Biblia Pauperum.* A Bible for the poor? On the last page he found the legend *De una manu,* and under it, the English translation: By one hand. Beneath that appeared the twisting vine device, enclosing Constance's name and a recent date. Clearly she was proud of her work, and why shouldn't she be? On leafing through the oversize volume, he discovered it to be an elaborately illustrated album of Bible stories, with quotations from the prophets ... in *English*!

Rainulf chuckled incredulously. English. She must have written this one herself. To have *conceived* of such a project was remarkable. To have actually executed it, in such ambitious fashion ...

A moan from beyond the leather curtain interrupted his reverie. Tucking the book back into its slot, he hurried into the bedchamber, to find Constance thrashing and yanking at her bedclothes, her flushed face glazed with perspiration, her eyes wild.

He touched her cheek, and she shook him off, but not before he felt how feverish she'd become. He growled a raw oath and crossed himself. Rushing outside, he drew a bucket of water, found a clean cloth, and returned to bathe her face and throat as he sat on the side of the bed.

After a while, her senses returned. She even smiled.

"I can still see," she said hoarsely, her eyes half-closed. "Father?"

"Aye?"

"Would you give me Last Rites?"

Rainulf held the cloth over the bucket and twisted it hard in his fists, wringing out every last drop until his hands trembled.

He drew a deep breath. "Of course," he said as her eyes drifted closed again. "I'll get what I need."

Constance heard her name whispered. Opening her eyes with some effort, she saw Father Rainulf, once again looking every bit the man of God in his white surplice and stole. Warm yellow lantern light provided the only illumination in the room, since it was night. On the bedside table, she saw, neatly laid out on a linen cloth, the items required for the sacrament of Extreme Unction. Her heart raced, and she felt queasy. She hadn't thought she was afraid of death, but now that it hovered so close, she wasn't so sure.

His large, cool hand closed over hers, and he squeezed gently. It aggravated the burning sensation, but felt so comforting that she was loath to ask him to release her. "Are you up to making confession?"

Constance nodded. Summoning all her strength, she confessed in a clear voice to her sinful relationship with Father Osred, but felt obliged to add, "It's not as if I was sinning all *that* much. I mean, Father Osred was an old man. And old men ... well ..." She shrugged.

"Yes, well ..."

"I mean, it's been months since he's wanted to—"

"Yes. I under—"

"And even before that, it was hardly what you'd even call *sinning,* if by sinning one means the pleasures of the flesh, because as far as pleasure was concerned—"

"You're forgiven, Constance. It's all right." His ears, Constance noted, had turned pink again.

Father Rainulf anointed her eyes, ears, lips, and hands with consecrated oil, his expression grave, his touch gentle. At his prompting, she spoke the words, "Into thy hands I commend my soul," and then he sat her up and supported her while he administered Communion.

"Now sleep," he said quietly, looking terribly sad.

Rainulf watched helplessly as Constance grappled with her ever-worsening delirium. It was close to midnight, by his guess. Unable to leave her in such condition, he'd decided to spend the night, but his cool compresses and whispered words of comfort seemed to be doing no good. From time to time, she regained her senses and spoke to him, as she had while he was giving her Last Rites, but those episodes were becoming shorter and less frequent, and he worried that, come dawn, he'd be carrying her to her newly dug grave.

From his time in the Holy Land, Rainulf knew Moslem physicians to be more educated about smallpox than their Western counterparts. Their theory was that the blood had a natural tendency to ferment, producing waste that must pass through the pores of the skin. Certain atmospheric conditions interfered with this process, resulting in outbreaks of this cursed disease. The treatment of choice in the Levant was to sweat out the excess fermented humors.

Constance groaned and muttered something. Rainulf sat next to her and laid a hand on her forehead. "Shh."

It grieved him to just stand by and watch her suffer—and, in all likelihood, die. Perhaps the sweating treatment had some merit; perhaps not. But it was the only remedy he knew of, so he had no choice but to try it.

Bringing the lantern outside, he chopped a great deal of wood and heaped it on one side of the central fire pit in the main room of the rectory. On the other side, he made a pallet of quilts and blankets, and then he built and lit a sizable fire. He tacked parchment over the windows that were not already sealed with it, so that the only opening in the room was the smoke hole above the fire pit. Returning to the bedchamber, he gathered Constance in her quilt, grabbed her pillow, and settled her on the pallet.

The great fire roared; Rainulf added more wood, flinching at the wall of heat that surrounded the blaze. In no time, the room became an oven, forcing him to shed first his tunic and then his sweat-soaked shirt. Still, perspiration ran in rivulets down his face and body. His damp chausses itched; unfortunately, he could not, under the circumstances, dispense with them.

Constance, also sweating heavily, grumbled unintelligibly and tried repeatedly to tear off the quilt in which she was wrapped. Weary of wrestling with her, Rainulf finally lay down with her on the pallet and pinioned her body with his. "I know you're uncomfortable," he said, although it was doubtful she heard him. "But you *have* to sweat. That's why I've gone to all this trouble. You have to get better."

She shivered and moaned, writhing beneath him as her body struggled to expel its scourge. The intimacy of their position suddenly struck him. It had been eleven years since he had lain atop a woman. The last time had been shortly before taking his vows, when the beguiling Lady Fayette had endeavored one last time to dissuade him from Holy Orders. She'd done a workmanlike job of it, too, he recalled with a smile. The memory of that night, and Constance's movements beneath him, stirred his loins. He shifted position and chastised himself for entertaining carnal thoughts at such a time.

Fayette had given it her best effort, as had her sister, Petronilla, before her. And then there had been their charming friend, Estelle ... But his mind had been made up. All his life he had known that he would become a priest. At one time, his faith had been pure and uncomplicated, his vocation a given. Now ... well, now was a very different matter, indeed.

Reflecting on his faith reminded him of the little reliquary in his saddlebag. When Constance finally lapsed into a fitful sleep, he retrieved it and placed it next to her head on the pillow. Then he added more fuel to the fire and lay down beside her in the rushes, thinking to rest his eyes for a moment.

"It's hot."

Rainulf awoke with a start, disoriented at first to find himself half-naked in a sweltering inferno, a bleary-eyed young woman lying next to him. Constance.

"Aye," he said, reclining on an elbow and wiping the sweat that ran into his eyes. "It's how the Moslems cure smallpox."

Her gaze lingered on his bare chest for a moment, and then she looked away, blotting her face with the edge of the quilt. "What can infidels possibly know of healing?"

He smiled crookedly. "A great deal more than we do, at times. It's partly why they call *us* the infidels."

That seemed to amuse her, for she laughed tiredly and sat up, the quilt falling around her waist. "What is this?" she asked, lifting the reliquary from her pillow and inspecting it closely. Firelight outlined her delicate body through the thin linen of her shift. High, petite breasts with dusky nipples were just visible beneath the drenched fabric.

Rainulf cleared his throat and combed both hands through his sodden hair. "It's a religious relic. Supposedly it's some hair from St. Nicaise." Rising, he tossed two more logs onto the fire.

Little frown lines appeared between Constance's graceful black eyebrows. "St. Nicaise . . ."

"The patron saint of smallpox sufferers."

She nodded and ran her fingertips reverently over the pearl-encrusted cross on the lid of the tiny silver casket. "It's the most beautiful thing I've ever seen," she murmured. "And to think it actually contains the hair of a saint!"

"Well . . . so they say."

"You don't believe it?"

He shrugged as he settled cross-legged next to her. "False relics abound."

"But you've no proof that this one is false."

"Nay, but—"

"Then I choose to believe it's real. What's more, I think you believe it, too, in your heart. You brought it here and laid it on my pillow, did you not?"

Rainulf shook his head, defenseless in the face of her particular brand of ingenuous perception.

She held the little token up and regarded it with an expression of awe. "Where did you get it?"

"Queen Eleanor gave it to me when I took up the cross. There's a great deal of smallpox in the Holy Land, and she'd hoped to keep me safe from it."

Constance gaped at him. "The queen of England gave you this?"

"She was still the queen of France at the time," he said. "It wasn't till after I returned from Crusade and took my vows that she divorced Louis and married Henry."

"But you know her?" Constance persisted, wide-eyed.

"We're distant cousins."

"Truly?"

Rainulf nodded.

"You're practically royalty, then."

He laughed shortly. "Hardly. As for the relic, I'm pleased if you find it comforting, but I'm not quite as convinced of its efficacy. After all, it didn't keep me from coming down with the pox when I was imprisoned in the Levant."

"Is that where you had it?" He nodded. She grinned smugly. "But you got better."

"Aye, but—"

"And you were left without scars."

"Not everyone ends up with scars."

"Nor did you go blind."

"Well . . ."

"So it worked for you," she concluded happily, and kissed the little silver box. "And it will work for me, as well. I feel much better already."

Her smile was rapturous, and more incandescent even than the blazing fire behind her.

"I'm pleased that you feel better," he said. Reaching out to touch her forehead, he added, "But you're still burning with fever." He pulled the quilt up over her shoulders. "You must stay bundled up until it breaks."

"But I'm sweating so." She shoved the quilt down.

Seating himself behind her, his long legs flanking her, Rainulf pulled it back up and wrapped his arms around her. "You're supposed to sweat. Try to go back to sleep."

"I can't. My skin feels like it's on fire."

Rainulf remembered the maddening sensation of flesh that felt as if it would ignite at any moment. "Just try. Lean back and close your eyes." She settled herself against him. Her plaited hair was soft as silk on his damp chest, and her weight felt wonderful against him. It had been so long since he'd held someone—anyone—He'd forgotten the simple pleasure of it.

"Do you think I'm going to die?" she asked.

He wanted to say, "No, of course not," but Constance, with her childlike wisdom, would only scoff at such an easy answer. "I don't know," he said slowly. "I don't think so, but there's no telling with this disease. If you *are* taken, have no doubt that the angels will welcome you into Heaven." He wondered if she could tell how empty those words of comfort really were, for it had been years since Heaven had had any real meaning for him.

"Oh, I know I'll go to Heaven," she said with seemingly complete assurance. "I mean, despite ... well, Father Osred and all that ... I've *tried* to be good. I think that counts for something with God. And, of course, I've just been shriven, so I'll die in a state of grace. I'm not worried. I'll go to Heaven, and then my soul will be free, and I'll be at peace."

Rainulf smiled inwardly. Ah, to have that kind of faith! That was *his* idea of Heaven: no more doubt, no more uncertainty to plague him.

"But," she added, "I don't quite like the idea of having to *die* before I can be free. Doesn't seem quite fair, does it?"

"Is anyone ever really free?"

"You are."

Rainulf just grimaced. If only she knew how wrong she was.

"As are many others," she continued. "Noblemen and the clergy and merchants are much freer to do as they like than *I* ever was. That's all I ever wanted—the freedom to go where I pleased and do as I thought best. I wish I'd been born a man, in some great city. Then I could ply a trade and earn a living and be happy. Instead, I was born female and the property of Roger Foliot of Cuxham, the randy old beast."

Rainulf suddenly felt chilly, despite the oppressive heat in the room. "Sir Roger ... did he force you to—"

"He tried. That's why I married Sully, and why I took up with Father Osred. I had no choice. Sir Roger is ... well, he's little more than a savage, if the truth be told. He beats the women he lies with, and if they run away, he's got someone he sends after them.

Someone even worse than him. They come back ...
He uses a knife on them, and ...."

She shuddered. Rainulf held her closer.

"The only reason he didn't come for me when Father Osred died was because I've got the pox. He hasn't had it yet, and he doesn't want to catch it. If I die, at least I'll be safe from Sir Roger."

"How will you protect yourself if you live?" Rainulf asked.

She yawned. "I don't know." She chuckled sleepily. "John Tanner's been sniffing around ever since Father Osred took sick. He's not old, either, and I think he actually wants to marry me." She curled into Rainulf's embrace and mumbled, "Only I don't know as I could take that smell of his day in and day out."

"Is that your only option?"

She shook her head. "There are two others, besides the tanner ... I'd probably have my pick."

Presently her breathing grew steady, and Rainulf knew she was sleeping. With careful movements he laid her back down on the pallet and made her comfortable. He fetched her *Biblia Pauperum* from the cabinet and sat with it by the fire, admiring the fanciful illustrations and struggling to decode the English text. Having little familiarity with the Anglo-Saxon tongue in written form, he couldn't pass judgment on the quality of the writing, but the pictures were extraordinary.

"Where did you learn to speak English?"

Rainulf looked up to find Constance staring at him, and wondered how long she had been awake. He reached out and stroked her face, still reddened but much cooler to the touch. Perhaps the sweat therapy had worked after all!

"I learned it on Crusade," he said. "After I was captured and imprisoned. One of my cellmates was an Englishman, and he taught it to me. His name was

Thorne Falconer. He's Baron of Blackburn now, and my brother by marriage."

"The Saxon baron," she said, sitting up and adjusting the quilt around herself. "Aye, I've heard of him. How long were you imprisoned?"

"A year. It was . . ." He shook his head. How could he possibly describe it? And why, after years of silence about that hellish time, did he want to speak of it to this woman he hardly knew?

Her eyes, shining with curiosity and compassion and native intelligence, searched his. "You must have very sad memories," she said quietly.

"My memories of the men I killed are far worse than those of imprisonment. I thought of them as infidels, as less than human. I thought 'twas God's will that they be slain." He swallowed the bitter reminiscence and shook his head. "I gained my freedom and returned to Paris, but my faith had been undermined. Mother Church had sent me halfway around the world to do an evil thing, and I found I could never trust her teachings again. Nothing was ever the same after that."

"Yet you took your vows."

He nodded. "I was educated for the priesthood, and I thought, perhaps in time, my faith would grow strong again. Instead, it slowly weakened, until . . ." He took in a lungful of hot air. "I returned to the Holy Land last year as a pilgrim, thinking that would help, but it's hopeless."

"All this melancholy because you killed trying to retake the Holy Land?" she asked. "Don't you think killing is justified sometimes?"

"Nay. Not anymore."

"How awful to live with such torment," she said. "And how silly."

Rainulf let out a disbelieving little laugh. "Silly?"

"You make everything so complicated, so troublesome. You can't accept anything for what it is."

"Constance . . . you really don't understand."

She laughed and waved her hand in airy dismissal. "I understand much more than you realize." Her gaze traveled to the book in his lap. "What do you think of it?"

He closed it and ran his hand over the lavishly embroidered cover. "I think it's extraordinary. Where did you learn to do such work?"

"Father Osred, of course. He used to copy books for himself, and also some to sell in Oxford. But by the time I came to live with him, his hands had become all gnarly and sore."

"So he taught you copying and illuminating," Rainulf finished. "And Latin as well, I take it?"

"Aye. I love making books—the pictures especially." She nodded toward the *Biblia Pauperum.* "I've just finished that one. It's my masterwork. If I do die, at least I'll know I've done something special first."

"It's very special," he said, rising to return the book to its cupboard. " 'Twas good of Father Osred to teach you this craft."

Constance regarded him thoughtfully as he replaced the volume and squatted next to the fire, stirring it up with the poker. She said, "You probably think . . . You must think I'm a . . . a common woman. A whore."

He set the poker aside and wiped his sweaty hands on his chausses. "It's not my place to pass judgment on you, Constance."

"Aye, but I know what you think."

He looked her straight in the eye and said quietly, "No, you don't." Moving closer to her, he gently tucked a stray hair behind her ear. "Our thoughts are private. And our actions, even if they be sinful, are rarely without cause. God understands this. It's men who don't."

She inspected him with discerning eyes. "You don't talk like other priests, Father."

"I'm not like other priests," he said soberly.

"Do you want to be?"

"Oh, yes. Yes. Very much. I want their easy faith, their unquestioning devotion. But instead, I question ceaselessly."

"Is that really so wrong?"

"I didn't use to think so. Do you know who Peter Abelard was?"

She shook her head.

"He was the greatest thinker in Europe, a man of extraordinary brilliance. I studied under him in Paris. He encouraged us to doubt what we were told. He said, 'It is not because God has said something that we believe it, but because we are convinced that it is so.'"

"What nonsense," Constance said.

Rainulf chuckled incredulously. "What?"

"Utter nonsense. No wonder you're miserable, having to struggle to *convince* yourself of things before you can believe them!"

"I'm not miserable."

"Of course you are. Look at you. I've never seen anyone so grim." She bit her lip, and then said, "Is it so very awful, being a priest who asks questions?"

He stared into the fire. "Yes, actually. It is. When I returned from pilgrimage six months ago, I went to Paris and immediately petitioned to renounce my vows."

Her brow knit. "To stop being a priest?" He nodded. "Can you do that?"

"No, not ... not ordinarily. It's very rare and exceedingly difficult."

"Ah, but not for a cousin of the queen, I'll wager. Was there royal intercession on your behalf?"

"There was," he conceded, amused at her savvy. "But it still wasn't enough. You have no idea what an outrage it is to ask for release from the priesthood. I had to come up with a better reason than my relation to the queen."

"And what was that?"

He sighed dispiritedly. "I claimed that the bishop who ordained me wasn't qualified to do so, because he was a heretic."

"Was he?"

Rainulf shrugged. "He was excommunicated for heresy, but only because he had dared to align himself with Abelard. All of Abelard's supporters were excommunicated after Abelard was condemned as a heretic by the Council of Sens. One of them—Arnold of Brescia—was even burned."

"Burned!"

"That's the punishment for the most serious forms of heresy. My sister, Martine, was condemned of heretical sorcery a year ago, and sentenced to the stake, merely for being a healer. 'Tis a miracle that she managed to prove her innocence."

"My God!"

"The bishop who ordained me was luckier. He got away with a flogging and banishment. I was loath to use this poor man's misfortune to benefit my own ends, but he himself encouraged me to do so. He said his reputation was already ruined—that I could do no more harm than had already been done. Still, I was consumed with guilt over the whole matter. And, of course, my petition has created quite a scandal. I'm a pariah in Paris. I used to teach there, but they've asked me not to come back. I knew that would happen, but I had to do it anyway."

She yawned and shook her head. "I'm sorry for your troubles."

"And I'm sorry for yours." He rested the back of his hand on her forehead and smiled. "Much better. I believe you're out of danger."

She took hold of his hand and brought it to her mouth, lightly kissing the palm. The warmth of her lips sent delicious shivers up Rainulf's arm. "Thank you. I think you may have saved my life."

He gently disengaged his hand from hers and urged her to lie back down. "You need your strength. Sleep."

She closed her eyes, and within moments was sleeping soundly.

"What's this?"

Rainulf looked up from the open saddlebag in which he was stowing away everything he'd brought. A portly woman stood in the doorway, backlit by a radiant dawn, hands firmly planted on her generous hips, her expression one of wary puzzlement. Her face seemed unnervingly familiar to him, which didn't make any sense until he realized where he'd seen it before—on one of Constance's window parchment angels.

Rainulf put a finger to his lips and tilted his head toward Constance, fast asleep on her pallet. "Don't wake her," he whispered. "Are you"—he struggled to recall the name—"Ella?"

Ella's eyebrows rose fractionally. "Aye," she said quietly. "And you'd be . . ."

"Rainulf Fairfax. *Father* Rainulf Fairfax."

Ella inspected his tunic and leggings with ill-concealed suspicion. "You don't—"

"Look like much of a priest," Rainulf finished wearily. He was exhausted, both mentally and physically. All he wanted was to sleep, yet he had to ride back to Oxford as swiftly as possible for an important lecture later that morning. He had just been awaiting Ella's arrival before he left, so that he'd know Constance would be cared for. "Yet, oddly enough, I am." As proof, he withdrew his folded stole for her inspection, then tucked it back in. "For the time being, at least."

Ella looked decidedly confused for a moment. Then, seeming to shrug him off like a fly, she approached her sleeping friend and squatted down next to her. "The pox have appeared."

"Aye." Rainulf followed her line of sight to the scattering of minuscule red pinpoints on Constance's cheeks and forehead, soon to be followed by many more.

Ella executed a solemn sign of the cross. "Pray God she don't scar."

Automatically Rainulf crossed himself as well, his gaze caressing that singular face. He hoped with all his heart that it would be spared. It was a face of such rare humor and intelligence; it would be a grave sadness indeed for it to be ruined.

"Is she ..." Ella hesitated, then looked up at him, grief and hope and fear in her eyes. "Will she ..."

"Will she live?" Ella nodded. "I'm not a physician. But I would think so. Her fever broke during the night, and she seems much better."

"Praise God," Ella breathed, crossing herself again.

Rainulf slung his saddlebag over his shoulder and looked down upon Constance. "Tell her ..."

Tell her what? That she's one of the most extraordinary people you've ever met? That you can't bear to think of never seeing her again? That you'll come back and make sure she's all right? And then perhaps again, and again ... ?

No. It would be very poor judgment indeed to allow himself to form an attachment of any kind with Constance of Cuxham. Attachments in general were something he'd avoided for quite a long time, as he'd retreated further and further into the comforting emotional void of academia. And an attachment to a woman—however innocent—would be particularly unwise, considering his plans should his petition for release from his vows prove successful.

"Tell her good-bye." Tearing his gaze from Constance, he strode quickly to the door and stopped, a thought occurring to him. Searching through his saddlebag, he located the tiny silver reliquary, brought it over to Constance, and knelt beside her. He rubbed his thumb over the little pearl-encrusted cross, kissed it, and tucked it into her open hand, closing her fingers firmly around it.

"God be with you, Constance," he whispered, and left.

Chapter 3

Rainulf saw the face in the open shopfront as he passed. Or, rather, he saw the hair, from the back—a swath of fiery copper—and mentally put the befreckled face to it as he walked by. It was that fellow who'd sent him to Cuxham two weeks ago. Pausing, he turned and looked back toward the shop—one of dozens lining narrow Pennyfarthing Street—above which hung a small sign announcing *Will Geary, Surgeon*. He retraced his steps and opened the door, jarring the bell that dangled overhead.

The surgeon turned to look over his shoulder as he deftly bandaged the arm of a young man sitting on the edge of a central table. "Well! If it isn't my poxy priest! Good afternoon, Father. What brings you to my humble shop? I hope you're not hurt."

"Nay. Just passing by, and I saw you in the window. I thought you were a *traveling* surgeon."

"I am, for the most part." Geary tied off the bandage, and the young man winced. "But I've had this shop for years, and I can't bear it give it up. Also, I live right upstairs"—he pointed toward a narrow staircase in the rear of the shop, near a stack of coffins—"so I don't fancy letting someone else conduct business down here. I like my privacy."

The oaken table on which the young patient sat was long enough for a man to lie upon, and featured a carved channel along the edge for blood, as well as leather restraints with buckles, not in use at present.

A smaller table laid out with surgical tools stood to the side, and cupboards lined the walls. The coffins in back attested to the difficulty and unpredictability of the surgeon's art. Rainulf doubted he would have the stomach for such work.

Geary assisted the young man off the table and helped him on with his cappa. "Keep that arm clean, boy," he ordered, then held out his hand. His patient withdrew his purse, made payment, and took his leave.

"By the way, Master Geary," Rainulf said, "it's not 'Father' anymore. I've just received word that the Pope has released me from my vows."

The surgeon frowned as he counted the coins. "I didn't know that was possible."

"Neither did I, until I did it."

"So this was something you wanted."

"Aye."

"Then you must celebrate. There's a public house next door. Let's share a pint, shall we? I'll even pay, providing you promise not to call me 'Master Geary.' " He grinned and pocketed the silver. "The name's Will."

The public house in question turned out to be the downstairs room of a brothel. As soon as the two men were seated, half a dozen working wenches gathered around their table, all silken smiles and undulating hips. The boldest—and prettiest—laid claim to Rainulf immediately, planting herself firmly on his lap and pressing his hands to her ample bosom.

"You're wasting your time, Hulda," said one of the other whores. "I recognize that one. He's a priest."

"Are you, now," Hulda purred as she wrapped her arms around him; Rainulf dropped his hands to her waist. "I've got some impure thoughts to confess, Father . . . thoughts I started having as soon as you walked through that door." Bringing her painted mouth close to his ear, she shared those thoughts in a voice throaty with sexual promise. She whispered things she could do to him ... things she'd let him do to her.

Will chuckled. "Your ears are turning the most remarkable color ... *Father*."

Rainulf's body reacted to her lewd suggestions, even as he sought some graceful way to extricate himself from her clutches. Hulda felt his grudging response. "Ah," she murmured, lifting her skirt and placing his hand between her warm thighs, "this is what you need."

"Yes," said Rainulf, realizing how pointless it would be to deny what was patently obvious. Nevertheless, he withdrew his hand and lowered her skirt. "But I'm obliged to resist." Grinning, he nodded toward Will. "Perhaps my companion ..."

"Him?" Hulda snorted in derision and rose from his lap. "That one never goes with any of the girls."

"They're diseased, most of them," Will said.

"Liar!" Hulda spat out.

Ignoring her, Will lifted his tankard. "I seek my ... diversion ... elsewhere, and if you value your health, I'd counsel you to do the same."

The girls dispersed in a huff, whereupon Will leaned across the table toward Rainulf and said, in a low voice, "If it's a woman you want, I'll find you a clean one."

Rainulf swallowed down a goodly portion of his ale. "Thank you, but that won't be necessary. I've resisted the temptations of the flesh for eleven years now. I think I can manage to continue doing so."

"But why should you? You've been released from your vow of chastity, have you not?"

"I'm sure you know that even lay teachers are, by custom, celibate."

Will chuckled. "You and I both know that's more a matter of appearances than practice. Half the teachers keep mistresses, and some are even married."

"Aye, but they're at a disadvantage for promotions."

He smiled. "Ah, so you have ambitions."

"I've been approached by the Bishop of Lincoln. He's got ultimate jurisdiction over Oxford and any teaching that goes on here. Right now we're just an informal little *studium generale*, loosely overseen by myself as Magister Scholarum, the Abbot of Osney, and the Prior of St. Frideswides. But Bishop Chesney thinks we'll someday be a great university. He wants to speed that process by appointing a chancellor to organize the masters into a guild and oversee the growth of the schools."

Will motioned for a refill of their tankards. "And he offered you this position?"

"Not yet, but I'm the leading candidate. It doesn't even seem to much bother him that I've renounced my vows. He wants a man the teachers will respect, and since they've already elected me Master of Schools, he feels that man should be me."

"They elected you Master of Schools after only . . . How long have you been in Oxford?"

"Just six months," Rainulf said. "But I had something of a reputation in Paris." *The most beloved teacher in Paris,* they'd called him. *A worthy successor to Abelard.* And now he could never go back. "Apparently that reputation preceded me. All the masters and Church officials here knew of me before I arrived."

Will nodded. "I'm impressed. But what has the chancellorship to do with your celibacy?"

"As Chancellor of Oxford, I'd no longer be a mere teacher—in fact, I wouldn't teach at all. I'd be an officer of the bishop, and therefore required to be chaste."

"Parish priests are bound by the same requirement, yet everyone knows what goes on behind the doors of their rectories, and no one much cares."

"Aye, but I'd be much more visible than your average parish priest. And I understand Bishop Chesney is especially uncompromising about the reputations of his officers. I'll be watched constantly, my behavior carefully monitored."

"But you haven't been appointed to the position yet."

"Nay, nor will I be for another five months. My lord bishop will make his decision at the end of the summer."

Will brightened. "Ah! So in the meantime—"

"In the meantime, I must conduct myself as befits the position for which I'm being considered. Any hint of impropriety, and my chances are ruined. I have no intention of jeopardizing this opportunity, Will."

"It means that much to you?"

"More than you can know."

Will looked at Rainulf curiously, but questioned him no further, for which he was grateful. He had no desire to discuss the self-doubt that had made teaching—once the joy of his life—so painful. He still craved the excitement of *disputatio*, the thrill of imparting knowledge to eager young minds. But his pleasure in teaching was one he had no right to, inasmuch as he was unfit for the task. His students trusted him, even revered him, hanging on every word from his mouth as if it were Gospel, even those who clearly couldn't fathom what he was talking about. They assumed he was a man of faith, a man sure of his convictions and fully qualified to guide them through the moral and intellectual complexities of logic and theology. In reality, he was a fraud. He didn't even know what he himself believed; what right did he have to train young minds when his own was filled with doubt and uncertainty?

All he wanted was to retreat from his students—from everyone—into the safe and undemanding administrative position to which Bishop Chesney seemed disposed to appoint him. In the meantime, he must do nothing to cause the bishop to question his suitability—certainly not consort with a whore in a Pennyfarthing Street brothel. In truth, he should have left the moment he realized what this place was. He would have, had he not been waiting for an opportunity to steer the conversation toward the subject that had obsessed him for the past fortnight.

Seizing upon a moment of silence, he asked, "Have you been back to Cuxham since I saw you last?"

Will nodded. "Just yesterday. I'm there quite a bit. Sir Roger frequently calls upon my services."

"How did you come to meet him?"

Will hesitated almost imperceptibly, as if weighing whether to answer the question, then cleared his throat. " 'Twas eight or nine years ago. I was traveling home through Cuxham, and I stopped by the manor house to ask for a bite of supper. Sir Roger seemed unusually glad to see me, when he discovered my profession. He told me he'd be happy to feed me if I'd set a villein's broken legs afterward. I told him I'd do it right away—that such a job shouldn't wait. 'Suit yourself,' he said, and he led me downstairs to the undercroft. He had a young man in irons—a young man who, it turned out, had tried to escape. I said, 'But there's nothing wrong with his legs.' Sir Roger just laughed. Then he picked up a mallet and smashed both legs, one after the other."

Rainulf lowered his tankard slowly to the table. "Good God."

"Indeed. Sir Roger said, 'Mind you do a good job on those legs. I want him back in the fields in time for the harvest.' So I set the legs, and then I ate my fill of stag and turnips and went on my way." He drained his tankard. "When I went back to take the boy's splints off, Sir Roger had another job for me. I don't remember what it was—probably someone had taken ill. And then there was another, and another. . . . He sends for me when he needs me. I seem to be the only surgeon he trusts."

Rainulf shook his head. "I wouldn't be too pleased about that, if I were you. He sounds like a monster."

Will laughed. "He'd love to hear you say so. He so desperately wants to strike terror in the breasts of all who know him. But the fact is, every man has his weakness, his secret fear—the thing that makes him vulnerable. In Sir Roger's case, it's Hell. He's an evil and petty creature, and he knows it. He's desperately afraid that he'll die and roast for eternity in everlasting torment. So, despite his wicked nature—or because of it—he's become something of a slave to the Church and her priests. It's all a rather pathetic effort to save himself when the time comes. The only man in Cuxham who had his respect was that old rector, Father Osred, and he's dead now."

"Aye, God rest his soul." Rainulf crossed himself and said, in a deliberately offhand way, "Do you happen to know what became of his housekeeper?"

"Housekeeper . . ." Will shrugged. "Didn't even know he had one. Sorry."

Rainulf sighed dejectedly. "Girl by the name of Constance. She had the pox, too. I was just wondering—"

"Constance, did you say?"

"Aye."

"She's dead." Will drank his ale and held his hand up for another.

Rainulf felt as if he'd been kicked in the stomach. He sat perfectly still, watching Will accept a new tankard and start in on it. "Are you sure?"

Will nodded and wiped his mouth on the back of his hand. "I saw her name on the tombstone myself. They buried her right next to the priest. What's wrong? You look pale."

Rainulf couldn't stop shaking his head. "But I don't understand. Her fever had subsided."

"Was it the first fever, or the second?"

Rainulf just stared at him.

"The first fever," Will explained, "comes before the rash. If the victim survives it, he generally feels much better afterward. But then a secondary fever sets in after the pox arrive, and it's just as deadly as the first. It must be this second fever that claimed the girl."

Nodding numbly, Rainulf rose from his bench. "I ... have to go."

Will stood, too, his manner solemn. "Sorry. I didn't realize you'd formed an attachment."

"I didn't," Rainulf said quickly.

"Was she pretty?"

"Nay." Then he remembered her eyes, full of laughter and wonder, and her smile ... "Yes. Listen ... I have to go."

Will grabbed for his arm, but he pulled away. "I have to go," he insisted as he bolted out the door.

"Can't you dig any faster?" growled Roger Foliot to the two villeins, visible only from the shoulders up as they steadily deepened the hole.

Hugh Hest drew in a calming breath and let it out slowly. "Patience, Sir Roger," soothed the reeve. "It won't be much longer now."

"Little bitch ..." the fat knight muttered. He ceased his relentless pacing and flicked his horsewhip against his leg, his porcine eyes fixed on the block of stone inscribed with a cross and a single word: Constance. "Little bitch."

His lapdog ran toward him, yipping and dancing about his heels. "Not you, Detinée," he purred, gathering the ratlike creature in his arms. "Another little bitch."

Drifting clouds shrouded the full moon, immersing the Cuxham churchyard in darkness. Hugh wished he had a lantern. He wished it weren't so chilly. But most of all he wished he were anywhere—*anywhere*—than in this damn graveyard in the middle of the night, overseeing the exhumation of poor Constance's body.

He'd thought Roger Foliot's fixation with the girl would die when she did, but he'd been wrong. During the past few weeks, he'd become obsessed with her to the point of derangement, culminating in this determination to unearth her corpse. What point he hoped to prove was quite beyond Hugh's ken. He prayed that the nasty business would be done with quickly, so that he could get home to Ella and his warm bed.

"Sir Roger," said one of the villeins in a coarse English accent; Hugh recognized the voice of the larger of the two men, a slack-jawed giant named Frick. "This may be it."

Hugh and his master approached the edge of the open grave as the moon emerged from cloud cover, illuminating a patch of unbleached linen peeking out from the dirt.

"Get out! Get out!" Sir Roger set Detinée down and whipped the two men frantically as they clambered out. The smaller one, Wiley, yanked the whip from his hand and raised it as if to strike him back. His hulking companion snatched it from him and tossed it aside, whispering a warning in English. Of the two men, Frick was by far the more obedient and hardworking. Little Wiley hadn't ceased to cause trouble since his arrival in Cuxham the previous fall.

Roger Foliot, usually alert to any form of impertinence, seemed barely aware of the incident, so preoccupied was he with the task of lowering his vast bulk into the grave. Once there, he unsheathed his sharp little eating knife and began hacking away at the partially buried shroud. Frick and Wiley exchanged a look and, crossing themselves, backed away from the appalling sight.

"*Aha!*" Grabbing the linen in his meaty fists, Sir Roger ripped it open. "Look, Hugh! Look! I knew it! I knew it!"

Steeling himself, Hugh leaned over to inspect the contents of the shroud.

It was filled with straw.

"What . . . ?"

"I knew it!" Even in the shifting moonlight, Hugh could see Sir Roger's face darken with fury, turning the color of an overripe plum. In a frenzy of rage, he stabbed at the straw-filled shroud, slicing it to ribbons. "You bitch! You little bitch! Make a fool out of *me*, will you?"

"But how . . . ?"

"She tricked me!" he exclaimed breathlessly. "She faked her death, the little strumpet! And I'll wager she had help doing it."

Ella had told Hugh that she'd been the one to bury Constance. She hadn't, of course; she'd buried a sack of straw instead. She'd lied to him, then, but he found he could summon no ire over it. It was a clever plan, and it had almost worked.

"Who filled in this grave?" Sir Roger demanded, clutching two quivering fistfuls of straw.

Hugh would be damned if he'd point the finger at his own wife. "I wouldn't know, sir. Someone traveling through, perhaps? Or perhaps Constance herself." Desperate to change the subject, he asked, "What made you suspect that this grave was empty?"

"You remember. You were with me when I saw her in Bagley Wood, going into that church. You told me it wasn't her."

"She had her head covered, and we saw her from such a distance. And when we got there, she was gone."

"Sneaked out the back," he growled. "Saw us and slipped away."

"And she . . . she was supposed to be—"

"She was *supposed* to be *dead*!" He crushed the straw in his fists, then flung it aside. "She's a crafty wench. But I'm craftier."

Looking up from the grave, he met Hugh's gaze, his eyes shining like black beetles in the moonlight. "Get Pigot."

"Pigot! Sir Roger, no . . ."

"*Get him!*" he screamed, spittle flying from his mouth. "Pigot will find her. Doesn't matter how far away she's gotten. Scotland, Wales ... He always finds them. He'll bring her back, and then I'll teach her a thing or two. I'll make her suffer for humiliating me."

"Sir Roger—"

"Get Pigot! Promise him double his usual fee. I'll sell her to a brothel after I'm done with her, and make it back that way." He held his hands toward Hugh. "Help me out." Together, the three men succeeded in hauling the obese knight from the hole.

"Sir Roger," Hugh began, "if I may ... I don't think it's such a wise idea, sending Pigot after Constance. That is, I don't think any brothel will want her after ... after he's done with her."

"Aye, he likes those knives of his." Sir Roger lifted Detinée and made kissing noises at her, whereupon she bared her teeth and lunged for his bulbous nose. He chuckled indulgently and scratched her behind her ears. "I'll order him not to ruin her face."

"He's a madman," Hugh objected. "You can tell him whatever you want, but he can't be controlled. Remember Hildreth? Didn't you tell him to spare her face when he found her? Yet look what he did to her! Poor girl drowned herself in the river rather than—"

"*Enough!*" Sir Roger bellowed. The little dog flinched and let out an indignant yelp. "I've told you to fetch Pigot, and by God that's what you'll do! You'll have him here by tomorrow afternoon or I'll see your neck in a noose. And try to figure out where Constance might have gone. Your wife was a friend of hers, wasn't she?"

"My wife?"

"Ella. She might know something about all this. She was probably the last one to see the bitch before she ran away. Send her to me. I want to question her."

"Nay! I ... I'll talk to her."

"And you'll send for Pigot?"

Hugh's shoulders slumped. "I'll send for Pigot. But for God's sake, don't call him that to his face this time. You know how it enrages him. Call him by his real name."

Sir Roger waved a plump hand in dismissal. "I'll call him what I damn well please! 'Twill remind him who's in charge."

Hugh considered arguing the point, but decided against it. If Sir Roger chose to make a personal enemy of this lunatic, so be it.

Sir Roger waved the two villeins over to the grave. They shambled toward him slowly, Wiley with an expression of disgust, Frick with one of wariness. "Fill this in so it looks exactly as it did." To Hugh, he said, "Make sure they do a proper job of it. Detinée and I are going to bed."

Late the next afternoon, Hugh, Sir Roger, Frick, Wiley, and Pigot stood hidden behind a copse of trees across the river from the churchyard, their eyes trained on a tall, fair-haired man standing beside the filled-in grave. He stood perfectly still, his expression solemn. Hugh, knowing the grave contained, not Constance, but a sackful of straw, felt a fair measure of unease watching this stranger mourn a woman who was, in fact, still alive somewhere.

"Anyone know who that is?" asked Sir Roger, cradling Detinée in his massive arms.

Pigot nodded, his penetrating gray eyes fixed on the stranger. "Everyone in Oxford knows him. His name is Rainulf Fairfax. He's Magister Scholarum."

"Master of Schools," Hugh translated, knowing Sir Roger's Latin to be no better than it should be.

"And," Pigot added quietly, "he's a former priest."

"*Former* priest?" Sir Roger exclaimed. "There is no such thing. Once a priest, always a priest. He took vows, for God's sake!"

"Well, it seems he's found a way to get out of

them," Pigot said in a bored tone. "He's the son of a powerful Norman baron, and a cousin of the queen. I'm sure that didn't hurt."

Sir Roger frowned, his eyes on Rainulf Fairfax as he sank to one knee and executed the sign of the cross. "Hunh. She was popular with priests, that one."

Wiley snickered. Elbowing Frick, he muttered something in English. They both erupted in laughter.

Across the river, the ex-priest lowered his head and began to pray.

"He was obviously attached to this woman you're sending me after." Pigot frowned at the two villeins, whose conversation was becoming loud and animated. "Hush, you two. I can't think." Frick quieted; Wiley went on as before.

"What do you suppose they were to each other?" Sir Roger asked.

Hugh's gaze returned to the man by the grave, who crossed himself again and reached out to touch the gravestone.

"I think it's safe to say they were close," Pigot said.

After some moments, Rainulf Fairfax rose and mounted his bay stallion. With one final melancholy glance at Constance's grave, he rode north along the river, disappearing into the woods.

"He seems to have been quite taken with her," Pigot said. "What does she look like? Is she pretty?"

Sir Roger nodded as he thoughtfully petted his dog. "Very. She's got the whitest teeth you've ever seen."

Pigot gazed skyward, then closed his eyes briefly. "You might want to elaborate on that description if you expect me to locate her. What color hair does she have?"

"It's dark," said Sir Roger. "And very long—down to her knees. And, let's see . . . she's quite slender. Very little up here." He cupped a hand over his chest, and Detinée snapped at it. "But quite a charming shape, nonetheless."

Wiley nudged Frick, and the two men snorted with laughter.

"If you want to keep your tongues," Pigot warned softly, "you'll hold them." He gave the satchel draped over his shoulder a meaningful pat. Frick paled, but the implied threat was clearly lost on Wiley, who sneered and mumbled something under his breath. Never having met Pigot before, he would have no inkling of the vast collection of knives housed in that satchel—nor of their owner's enthusiasm for wielding them. He would have no idea that Pigot was quite thoroughly and completely mad. It was what made him so unpredictable ... and so very good at what he did, which was finding people who'd gone to very great lengths to hide themselves, people who had no reason to think they'd ever be found.

Pigot could do this because of his gift, a gift peculiar to a certain variety of madman. It was the gift of adopting whatever persona most suited the particular search on which he was embarked. He could appear entirely harmless, even charming, when he chose. He could play the bored nobleman, the mendicant friar, the jolly butcher ... whatever enabled him to get close to his prey. And then, like a snake, he would attack—swiftly and mercilessly and utterly without conscience. Like Sir Roger, he derived pleasure from dispensing pain, but unlike the petty knight, he had refined this cruelty into a kind of hellish art form. In truth, he seemed to regard the mutilated women he returned to Cuxham as something akin to creative accomplishments.

"You might do well to keep track of this magister who used to be a priest," Sir Roger said, seemingly oblivious to Pigot's growing impatience with his men, "in case she seeks him out."

Pigot stared him down, his eyes like chips of ice. "The thought had occurred to me."

Wiley said something that prompted his friend to whisper, "Shh!"

Turning to face the two men, Pigot reached into his satchel. "You," he said to Frick.

"Me?"

Pigot withdrew a small, curved knife, which glinted in the late afternoon sun. The big man backed away, his eyes wide. "Wait, I—"

"Hold him down," Pigot ordered Frick, pointing toward the smaller man.

The two villeins looked at each other, Wiley shaking his head, Frick wearing a dumbfounded expression. "Sir Roger?" the big man said. "What . . . what should I—?"

"Christ," Hugh muttered. "Sir Roger, don't let him—"

"*Now!*" Pigot commanded, advancing on the two men.

"Uh, Pigot," Sir Roger began, "must you really—"

"*Don't call me that!*" Pigot roared, whirling on the obese knight, the knife upraised.

Sir Roger, clutching the little dog, stumbled backward. "Do it!" he ordered Frick, who hung his head, then nodded grimly.

Wiley tried to run, but Frick overtook him easily. "I'm sorry. Truly I am." Seizing his friend's arms, he muscled him to the ground and held him down for Pigot. "Be quick about it, all right?"

"*No!*" the little man screamed as Pigot straddled his thrashing legs and pried his mouth open. "*No!*"

"Sir Roger!" pleaded Hugh. "For God's sake!" But the knight only shrugged helplessly and squeezed Detinée against his chest.

Wiley's screams tore through the woods. Pigot, his back to Hugh, made an abrupt movement. Frick turned his head, his face contorted in anguish, as the screaming was replaced by an eerie, guttural moan.

Pigot rose and crossed to Sir Roger, holding something outstretched in his bloody hand. "Here."

The astonished knight accepted the offering, which Detinée sniffed at eagerly. With a cry of disgust, he flung it away. The little dog leapt from his arms in zealous pursuit of the morsel. "No, Detinée!" Sir Roger shrieked as the dog pounced on Wiley's tongue and swallowed it whole.

Pigot retrieved a scrap of linen from his satchel, cleaned the blade carefully, and put it away. Then he washed his hands in the river. Rejoining Sir Roger and Hugh, he glanced toward Frick, cradling Wiley in his arms and stuffing a rag in his mouth. "He didn't need that tongue. They're a nuisance in a villein." He held his hand out to Roger Foliot. "Half now, correct?"

"Half? Ah. The payment." With a trembling hand, Sir Roger withdrew a sack of silver from beneath his mantle and handed it to Pigot. "A pound sterling." Pigot poured the coins into his palm and counted them.

Sir Roger cleared his throat. "You'll get the other pound when you bring her back." He puffed out his stout chest. "With her face intact."

Pigot pinned the obese knight with an unblinking stare.

"Please," Sir Roger added sheepishly.

The corners of Pigot's mouth turned up in a smile that never reached his eyes. "Don't I always bring them back?"

"Aye, but—"

"And I'll bring this one back, as well."

"Aye, but I don't want her—"

"Good day, Sir Roger . . . Master Hest." He turned and began walking away.

Sir Roger sighed heavily. "Good day, Pig—" He winced. "G-Good day."

Pigot paused, his head cocked to the side as if he were contemplating something; then he continued on his way.

*   *   *

"But what of Plato?" challenged a familiar voice from within the multitude of black-clad scholars crowded into dimly lit St. Mary's Church. Rainulf sighed and rested his elbows on his lectern as Victor of Aeskirche, always overeager for confrontation, climbed onto his bench and planted his hands on his hips. "This 'conceptualism' of yours—this notion of universals as mere words—is in direct opposition to Plato's teachings."

"Had you listened more carefully," Rainulf countered wearily, "you would know that conceptualism is not my notion at all, but that of Master Abelard— and, I might add, of Aristotle. And incidentally, the point I've been making all evening is that universals are neither realities nor mere names, but concepts. I welcome debate, Victor, but in the future I would recommend that you get your facts straight before you go to the trouble of climbing atop your bench."

There was some laughter at Victor's expense, and several of his fellows called out to him to take his seat, which he did, rather sullenly.

"That will be all for tonight," Rainulf announced, abandoning the Latin he used for his *disputatio* for French. "Those who care to may join me tomorrow morning in my home for a discussion of nominalism and how it relates to the doctrine of unity in the Trinity. The discussion will commence at terce."

The scholars—ranging from grammar students of ten to doctoral candidates in their thirties—filed out into the rainy April evening, leaving Rainulf alone in the candlelit church. Or not quite. As he gathered his notes and books, he saw again, half-hidden behind a pillar in the nave, the shadowy figure of a young man clad in a coarse gray mantle, its hood drawn low over his forehead, a large satchel on his back. He had noticed the youth several times during the evening, and wondered why he had chosen to stand, although two benches were empty in the rear of the church. Perhaps he felt awkward because he lacked the black academic robe of the Oxford students, but he wouldn't have been alone in that regard. Some of the better-educated locals—even a few of the ladies—frequented Rainulf's *disputatios,* and none of them wore the cappa.

"A triumph, as usual." Rainulf turned to see Father Gregory emerge from behind the altar.

"Have you been listening this whole time?"

"I frequently do." Gregory leaned on the lectern and smiled, his kind eyes lighting with an almost mischievous humor—incongruous in a man of his advanced years. "You're the most exceptional teacher I've ever known . . ."

Rainulf groaned. *Here it comes . . .*

"Brilliant, perceptive," Gregory continued. "The students worship you."

"'They might save their worship for a worthier sort. You, of all people, know of my many flaws." As Rainulf's intimate friend and confessor, Father Gregory was the only man in Oxford privy to the crisis of faith that had driven him from the priesthood.

"I know that you're but a man, with a man's weaknesses . . . and strengths. Your strength is in teaching, Rainulf. It's a gift from God. A man with such gifts shouldn't waste them in administration."

"The chancellorship—"

"Will smother you," Gregory stated flatly. "And it will deprive Oxford's scholars of their most valuable resource."

"Anyone could do what I do."

"But not nearly as well."

Rainulf shouldered his bag and turned to leave. "I doubt that."

Gregory held him back, placing a hand on his arm. "You doubt *yourself,* friend. It's all right to doubt what you're taught. Brilliant men can't help but question what others unthinkingly believe. Such doubt is understandable, even expected. But when they doubt themselves, and retreat from the world, as you're trying to do, their brilliance fades ... and the world is poorer for it."

Rainulf raked a hand through his hair. "Gregory, you don't know how frustrated I've been, how desperately I need this change—"

"Perhaps not," his friend said quietly. "But just promise me one thing. Promise me you'll take the time to consider whether this chancellorship is really what you want. You have all summer, and there's no reason you can't turn it down, even if it is offered to you. Will you promise me that, as a friend?"

"I don't understand," Rainulf said. "You're the bishop's representative. You're supposed to encourage me to accept this position, not turn me against it."

Gregory shrugged and smiled sagely. "I'm God's representative, too. And I can't help but think He would want you to continue teaching." His expression sobered, and he closed his hand over Rainulf's shoulder. "Just think about it. That's all I'm asking."

Rainulf knew in his heart there was nothing to think about—he *needed* the chancellorship—but out of politeness, he nodded in agreement before bidding the elderly priest good night and taking his leave. As he passed the nave, a movement in the shadows behind a pillar caught his attention.

"Father Rainulf?"

The magister paused and peered at the cloaked figure waiting in the darkness—the young man who had declined to take a seat. "It's not 'Father' anymore," Rainulf said.

The hooded head nodded. "Aye, I meant 'Master Fairfax,' " he said in English.

The sandy voice was familiar, but before Rainulf could recall where he'd heard it before, the youth extended his hand, in which he held something shiny. "This is yours."

Rainulf took a step closer and accepted the small

object, turning it over in his hands. It was the tiny silver casket with the pearl-encrusted cross on top, the reliquary containing the hair of St. Nicaise.

"It worked." A hand reached up and lowered the gray hood. "I got better."

Chapter 4

He saw the warm brown eyes, wide in the dusky nave, smiling at him; he saw the gleaming white teeth. Rainulf stopped breathing for a moment. The reliquary slipped from his fingers and clattered on the stone floor. He and his visitor both crouched to pick it up, their hands meeting on the little silver box. The skin that Rainulf touched was warm and smooth, the skin of a woman. Rainulf looked up at the face just inches from his. "My God! Constance?"

"It's Corliss now." She glanced around furtively. "You mustn't call me Constance."

Rainulf's incredulous gaze took in her wavy black hair, now shorn to chin length, and her face—her very singular face—free of any scars that might betray her bout with the pox ... and her clothes! With her slight build, and her heavy tunic and chausses, she looked remarkably like an adolescent boy, if a delicate one.

He shook his head in grateful disbelief. "I ... my God! I don't believe it!" His bag slipped off his shoulder; his arms encircled her without his willing it, and he drew her close. She set down her satchel and returned the embrace. For a precious, mindless moment that seemed to stretch beyond time, he held her tight, reveling in the feel of her in his arms—her substance, her solidity, the faint tickle of her warm breath on his neck. With a curious detachment he saw himself, as if from above, holding this woman as one would a lover. His rational mind, long accustomed to absolute au-

thority over his actions, scolded him for imprudence;
but an unfamiliar force deeper within him—an urge
both elemental and profoundly needful—refused to let
her go.

"You're real," he whispered. "You're alive." His
fingers threaded themselves through her hair; he
breathed in the scent of green herbs and sweet blossoms. An astonished chuckle rose from his throat. It
was the first time in a long time that he had laughed,
and it enhanced his feeling of unreality—the impression that this was all happening to someone else.
"You're alive!"

"Aye," she murmured into his chest.

"My God, Constance, I thought you were dead. I
thought—"

"Don't call me that." She pulled away from him
and stood, raising her hood as she retreated behind
the pillar. "Please. No one must hear you call me
that."

Feeling unexpectedly bereft at the loss of contact,
Rainulf retrieved the reliquary and slowly gained his
feet. "You're in hiding?" he asked her. She nodded.
"From Sir Roger?"

"From the man he sends out to capture runaways.
I don't know who that is."

"How did you manage to ... I mean, there's a
gravestone with your name on it!"

"Ella helped me. It wasn't hard. We filled a shroud
with straw so that anyone passing would think she was
burying me." She shrugged. "No one questioned her,
and I merely waited until dark and went on my way."

"Where did you go?"

"I have a cousin in Bagley Wood, who I stayed with
for a few weeks. But I should have known better than
to remain so close without a disguise. About a week
ago, I got careless. I was heading into church for mass
when I saw Sir Roger, along with Hugh Hest, coming
down the road. I think they saw me, too."

"What did you do?"

"I slipped out the back and ran as hard as I could," she said. "Came here to Oxford." She fingered the short tendrils of hair framing her face. "Cut my hair, traded my kirtle for chausses." Grinning, she extended her booted leg. "What do you think?"

Rainulf shook his head helplessly. "I don't know what to think. How long do you propose to maintain this disguise?"

"Until Sir Roger gives up on trying to find me. It may takes months—perhaps years—but eventually he'll tire of the search. If I stay here in Oxford, perhaps I can keep track of his progress through my friend Ella. If I were to flee to some far-off place, I'd lose that advantage, and most likely I'd still be found."

"Where have you been staying?" Rainulf asked. "Have you any silver?"

She shook her head. "What little I had is long gone. I've been sleeping in an alley off Beefhall Lane till I can find work."

"An alley! You could get your throat cut in your sleep! And what do you do when it rains?"

"The weather's been fair. I've been lucky . . ." She glanced toward the downpour visible through the open front door of the church. "Until now." She shrugged. "Perhaps Osney Abbey will take me in for the night."

Rainulf conjured up a disconcerting mental picture of Constance—or rather, Corliss—bedded down in the straw in a monastic guest house with dozens of indigents . . . all male, and many the lowliest form of knave. Granted, she passed amazingly well for a boy, but that alone wouldn't protect her as much as she seemed to think. There were those who would just as soon force themselves on a defenseless-looking youth as on a girl. And when they discovered her true sex, she'd be fair game for them all. Doubtless the young woman standing before him, so secure in her tunic and chausses, knew little of such matters.

"I'd better go now," she said, "or they may not have room for me by the time I get there." She nodded toward the reliquary clutched in his fist. "I just wanted to give that back. Thank you for ... everything." She looked down momentarily. Even in the shadowy nave, Rainulf thought he could see a slight blush suffuse her cheeks. "I was sad to wake up and find you gone."

"I was sad to leave," Rainulf said quietly. She looked directly at him, her eyes huge in the darkness, as if his declaration had surprised her. He cleared his throat and held the reliquary out to her. "I'm not taking this back. It was meant as a gift. It's yours now."

"Mine?" Her disbelieving gaze met his. "Nay, I couldn't keep it!"

"Whyever not?"

"It's ... it's much too fine."

"You deserve fine things." He took her hand, opened her fingers, and closed them around the reliquary. "Keep it." Wrapping both his hands around her small fist, he added, "Please."

She nodded gravely, her gaze locked with his. "I'll treasure it. 'Twill be a reminder of you and ... and everything you've done for me. And perhaps it will continue to bring me good luck."

Rainulf looked down at his hands enclosing her small fist. He didn't want to release her, but he did, and took a step back. Constance—*Corliss*—stepped back as well. Lifting her satchel from the floor, she secreted the little reliquary in it. For a moment they simply looked at each other, and then she said, "Good-bye, Master Fairfax."

She walked to the front door, adjusted her hood, and stepped into the driving rain.

"Wait!" Rainulf crossed to the door in two long strides and pulled her back into the church.

She looked startled. "Is something wrong?"

"No. Yes. It's not safe, you staying at Osney. I don't like it. You need proper lodgings."

She wiped the rain from her face with the edge of her mantle. "Proper lodgings cost money. I hope to be earning some soon, but in the meantime—"

"Come home with me."

She blinked at him.

"For a decent meal," he hastily added. "How long has it been since you've had one?"

She smiled a little self-consciously. "Too long. But I couldn't trouble you after everything—"

"It's no trouble. And while you're eating, I'll set my mind to the problem of your lodgings."

She nodded slowly, then smiled her extraordinary smile; it was as if the dusky church had just been flooded with heavenly light. "All right."

Corliss paused in the middle of muddy St. John Street and stared up at the building to which Rainulf Fairfax had led her—a massive two-story stone edifice that dwarfed the adjacent timber houses, looming darkly against the night sky. Shielding her eyes against the rain, she could make out a long row of large, arched windows on each of the two floors; warm, inviting light glowed around the edges of their closed shutters. Smoke drifted from a chimney on the far left side of the shingled roof.

There were two doorways at street level. Master Fairfax opened the one on the right and motioned her to precede him up a steep, narrow staircase.

"Where does the other door lead?" she asked as she climbed the stairs.

"To my lecture hall, which is half below ground. It's where I teach smaller groups."

That he had his own lecture hall here came as a surprise to Corliss. But even more of a surprise was what she found when she got to the second floor. She had expected a corridor leading to a number of apartments, one of which would be the magister's. Instead, she found herself in one long rectangular hall with a high, vaulted ceiling and whitewashed walls, majestic in size but sparsely appointed. To the right, a leather curtain spanned the width of the space, so it was clearly even larger than it first appeared.

A savory aroma made her mouth water. Her gaze sought out the cavernous fireplace on the far left wall, in which an iron cauldron hung over a sputtering fire. Fish stew, if she had to guess, with plenty of wine and spices and leeks—a good Lenten supper. She hadn't eaten since yesterday and felt hungry, exhausted, and soaked to the bone. Thank God she'd finally get to sit down in a warm place and partake of a decent meal!

In front of the hearth stood a table, at which two black-robed scholars sat before tankards of ale and soggy trenchers of snowy white bread with thick crusts. "Hello, Master Fairfax!" called the sandy-haired one, laughing. He and his companion, a pleasant-looking youth with dark, cropped hair, greeted the teacher in slightly slurred French.

Master Fairfax tossed his bag in a corner. "Corliss, these drunken mongrels are Thomas and Brad, two of my most leechlike students."

She cleared her throat and tried to speak in a low pitch. "Pleased to meet you."

"I don't believe I've seen you before, Corliss," said Brad, the dark one. His English accent pleased her; he was a Saxon, like her. "What do you study?"

Corliss hesitated. "I . . . I came to Oxford to work, not to study." She set her satchel on the rush-covered floor, retrieved her *Biblia Pauperum*, and handed it to Brad. "I'm an illuminator."

The young men praised her workmanship, and she flushed with pride. "You must go to Catte Street," Thomas said. "That's where the booksellers, scribes and such have their shops."

"I know," she said, taking back the volume and

carefully replacing it in the satchel. "I went there today, but had no luck. Perhaps tomorrow."

The magister nodded toward the empty trenchers. "Have you two eaten all my supper again?"

Thomas shook his head, grinning. "Luella has taken to cooking extra. She's used to us by now."

"Where is she?"

"Downstairs," Brad said.

Master Fairfax crossed to an arched opening in the corner to the right of the hearth, through which Corliss could see a spiral staircase leading to the lower level. "I'm home, Luella!" he called down.

An odd twist of discomfort burned in Corliss's stomach. She had wondered about women, had considered the possibility that the robust priest—now ex-priest—kept a mistress in some convenient place. What more convenient place than one's own home?

As if sensing her speculation, the ex-priest in question said, "Luella is my housekeeper."

Just as I was Father Osred's housekeeper. Corliss heard footsteps ascend the curving staircase. Slow and heavy footsteps, she realized as they neared, and accompanied by stentorian breathing.

"It's about time!" came a gravelly, English-accented voice just as its owner—a very large, red-faced, and breathless woman of advanced years—appeared at the top of the stairs. "I was just tidying up the lecture hall for tomorrow, though I don't know as I should bother, seeing as how it'll look once that herd of yours is done with it." Her sharp little eyes settled on Corliss. "Who the devil are you, young man, and what are you grinning at?"

Corliss swiftly composed her features. "I didn't mean to stare, mistress. My name is Corliss."

Luella crossed her arms and raked Corliss with a coolly assessing gaze. "Another mouth to feed, eh, Father?" She stalked inelegantly to the table and gathered up the used trenchers, tossing them in a pail in the corner. "*And* clean up after!" she added, spearing Thomas and Brad with a censorious frown. She grabbed a large spoon from a hook and stirred the contents of the cauldron, releasing more of its seductive aroma into the room.

"Do stop calling me 'Father,' Luella. And yes, I do intend to feed Corliss, but we'll clean up after ourselves. I thought you might be ready to go home. Thomas and Brad will be happy to walk you back to Grope Lane." He cast a meaningful glance in their direction. "Won't you, boys?"

The two youths assented with a decided lack of grace, then swiftly gulped down the remainder of their ale and rose unsteadily.

"Lots of good they'll do me in *their* condition," grumbled Luella as Rainulf helped her on with her shawl.

"I was hoping you could protect *them*," the magister said. Luella hooted with laughter, the boys rolled their eyes, and the three took their leave.

The big hall rang with silence once Corliss and Master Fairfax were alone together. He said nothing, simply leaned back against the table, crossed his arms, and scrutinized her, as if inspecting a strange new type of creature he'd never seen before. Corliss began to shiver, as much from nervousness as from her sodden clothes. She licked her lips and looked around, observing the bare walls, the minimal furniture, the very vastness of the place.

"This whole house is yours?" she asked.

"Aye," he said without taking his eyes off her.

"It must have cost a fortune."

He appeared to ponder that. "I suppose that would depend on your definition of a fortune."

She detected a slight shift in the atmosphere between them, a subtle disquiet, and wondered at its cause. "That's not an answer."

"You didn't ask a question," he pointed out.

"Is this how academics converse?" she asked testily. "I hate it. Why won't you just tell me how much the house cost?"

"One isn't supposed to ask such things." He smiled oddly. "It cost thirty-eight pounds sterling."

Her jaw dropped open. "You have that much money?" Before he could answer, she said, "Of course you do. You're a cousin of the queen. You must be terribly wealthy, priest or no priest."

"I'm not a priest," he said a bit irritably, pushing away from the table, but keeping his eyes trained on her.

She took a step back. "Why do you keep staring at me like that?"

He almost smiled. "Father Osred was right. You *are* like a little child, always asking questions."

She raised her chin. "Well?"

After a moment's hesitation, he said quietly, a note of amazement in his voice, "They thought you were a boy."

So that was it. He couldn't believe her disguise actually worked! "That's the point of all this," she said, indicating her masculine garb with a sweeping gesture.

"No, but they really believed it. They have no idea you're a woman. None whatsoever."

She grinned. "You see? I could probably live this way for years, and none would be the wiser."

He turned his head toward the fire, clearly still engaged in his private ruminations. She followed his line of sight, her gaze lighting on the cauldron; she wondered how soon they would eat.

He rubbed his chin thoughtfully, his eyes distant and unfocused. Whatever he contemplated with such absorption was lost on Corliss. Her stomach groused impatiently. "Master Fairfax?"

His gaze darted to her, as if he'd forgotten she was there.

"Are we going to eat?"

"Yes, of course." But he made no move to serve supper. Instead, he said, "I'd prefer if you called me Rainulf."

She smiled slowly, finding herself inordinately pleased by this. "Are you sure?"

"Absolutely. There's no need for formality between us. Especially if ... that is, I was thinking ..." He dragged both hands through his hair. "I was thinking, since you've no place to live, and you pass so well for a young man ..."

"Yes?"

He took a deep breath. "It occurred to me you might want to live here. With me."

They stared at each other for a moment.

"With you?" she said.

"If you like. You'd be safer living with me than living alone—and not only from Sir Roger. Oxford is like any city—it's teeming with brigands and cut-purses. Of course, you'd have to be careful. We both would. 'Twould be scandalous if I were discovered to be living with a woman, but in your case, with your uncanny disguise ..." His gaze traveled over her rain-soaked mantle, and his expression darkened. "Oh, for pity's sake. Come."

It was with a certain wariness that she followed him to the leather curtain, which he pushed aside enough for the two of them to pass through. The section of hall on the other side—smaller than the main hall—had been furnished as a bedchamber. Constance felt a prickle of foreboding and stood utterly still, taking in the huge bed—the largest she had ever seen, easily capable of accommodating an entire family. Its saffron damask curtains were tied back, revealing several layers of quilts and a mountainous tumble of pillows. She assumed it had a feather mattress.

"It came with the house," Rainulf said, noticing the direction of her gaze. "I always felt it was just too big, too. . . ." He spread his hands and made a small, wry smile. "Perhaps you'll like it better."

Her mind instantly conjured up a picture of Father Osred, standing in his bedchamber dressed in nothing more than his shirt. *I don't imagine you've ever lain on a feather mattress. . . .* Did all priests sleep in such luxury? she wondered. *You can hang your things up here. . . .* Did *all* of them keep mistresses?

Of course, Rainulf Fairfax was no longer a priest, she reminded herself. Even if he had been chaste before renouncing his vows, there would be no need for chastity now.

"Here." He reached for her, and she flinched. His eyes met hers, and he smiled reassuringly. "Did I startle you? I just wanted to help you off with this." She watched his face as he unfastened her mantle, studied the concentration in his eyes as he worked on the complicated clasp; noticed the little vein on his forehead, pulsing through the smooth, golden skin. He smelled of rain and wet wool and clean male. Heat from his hands warmed her throat, and she swallowed hard, striving to keep her breathing steady.

Rainulf swept the mantle off her shoulders and draped it on a hook, then removed his drenched cappa and hung it up, as well. He unbuckled his belt and tossed it onto a finely carved chest, then pulled his damp tunic off over his head, leaving himself in shirt and braies. Turning his back to her, he squatted down, rolled up the loose trousers, and began unwrapping the long linen strips that bound his woolen hose. "You can put your boots in the corner there, and hang your other things on the wall."

Motionless, Corliss watched the muscles of his back and shoulders strain and flex beneath the linen of his shirt as he undid his hose. The sight was strangely captivating. She wondered what it would be like to share a bed with a man like Rainulf Fairfax; surely, were she to remain here, she would soon find out. The prospect was both compelling and disconcerting.

Most disconcerting.

Don't let yourself be tempted by his comeliness and his appealing ways, she warned herself. *'Twill be but more of the same. You'll be naught but a whore again, bartering your body for protection. You'll never know freedom.*

Would he let her go willingly, if she refused him? On the one hand, he was a good man; she knew that unequivocally. On the other, *all* men were beasts when aroused, and ruthless with women they believed to have led them on; Ella, very wise about such matters, had assured her of this many times. Corliss had no reason to doubt her, her own experience being limited to Sully and Osred, old men with waning sexual appetites. Rainulf Fairfax was not old, and he was a man of great strength. If he was determined to have his way with her, she'd be powerless to stop him.

Holding her breath, she backed up slowly, taking care to step cautiously in the rushes, so as not to draw his attention. Once past the leather curtain, she made a quick dash for her satchel, then darted into the stairwell, bounding down the steps in a blur.

Rainulf heard the pounding footsteps in the stairway and whipped his head around. "Corliss?" He rose and, frozen in bewilderment, listened to the sound of booted feet racing down the stairs, the dull thud of the front door slamming. "What the devil . . . ?"

In his mind he re-created the events of the last few minutes, searching for some reason for her sudden flight. Surveying the bedchamber, his gaze lit on the big, ridiculous bed, in which he had never once slept . . . his belt dangling off the edge of the chest . . . his discarded tunic and cappa, hung up next to her mantle—the mantle she hadn't even bothered to put back on before she fled out into the rainy night. He looked down at the woolen hose in his hand, then groaned, awareness dawning on him.

You fool, Rainulf Fairfax. Aye, she had fled. From him!

"Damn!" Flinging the hose aside, he sprinted to the stairwell, descended the steps three at a time, and ran out into the middle of St. John Street. The rain had died down to a drizzle, but it was chilly out—and dark as Hades, save for the occasional patch of light from a town house window. He spun around, peering through the gloom, his bare feet slipping on the muddy surface of the road. There she was—a small, receding figure running west toward the center of town.

"*Corliss!*" he shouted, but she didn't pause or turn around. Perhaps she hadn't even heard him.

With a muttered curse, he darted after her, mud spraying in his wake, his shirt and braies clinging wetly to him. With his lengthy strides, he swiftly gained on her. "*Stop!*" he called out when he knew she was within hearing distance, but this only encouraged her to pick up her pace.

At the corner of Shidyerd Street, he overtook her, grabbing on to her tunic as he battled to maintain his footing on the treacherous roadbed. It didn't work; his feet slid out from under him and he fell heavily, pinning her beneath him.

"Be still!" he demanded, as she struggled violently, thrashing to and fro and demanding to be let go. They grappled briefly in the rain and the mud, she lashing out with her fists and feet, he striving to subdue her without hurting her. Finally he seized her hands and pinned them next to her head. "Stop this! I'm not going to hurt you. I just want to talk to you."

"You want more than that," she spat out, her expression fierce through the mud spattered on her face. "But I assure you, Master Fairfax, I've had quite enough of playing the willing whore."

She writhed and strained to free her hands from his

grip; he tightened it. She brought one knee up sharply, but he moved aside to avoid it, then readjusted his weight so that his body pressed hers down, immobilizing her. Through his thin, sodden shirt he felt the rapid rise and fall of her chest, and fancied he could sense the birdlike racing of her heart, despite her heavy tunic.

"Corliss, listen to me!"

"If I'd been willing to trade my body for protection again, I'd have said yes to John Tanner. He wanted to marry me! All you want—"

"Is to help you."

"Hah!"

Rainulf drew in a deep lungful of air and let it out slowly, willing composure on himself. As soothingly as he could, he said, "I know what you thought, back there. I know how it looked. . . . I'm . . . unused to dealing with women, or I wouldn't have been so . . ." He shook his head helplessly, noting that she had grown still and alert. The rain had ceased while they were wrestling. A great silence descended over them, punctuated only by their ragged breathing.

"I was a fool," he continued quietly. She looked him in the eye as he spoke, the subtleties of her expression impossible to decipher in the dark. "It's been eleven years since I've had a woman in my home, Corliss. For eleven years I've been . . . well, a priest. And fully observant of my vows."

There was a pause while she digested this. Her head moved in a small nod, but then her eyes, wide and watchful, narrowed slightly. "Aye, but you're no longer a priest. I thought . . . when you began to undress, I thought . . ."

"Well, I *didn't* think. That was the problem. Believe me, I'm at fault." He sighed and shook his head, then loosened his hands from her wrists experimentally. When she didn't renew her struggles, he released her, supporting himself with his arms braced on either side of her head.

"Truly," he said, with all the conviction he could muster, "all I wanted was to get out of my wet tunic ... and I thought you might want the same. Perhaps it's because you pass so well for a boy that I didn't consider ... how it would all look to you. That you would think I was trying to ... well ..." His ears grew warm.

"Seduce me," she provided, a little spark of amusement lighting her eyes.

"Rest assured, I have no such plans," he said firmly.

Perhaps a little too firmly, for he detected just the briefest flicker of hurt in Corliss's expression before she marshaled her features and said, "That's very reassuring. Now, may I please sit up?"

He eased off her and rose, offering her his hand. She accepted it with a neutral expression and allowed him to help her to her feet.

"I didn't mean that the way it sounded," he assured her. "It's not that I'm not ... that I don't find you ..." He raked the fingers of both hands through his hair before realizing that they were covered with mud. Corliss looked up at him and giggled; Rainulf smiled, thinking he had never heard a lighter, more melodious sound. "In truth," he began sincerely, "you're a very attractive ..." He inspected her from head to foot, grinning to find her more mud-covered than not. "That is, *usually* a *most* attractive ..."

Laughter bubbled up from her. He laughed as well, marveling in the feel of it as it shook his chest, the sound of it, blending with hers.

He reached out and tried to wipe the mud off her face with his fingers, but that only made it worse.

"Do you have a bathtub in that wonderful big house of yours?" she asked.

"I do indeed. Would you like to go first?"

"You can. I'd rather eat first."

"It'll be cooked to the bottom of the pot by now."

"I'll eat it anyway," she said.

"As you wish." With a light hand on her arm, he turned her around and guided her back in the direction from which they had come.

The man called Pigot watched from a narrow, unlit alley as the ex-priest and the dark-haired youth walked back up St. John Street and disappeared into the enormous house.

So . . . the Magister Scholarum of Oxford likes boys. Then why, Pigot wondered, had he appeared so grief-stricken at the grave of the old rector's young mistress? Perhaps he was one of those whose passions encompassed both sexes.

Even so, he mused, a man like Rainulf Fairfax could do better than a whore like Constance of Cuxham. And not just a whore, but a tricky one—devious, deceitful, cunning. How well he knew her kind. He could teach her a lesson or two, he and his steel.

But first he had to find her. His instincts told him to keep a close watch on Master Rainulf Fairfax, because sooner or later, she'd come to him. . . .

And Pigot's instincts had never failed him yet.

Chapter 5

Corliss woke up slowly, surrounded by softness. *I'm in a cloud,* she thought dreamily, her eyes still closed. *I'm in Heaven.*

Heaven smelled lovely, like fresh laundry hung out to dry in fragrant breezes. It sounded like the giggly, careless chattering of birds. And it glowed with a rapturous golden light that she could see even through her closed eyelids, a light that surrounded her, soothed her, warmed her. . . .

If I open my eyes, 'twill all be gone. For long, peaceful moments she lay motionless, cocooned in her golden paradise. Gradually a sense of wakefulness—of reality—stole upon her, yet the birds still laughed and sang, the light still glowed.

"Ah," she breathed, remembering where she was.

Opening her eyes, she saw morning sunlight sifting through the saffron damask of the drawn bed curtains, illuminating the space they enclosed—as sizable as a small room—with extraordinary yellow light. *This is my bed now,* she thought with an awestruck grin. *My bed! Mine alone!* She yawned and stretched like a contented cat, then lay still, remembering last night, after she had fled and Master Fairfax—*Rainulf*—had brought her back.

The first thing he'd done—thank a merciful God!—had been to cut her a thick slice of bread and heap it high with fish stew. While she ate her fill, much too quickly, he set up a wooden tub in front of the fire-

place and put a pot of water on to boil. They took
turns bathing, shielded from each other's view by a
portable screen, then sat at the table and talked well
into the night.

They talked about her plans to find work as an illuminator. Rainulf told her everything he knew about
Catte Street, where most of Oxford's books were produced. They talked about this small walled city and
the changes it was undergoing, with the recent influx
of scholars and masters. They talked about teaching,
and how troubling it had become for Rainulf; about
the chancellorship he so desperately wanted, and the
necessity for his remaining celibate in order to secure it.

So you see, Corliss, he had reassured her, *you're
perfectly safe with me. I'd never jeopardize this opportunity by making you my . . . trying to make you my . . .*

Mistress?

He'd looked away quickly, nodding. *Not even in secret. Discretion is pointless. The truth is very stubborn,
and people always discover it. I've seen more than one
churchman stripped of his position—ruined—over a
woman. 'Twill never happen to me.*

His vague discomfort had both amused and in-
trigued her. How, she wondered, could a man like
Rainulf Fairfax have gone eleven years without suc-
cumbing to the temptations of the flesh? She pictured
him in her mind—his impressive stature, his lean and
muscular body, his fair-haired good looks, and those
gentle and perceptive eyes the color of a stormy lake.
Surely there had been women during those eleven
years who'd tried to coax him into violating his vow
of chastity. Yet, if she was to believe him—and she
did—he had never done so.

Eleven years . . . She snuggled deeper into the
downy mattress and pulled the sweet-smelling covers
up to her chin, reveling in the finely woven linen,
smooth as silk. *'Tis a frightfully long time for a man*

to go without sex. It would be no hardship for her, of course, the act being more a matter of duty than pleasure for women; but men seemed to need a good tupping on a fairly regular basis, or they got cranky. Perhaps, despite his seeming virility, Rainulf Fairfax didn't care for women—that way. Perhaps, like some priests she'd heard of, he preferred men and boys to the fairer sex.

Corliss squinted up at the expanse of yellowish damask overhead and contemplated that possibility. On the one hand, Rainulf had called her "attractive." And last night, after they'd bathed, when she'd sat across from him wearing naught but his own thin linen wrapper, his gaze had more than once strayed downward toward her breasts. Mayhap, she thought sourly, he was simply astounded that a grown woman should have so little where others boasted so much. It would be the height of conceit to think he'd find her most unappealing feature alluring.

The more she thought about it, the more likely it seemed that the handsome, engaging magister reserved his affections for those of his own sex. *A pity . . .*

Or perhaps not. *The last thing you should want,* she reminded herself, *is for Rainulf Fairfax to lust after you.* If he did—really did—could she resist him? And then what would happen to her precious freedom?

She closed her eyes and saw him as he had been that night in the rectory, after he'd built the great fire that was supposed to cure her of the yellow plague. Superstitious nonsense, of course; it was the hair of St. Nicaise that had cured her, not some absurd heathen sweating treatment. Yet it moved her deeply that he had gone to all that trouble for her. And he had looked so . . . untamed . . . when she'd awakened and found him next to her, bare-chested and sweating, his face flushed from the heat. He'd looked as if he'd just lain with a woman . . . and enjoyed it.

At least, that's what she'd thought at the time. Now

that she knew of his many years of celibacy, and his seemingly untroubled decision to remain chaste, she doubted that he had *ever* been with a woman; she doubted, moreover, that he had ever wanted to. This knowledge brought her some measure of relief, for she knew now that she could live here without fearing for her ... virtue?

A little late to try and salvage that! Crawling to the edge of the enormous bed, she swept aside the curtains, startling a handful of little brown house sparrows gossiping on the sill of an open window—the source of all that merry chirping. They scolded her irately as they fluttered away, leaving the sun-flooded chamber completely silent. She sat on the edge of the bed for a minute, thinking, *I live here now! This big bed, it's all mine!* She could scarcely believe her ears last night when Rainulf had given it to her—given her the whole bedchamber! *But where will you sleep?* she had asked. *Where I've always slept—on a straw pallet in front of the fireplace.* How odd, she'd thought, that he would eschew such delicious luxury for a straw pallet; but how lucky for her!

Crossing to the open window to breathe in the cool air, she gazed down at the rooftops of Oxford—many, like that over her head, covered with handsome oak shingles. There were even a few, over in the Jews' quarter, made of lovely, rust-colored curved tiles, and one that looked like it might be slate! *I'm a long way from Cuxham.* She closed the shutters. Even the grandest dwelling in the village of her birth—Sir Roger's manor house—was roofed with humble thatch.

Grateful to find water in the pitcher on the washstand, Corliss scrubbed her face. Then she used the chamber pot; there was a privy in the stable yard, but she didn't want to venture outside in the daylight wearing just the nightshirt Rainulf had lent her. She rummaged in her satchel for her big whalebone comb and quickly tidied her hair. *How wonderful not to have to plait it into those tedious braids,* she thought as she stowed away the comb. She pulled the nightshirt off over her head, then retrieved a fresh shirt and chausses.

The leather curtain that separated her bedchamber from the main hall began to part. "Someone in there?"

Luella! Clutching her clothes to her bare breasts, Corliss jumped onto the bed and yanked the curtains shut. "Uh . . ." She cleared her throat and consciously lowered her voice. "It's Corliss."

A slight pause. "Who? Show your face!"

Corliss poked her head out from between the curtains and forced herself to smile at the scowling housekeeper, who held her broom with both hands, as if ready to swing. "Corliss. From last night?"

"Oh. You." Luella lowered the broom. "Father let you sleep *there*?" She grunted and shook her head. "Figures. Come on out of there, then, and let me make up that bed."

Corliss shrank back and pulled the curtains closed, then began furiously wriggling into her chausses. "I . . . I'm not dressed."

Luella snorted with amusement. "I raised seven sons of my own, young man. You haven't got anything that'd shock *me.*"

I doubt that, thought Corliss, with a glance down at her half-naked body. "Please, Luella. Leave me and I'll dress quickly and then you can do whatever you need to."

Luella sighed heavily. "All right," she growled, leaving and closing the leather curtain behind her. "But make it quick!"

With more speed than she knew she was capable of, Corliss shimmied the chausses up over her small hips and tied the waist-cord, then tugged on her boots. She wrapped her breasts in a length of linen to compress them, then donned her shirt and tunic, just as Luella flung the curtain aside and stomped toward the bed.

"There's some wine and bread out there if you want," the old woman said as she briskly straightened the bedcovers.

"Thank you. Is Rain—er, Master Fairfax ... is he—"

"Father's been downstairs all morning, talking his ungodly gibble-gabble with all them so-called students of his."

"All morning?" asked Corliss, appalled. She had never slept so late in her life, except when she had the pox. "How late is it?"

Luella grunted. "Too late for a healthy young man to be lying abed, that's for sure. Father'll be wondering how come you're not down in the lecture hall with the rest of them."

"I'm not a scholar," Corliss admitted. "I'm looking for work."

"Glad to hear it! They're like packs of begging dogs, those *scholars*. Half of them'll be up here looking for a handout afterward. Master Thomas and Master Brad will, at any rate. Idle young good-for-nothing ..."

"Why do you still call him 'Father'?" Corliss asked. "He's not a priest anymore."

"Hmph!" Luella punched the pillows up, one by one, and piled them against the headboard. "You can't undo something like that just by wishing it so. Once a priest, always a priest. The idea ... thinking he can just wake up one day and ..."

Corliss stole out through the leather curtain while Luella griped and muttered. On the table in front of the fireplace she found a pitcher of watered wine, a loaf of crusty bread, and a wedge of cheese. She ate quickly feeling all the while like an impostor—which, in fact, she was. If Luella—or anyone else—knew her true sex, Rainulf Fairfax would be ruined.

Voices from downstairs drew her to the corner stairwell. She strained to hear the words from below, but couldn't make them out, so she descended on silent, soft-soled feet to the bottom of the circular stairs.

The lower level, like the upper, was all one huge room. The windows downstairs were smaller and higher than those upstairs, and there was no fireplace; otherwise the two halls were much the same. Corliss had thought Rainulf's living quarters austere, but his lecture hall was even more bare, containing but one piece of furniture—the lectern at the far end of the hall, at which Rainulf stood. The several dozen students crowded around him sat in the straw on the floor.

"And therefore," Rainulf was saying in Latin, "it falls to nominalism to apply the test of reason to the mysteries of the faith, including that of the Trinity." The magister noticed Corliss, and his demeanor changed, ever so subtly. He stood a bit straighter, seemed slightly more alert, more *there*. "Corliss."

Every head turned and stared at her; she backed up into the stairwell.

"Don't go away," Rainulf said, stepping out from behind the lectern. "We're done here." To his audience he said, in French, "Those who are interested may hear more on this subject tomorrow morning. And tonight at St. Mary's, we'll debate the relationship between logic, physic, and metaphysic."

His audience stood around and chatted for a few minutes as they swatted the straw from their black robes. Rainulf strode through the milling crowd and came straight to Corliss, with Thomas and Brad tagging behind. "A pity you missed the lecture. I think you would have enjoyed it."

Corliss gave a sheepish little laugh. "Do you think I would have understood it?"

He leaned down to whisper in her ear, "Better than most of these fellows." His breath was warm on her ear; little shivers of pleasure skittered through her body.

I'm such a fool. If Rainulf knew how she reacted to his touch, he'd surely laugh, unmoved as he was by the charms of her sex.

"What are your plans for the day?" Thomas asked her.

"Another visit to Catte Street," she said. "Late yesterday, someone told me about a widow named Enid Clark who's got a copying shop. They say she's looking for illuminators for a big job."

"Brad and I are going in that direction," Thomas said. "We'll walk with you as far as St. Mary's."

She was about to say yes, but Rainulf's furrowed brow stilled her tongue. "I'll accompany Corliss," he told the boys. "Why don't you two go upstairs and have some breakfast?"

Thomas and Brad eagerly took him up on the offer. Corliss emptied her satchel of everything except her *Biblia Pauperum,* slipped the little reliquary into her belt pouch—for luck—and set out with Rainulf for Catte Street. The weather had cleared up overnight, but the roads were narrow avenues of mud—until they came to High Street, which was more of a grand, wide avenue of mud, teeming with people. Many of them—not just academics, but townspeople!—waved to Rainulf, and he waved back, often greeting them by name. Everyone in Oxford seemed to know and like the handsome Magister Scholarum.

Corliss loved the controlled pandemonium of Oxford, so different from Cuxham's unchanging sameness. There was an atmosphere of lively expectation here, a sense that anything was possible—that one could unravel the mysteries of the universe if only one applied one's mind to the task. The very air here crackled with intellectual curiosity; it buzzed all around her, infusing her with its fervor, making the blood run swifter in her veins.

To the west, rising above the overhanging shops and town houses, loomed the great square tower of Oxford

Castle, the city's most prominent landmark. In that direction also stood dozens of market stalls, many clustered around St. Martin's Church, where the townspeople worshipped. During the week she'd spent in Oxford, Corliss had seen how the city's residents avoided the scholars. From all appearances, they despised them, despite the outrageous profit they made from renting them their rooms and selling them their food and drink. This antagonism struck her as odd and foolish. The scholars, after all, were what made Oxford so special; the merchants should welcome them with open arms, not overcharge them and treat them with contempt.

Corliss was not so lost in her own thoughts that she didn't notice Rainulf's pensive silence. He'd been out of sorts ever since they'd left the house. "Why didn't you want Thomas and Brad to come with me?" she asked as they crossed High Street.

Rainulf tossed a coin into the cap of a mendicant scholar begging outside St. Mary's. "I'm afraid to let them—or anyone—spend too much time with you."

"You're afraid I'll be found out," she guessed. "That I'll give myself away somehow."

At the corner of Catte Street he paused, frowning down at her. "It's exhausting to have to hide one's true nature for any length of time, Corliss. Believe me, I know. One day you may slip. You may say something, do something ... and you *will* be found out. You must take no chances—*none*. 'Twould be disastrous for me."

"For me as well," she pointed out, sounding more petulant than she would have liked. "I only adopted this disguise to protect myself. If it fails, I'm at Roger Foliot's mercy."

"Aye, and from all I hear, he doesn't know the meaning of the word. Do be careful," he cautioned, briefly laying a hand on her arm.

Her heart quickened at his touch. *Fool!* she chided herself. "I will."

They turned the corner and began walking north along Catte Street. "A few years ago, none of this was here," Rainulf said, indicating the businesses lining the street—parchmenters, writers, scribes, binders, and booksellers—with a generous sweep of his hand. "All the books came from the monasteries. Now most of them—most that are used in Oxford, at any rate—are made on Catte Street. There's a similar district in Paris. . . ."

Rainulf continued on in this manner as they walked, describing the rise of the great centers of learning and the corresponding demand for books: textbooks and sacred books; books of theology, philosophy, logic, and astronomy; tales of ancient battles and tragic romances; law books from Bologna, medical books from Salerno; books by so-called pagans and infidels, banned for centuries in Paris, but displayed proudly and openly in the bookshops of Oxford's Catte Street.

He'd slipped into the role of teacher, Corliss realized. It was so natural to him that he didn't even seem aware of it, seemed hardly to notice that he wasn't making conversation, but presenting a lecture. His eyes glittered as he delivered his discourse; his whole countenance seemed to glow with an inner light. She smiled sadly to herself. Teaching was in his blood; it was fundamental to who he was. How could he think of giving it up?

The used-book shops seemed irresistible to Rainulf, and he insisted on visiting nearly every one. The proprietors all knew him, and would lead him to whatever volumes they'd managed to acquire since his last visit—all either locked in cages or tethered by chains to heavy reading tables. He made two purchases: a fairly new copy of *The Antidotarium* by someone called Nicholas of Salerno, for which he paid the staggering sum of sixty shillings; and a rather shabbier *Ars*

Medicinae by one Constantinus Africanus, which cost half as much.

"They're for my sister, Martine," he explained. "She's interested in the medicinal uses of herbs. I'll be visiting her and Thorne soon. She's expecting their first child, and I promised I'd try to get to Blackburn before the birth. I've only seen her once, briefly, since I returned from pilgrimage. We're due for a long visit together."

Corliss didn't ask how soon he'd leave, or how long he'd be gone, although the questions rose to her lips. Nor did she ask if she could remain at the big house on St. John Street during his absence. She had no claim of any kind on Rainulf Fairfax or his home, and she'd best get used to that fact.

"There it is," she said, pointing to a large, two-story shop with the legend E. CLARK, SCRIPTORIS painted in graceful red lettering over the open door. To one side of it was nailed a thick parchment poster displaying specimens of eight different scripts, all flawlessly penned.

Rainulf indicated that she should precede him into the shop. Swallowing hard, she dusted off her tunic and walked inside. At sloped writing desks next to the windows sat two young men and a girl, hunched over their parchment. Each had a penknife in one hand and a quill in the other, with which they were industriously copying the text from books propped open with lead weights. All three looked up at her as she entered. The youths nodded in a preoccupied way and returned to their work, but the girl—a fragile honey blonde of perhaps fourteen—stared at Corliss, her quill poised in the inkhorn. Corliss smiled at her, whereupon her cheeks stained scarlet. She looked down momentarily, then shyly returned the smile and looked down again.

"Felice!" barked a woman from the back of the shop.

The girl started and jerked the pen out of the horn,

spattering her half-finished page with ink. Groaning, she slumped in her seat. "Sorry, Mama. I think it's ruined."

Her mother sighed. "Try to scrape it off. That took you all morning to do. May I help you, gentlemen?" Her gaze lit on Rainulf. "Ah, it's the Master of Schools himself. What can I do for you, sir?"

"You can spare a few moments of your time for my friend, mistress." Guiding Corliss with a gentle hand on her back, Rainulf urged her toward the woman. She wore the wimple and veil of a respectable widow, beneath which peeked out hair like polished bronze. The vivid green of her kirtle emphasized her emerald eyes; she was an older version of her daughter. Like the others, she was busily reproducing an exemplar held open on her large and elaborate desk.

Taking a deep breath, Corliss said, "Are you Mistress Clark?"

"I am."

Corliss took her *Biblia Pauperum* out of the satchel. Enid Clark laid down her pen and knife and held her hand out. Corliss hesitated, noticing the woman's ink-stained fingers.

"It's dry," Mistress Clark assured her as she took the book out of Corliss's hands. Her eyebrows rose when she opened it and began reading. "English?" She studied it carefully, taking her time and peering closely at every intricate illustration.

She glanced up at Corliss. "I'll give you a hundred shillings for it."

"What?"

"A hundred twenty, then." Closing the volume and running her fingers over the embroidered cover, she said, "I don't usually trade in used books, mind you, but I'll make an exception for this one." Her soft smile rendered her much less intimidating in Corliss's eyes.

"Mistress, I really couldn't—"

"She couldn't take less than eight pounds sterling for it," Rainulf interjected.

Corliss gasped; he closed a hand over her shoulder and squeezed sharply, but she refused to be silenced—*or* to have him negotiate for her, as if she couldn't manage her own affairs. "Thank you, Mistress Clark, but I have no intention of—"

"Seven and a half," the lady scribe countered.

Rainulf shook his head. "Seven and—"

"*Stop!*" The two hagglers fell silent. "Thank you, but I can't sell it. I can't. It's . . ." She shook her head; words were inadequate. When she reached for the book, Enid Clark met her gaze with a look of understanding and placed it carefully in her hands. Corliss returned it to her satchel.

"It's special," the woman said quietly. "Yes. It is, indeed. I envy you your ownership of it. Where did you acquire it?"

The question made Corliss laugh. "I made it!"

The scribe stared at her. "You mean you copied the text yourself? What exemplar did you use?"

"I wrote it myself, and illuminated it, too."

"Who bound it?"

"I did."

Mistress Clark grinned and shook her head. "Did you slaughter the sheep and make the parchment, too?"

"Nay, but I know how."

"I have no doubt that you do. It seems you're a young man of many and diverse talents. What brings you to my shop today?"

Rainulf stepped forward. "My friend is looking for work as an illuminator."

Corliss grabbed his arm and drew him back. "Your friend has a tongue," she whispered—too loudly, for Mistress Clark heard and chuckled. "They tell me you need illuminators," Corliss said.

Mistress Clark nodded. "A very important client has

commissioned a rather ambitious project—all the
books of the Bible in one volume. Everything . . .
Psalms"—she indicated the exemplar on her desk, a
monastic psalter—"gospels, minor prophets . . . What
normally fills twenty or more volumes will all be
bound into one huge book."

Rainulf let out a low whistle. "Is that possible?"

Mistress Clark shrugged. "We'll find out. We're
using the finest uterine parchment, so thin you can see
through it." She held out the sheet she was working
on for Corliss to touch; it was soft as Sicilian wool,
and nearly transparent. "If it can be done, we'll do it.
But I'll have to hire on extra copyists, and I can use
all the illuminators I can get"—she fixed her gaze on
Corliss—"but they have to be good."

"I'm good," Corliss stated flatly.

Mistress Clark smiled, clearly pleased at the lack of
false modesty. "You're more than good. But I need
someone who can apply gold. I noticed there's none
in that *Biblia Pauperum* of yours."

"Only because it's so dear. I know how to use it."

"Leaf or dust?"

"Both."

The older woman nodded slowly. "Do you have
someplace to work? I'll provide you with your supplies, but I'll have no room here after I hire the new
copyists."

"I . . ."

"Aye," Rainulf inserted. "Sh— He has everything
he needs at home."

At home. Corliss liked the sound of that, as if his
home—his wonderful home with its grand, soft bed—
were really hers.

"All right, then," said Mistress Clark. "I pay four-
pence each for a large gold initial. The small ones are
three for a penny. Paragraph marks are ten for a
penny. You'll get a shilling for every full-page illumi-

nation, sixpence for half a page. I'll expect you to work quickly."

Rising, she gestured for Corliss to follow her to a large table in a back room, on which were stacked dozens of signatures ready for illuminating. The gatherings of double pages were fully lettered but unsewn, and numbered so that they could eventually be bound in the proper order. "The scribes have left spaces for the illustrations, and they've written margin notes as to what should go into them." She slipped a signature into a leather sheath and gave it to Corliss, who stowed it in her satchel. Mistress Clark then handed her a slim book from a stack of identical volumes. "Copy the artwork from this pattern book."

"Oh." Corliss leafed dejectedly through the book, which contained decorative capitals in ascending sizes, as well as sample illustrations: angels, stars, birds, rabbits, stags, herons. In the back were pictures of various mythical beings: unicorns, lions, monkeys, and assorted grotesques. "I thought . . ." Corliss began.

"Yes?"

"I thought I could make up the pictures myself." That sounded like whining, she realized, so she opted for a different approach: "Such an important book ought to have original pictures, don't you think? I'm an excellent draftsman."

"You are that." Mistress Clark looked thoughtful for a moment. "Very well. You may do as you wish with that signature. But if I'm not pleased when you bring it back, you'll have to recopy the whole thing for free, *and* reimburse me eightpence for the parchment."

Corliss grinned and handed back the pattern book. "Thank you, mistress. And you *will* be pleased—I guarantee it!"

Rainulf said, "How long do you think it will take to complete this Bible?"

"Probably around four months," the scribe answered as she gathered together the various pigments Corliss would need for her work: black and red inks, vermilion, lead white, yellow volcanic earth, green malachite, even a tiny pot of precious lapis lazuli, known as ultramarine, and gold leaf. "It could take as long as half a year, perhaps longer. And it's all we'll be working on. Of course, Master Becket's making it worth our while. We're getting forty pounds for it."

"Master Becket?" Rainulf said. "Thomas Becket— the king's chancellor? That's who commissioned this Bible?"

"Aye. And the job couldn't have come at a better time. I'm tired of this business, tired of living in two rooms over this shop. I want to move out of Oxford and raise goats and chickens. I've been wanting out ever since my husband died two years ago, but I couldn't afford to leave. Now I'll be able to."

"I'm very proud to be working on Thomas Becket's Bible," Corliss said as she latched her heavily laden satchel. "Thank you for giving me the opportunity."

Rainulf thanked her, too, and they took their leave. Corliss noticed young Felice gazing at her rather wistfully as she crossed to the door. One of the young men—a large fellow with dark, curly hair—scowled at Corliss and gripped his penknife in a white-knuckled fist.

"Bertram," Mistress Clark admonished, "get back to work. You, too, Felice."

They left the shop and began walking down Catte Street, but Rainulf stopped in his tracks, his expression alert and wary. "Did you see that?" he asked, pointing across the street. "Someone ducked into that alley as soon as we came out."

"Who? Do you know him?"

"I didn't get a good look at him, but he backed up quickly, as if he didn't want us to see him."

"You're making much out of nothing," she said.

"I think not. You stay here."

"Rainulf—"

"Stay here," he repeated. "I'll be right back." He crossed the street and disappeared into the alley.

Corliss sighed impatiently and waited in the street. After a minute she felt a hand grip her shoulder hard and wheel her around. It was the dark-haired scribe, the one called Bertram.

"Stay away from Felice," he demanded.

"What?"

"You heard me. I saw how you were looking at her."

"Wait, you've got it all—"

"Just stay away from her. Her and me are going to be married next year. I already arranged it with Mistress Clark."

"Does Felice know that?"

"That's none of your affair. *She's* none of your affair. I love her and I'm going to marry her, and you're going to keep your distance from her. Understand?"

The panic in his eyes startled Corliss. *Good God, he really is in love with her!*

"I've no interest in her," Corliss assured him.

Bertram backed up slowly toward the shop. "Just you see it stays that way," he warned as he went inside.

"My, my." Corliss turned to find Rainulf standing behind her, arms crossed, a glint of amusement in his eyes. "It would seem you pass rather well for a man, after all."

"I *told* you!" she snapped as they began walking south on Catte Street. "Did you find your mysterious man?"

"Nay. He eluded me. But I know he was there. Watching us."

"Mm-hm."

Rainulf speared her with a sideways glance. They walked in silence until after they came to High Street. "Why didn't you sell her the book? She'd have given you almost eight pounds! You could have lived off that for a long time."

" 'Twas tempting," Corliss admitted. "But I couldn't bear to take money for something I'd put so much love and effort into. And I'm not looking to live a life of idleness. I want to work! I want to illuminate books." She shrugged. "At least now I know that I *can* sell it if I ever find myself without resources."

He made a sound that might have been the beginning of a laugh. "I can't imagine you ever being without resources, Corliss. You're the most resourceful person I've ever known. The most remarkable, the most . . ." He paused on the busy street and looked down at her for a moment, then looked away, seeming strangely ill at ease.

"Rainulf?"

Presently his gaze refocused on her and he smiled, but it looked forced. "Have you ever been to an alehouse?"

"An alehouse? Of course not!"

He grinned and steered her by her arm diagonally across the wide avenue. "There's a fairly unobjectionable one on Blue Boar Lane. Let me buy you a pint. Then we can go hunt you up a desk for your work."

Chapter 6

"Exquisite." Corliss whispered the word out loud as she walked in a daze from the shop on Catte Street to the house on St. John. That was the word Enid Clark had used when Corliss had handed her the completed signature, fully illuminated. *This is exquisite work. And it took you less than a week! I'm so pleased to have found you.* Then she'd filled Corliss's hands with money and given her another signature to work on.

Corliss fingered the pouch on her belt, heavy with silver coins and the little reliquary, whose good fortune had not failed her yet. She sprinted up to the big stone house, threw open the door, and bounded up the stairs, filled with a heady excitement. *So this is what freedom feels like!*

Thomas sat with a tankard of ale at the table in the main hall, looking a good deal more disheveled than usual. His sandy hair was unkempt, and his shirt hung loose over his chausses.

"Corliss!" He stood abruptly and nervously finger-combed his hair. "Back already? It's not even noon."

Cappas, tunics, belts, and boots lay strewn about the floor. "This place is a mess," Corliss said, setting her satchel down on the chair attached to her big desk. "Where's Luella?"

"Out marketing. Uh, Corliss—"

"I've got good news, Thomas!" She crossed to the

leather curtain and swept it aside. "Mistress Clark liked my—"

"Corliss, wait!"

Someone moaned. Corliss froze on the threshold of her bedchamber, listening. Low, masculine murmurs ...

A woman's voice, from behind the drawn curtains of the big bed: "Do you like it like this?"

The man gasped. "Oh, yes! That's it. Yes!" Corliss recognized Brad's English-accented voice.

There began a muffled rhythmic squeaking of the ropes that supported the huge mattress. The yellow damask curtains shifted in time to the sound.

Corliss turned to find Thomas behind her, grinning sheepishly. "Don't be mad. We'll let you share her."

"*What?*"

The squeaking stopped. A plump female hand reached out and parted the damask, revealing the couple within. The woman—a frowsy blonde—was on top, her front-lacing kirtle undone and gaping open. Brad lay beneath her, cradling one enormous breast in each hand; he muttered a low Anglo-Saxon curse upon seeing Corliss.

The woman's gaze swept Corliss from head to foot, sizing her up. "You'll have to wait your turn, love. And it'll cost you tuppence. *Ahead* of time." With that she yanked the curtain closed, and the bed promptly recommenced its steady rocking.

"I don't believe this," Corliss told Thomas as he led her into the main hall, reclosing the leather curtain. "That's *my* bed. *Mine!*"

He shrugged as he tucked his shirt into his chausses. "We can't bring wenches back to our rooms. The landlady won't permit it."

"Does Rainulf know you bring them here?"

Thomas blanched. "Nay. He'd never allow it."

Even through the leather curtain, Corliss could hear the increasingly hectic creaking of the bed.

"Of course he wouldn't!" Corliss said. "He'd be

outraged if he knew. He's got a reputation to maintain, Thomas. He could be ruined if people found out that kind of woman had been here. Did anyone see her come in?"

"I don't think so."

Brad released a satisfied groan, and then the creaking ceased.

"You don't *think* so?" Corliss spat out.

"Don't be angry," Thomas pleaded. "And please don't tell him. Come on—be a sport. You can have her for free. I'll pay the tuppence myself."

"I don't want her."

"Don't be too hasty." Thomas grinned. "Alfreda is very . . . talented."

"I'm not interested. Just get her out of here."

He adopted a conspiratorial air and lowered his voice. "She's got a *very* clever mouth, if you know what I mean."

Corliss had no idea what he meant.

Her ignorance must have shown on her face, for Thomas said, "Have you ever even bedded a woman?"

Corliss felt heat sweep up her throat and suffuse her face. "Of course."

Thomas eyed her knowingly. "No, you haven't. A sad state of affairs, I'd say." He located his purse among the discarded clothing and shook two pennies into his palm. "But one easily remedied."

The leather curtain opened and Brad stepped through, tying his chausses. He nodded to Corliss. "She's waiting for you."

"She'll have a long wait," Corliss said, backing up.

"Come on," Thomas urged, grabbing her by the arm and pulling her toward the bedchamber. "It's my tuppence! Give her a go!" As an aside to Brad he added, "He's nervous. It's his first time."

"Truly?" Brad laughed and took her other arm.

"You could do worse than lose your virginity to Alfreda. She knows every trick there is."

"No!" Corliss howled as they drew her into the chamber and toward the bed. The curtains were open. Alfreda reclined against the mountain of pillows, yawning, her breasts still exposed, the skirt of her kirtle raised up above her stout white thighs. She held her hand out and Thomas put the two pennies in it.

"Come to Alfreda, love," the whore coaxed tiredly, her arms extended.

Thomas and Brad pushed her onto the bed and closed the curtains around her. A ripe scent comprised of cloying perfume and unwashed flesh filled Corliss's nostrils. Alfreda reached for her. She scrambled backward, turned, and tore the curtains open. "Get her out of here *now,* or I'm telling Rainulf!"

The two young men gaped at her. "He's serious," Brad concluded.

"Leave now," Corliss said, jumping down, "and never bring another woman here, and I'll keep quiet. Otherwise, Rainulf finds out everything!"

Thomas and Brad exchanged a look, and then Thomas said, "We'd better get going, Alfreda. It seems young Corliss is determined to remain pure and unsullied despite our best efforts to corrupt him."

"I'm keeping the tuppence," Alfreda announced as she retied her kirtle.

Thomas sighed. "And welcome to it, my dear."

When they were finally gone, Corliss whipped the quilts off the bed and stripped the sheets for Luella to wash when she returned. As she struggled to tie them into a bundle, a knock came at the front door. Muttering an oath—something she'd never once done while she still wore kirtles—she kicked the wad of sheets across the bedchamber, then pounded down the stairs and opened the door.

A man stood there—a large man, hunched beneath the satchel on his back, in coarse braies and a short hooded cloak with a pointed cowl pulled down low. With his head partly bowed, and that cowl, his face was lost in shadow, despite the glaring noon sun.

"Yes?" Corliss said testily.

The man nodded slightly without raising his head. "Good-good ..." He hesitated, as if struggling with the words. "Good day, m-mistress."

"Mistress?" Her scalp tightened. "Why do you call me mistress?"

The man stood unmoving for a moment, as if gathering his thoughts. "Y-you seemed like ... th-that is ..."

He hadn't once looked at her. "Raise your head," she said. "Look how I'm dressed. Do I look like a woman to you?"

The man hesitated, then slowly raised his head—very slowly, as if lifting a heavy burden. As the sunlight played over his features, Corliss stifled a gasp. His broad, fleshy face was deeply pitted, all over, with hundreds of pockmarks—the worst Corliss had ever seen. He looked like one of the grotesques in Mistress Clark's pattern book—an imaginary creature surely inspired by the ravages of leprosy. In fact, she might have thought this man a victim of that disease rather than the pox had his scars been deeper and more irregular.

She bit her lip, contrition gnawing at her. Had the hair of St. Nicaise not protected her during her own bout with the yellow plague, she could have ended up looking like this man. Beneath his disfigurement, she reminded herself, he was just a man like any other—a peddler, judging from the satchel on his back.

"I'm sorry," she said. "I've been rude. I was out of sorts and I took it out on you."

She saw surprise in the peddler's eyes, as if kind words were foreign to him. What must it be like to go through life regarded as less than human? On impulse she asked, "What's your name?"

He paused. "My r-real name, or"—his expression

became grim—"what-what-what"—he shook his head in evident exasperation over his stuttering—"what they c-call me?"

God only knew what vile nickname the people of Oxford had thought up for this poor creature. "Your real name."

"Rad," he said presently.

"Rad," she repeated. "I'm pleased to meet you, Rad. My name is Corliss." She nodded toward his satchel. "What have you to show me?"

The peddler thumped his big satchel down and opened it, pulling out a large blue cloth, which he spread out on the ground at her feet. On this cloth he arranged a dizzying display of goods, some new and some clearly secondhand: battered pots and pans, fireplace pokers, spoons of all sizes, small bolts of cloth, skeins of colored silk, kid slippers, fur-lined gloves.

A hairbrush caught her eye, and she knelt down to examine it. "Oh, how lovely." It had stiff boar bristles and a handle of intricately carved ivory.

"It's n-new," Rad offered.

"What do you want for the brush and these ribbons? Oh, and this piece of lace."

He squatted down so they were eye to eye. "Four-p-p-pence for the lot."

"It's worth sixpence if it's worth a penny," she said. "You're just being nice to me. What else have you got in that bag of yours?"

"N-nothing as f-fine as that."

"No?" Leaning over, she peered into the open mouth of the satchel and saw the glint of steel. "Knives, I see. You've certainly got a lot."

"You-you-you n-need knives?" he asked.

"No, Rad, thanks just the same. Perhaps if I had a kitchen of my own, but I'm really just a guest here. Master Fairfax has been kind enough to take me in—"

"What have we here?"

Corliss squinted up to see Rainulf standing over her, silhouetted against the bright sky. He was staring fixedly at the huge collection of knives. She stood and held out the brush for him to admire. "Look—isn't this pretty?"

He glanced at it briefly, then turned his hard gaze on the peddler, who proceeded to gather up his wares. "How much?" the magister asked, withdrawing his purse.

"S-sixpence," Rad said without looking up.

"Here." Rainulf withdrew the coins, but Corliss grabbed his wrist.

"They're my things. I'll pay for them." She retrieved the sixpence from her pouch and gave it to Rad, who stowed it away without looking at her.

"Be on your way," Rainulf told the peddler.

Corliss glared at him, but he wouldn't meet her eyes. Arms crossed, he watched Rad pack up his things and shamble down the road.

"What's gotten into you?" she asked.

"I might ask the same of you." He frowned at her purchases. "Ribbons? Laces? A lady's hairbrush? Do you *want* to be found out?" He stepped through the doorway and stormed up the stairs.

He's right. She ran her fingers over the carved ivory, the dainty strands of silk. She'd been indiscreet. What would he say if she knew Rad had called her "mistress?" She pondered the situation as she slowly climbed the stairs to the main hall. He may have been right about the ribbons and such, but still he'd been unforgivably rude to Rad. She would never have expected such discourtesy from Rainulf Fairfax. Perhaps she didn't know him as well as she thought.

Rainulf stood at a window and gazed out at the rolling pastures beyond the north wall of Oxford. He heard Corliss come upstairs and go into her bedchamber, presumably to put away her new things. Presently she came out again.

"You had no right to talk to Rad that way," she said. "He meant no harm. He's just a peddler trying to make a living."

"How do you know?" he challenged, turning to face her. She stood there in her tunic and chausses, with her feet apart and her hands fisted at her sides, ready to take on the world. She looked amazingly like the young man she pretended to be. Only Rainulf knew otherwise—and Father Gregory, of course, to whom he confided everything. And now, perhaps, this Rad.

"Really, Rainulf. First it's shadowy figures in alleyways. And now, every person I befriend becomes suspect—"

"You have no business befriending people like that peddler."

"Why? Because of how he looks? I can't believe you, of all people, would judge a man on the basis of—"

"You should know me better than that, Corliss. His appearance means naught to me. And it *should* mean naught to you, but in fact, you seem to assume some innate goodness in him *because* of his misfortune. Life isn't always like that. People who've suffered can be evil, too. Certain kinds of suffering can even bring out wickedness in those of weak character."

"Oh, for Heaven's sake, Rainulf. The man is harmless."

"No one of that size is harmless."

"He's simple-minded . . . I think."

"But you don't know for sure." He strode over to her and grabbed her upper arms. "All you really know is that Sir Roger has sent someone to find you. Someone who will not only return you to Cuxham, but do serious harm to you in the process. You ought to have more sense than to expose yourself to strangers this way. You're making yourself too visible, Corliss. You lark about on your own, in all precincts and at all hours. This morning Father Gregory told me he saw you last night with a group of scholars outside St. Mary's, listening to that hothead, Victor."

She wrested out of his grip and rubbed her arms. "I thought he pointed out some genuine concerns."

Rainulf grunted. "Pointing out concerns is easy. Doing the right thing about them is hard. Victor invites trouble. I think he may actually want to die. They tell me he used to be quite the ruthless mercenary—completely bloodthirsty. Perhaps he thinks he's sinned so badly that he must atone with his own death."

"That's preposterous."

"Perhaps. Nevertheless, you mustn't fall in with his crowd, Corliss—or any crowd. You mustn't go out at night so much, or talk to strangers, or trust *anyone*. One of these days someone may take a good hard look at you and realize you're not what you seem."

She smiled dismissively. "No one pays any attention to me. I'm just another adolescent boy roaming around Oxford—one of hundreds. Don't you understand? For the first time in my life, I'm free to go where I please and do what I want, and no one tries to stop me—except you."

He dragged his hands through his hair. "I just don't want to see you get hurt."

She raised her chin. "You just don't want to lose the chancellorship, and you're afraid that's what will happen if people find out you're living with a—"

"It's not just that, Corliss. I'm worried about you. If anything happened to you ..." He sighed heavily. "I'm going to have to forbid you to continue exposing yourself to danger in this manner."

"What do you mean?"

"I won't permit you out after dark anymore."

Outrage flared in her wide brown eyes. "*What?*"

He tried to gentle his voice. "Not unless I'm with you. And you'll have to limit your movements and associations—"

"You can't be serious." She gaped at him, her face a mask of disbelief. "Please tell me you're not serious."

"Corliss . . ." He reached for her, but she backed away from him.

"I can't believe you're saying these things to me. I can't believe you're doing this to me."

"Corliss!"

"I didn't come to Oxford to be told what to do and when to do it, where to go and who to talk to."

"It's for your own good, Corliss."

"I thought you were different," she said, her voice quavering. "But you're like every other man I've ever known. You think you have the right to tell me what to do, just because of what hangs between your legs. You know, when you come right down to it, you're little better than Roger Foliot."

"Corliss . . ."

She swept past him and into her bedchamber, tugging the leather curtain closed behind her.

He listened outside the chamber for several minutes. She was moving about in there. "Corliss?"

No answer. He parted the curtain. Her satchel lay open on the unmade bed. Within it he saw her clothes and the *Biblia Pauperum.* She picked her comb up off the washstand and tossed it on top, then buckled it and slung it over her shoulder.

"It's not that I don't appreciate everything you've done for me," she said, calmer now. "But I can't live the way you want me to live. Not anymore. I'll come back for my paints and inks and things as soon as I find my own place."

She tried to walk past him, but he blocked her way. "You can't afford a decent place, Corliss—not yet, anyway."

"I'd rather live in the most dismal rented room, and be free, than to stay here."

"I thought . . ." A strand of hair hung in her eyes;

he brushed it aside and saw her bite her lip. Very quietly he said, "I thought you liked it here."

"I love it here," she replied softly. "I never thought I'd live in such a grand house. And you've been ..." She looked down. "You've been very kind. But if the only way I can live here is to give up my freedom, I'm no better off than a bird in a cage. A very grand cage, to be sure, but a cage nonetheless. Good-bye, Rainulf."

She tried to walk around him, but he seized her shoulders. "Corliss, don't."

She tried to twist out of his grip. "Rainulf, please. Let me go."

"No." He held her tighter.

"Why not?"

"Because I don't want to." With one hand wrapped around her back and the other holding her head against his chest, he murmured, "I don't want you to go."

He could barely hear her when she spoke, but he thought she said, "I don't either."

His heart thundered in his chest. "Then don't."

"I have to."

"No you don't." He closed his eyes and rubbed his cheek against her glossy hair. "You don't. Stay."

"But—"

"I won't tell you what to do," he promised in a hoarse whisper. "I won't tell you where to go."

She backed away slightly. Her arms encircled him, he realized; when had she returned his embrace?

"Really?" she said. Her warm breath tickled his face. She was so close.... He felt her chest rise and fall with every breath she took.

He nodded. "Just promise me ... promise me you'll be careful."

Those charming little frown lines appeared between her eyebrows. "Nay," she said, "I refuse to be careful." He blinked, and she burst out laughing. "You are so dreadfully serious, Rainulf Fairfax. I must try to cure you of that."

He found himself smiling. "Then you'll stay?"

"Aye."

He squeezed her tight and kissed the top of her head. She looked up at him; his gaze traveled from her eyes to her mouth, slightly parted. He felt breathless, light-headed. . . .

I could lower my mouth, he thought crazily, *until it touches hers. I could kiss her.* It would be the most natural thing in the world.

And the most foolish.

He released her—somewhat abruptly, he realized—and stepped back. "Good," he said gruffly. "You'll be safe here."

A fleeting trace of sadness darkened her eyes, and then she smiled stiffly and nodded.

From beyond the leather curtain he heard the groaning of stairs, and then a voice from the main hall, Luella's voice: "Father Rainulf? Corliss? Anybody home?"

They drew farther apart, just as Luella flung the leather curtain open. "Here you are! I've got nice, fresh bread for dinner, and some lovely sausages. Shall I cook them up now? Are you hungry, Father?"

Rainulf let out a long, ragged sigh. "Do stop calling me 'Father,' Luella. And yes, I'm hungry . . . terribly hungry."

Chapter 7

"Shall I begin?" Rainulf asked, pulling up a chair next to Corliss's desk and unfolding the sheaf of parchment.

"Go ahead," she said, "but move your chair back a bit so your breath doesn't disturb the gold leaf." He did as she asked. In truth, there was little risk in having him sit so close—except to her composure. During the month they'd been living together, the foolish attraction she felt for him had not diminished in the least; in fact, it grew stronger day by day. To attempt the tricky business of applying gold leaf with Rainulf Fairfax mere inches away was more of a challenge than she felt up to.

He cleared his throat and began to read Abelard's letter of consolation to his friend. " 'There are times when example is better than precept for stirring or soothing human passions; and so I propose to follow up the words of consolation I gave you in person with the history of my own misfortunes, hoping thereby to give you comfort in absence.' "

"Comfort?" she said as she arranged her tools and materials on the flat desk for easy access. "What made him think his own problems would give anyone comfort?"

"Well—"

"Was this a real letter? It doesn't sound like a letter to a friend. Sounds more like an excuse to talk about himself ... to whine about his problems."

Rainulf gave an astonished little gasp of laughter. "Peter Abelard didn't *whine*. He was the greatest—"

"The greatest thinker in Europe," she finished, mocking his sober tone. "A man of extraordinary brilliance. And, it would seem, something of a whiner."

Avoiding Rainulf's gaze, she made a show of leaning over the double page on her desk to examine the miniature she was preparing to gild. Hard as she tried, she couldn't keep from smiling at Rainulf's outrage. He took everything so terribly seriously. She knew she oughtn't goad him so much, but he made it so irresistible. A glance revealed that he was smiling, too. *Ah! Progress!*

"As it happens," he said, "you're right about this being more than a simple letter. It's generally agreed that Abelard intended it to become public and set the record straight about his supposed heresy and his love affair with Héloïse. I understand it's been in circulation for nearly three decades, although this is the first I've seen of it. I'm curious as to how he's going to explain away Héloïse. As a teacher, he was supposed to remain celibate." He found his place in the document. "Shall I continue?"

"Please."

" 'I was born on the borders of Brittany, about eight miles I think to the east of Nantes. . . .' "

Corliss took a long, critical look at the drawing she'd inked but not yet colored—St. Luke at a writing desk, with an angel peeking out of a cloud above—and felt inordinately pleased with herself. The lines were fluid and natural, the folds in Luke's robe the best she'd ever drawn. His face had come out particularly well—handsome yet thoughtful, almost grim. The nose was straight and aristocratic, the jaw strong, the eyes kind and intelligent. Her instructions had been to give the saint long, flowing hair and a beard, and this she had done; but for them, the face staring up at her from the parchment was none other than the face of Rainulf Fairfax.

She glanced from the portrait to the man himself, absorbed in reading his beloved Abelard's rather self-indulgent *Historia Calamitatum.* " 'At last I came to Paris, where dialectic had long been particularly flourishing. . . .' "

His face glowed with a light sheen of perspiration. It was dreadfully hot for May, and she'd had to tack parchment over the window by the desk so the warm breezes wouldn't disturb the gold leaf. He wore an untucked white shirt over his chausses, the open neck of which revealed the mat of black hair on his upper chest—not wiry hair, as Sully's had been, but soft and smooth. Just as a creature with silken fur invited petting, so Rainulf's chest cried out to be touched. Her fingers hummed with a restless urge to stroke it. . . . She ached to lay her cheek against its sleek heat and hear the heartbeat within.

Corliss, you idiot! Holding her breath, she carefully lifted a weightless, shimmering piece of gold leaf with a thin brush and let it fall atop her gilder's cushion. It fluttered down like a wrinkled silken sheet, and she gently blew it out flat.

" 'Thus my school had its start and my reputation for dialectic began to spread. . . .' "

Corliss bit her lip as she painstakingly cut the gold leaf with a tiny, sharp knife into the crescent shape of St. Luke's halo. What an idiot she was to have taken a fancy to Rainulf Fairfax. For one thing, there was no question of her feelings ever being reciprocated, given Rainulf's disinterest in women. Only once during her stay here had she had cause to question that disinterest—when she'd packed her things and tried to leave, after he'd attempted to restrict her movements. He'd embraced her, kissed her hair, all but begged her to stay. . . . *Have I misjudged him?* she'd wondered, elated by the possibility that he might care for her.

But no . . . No sooner had she agreed to remain in the house than he once again assumed that distant politeness with which he treated all women. It was clear that any affection he might harbor for her was, at most, that of a brother toward his sister. That this disappointed her shamed her intensely. The last thing she wanted was an affair of the heart with Rainulf. It would compromise her freedom. Yet at the same time, she miserably conceded, it was *all* she wanted, all she thought about when she wasn't working. Her gaze settled on St. Luke's all-too-familiar face, and she smiled sardonically, for in truth, the handsome magister appeared to be all she thought about even when she *was* working.

" 'My own teaching gained so much prestige and authority from this that the strongest supporters of my master who had hitherto been the most violent among my attackers now flocked to join my school. . . .' "

Corliss wiped her brow with her tunic sleeve so that sweat wouldn't fall on her work, and then leaned close to the drawing and carefully examined the area to which the gold leaf would be applied. The pinkish gesso she had laid down on the halo yesterday had dried, and now she took up another little knife and scraped the raised surface smooth. Bringing her mouth close to the page, she breathed onto the gesso, the dampness of her breath making it slightly sticky. Working quickly, she lifted the little crescent of gold leaf and settled it onto the gesso, then grabbed a square of silk and pressed the infinitely thin gold onto the raised medium with her thumb.

" 'But success always puffs up fools with pride,' " Rainulf read, " 'and worldly security weakens the spirit's resolution and easily destroys it with carnal temptations. . . .' "

Picking up her burnisher—a dog's tooth attached to

a stick—Corliss rubbed the convex little halo, careful to use just the right pressure. Presently the gold's rather dull gleam began to take on a blindingly brilliant shine, and she smiled to herself, proud of her efforts.

" 'There was in Paris, at the time, a young girl named Héloïse, the niece of Fulbert, one of the canons, and so much loved by him that he had done everything in his power to advance her education in letters.' " Rainulf looked up from his reading. "You know, Corliss, Héloïse was a remarkable woman in her own right, even before she met Abelard. At seventeen, she was already renowned for her learning. They say she knew Greek and Hebrew as well as Latin. . . ." He fell silent. When Corliss glanced up from her work, she saw him staring at the ever-brightening halo, his expression rapt. "So that's how it's done."

Rising, he came to lean over her, one hand on the back of her chair and the other on the edge of her desk. She continued polishing the gold, her eyes on her work, her thoughts on Rainulf Fairfax. His loose shirt hung down, brushing her lightly. With every breath he took, she felt the linen shift against her.

"That's quite extraordinary," he said. "Is there anything you can't do?"

I can't stop thinking about you, she wanted to say. Instead she merely shrugged and kept burnishing the gold, even after it had attained its maximum shine.

"You're exceptionally talented, you know," Rainulf said quietly. "And very clever. More than clever. I watch you when you come to my lectures . . . standing there in the back, as if you're afraid to sit down. You follow every word I say—I can see it in your eyes, that light of understanding, that intellectual curiosity. That's more than I see in a lot of my students, I assure you. And you're quite accomplished for a woman, especially one of your background. You know how to read and write. You're fluent in three different languages—"

"My French is abominable," she said. "I speak it like an Oxfordshire peasant."

He sat down again, smiling. "You *are* an Oxfordshire peasant."

"Not anymore," she said crossly.

Rainulf sat forward. "I didn't mean—"

"It's just that I don't fancy sounding like one of Roger Foliot's villeins every time I open my mouth. Everyone in Oxford speaks such elegant French, with no accent."

He regarded her thoughtfully for a moment. "You could lose your accent. It wouldn't be difficult."

"Really?"

"Why not? It's just a matter of training yourself. You've got one of the quickest minds I've ever seen. I'll help you. You can read aloud from books of Frankish literature and history, and I'll correct your pronunciation. And in the meantime, you'd be learning something."

She twirled the burnisher absently between her thumb and forefinger. "I wouldn't mind learning a bit of history."

He sat on the edge of his seat and leaned on her desk, the light of excitement in his eyes. "You can learn other things, too, if you like. I could tutor you in the *trivium* and the *quadrivium*. Grammar, rhetoric, logic, geometry—anything you want. You could become an educated woman, a woman of letters, like Héloïse."

She could be like the great and learned Héloïse. Was that possible?

He rested a hand on her arm. "I'd love to teach you. Tell me you'll let me."

She chewed her lip. "You want to remake me. To create a new person."

He removed his hand, shaking his head. "Not a new

person. I'm quite fond of the person you are. I just want to ... polish you a bit. The way you polish the gold leaf with that tool of yours, to make it even shinier. Isn't that what you want? Isn't that why you came to Oxford and sought your freedom? To change yourself? I'd only be refining what you started."

Corliss nodded slowly. "All right." She allowed herself a wicked little smile. "Under one condition. You've got to let me do something about this hall."

He shook his head resolutely; this was an old argument between them. "I like it the way it is," he insisted, looking around at the bare, whitewashed walls. "I don't want angels and unicorns and trailing ivy everywhere I look."

"I wouldn't do anything undignified. You'd love it."

"It's just not necessary. I'm happy with my home the way it is."

"Happy? Rainulf, in the five weeks we've been living together, I've seen you smile perhaps half a dozen times. I've heard you laugh exactly twice. You don't know the meaning of happiness." She grinned and leaned toward him. "Let me paint a circle of dancing monkeys around this window."

A burst of laughter escaped him. "Dancing monkeys? *That's* dignified?"

"You see? It makes you happy just to *think* about those monkeys. If you could actually see them every time you glanced at this window, think how it would lift your spirits!"

"Corliss," he chuckled, shaking his head. "Oh, Corliss. Sometimes you seem so innocent and naive— wide-eyed in wonderment over everything. And then, other times you're so frighteningly astute. But when you're both at the same time, as now ..." He held his hands up, grinning. "You disarm me. I have no defense against you. Go ahead. Paint all the monkeys and unicorns you like."

She fairly jumped out of her seat. "Really?"

"Really." He nodded toward her work. "Are you finished there?"

She shook her head. "I still have to do the angel's halo."

He settled into his seat and crossed his long legs. "Then I'll continue reading . . . unless it's boring you."

"Nay," she lied. "It's fascinating." It was Rainulf's company she wanted, of course, and not more of Master Abelard's treatise on himself. But she was quite happy to put up with one in exchange for the other. What enervated her wasn't the dullness of the *Historia Calamitatum,* but the heat. Her tunic was stifling; sweat trickled between her bound breasts, making her squirm.

Why suffer? she decided. *If Rainulf can relax at home in just a shirt and chausses, so can I.* Rising, she flung aside her belt and pulled the heavy wool garment over her head, then untied the neck of her shirt, reached in, and unwound the strip of linen from around her breasts. Rainulf stared, but said nothing.

"Ah," she breathed, taking her seat once more, "that's better." She picked up her tiny knife and proceeded to cut the angel's smaller halo out of the sheet of gold leaf.

Rainulf cleared his throat and read Abelard's account of having contrived to live in Canon Fulbert's home and tutor his niece, for whom he was "on fire with desire."

" 'Need I say more? We were united, first under one roof, then in heart; and so with our lessons as a pretext we abandoned ourselves entirely to love. Her studies allowed us to withdraw in private, as love desired, and then with our books open before us, more words of love than of our reading passed between us, and more kissing than teaching. My hands strayed oftener to her bosom than to the pages.' "

Rainulf paused, frowning at the manuscript in his hand, his ears crimson.

"Go on," Corliss said. He licked his lips and continued reading as she softened the gesso with her hot breath and positioned the delicate gold leaf.

" 'In short, our desires left no stage of lovemaking untried, and if love could devise something new, we welcomed it. We entered on each joy the more eagerly for our previous inexperience, and were the less easily sated.' "

He refolded the sheaf of parchment. "That's enough for now. You're not really interested in all this."

"Yes I am," she said—quite truthfully this time. "Please go on."

Rainulf studied Corliss as she went back to burnishing the gold leaf. Was she just having a bit of fun at his expense by embarrassing him? His gaze was inexorably drawn to her shirtfront, open to midchest, revealing the ivory flesh between her breasts. Their perfect roundness was evident through the filmy linen. . . . They were just the right size to fit in the palm of a hand.

My hands strayed oftener to her bosom than to the pages, Abelard had written. *In short, our desires left no stage of lovemaking untried. . . .* If Héloïse's charms had been comparable to those of Corliss, Rainulf could easily imagine the great man losing his head over her—and suffering mutilation and disgrace as a result.

Rainulf sat back and rubbed his damp palms on his wool-encased thighs. Perhaps he'd been rash in proposing to tutor Corliss. It seemed suddenly unwise to think of their bending their heads together over the same book, hour after hour. Unwise, but . . . a most enchanting prospect nonetheless. He liked being with her. Whenever he came home from a lecture, he hoped she was here. When he saw her, his spirits lifted. When she smiled that dazzling smile of hers, they soared. Colors seemed more vivid when he was in her company; things that he touched felt different, more ... *there*. Her very presence heightened his senses, made him more alive than he could ever remember having been. He craved her companionship as some men crave strong drink.

"Well?" she said without looking up from her work.

He found his place in the *Historia Calamitatum* and read on a bit to himself, finding no more descriptions of ardent lovemaking, at least for the next page or so. " 'Now the more I was taken up with these pleasures, the less time I could give to philosophy and the less attention I paid to my school. ...' "

While Corliss labored over her miniature, Rainulf recounted the horror of the lovers' discovery "in the act," Canon Fulbert's rage, the birth of their son, their secret marriage, and the canon's revenge, carried out by some of his friends and relatives: " 'They cut off the parts of my body whereby I had committed the wrong of which they complained.' "

Corliss sat motionless for a moment, holding the burnisher poised above the angel's radiant halo. "Now ... when he says, 'the parts of my body whereby ...' "

"They castrated him," Rainulf said softly. "They bribed his servant to let them in during the night, and—"

"My God."

"Yes."

"Was he asleep?"

"Well ... at first. But I imagine one could hardly sleep through ... that."

"How many were there? In the group that attacked him?"

"I don't know."

"Was Abelard a large man?"

"Aye. Tall and well built. Why do you ask?"

She set the tool down and crossed her arms. "Well, it seems to me that, if he were awake, and if he were a man of some strength, and if his enemies were not too numerous—"

"Then he could have defended himself?" Rainulf asked. "Fought off his attackers?"

"Aye. From his position on the bed, he should have been able to kick one or two in the stomach, perhaps punch . . . Why are you shaking your head like that?"

"How little you know of fighting, Corliss."

"I know enough."

"You know hardly anything," he said grimly. "In point of fact, Abelard was outnumbered and caught by surprise. But even if it had been broad daylight, and a fair, one-on-one fight, I doubt he would have prevailed, regardless of his size. He was an academic, Corliss. A creature of the mind."

"He was also the eldest son of a knight of Brittany."

"Aye, but he renounced his birthright, and was never trained as a soldier. Without the proper training—or its equivalent in experience—one can't hope to defend oneself physically against any but the weakest opponents. I saw too many wellborn, inexperienced men on Crusade. They all met early deaths."

"But you didn't."

He hesitated, never eager to discuss this part of his past. "I knew how to fight," he said tersely. "Even though I was a second son, and destined for the Church, my father insisted on training me. As a soldier is trained—to kill or be killed." A memory surfaced in Rainulf's mind—a hazy image of a small, tow-headed child and the golden giant who had sired him, squaring off in a castle courtyard. The yard had been paved with slate, and his father hurled him onto it repeatedly and ruthlessly; he was often bruised head to toe during his youth.

"And then," he continued, "I got in plenty of practice at the University of Paris. There was always one scrape or another."

"You?" she asked incredulously. "Getting into scrapes? Over what?"

Women, mostly. "This and that." He held up the sheaf of parchment. "Shall I continue reading?"

"Nay. I'm done here, and ..." Color rose in her cheeks. "Would you be willing to ... that is . I was wondering if you'd teach me how to fight."

He blinked at her. "You're a woman."

"All the more reason I should know how to defend myself, wouldn't you say?"

He must have hesitated too long, because she shrugged and turned away, saying, "If you don't want to, that's all right. I don't plan on courting danger."

"But you do court danger, Corliss. Every time you join in the crowd that gathers around Victor, or share a pint with one of his followers, you're drawing unwanted attention to yourself."

"I just like to hear what they have to say. That doesn't make me some kind of fanatical—"

"It makes you appear so to those who don't know you well. And then there's that peddler."

She groaned. "Rad is harmless. I've told you that a thousand times. He's like a child."

"I don't like the way he keeps coming around, hoping to find you here, even when he's got nothing new to sell you. And the way he looks at you .. There's something in that look. He sees too much. Why do you encourage him?"

She shrugged. "I like him. I feel a little sorry for him, too. Everyone treats him like some kind of animal. He only seeks me out because I'm nice to him."

"Look, Corliss, I try not to worry, but I do. I can't help it."

"Well, don't. Even if something happened, I really do think I'll be able to take care of myself. I've decided I'm going to buy a dagger."

"Oh, for pity's sake."

Her eyebrows rose. "Ah, so it's unladylike to carry a weapon, as well as to learn how to fight? This is beginning to sound like some grand scheme on the part of men to keep us as weak and helpless—"

"It has nothing to do with your being a woman," he said. "Have you ever handled a dagger?"

She hesitated. "Nay, but—"

"That takes practice, too. Do you know what would happen if you started waving one in front of an attacker? Chances are he'd take it away from you and use it on you." He sighed in frustration. "It'd be safer if I taught you how to defend yourself with your fists and feet. Perhaps I *should* show you one or two moves."

"It really isn't necessary," she said, tidying up her desktop.

He stood. "Nay, I insist." She wouldn't meet his gaze. He noticed she seemed to be trying not to smile. "Why, you little . . . How did you do that?"

"Do what?" she asked disingenuously.

"Turn things around so smoothly. Got me trying to talk *you* into it."

"Is that what I did?"

He grabbed her arm and lifted her to her feet. "Come along before I change my mind. We can do this out back in the stable yard. All that clover will cushion your falls."

"And yours," she added, grinning.

"All right, now you try it," Rainulf said, lifting the hem of his shirt to wipe the sweat from his face. He wished it weren't so damn hot. "Like I showed you."

Corliss nodded and fingered her sweat-soaked hair out of her eyes, then grabbed her own shirt by its hem and flapped it, fanning herself. She hadn't an ounce of pretense, and he found that oddly fetching. Back before he'd taken his vows, his taste had run to women of refined and calculated beauty—women who painted their faces and laced their kirtles tight, who rubbed fragrant oils into their skin and bedecked themselves with jewels before a tryst. It used to excite him to think that a woman had taken pains to make herself alluring just for him.

None of those women would ever have asked him to teach her how to fight, that's for sure. So far this afternoon he'd shown her how to break a man's fingers, nose, and kneecaps. She'd proven an eager pupil and a fast learner, and she was stronger than she looked. Still, it was clear she was tiring. He'd make this the last demonstration of the day.

She turned her back to him and adopted a ready stance—feet spread, hands at her sides. "Go ahead."

He came at her from behind and wrapped his arms around her upper chest, tight.

"Like this?" Corliss gasped, shoving her fists beneath his arms and pushing.

"Does it *seem* like it's doing any good?"

She grunted with the strain of trying to dislodge his arms. "Nay."

He released her and turned her around by her shoulders. "That's because you did it wrong. This is what I showed you." He crossed his arms over his chest, slid them up, and flung them out wide. "That'll work on any but the strongest opponent. Try again?"

Breathless, she nodded and turned around. Again Rainulf locked his arms around her. This time she executed the maneuver perfectly, breaking his hold and wheeling around to face him, laughing delightedly.

"Do your worst!" she challenged. "Come on. I can take you!"

He smiled. "Ah, you're invincible now, are you?" The prospect of grappling with Corliss was inviting—too inviting. The lesson—with its unavoidable physical contact—had been trying enough in its own way. He wiped his forehead with his sleeve and turned back toward the house. "Perhaps tomorrow. We're both tired."

Cackling with glee, she charged him, nearly knocking him over as she grabbed his arms and hooked a leg around his. He struggled to keep his balance, but it was no use. Down they went, a tangle of arms and legs, landing in the white-flowering clover that blanketed the ground. Laughing breathlessly, she made a fist and aimed for his nose, stopping just short of smashing it. "I win!"

"No you don't," he growled, seizing her wrist. "A man with a broken nose can still do this." He pinned her hand to the side as he lowered his weight on her.

She twisted frantically, pounding on his shoulder with her other hand. He grabbed it as well and held it down on the other side. "*I* win," he rasped, pushing himself up on his elbows, but keeping a firm grip on those wrists; she was unpredictable. "You're a quick study, but you have much to learn yet."

She nodded and closed her eyes, gulping air. Her hair stuck in damp curls around her face. Such an extraordinary face, he thought, taking advantage of this opportunity to gaze upon it at close range. She had the kind of translucent skin that showed so much underneath, if one only looked hard enough. Right now a flood of red burned beneath that sheer skin, the product of her exertions. Her lips, as well, seemed suffused with blood; they were dark as cherries.

His gaze traveled down her throat, and lower. He stilled, his grip on her hands tightening, dimly aware of her eyes blinking open in confusion. Her struggles had twisted her shirt to the side. The neckline gapped open widely, revealing the left side of her heaving chest. Aware now that she was watching him, but unable to control the direction of his gaze, he followed the creamy curve of the exposed breast to its tip. The nipple, small and rosy, became erect under his scrutiny.

A powerful rush of arousal uncurled in his loins and strained at his chausses. He felt himself move without his willing it, as if his body had taken over and his mind were shutting down. His hips shifted, seeking the warm cradle of her thighs, their soft juncture—seeking relief from the pain of this sudden, shocking need. Like an animal, his natural urged clawed for dominance within him. With what little rational thought he still possessed, he fought the overwhelming urge to thrust against her.

Chapter 8

Astonished, Corliss felt the rigid male flesh press against her through the wool of their chausses. When he shifted, she followed suit, fitting her hips to his as naturally as if they were longtime lovers—all the while utterly amazed that this was happening, that she had the power to arouse him. She knew she shouldn't want this, but she did, desperately. She had wanted it for weeks.

Gazing up at him, she saw a raw hunger in his eyes. His face was flushed. That little vein on his forehead throbbed in time to the pulsing heat between her legs—his heat . . . and hers, too. It was a strange, liquid heat—a heat she'd never felt before, at least not to this degree. It was like an itch that needed scratching, that needed his touch, an itch that made her arch her hips, striving for closer contact.

He squeezed his eyes closed, his body taut, his fingers digging painfully into her wrists. "Corliss," he whispered harshly. Opening his eyes and meeting her gaze, he shook his head forlornly.

He looked down at her open shirt, then released one of her wrists and slowly brought his hand to her uncovered breast. She thought her heart would explode through her chest as his palm hovered over her bare flesh. His jaw clenched, and then he took hold of a handful of her shirt and drew it back across her chest, concealing her once again from his view.

Raising himself off her, he stood and dragged his

fingers through his hair. She sat up and retied her shirt with trembling hands, then examined her wrists, reddened and swollen.

Squatting down, he took her hands in his, frowning at the red marks. "Damn." He shook his head and looked away, then froze, his eyes narrowed in the direction of the stable.

Corliss felt the sudden tension that surged through him. "What is it?"

"Someone was there," he said tightly. "Just now. Watching us."

"Rainulf, no one was—"

"Go inside." He sprang to his feet and strode across the yard toward the stable.

"Rainulf!" she yelled. "There's no one—"

"*Go!*" he yelled over his shoulder as he broke into a sprint and took off.

Rainulf raced through the neighboring yard, arms and legs pumping, scanning the area for the intruder. *There*—a dark figure, vanishing into a narrow alley between two houses. "Stop!"

He turned in to the alley and tripped over something, falling face-first onto the hard-packed earth. As he scrambled to his feet, he glanced back at the big satchel he'd stumbled over, from which dozens of assorted knives had spilled out.

Rad. "You bastard!" he yelled as he tore off down the alley in pursuit of the peddler. "Come back here!"

He darted across Kibald Street, right in front of a cart loaded with wine barrels. "Whoa!" screamed the carter, and he yanked on the reins. The two horses squealed and bucked as Rainulf hurriedly sidestepped them. A barrel rolled onto the road and crashed open, spraying its crimson contents in every direction. "Come back here!" the carter bellowed. "You've got to pay for this!"

A shadowy figure disappeared around the corner,

and Rainulf followed it. Grope Lane was more populated than Kibald today, but Rainulf easily picked out
Rad's ponderous form, glancing back over his shoulder as he ran with surprising speed. Rainulf, however,
had always been fast on his feet, and he easily overtook the peddler, grabbing him by his cape and spinning him around roughly.

Rad ducked and crossed his arms in front of his
face. "D-don't hur-hur-hurt—"

"Why were you watching us?"

"D-don't . . ."

Rainulf shook him hard. "Talk! What were you
doing sneaking around behind my house?"

Rad just shook his head, cowering. Passersby stared
openly. Growling a curse, Rainulf dragged Rad into
the recessed entryway of a poulterer's shop and
slammed him against the door. "Tell me why you were
spying on us."

"I . . . I m-meant no h-h-h-harm."

Rainulf made a fist. "*Tell me!*"

The peddler's grotesque face took on an abject expression. "I th-thought you might h-hurt her."

"Her."

"Cor-Corliss."

Her. "Oh, shit." Rainulf lowered his fist, recalling
the sight of Corliss, her shirt askew, one breast exposed. Any doubts Rad might have harbored as to
her true sex would have been laid to rest that afternoon. "You were trying to protect her?" Rad nodded.
"From me?" He nodded again. "I wasn't hurting her.
I was trying to teach her how to defend herself."

Rad nodded. Even when Rainulf stepped back, he
continued to press himself against the door, twitching
nervously. The magister studied the peddler for a minute, and then said, "Did you suspect she was a woman
before today?"

Rad shook his head, and Rainulf relaxed a bit,

grateful it wasn't *that* obvious—until Rad said, "I knew."

"You *knew*? Since when?"

"A-always. E-e-even before I s-saw her face, I saw her light. And I knew."

"Her light?"

Rad nodded. " 'T-twas silver. A w-woman's light. A-all around her, b-bright as anything and sh-shimmering in waves. S-silver."

"I see." He did. The hulking, disfigured peddler was mad. Had he been merely dull-witted, he'd be no threat, for Rainulf believed him when he claimed to be watching after Corliss, to whom he seemed to have taken a fancy of sorts. But this talk of a shimmering silver light boded ill.

Rainulf knew more than he cared to of madmen. Of the many prisoners chained into that fetid hole in the Levant, only he and Thorne had retained their senses. The rest howled, wept, laughed endlessly ... and attacked one another at regular intervals, for no reason other than that their minds had snapped. Violence was part and parcel of who they were; seven of his cellmates had died at the hands of fellow prisoners.

"C-c-can I go?" Rad asked.

Whether this pathetic creature meant to or not, he could easily end up doing harm to Corliss. It was a possibility Rainulf did not intend to invite. "You can go," he said, "but you must never come back to the house. Do you understand?"

Rad just stared at him, his eyes wide and sad.

Steeling himself, Rainulf said, "You must never see Corliss or talk to her again. Or I'll ..." God, how he hated this. "I'll have to hurt you. Tell me you understand."

Rad looked all around the little entryway, his eyes growing moist. Finally he nodded and said, "I un-un-un ..." He shook his head vigorously, like a dog shaking off water. "I understand."

Rad stared at the ground. Rainulf backed away, feeling like the lowest form of knave. "Your satchel's in that alley off Kibald Street. Go and fetch it, and then don't ever come that close to the house again."

The peddler nodded miserably. Cursing under his breath, Rainulf turned and walked away.

When he rounded the corner, someone yelled, "There he is!" It was the carter, the one whose horses Rainulf had spooked. A flock of ragged children were clustered around the shattered barrel, frantically dipping their hands in what remained of the wine and slurping it up. The carter stalked toward Rainulf, his expression fierce. "You owe me four shillings. That there was good Rhenish wine. Four shillings, and not a penny less."

It was an outrageous sum, even for Rhenish wine, but Rainulf hadn't the heart to debate the matter. With a resigned sigh, he pressed the coins into the wide-eyed carter's open palm, and slowly walked home.

She'd been wrong about him, Corliss reflected as she watched Rainulf and a dozen others—masters and scholars, all shirtless beneath the glaring noon sun—line up for the race. The starting line had been scratched into the dried mud at one end of High Street, in front of East Gate. The finish line was the entrance to Oxford Castle, more than half a mile to the west. Between the two points, hundreds of scholars and a handful of townspeople lined either side of the wide avenue, impatiently waiting for the race to begin.

Aye, she'd been very wrong, indeed. Three weeks had passed since the incident following the fighting lesson—since she had felt his body respond to hers and realized that Rainulf Fairfax was a man like any other, a man with the same physical needs, the same desire for a woman's touch. Afterward, neither of them had spoken about it, as if trying to pretend it had never happened, which was probably for the best. Since he hadn't offered any more fighting lessons, she'd gone ahead and bought a dagger. Not wanting his disapproval, she hadn't told him about it, but kept it hidden in her boot at all times.

Squinting against the sun, she watched him plant a booted foot against the great stone gate and lean forward, his thighs and calves hard and well defined beneath his snug chausses. Grateful for the chance to stare openly, she admired the way his back and arm muscles stood out in sharp relief, the way his wide shoulders and narrow hips and strong limbs all balanced together to create a flawlessly proportioned whole. He was the very image of masculine perfection. How could she ever have thought him less than completely male?

In her mind she contrasted the virile, handsome Oxford master with the two old men she had buried. They'd both had hands as cold as ice, and their attentions were always a vague irritant. Rainulf's hands—what little she had felt of them—branded her with their heat, scalded her blood, made her heart pound with fevered longing. Neither Sully nor Osred had ever made her feel this strange exhilaration, even when they'd bedded her. Observing the flexing of Rainulf's muscles, and contemplating his vigor and strength, she couldn't help wondering what it would be like to lie with him. Imagining him on top of her, inside her, stirred her in ways she'd never felt before.

Thomas nudged her, ale spilling from his tankard onto the ground. "Sixpence says Master Fairfax finishes last."

"Last!" Corliss exclaimed. "How disloyal of you!"

Brad elbowed her from the other side. "That's what *I* said," he declared thickly. "He'll place in the middle of the pack, I'll wager."

"Shame on both of you! He's your teacher. You ought to put your money on his winning."

The two young men laughed. "He's six-and-thirty, Corliss," said Brad, "twice the age of some of the others. He couldn't possibly win."

Shielding her eyes, she studied the tall magister as he whipped his powerful arms back and forth, back and forth. "I wouldn't be so sure about that."

Rainulf appeared to be scanning the crowd. His gaze rested on her and his entire being seemed to find its focus. He ceased his stretching to reach up and run his fingers through his hair, pale and fiery in the bright sun. Even from this distance, she saw his lake-colored eyes ignite from within. A hint of a smile played on his lips, and then someone spoke to him and he turned away quickly, with an uneasy look.

She wondered whether the look had to do with her or the race. He and Father Gregory had organized it as a way of involving both the people of Oxford and the scholars in a social activity—only, at the last minute, Victor had entered the race, and all the townsmen had dropped out in protest. That left just twelve academics, including Rainulf. He had never wanted to participate, for reasons not entirely clear to her; perhaps it just came down to that dreadful *dignity* of his. Finally Corliss and Father Gregory, working together, had been able to talk him into it.

She liked the elderly priest. Although he never seemed quite sure how to act with her, being the only person besides Rainulf who knew her true sex, he seemed fond of her as well. He probably suspected that she and the Magister Scholarum were secret lovers, despite Rainulf's assurance in confession that their relationship was innocent. Even priests knew—perhaps better than anyone—that the flesh was weak and subject to powerful urges.

Yes, Rainulf had urges of the flesh, and those urges were directed toward women, but Corliss was as convinced as ever that he had little in the way of sexual experience. It was entirely possible that he had never lain with a woman. She knew that many priests went their whole lives without sex, abstaining with apparent ease from something most men couldn't seem to live without. Perhaps this was because never having experienced such pleasures they simply didn't know what they were missing. Given Rainulf's willingness to maintain his celibacy, she thought it more than likely that he was one of their number.

"*Corliss!*" Thomas was yanking at the sleeve of her tunic, and swaying on his feet as he did so.

Brad chuckled drunkenly. "Are you awake, boy?"

"I asked you," Thomas pronounced slowly, "if you had six pennies to back up your confidence in Master Fairfax."

"I have twelve," she said. "A shilling says Rainulf Fairfax comes in first." She produced the coin and held it up; it glinted in the sun.

The two scholars exchanged grins of disbelief. Thomas grabbed at the shilling. Corliss held it out of his reach, and he toppled dizzily to the ground. Brad howled with laughter.

"You two get this shilling when and if Rainulf loses," she said as Thomas awkwardly gained his feet and dusted off his cappa. "And if he wins, you *each* owe me sixpence."

Thomas and Brad agreed to the bet, and presently Father Gregory called the participants to the starting line.

"Ready . . . and *go!*"

The racers shot forward like a volley of arrows, kicking up a storm cloud of dust as they tore down High Street. Corliss coughed and shielded her eyes. When she uncovered them, the runners were out of sight, the onlookers sprinting after them.

"Come on!" Tossing their tankards aside, Brad and Thomas each grabbed a sleeve and pulled her along with the crowd, but she couldn't run as fast as them, and kept stumbling.

"You two go on ahead," she said, tugging her tunic out of their grasp and giving them each a push. "I'll catch up with you."

Brad shook his head uncertainly. "Master Fairfax told us to stay with you."

"Just to keep me company," she lied. Rainulf, who'd worried overmuch since Rad had spied on them, now frequently asked Thomas and Brad to "keep her company." *If they haven't figured out yet that you're a woman, they never will,* he'd said. "But I don't want your company, if it means trying to keep up with you. Go ahead."

Thomas and Brad looked at each other and shrugged. "All right," said Thomas as they jogged on ahead. "See you later."

They disappeared from sight, with the rest of the throng, where High Street curved in front of St. Mary's. Corliss and a few dozen other stragglers walked at a more leisurely pace.

"Corliss!" She looked across the street and saw young Felice, along with her mother and Bertram. The girl waved and grinned; Mistress Clark looked on with a bemused expression, Bertram with one of suppressed rage. "Will you be coming to the shop today?" Felice called out.

"Nay. Not today."

Her shoulders sagged. "Oh."

"Come, Felice," her mother urged, guiding her by the arm up Catte Street. "Good day, Corliss."

"Good day, mistress."

Bertram's hands balled into fists. He speared Corliss with a threatening glare, then turned and followed the two women.

From the direction of the castle rose the sound of hundreds of voices shouting "Hurrah!" The race was over, and the winner was being cheered. She thought about that shilling in her pocket, and wondered casually whether she'd get to keep it. Two months ago she never would have believed she could take such liberties with a whole shilling! To be earning such money doing what she loved the most was like finding Heaven on earth. In the beginning she'd spent it as soon as she earned it—mostly on clothes and supplies for her work. Now, however, she saved all but a small allowance in an old, cracked saltcellar under her bed. She smiled; soon she'd have to find a larger container for it.

A familiar-looking shape drifted in and out of her field of vision to the left. *Rad.* She'd noticed him earlier in the crowd, but had paid him little heed; he hadn't been the only townsperson watching the race. But now she couldn't deny the fact that he was following her. His pace matched hers exactly, although he kept back a bit and hugged the buildings on the edge of the street.

When she reached the corner of Shidyerd, she turned to face him squarely. "I see you."

He shrank back into the doorway of a wine shop. She walked directly up to him. "You mustn't do this, Rad. Rainulf wouldn't like it. He told you not to come near me."

Rad shook his big head helplessly. "J-just w-w-want to k-keep you safe."

"From what?"

"There are b-b-bad people." He scowled as if to emphasize his point. "Bad people. I know."

Corliss was sure he did. She shuddered to think of the abuse he'd come to accept as an everyday thing. "No one wants to hurt me, Rad." Perhaps not quite the truth, but Rad knew nothing of Sir Roger and his plans for her; why worry him?

"Some b-bad men hurt w-w-women."

She lowered her voice and glanced around. "Everyone thinks I'm a boy, Rad."

"*I* kn-knew you weren't."

Rainulf had told her about the silvery, feminine light Rad claimed she emitted. "Yes, well . . ."

"Others must kn-know as well."

"No one knows, Rad. No one but you and Rainulf and Father Gregory. I'm perfectly safe. You must stop spying on me all the time. I see you watching the house when Rainulf isn't there. And I see you sometimes, walking behind me when I go to Catte Street, or to St. Mary's for a lecture."

He blinked in surprise.

"Oh, I see you, all right. I know you're there. And I know you don't mean any harm. I know you just want to look after me, but you *mustn't*. If Rainulf knew, he'd . . . I don't know what he'd do."

He nodded furiously, twitching.

"Rad, please. Promise me you'll stop this."

He hunched his shoulders up, shaking his head fractionally. "Got to k-keep you—"

"No, you don't!" she said more firmly. "I have Rainulf to protect me. And when he's not there, he always gets someone . . ."

Rad adopted a surprisingly astute look that could only be described as skeptical, and glanced around. Corliss followed his gaze to the sparsely populated street behind her. "Ah . . . right. There's no one with me now. You see, Brad and Thomas . . ."

His eyebrows shot up, and she smiled and shook her head. "Brad and Thomas fell down on their duty, I suppose. And I encouraged them to. But that doesn't mean you have to—"

He nodded vigorously.

"Rad, please . . ."

A din of raised voices advanced steadily from the west. The crowd was returning. She backed away from the wine shop. "Go, Rad. Rainulf may be with them. Go before he sees you."

Rad pulled his cowl down over his forehead and

ducked between two buildings just as the black-clad horde appeared. The group in front, which included Thomas and Brad, were laughing and cheering . . . and carrying Rainulf on their shoulders!

He won! Rainulf won! The sheepishly grinning victor wore an ermine-lined mantle and a crown of something resembling laurel. On another man, such trappings might have seemed ridiculous, but they only enhanced Rainulf's aristocratic good looks. With his silver-blond hair, broad shoulders, and natural poise, he looked like a warrior chief of the Northmen, being honored by his people after a glorious victory in battle.

His regal costume made it easier to remember that he was, in fact, of noble blood—the son of a Norman baron, and a cousin of the queen. He came from the very top of the inviolable social order, she from the bottom. It was pointless to deny her feelings for him to herself, but she must be careful to keep them in their place.

The most difficult time to remember this was during their lessons, when he had her read aloud in French, or tutored her in the seven disciplines. It was always a challenge to keep her mind on her work, with him hovering so close, watching her with those perceptive eyes, instructing her endlessly. Teaching was an ingrained passion with him, and once he got started on remaking her, he couldn't keep himself from refining her demeanor, as well as her accent: *If you're going to speak like a wellborn lady, Corliss, you may as well sit like one. Tilt your chin up just a bit . . . That's right. Now, straighten your back. You look lovely!*

Those occasional compliments were what kept her going, try as she might not to read too much into them. Even if Rainulf were of a mind to take a mistress, and willing to risk the chancellorship by doing so, he wouldn't want a simple peasant like her, no matter how well she'd been trained to speak and carry herself—and regardless of fleeting urges in stable yards. And if he did, what would become of her independence? The best way to protect her precious freedom was to avoid entanglements with men.

Rainulf caught her eye, and to her astonishment, the grin widened. Someone thrust a tankard into his hand. "Drink! Drink! Drink!" the crowd chanted. He upended the vessel and swiftly drained it to a roar of approval. It was snatched away and quickly replaced by another.

"Look at him." Corliss turned to see Father Gregory standing next to her, gazing in Rainulf's direction. "I think he's actually happy."

Corliss chuckled disbelievingly. "You may be right."

The priest smiled at her. "It's your influence, you know. Somehow you've managed to crack that armor of his. As well as I know him, and as hard as I've tried, I could never even dent it."

"I hardly feel as if I know him at all," Corliss said, watching the subject of their conversation being lowered to the ground and dragged into Burnell's Tavern. "He's something of a mystery to me."

"And to himself as well, I think," said Father Gregory, leading her across the street, toward the tavern. "Come." He grinned. "He'll want you to be there with him in his moment of glory."

Burnell's wife tilted the pitcher over Rainulf's tankard, but he covered it with his hand. "I've had enough."

"Aye, and that's just the problem!" exclaimed Walter Kent, the young master of dialectic who'd finished second in the race. "You've 'had enough,' when you *ought* to have had far too much!" He emptied the contents of his own tankard into that of the Magister Scholarum.

"Hear, hear!" cried the others, all of whom, with the exception of Corliss and Father Gregory, were reeling drunk. It was a condition Rainulf had not experienced since his university days. He'd come to hate that out-of-control, off-balance feeling brought on by an excess of drink. It made him feel helpless—no, terrified—to have his unchanging, orderly world replaced by one that spun and shifted, to have his most secret, deeply buried thoughts and feelings push through to the surface.

He glanced across the table at Corliss, laughing as she accepted her shilling from Thomas and Brad, her eyes alight, her teeth glowing like pearls in the dim tavern. In public, she acted the part of the amiable young man; in private, she was becoming more and more the lady. Her gestures had had a natural grace to them even before he'd taken it on himself to refine them; under his tutelage, they were developing a polished layer of elegance that he found enchanting. And her accent had faded remarkably in quite a short time, replaced, for the most part, by the cultivated tones of an educated member of the nobility.

"Nay, I must be leaving," he said, rising and straightening his leafy crown, which they hadn't let him take off. He had, however, exchanged the ermine mantle for a blessedly ordinary shirt and tunic. He couldn't believe he'd let Corliss and Gregory talk him into this. Not that he hadn't enjoyed the race. In truth, it had been exhilarating, and he could think of worse ways to have spent the rest of the afternoon than in an alehouse, celebrating his victory. The only unpleasant moment had occurred about an hour ago, when Victor had shown up and leaped onto a table. Three men had had to hold Burnell back, but the young firebrand never once mentioned unfair prices or rancid meat pies. Instead, he bowed dramatically in Rainulf's direction and made a surprisingly gracious speech congratulating him on the win. Then, with another grinning half bow toward the incensed tavern keeper, he quickly took his leave.

Corliss stood, as well. "I'll walk back with you."

Rainulf breathed a sigh of relief. He hated to think of her on the streets alone, even during the daylight hours. In truth, he should have continued her fighting lessons, only that seemed most unwise after what had happened in the stable yard. Since she was ill equipped to defend herself, he felt obliged to escort her whenever possible.

As soon as they were outside, Rainulf swept the crown off and, on impulse, placed it on Corliss's head. It made her look like a forest sprite—a childlike creature with extraordinary powers. He smiled. "It suits you." Her musical laugh was absurdly gratifying.

"Good afternoon." They turned to find Will Geary leaning against the outside wall of the tavern.

"Will! Were you waiting for us?"

Will nodded, his expression growing sober. "I asked around, and they said you were here. Have you got a moment?"

"Of course."

The surgeon's gaze lit on Corliss and her crown. She took it off as Rainulf introduced them.

"I'll walk with you," said Will, glancing around.

"As you wish."

Will said nothing until they'd crossed High Street and turned down Grope Lane. Twice he looked back over his shoulder, before saying, "I just got back from Cuxham. First time I've been there since I saw you last."

Rainulf nodded, feeling a cold wave of trepidation. "Aye?"

Will inclined his head toward Corliss, walking in front of them, and directed a questioning look toward Rainulf.

"You can speak freely in front of Corliss," Rainulf assured him.

"I just thought you should know that Roger Foliot's been talking about you."

"Really?" said Rainulf, trying to appear unruffled. "I don't even know the man."

"Well, he knows you. Or *of* you, at any rate. He seems to think you were somehow involved with that woman named Constance, who kept house for the rector you delivered Last Rites to." He raised an eyebrow. "Served him in other capacities as well, if you believe the talk."

Rainulf felt the hairs on the back of his neck spring up.

"Is it true?" Will asked. "Was she the priest's whore?"

Rainulf's hands curled into fists; he saw Corliss's back stiffen. "She did not strike me as a whore."

Will shrugged. "Well, Sir Roger seemed to think she was letting the old fellow under her skirts." He paused, adding quietly, "And perhaps you, as well."

Rainulf stopped walking and turned to face Will. Corliss stood stiffly, her back to them. "That's preposterous."

The surgeon held his hands out. "Easy. I'm only reporting what I heard. I thought you should know—"

"Of course," said Rainulf. Corliss looked back over her shoulder at them; he saw that the color had leached from her cheeks. "I appreciate your telling me this. Is that all?"

"Hardly." With another furtive glance behind him, Will motioned for them to continue walking. "Apparently the girl faked her death and ran off. Hugh told me all about it. That's Hugh Hest, his reeve—a decent fellow. He said Sir Roger's foaming at the mouth over it. Seems he'd wanted a piece of her for himself. Still does. Anyway, he seems to think she might come to you."

Damn! Rainulf maintained a granite silence as they turned onto St. John Street. *He knew she'd come to me! How could he have known?* Corliss crossed her arms and hugged her chest as she walked.

"If that's likely," Will continued softly, "then you'd best watch your back. Hugh says he's sent someone after the girl. A human bloodhound, by all accounts, and a crazy bastard to boot. He's supposed to be watching you, hoping the girl shows up."

Dear God, I was right all along. Someone's watching us. Rainulf said nothing until they stopped in front of the big stone house. "Thank you for telling me this."

"Like I said, I thought you should know. It's my fault you got involved in this mess in the first place. I'm the one who sent you to Cuxham."

"Don't blame yourself," Rainulf said. "You couldn't have known how it would turn out." He waved a hand toward the front door. "Will you come inside and join us for some supper?"

"Thanks, but I have a patient waiting for me." Raising a hand in farewell, he walked a few paces in the direction from which they'd come, then turned and added, "Be careful, Rainulf. Don't trust a soul."

Corliss studied Rainulf as he picked at his spiced meatballs, a dish he normally made short work of. He'd said hardly a word throughout supper. Now he pushed his trencher back and gazed with preoccupied eyes toward the fire.

Presently he expelled a great lungful of air, as if he'd been holding his breath. "I want you to come to Sussex with me."

"Sussex?"

"Blackburn Castle."

"Ah, Blackburn ..." He'd mentioned the planned visit to his sister's home only once, quite some time ago. "When? And for how long?"

"Next week." He poured them each some brandy. "For perhaps a fortnight. Perhaps longer. I won't want to leave until Martine's baby is born."

Corliss sipped some of the dark amber liquid; it left a trail of honeyed fire as it trickled down her throat.

Blackburn Castle. She'd never been in a castle before, never even seen people of Thorne and Martine Falconer's rank, much less spoken to them. "Would I have to maintain my disguise?"

"Only while we travel. It's a two-day ride. Once we're at Blackburn, you'll be in no danger. You can wear a kirtle again. Would you like that?"

"I don't own a kirtle."

"Martine will find you one."

"Do they know about me? Your sister and her husband?"

"Nay."

"Won't they be shocked when you arrive with me in tow?"

He smiled, and as always, it struck her how devastatingly handsome he looked when he wasn't frowning. "They're not easily shocked, either one of them. Don't trouble yourself over what they'll think."

She bit her lip, and now it was she who scrutinized the leaping flames. "What of my obligation to Mistress Clark?"

"She doesn't own you, Corliss. She'll simply have to do without your services for a fortnight." His brow furrowed. "Don't you want to come?"

She took a deep breath. "Will I be a guest, or ..." Heat scalded her face as Rainulf stared at her, his eyebrows gradually rising.

"Or what?" he asked, leaning forward on his elbows. "Sleep in the barn with the stablehands? Of course you'll be a guest. I'll have brought you. You'll be treated as my ..." He appeared to be groping for words. "You'll be treated as a guest."

Rising, he grabbed his trencher and tossed it in the bucket, then stood with his back to her, hands on his hips, inspecting the fire. "I can't leave you here, Corliss. It's not safe. Especially after what Will told us today. Sir Roger *knew* you'd come to me! I can't imagine how, but ..." He shook his head. "I can't leave you alone in Oxford. And I must go to Blackburn to be with my sister."

He turned to face her. "Please come with me. I couldn't bear it if ..." Shaking his head again, he turned around. "I don't want anything to happen to you," he said gruffly. "I just want to keep an eye on you, that's all."

She thought about it for a moment, but in truth she had known all along what her answer would be. "All right," she said. "I'll come."

Chapter 9

They set out at dawn on the first of July. It was cool for the time of year, and Corliss was glad of it; the weather made for swift traveling. It was also overcast, although thankfully it didn't rain until that night, and by then, they'd found shelter in a monastic guest house. Rainulf's rank should have assured them of private chambers in the abbot's lodge, but those had already been granted to a passing bishop and his entourage.

"This isn't so bad, is it?" he asked her as he unrolled his blanket in the straw that covered the earthen floor of the guest house.

Corliss cast a quick glance over her shoulder at the motley assortment of indigent travelers, beggars, and knaves bedding down around them. The quarters were close, forcing perfect strangers to sleep pressed up against one another. They smelled like what they were—men who'd lived and slept in the same clothes without bathing for months, perhaps years.

"Lay your blanket out here," Rainulf said, indicating a narrow space between him and the stone wall. He raised his eyebrows fractionally and glanced meaningfully toward the other guests. His message was not lost on her: Better to sleep squeezed between Rainulf and the wall than between two strange and possibly dangerous men.

She nodded and spread out her bedroll. Someone extinguished the single hanging lantern, and she closed her eyes and tried to get comfortable. For some time she lay awake, her senses focused solely on Rainulf's closeness—the heat from his body, the whisper of his breath, his *presence,* so near. Unable to sleep, she tried to think of other things, anything but Rainulf sleeping mere inches away. She listened to the tapestry of sounds surrounding her: Rain pattering softly on the thatched roof ... straw rustling beneath fitful bodies ... snores and grunts and coughs.

Presently the rain eased off and ceased, and another sound replaced it—a high, stately chanting that drifted on the night breezes through the small window above her head. She opened her eyes, startled to find Rainulf sitting up and gazing out the window. Watery moonlight bathed his face, adorning his broad forehead and straight nose and resolute chin with soft brushstrokes of silver. His eyes, transparent as clear gems, shone with some emotion she couldn't identify—not sadness, but something close. Regret? Longing? Remembrance?

He looked down at her and whispered, "I can't sleep, either." He nodded toward the window. "It's the midnight service. Matins."

She turned her head toward the window. "It's lovely."

"You should hear it up close." Something almost mischievous flickered in his crystalline eyes. He took her hand in his and rose, pulling her to her feet. "Come with me."

"What?"

"Shh ..." He guided her carefully through the somnolent bodies and out the door, into the damp night. "This way." As he led her by the hand across the abbey's public courtyard, she reflected on how relaxed—almost carefree—he had seemed all day. Almost like a different person. Father Gregory seemed to think she was responsible for the lifting of Rainulf's melancholy, but she doubted she had that much influence over him. More likely, it was simply being away from Oxford that had done the trick.

He guided her into the church and closed the door behind them. Sound blossomed around her, and she gasped, momentarily stunned by its beauty and power. She caught a quick glimpse of rows of hooded monks and dozens of lit candles before he quickly pulled her into one of the nave aisles, where they wouldn't be seen. "We shouldn't be here," he whispered. "I just wanted you to hear this."

The chanting—amazingly loud, yet ethereal as a silken veil—resonated throughout the enormous church. Corliss had never heard anything quite like it. Rainulf released her hand and grasped her upper arms gently from behind. "Close your eyes," he murmured into her ear. "Let it inside you."

She did as he instructed, opening her ears and mind and body to the celestial tones of a hundred voices raised in sacred song. He held her pressed back against his chest, and she felt the drumming of his heart in primitive counterpoint to the airy chanting. The steady heartbeats reverberated throughout her as the voices rose in unison, filling her up, lifting her to a place of weightless serenity, of earthly ecstasy and holy perfection.

All too soon it ended, and the brothers filed out through the transept. Rainulf's hands eased their grip, and he lightly stroked her arms, causing her heart to trip wildly. "What did you think?" he whispered, his hot breath tickling her ear.

She turned to face him. "It sounded . . . amazing. Like Heaven."

He glanced over her shoulder, then abruptly seized her and pushed her back against a pillar, pressing himself against her.

"Rainulf! What—"

He clamped a hand over her mouth and lowered his mouth to her ear. "The abbot."

Corliss listened and heard soft, sluggish footsteps advancing toward them. Rainulf touched her lips with a finger and she nodded. The footsteps passed excruciatingly slowly, the abbot being well advanced in years. Rainulf flattened himself against her in an effort not to be seen. With the cold, hard marble at her back, and his unyielding warmth in front, she could barely breathe. A flood of giddy intoxication overcame her, and she stifled a giggle that bubbled up in her throat.

He covered her mouth again, whispering, "Shh," but she felt his chest shake, and knew that he, too, fought to maintain his composure. A kind of gasping chuckle escaped him, and she slapped her hand across his mouth. The absurdity of the situation—each of them covering the other's mouth—struck them both at once, and they fairly choked with laughter, spurred on as much by fatigue as by their predicament.

They both peeked around the pillar and watched the old abbot shuffle down the nave and out of the church, seemingly oblivious to their presence. "He must be hard of hearing," Rainulf said.

"Thank goodness."

He took her hand and drew her to the door. They watched until the abbot disappeared into his lodge, then sprinted across the courtyard, holding hands and laughing like prankish children. At the door to the guest house, he turned her to face him and rested his hands on her shoulders. He was breathless, and still smiling. Regardless of the cause of his surprising good humor, it utterly delighted her.

"Shame on you, Corliss."

"What?"

"You're a bad influence on me."

"It was your idea!" she pointed out huffily.

"I never would have done it with anyone but you." He trailed the back of one hand down the side of her face, his gaze wandering from her eyes to her mouth. She saw his lips open slightly, and thought—or imagined—that he moved a hairsbreadth closer to her. Then his smile faded, and he backed away. "We'd better get some sleep. We've another long ride ahead of us tomorrow."

She nodded, not trusting herself to speak, and followed him into the guest house.

It was late the next afternoon when she first saw the round, whitewashed castle keep rising in the distance above the rolling pastures and woodlands through which they rode. A crenellated stone wall surrounded the castle, and a banner snapped on its high tower.

"Is that Blackburn?" she asked in a small voice.

"That's Blackburn. We have just one stop first." He pointed, and Corliss saw, nestled in the river valley below them, a low arrangement of neat stone buildings.

"Another monastery?" she asked.

He nodded. "St. Dunstan's. The prior, Brother Matthew, is an old friend of mine from university. We'll just say a quick hello and be on our way."

A black-haired monk was waiting for them as they rode through the front gates.

"Matthew! How goes it?" Rainulf leapt down from his horse and embraced the prior.

"I'm well. And very happy to see you!"

Corliss dismounted and tried to be inconspicuous, but the prior's keen, dark eyes quickly settled on her. "Is this boy with you? Do famous magisters have pages now?"

"This is Corliss," Rainulf said, then hesitated, glancing uneasily at the monks, lay brothers, and servants who'd gathered around. "Corliss is ..." He met her eyes; she grinned and shrugged, as if to say, *Tell them.* "Well, it's a rather involved story, but Corliss is actually—"

"Look!" cried a young monk, pointing to the road that led from Castle Blackburn to the priory. A horseman was tearing toward them at breakneck speed, his enormous white mount kicking up a trail of dust.

Matthew chuckled and shook his head. "He must have seen you and couldn't wait for you to come to him. Thorne's got an impatient streak."

"Aye," Rainulf agreed. "We'll have to save our visit for some other time, Matthew." He walked to the gate and waited, hands on hips, as his friend rode toward him.

The big white stallion snorted and danced as he was reined in. Thorne Falconer dismounted and wrapped Rainulf in an enthusiastic bear hug. Corliss gaped, taking in the Saxon's size. He was taller even than Rainulf, with the most massive shoulders she'd ever seen—a human warhorse. His long, golden brown hair and humble tunic enhanced his slightly barbarous image. He wore no fur or sword to signify his rank. All this was odd enough, but when he asked Rainulf how his journey had gone—in *English!*—her jaw dropped open. She'd never thought to hear a baron speak her native tongue. Never mind that it was his native tongue as well. The ruling class of England spoke French exclusively; she'd never heard of an exception.

He spoke to Brother Matthew in French, but reverted to English as he got back on his horse. "Martine's been anxious to see you, Rainulf. I promised I'd bring you back right away. You don't mind, do you?"

Rainulf exchanged a grin with the prior. "I wouldn't want to disappoint Martine." He remounted, and Corliss followed suit.

The baron's vivid blue eyes assessed her curiously as they rode slowly back up the path toward the castle, three abreast with him in the middle. "I must say, Rainulf, I never thought to see the day you'd be traveling with a servant. What happened to that famous humility of yours?"

Rainulf sighed and cast her a slightly apologetic

look. "Corliss is ... a friend, not a servant. And there's something—"

"Corliss, eh?" He regarded her skeptically. "Isn't that a woman's name?"

"Not always, my lord," she said. "It can be either a man's or a woman's."

"None of that 'my lord' business, boy," the big Saxon remonstrated. "Friends of Rainulf's must call me Thorne."

"Thank you ... Thorne." She caught Rainulf's eye and mouthed *Tell him,* but before Rainulf could speak, Thorne reached over and punched him on the arm.

"Look at you! You're not a priest anymore! I'm still not entirely sure how you managed to get out of it."

"Neither am I," Rainulf conceded.

Thorne shrugged. "Mayhap it's just because everyone likes you so much." He turned to Corliss and said, "He's always been able to get away with things no one else could. His charm has earned him special favors all his life." His voice took on a low, conspiratorial tone, and he winked at her. "Especially from the fairer sex."

Corliss sat up straighter in her saddle. "Really?"

"Aye." Thorne chuckled good-naturedly. "He was reputed to be quite the swordsman in his university days."

Corliss frowned. "Swordsman?"

"In bed."

"Thorne—" Rainulf began.

"Of course, I didn't know him back then. I met him when they chained him next to me in a prison hole in the Levant. After a year, Queen Eleanor bought our freedom, and we returned home along the overland route. That's when I first became aware of his amorous skills. We were traveling through the Rhineland—"

"Thorne," Rainulf interjected, "there's something you should know about Cor—"

"Later!" said Corliss, knowing she'd never get to hear the story once Thorne found out she was a woman. Rainulf shot her a look, but she ignored him. "What happened in the Rhineland?"

Thorne leaned toward her with a grin. "There was this sweet young farmwife who let us sleep in her loft. Can't remember her name . . ." He glanced over his shoulder. "You were always so good with names, Rainulf."

"Sigfreda," Rainulf said, staring straight ahead.

"Sigfreda! That's right. Lovely. Hair the color of ripe wheat. Rainulf and I had picked up enough German from our cellmates to be able to talk to her. Turned out her husband had gone on Crusade and never returned. She was . . . lonely." He shrugged. "We stayed with her two nights. The first night, I slept upstairs in the loft and Rainulf shared Sigfreda's bed. The next night, Rainulf got the loft, and I got Sigfreda."

"Ah," Corliss said.

"That first night," Thorne said, "I lay up there in the hay listening to the most astonishing sounds from below."

Rainulf groaned. "Thorne . . ."

"All the more astonishing because of my own inexperience. I'd been a pious and chaste youth when I took up the cross. Two years of battle and imprisonment had cured me of my piety, but left my chastity intact. So I lay awake for hours, wide-eyed in the hay, wondering at every little gasp and giggle, every crackle of the straw. And then, when the screams came—"

"Screams?" Corliss stole a glance at Rainulf; his ears were purple.

"Every once in a while," Thorne explained, "Sigfreda would let loose with the most alarming . . . I hardly know how to describe the sound. At first I thought the imprisonment had gotten to Rainulf, after all. I thought he'd gone mad and was killing her in some slow, torturous way. Then I realized she was just, well, enjoying herself. Very much. I was impressed." He laughed. "So was she."

Turning to Rainulf, he said, "You ruined her for me, you know. The next night, when it was my turn, all she could talk about was you. Your endurance, your vigor, your ... 'sorcerer's hands,' I think she called them."

A small smile crept past Rainulf's stony defenses. "I knew I'd be taking a vow of chastity soon. I was inspired."

"Well, your inspiration was my downfall," Thorne said. "I'd never been with a woman, and I finally decided I must be incompetent, because I couldn't get her to scream like you did. She assured me I wasn't doing it wrong—I just wasn't doing it as *right* as you had. When I told her you were taking Holy Orders, she burst into tears." To Corliss he said, "Not an uncommon reaction, as I understand. I'm told the ladies of Paris went into mourning when Rainulf took his vows."

Corliss looked back and forth between the two men, gathering her thoughts. Certain aspects of the ribald anecdote confused her—that a woman should scream during sex made no sense—but one thing was clear. Her image of a virginal Rainulf was clearly off the mark—way off the mark. She cleared her throat and tried not to sound as astonished as she felt. "I had no idea our Magister Scholarum was quite such a legend," she said with forced nonchalance.

"Aye, 'legend' is the right word," Thorne said. "And now that he's renounced his vows, perhaps the legend can continue. What say you, Rainulf? Are you ready to enslave the ladies of Oxford as you once did those of Paris?"

"Enslave?" said Rainulf.

"You enslaved their hearts, only to break them when you became a priest."

"That's ridiculous."

"Oh, I heard all about you at the queen's court in Paris, before I returned to England. The ladies would whisper of your extraordinary seductiveness, of the deep and reckless passion hidden beneath your scholarly robes. They'd confess how they'd given themselves to you eagerly, even knowing you didn't love them. And then they'd ask me why a man like you would want to be a priest, and they'd weep."

"I do hope you comforted them," Rainulf said dryly.

Thorne smiled. "What else could I do?"

Both men laughed easily, and Corliss shook her head in astonishment, thinking, *I really don't know Rainulf. I don't know him at all.*

The horses' hooves clattered on the drawbridge, and Corliss swallowed hard, staring up at the spectacular majesty of Blackburn Castle as it loomed over them. She whispered a hurried prayer—"Please, God, don't let me throw up from nerves before I even get inside"—and crossed herself as they rode single file through an opening in the great oaken door. The outer bailey—with its stone-and-thatch structures surrounding a central fishpond—reminded her of Cuxham. Or it would have, except that everyone here seemed content, even happy, whereas smiles were rare within Roger Foliot's domain.

The inner bailey was a maze of gardens, both utilitarian and ornamental. Against the far side of the wall from the keep stood an enormous stone dwelling, which Thorne identified as his hawk house.

"*Birds* live in there?" Corliss asked. It was as large as Sir Roger's manor house!

Rainulf laughed. "Thorne's falcons are his babies. He lives for them."

"I live for Martine," Thorne said, a statement so

matter-of-fact, yet so intimate, that Corliss hardly knew how to respond. "I keep falcons merely to amuse myself when she's had enough of me."

As they dismounted in the tree-lined courtyard outside the keep, Rainulf said, with a smug grin, "By the way, Thorne, there's something I didn't get a chance to tell you about Corliss before you launched into that bawdy story of yours."

"Something about Corliss?" Thorne glanced at two young women hauling baskets of laundry down the wide steps of the keep's forebuilding, and lowered his voice, grinning. "Is the boy an innocent? Too delicate for tales of Sigfreda?"

"The boy's a woman," Rainulf said mildly. "And by her very nature too delicate for such tales."

The big Saxon blinked at Rainulf, and then turned to stare at Corliss, taking her in head to toe. When he met her gaze, she broke into a wide grin and shrugged. "It's true, my lor—I mean, Thorne."

He blanched, then turned to glare at Rainulf. "Why didn't you tell me?" he demanded in a fierce rasp.

"I tried. You were too busy describing Sigfreda's screams of ecstasy to—"

"Rainulf!" Thorne cast a horrified look in Corliss's direction.

"She's heard it already," Rainulf pointed out. "From your own mouth. Too late to worry about her feminine sensibilities now."

"Too late to worry about *whose* feminine sensibilities?" They all turned toward the soft voice, which belonged to a young woman standing at the top of the stairs. Corliss instantly knew that this was Martine Falconer. She had her brother's impressive height, flaxen hair, and regal good looks. A band of hammered silver encircled her head, but she wore no veil, her two long, thick braids hanging down on either side of the largest stomach Corliss had ever seen on a pregnant woman. In the curve of one arm she held a black cat with white boots. Smiling, she lifted the hem of her voluminous blue silk tunic, descending the steps with a good deal more grace than Corliss would have thought possible.

Thorne raced up the steps to take her arm, closely followed by Rainulf. "Martine!" Her brother kissed her on both cheeks. "You look wonderful. Full of health." She did; her deep blue eyes sparkled, her face glowed.

She laughed. "I look like some great sow that's been fattened up for just a bit too long." Like Rainulf, she spoke the Anglo-Saxon tongue with a pronounced Norman-French accent.

He studied her vast belly with an expression of wonderment. "Nay, you look . . ."

She laughed again and petted her cat. "Fat. Say it."

Shaking his head, he murmured, "Beautiful. More beautiful than ever."

Corliss felt an irrational stab of jealousy, despite the fact that Martine was Rainulf's sister. Perhaps it was her very womanliness, her fecundity—and Rainulf's awestruck reaction to it—that so discomfited Corliss. She fingered her chin-length hair and looked down at her dusty chausses, feeling suddenly self-conscious, even a bit foolish in her masculine garb.

"So, whose sensibilities has my husband bruised?" Lady Falconer asked with a smile. "Whom has he insulted now?"

"Corliss." Rainulf gestured to her to step forward. "I hope you don't mind an unexpected guest, Martine."

"Of course not."

"Thank you, my lady," said Corliss.

"It's Martine," the young baroness corrected, looking a little confused. "I must have misheard Rainulf. I thought he said something about feminine sensibilities."

Thorne leaned down and whispered something in her ear, whereupon Martine fixed her widening eyes on Corliss. The cat leaped from her arms and darted away, though she seemed scarcely to notice. "Oh."

"Yes," said Corliss miserably. "Perhaps Rainulf should have written ahead of time . . ."

"Nonsense." Martine held out her hand, and Corliss bounded up the stairs to take it. "I'm very pleased to have you. Just a bit"—her gaze sought out her brother, and she raised her eyebrows teasingly—"unaccustomed to Rainulf's having a . . . female companion."

"It's not what it looks like," Rainulf said.

Martine's amused gaze swept Corliss from top to bottom. "I'm not quite sure what it *does* look like."

"I mean, we're not . . ." Rainulf began. "Corliss lives with me, that's all."

Thorne and Martine exchanged a look. The Saxon grinned knowingly and reached behind his wife to slap Rainulf on the back. Corliss rolled her eyes.

"This isn't coming out right," said Rainulf.

Martine chuckled. "There will be plenty of time to explain it over supper. Meanwhile, you and Corliss can rest up a bit from your journey. I'll show you to your chambers."

Once alone, Rainulf stripped completely, then lay on the too large bed they'd given him and threw an arm over his face. An image of Corliss materialized before him—Corliss as she had looked last night while she listened to the monks chant, her eyes closed, her mouth slightly parted, her head back. She'd looked transported. He imagined her looking like that as she lay beneath him, and his body reacted instantly. Growling, he leaped from the bed and poured a basinful of cold water, then lathered up a bar of soap, and vigorously washed off the dust of the road.

As he dried himself off, he became aware of muffled voices—not from the hallway, but from another door, one that he had assumed to be a dressing alcove or closet. Silently turning the handle, he opened the door a crack and peeked through.

"Which one?" Through the narrow opening, he saw a flash of purple silk, and another of green, as Martine held up two shimmering, jewel-toned kirtles.

He heard water splashing and eased the door open just a fraction more, then stilled, his heart quickening. A pale, curved ribbon of flesh—Corliss's flesh—was just visible. She stood in a bathtub as someone poured steaming water over her. He saw her arm rise as she lifted her damp hair off the back of her neck, saw the delicate contour of a breast, the slope of a hip....

Another woman spoke. He recognized the voice of his sister's personal maid, Felda. "Take the purple gown, Lady Corliss. It suits you. I'll hem it, and we can lace it up so it fits like it was made for you."

Lady Corliss?

Rainulf closed the door with a silent, careful movement, then leaned his forehead against the cool, polished wood and let out the breath he hadn't realized he'd been holding.

They'd given Corliss a chamber adjoining his. That was surely no accident. They—Martine and Thorne—assumed she was his mistress. They'd thought to please him with this discreet arrangement—separate chambers that connected, a winking nod in the direction of respectability.

He heard Martine's gentle laughter, and the louder laughter of Felda, and knew that they harbored no doubts whatsoever that he and Corliss were lovers. Closing his eyes, he pictured again that fleeting, partial view of Corliss in her bath ... the sliver of creamy flesh, steam rising from her smooth, wet body ... and wished, with sudden, staggering force, that it were so.

Fool!

Pushing away from the door, he dressed quickly and bolted from the room. He'd go to the stables and choose a horse—one of Thorne's giant, half-mad stallions—and ride until his bones were too weary and his mind too numb to think of anything but supper and bed.

Pigot knew something was wrong. He'd seen neither Rainulf Fairfax nor his young housemate for two days, and that made him nervous.

The housekeeper still cooked and cleaned in the big house on St. John Street. And those two scholars who hung on his cappa still treated their magister's home as their own, although they had long ago stopped entertaining their whores there; Fairfax must have discovered the practice and put an end to it. But he and Corliss were nowhere to be seen.

Had Fairfax caught on, discovered that he'd been watching, waiting? Was his quarry even now being stowed aboard a ship bound for Normandy, or escorted north into the Scottish Highlands?

He'd never failed to bring back his prey, and he'd be damned if he'd fail this time.

You'll be damned anyway, he thought with a humorless smile as he watched the front door of the magister's house open and the old housekeeper emerge. He retrieved his leper's mask—a sack of coarse linen with a hole for one eye and another for his mouth—and drew it down over his head. Next came ragged gloves, a pair of shabby, oversize boots, and a tin cup. Shrugging his satchel onto his back, he shuffled out of the alley and followed the housekeeper down St. John Street, catching up to her at the corner of Shidyerd.

He shaped his throat so that his voice would emerge as a gravelly rasp. "Mistress?"

She turned around and started, then pressed a fleshy hand to her bosom. "Aye?"

He held the cup out, his head lowered. "Alms for a cursed soul?"

Grimacing, she fumbled in her purse for a penny

and dropped the coin with a metallic clatter into his cup. He peered inside and said, "Master Fairfax gives me tuppence."

She frowned. "Father gives you money?"

Father? "Every day."

Planting her hands on her hips, she said, "Then how is it I've never seen you before today?"

"I'm usually outside St. Mary's. That's where I see Father Rainulf. I came here looking for him." He shook the cup; the coin rattled around inside. "He gives me tuppence."

"Aye, well, Father's far too generous for his own good. 'Twill serve him ill someday. Be off with you."

She turned to leave. Pigot grabbed her arm, and she shrieked as she wheeled around. She stared at the spot he'd touched, her expression a mixture of fear and fury. "You've got no business touching me. Now I'll have to burn this kirtle."

"Father Rainulf always gives me tuppence," he repeated, jiggling the cup.

She backed away, her eyes on him as he slowly advanced. "Well, Father Rainulf's not here. I am, and I give beggars a penny, if I give anything. Now, off with you!"

"I need my tuppence. I'll wait here for Father Rainulf."

"You'll have a long wait. He's visiting family in Sussex and won't be back for a fortnight."

"Where in Sussex?"

She laughed shortly. "And what business is that of yours?" She spun around. "Be off before I put the sheriff on you."

He let her go, and returned to his hiding place in the alley across from the big stone house to take off his disguise.

Visiting family, eh? He might be. Or he might be hiding Constance of Cuxham. There was no way for Pigot to know unless he found out where these Sussex relations lived and followed him there. If, indeed, Fairfax *was* just visiting family, the journey would have been for naught, and he'd have risked exposing himself. If Fairfax wasn't there—if he *was* spiriting the priest's whore out of the country—the trip would still be a waste of time, and he'd be no closer to apprehending her.

Traveling to Sussex was pointless. The prudent move now was to wait for the magister's return. If the whore was with him, he'd make his move the instant she was alone. If she wasn't with him, he'd damn well find out where she was. This endless watching and waiting was a waste of his valuable time.

He took the coin from the cup and tossed it in the air. At least this afternoon had proved fruitful, if only to a small degree. He'd saved himself two weeks of worthless surveillance ... and earned a penny in the process. He'd keep it, he decided, slipping it into his boot. Perhaps it would bring him luck.

Chapter 10

"Peter stared at Rainulf as if he were mad. "You went *riding*?"

"You've just spent two days on a horse," Guy pointed out.

Rainulf shrugged distractedly and drained his pre-supper brandy in one burning gulp as the two knights—sitting across from him at the high table in the great hall—exchanged raised eyebrows. In appearance, they were the antithesis of each other. Peter was tall and Nordic, with kinky blond locks that tumbled halfway down his back; his shorter, burly companion wore his dark hair cut close to his scalp in the Norman style. Where it mattered, however, they were much the same. They shared a consummate mastery of soldiering skills and an unwavering dedication to their friend and overlord, Thorne Falconer. Thorne insisted that they—along with all of his vassals and villeins—speak English, a tongue they pronounced with thick Norman accents.

Thorne, sitting to Rainulf's right, beckoned to the page with the jug and asked him to pour them each a refill. Rainulf thought about refusing it, as he had an empty stomach, but he let the boy fill the little cup to the brim.

"Rainulf is a creature of the intellect," Thorne laughingly told his men. "He doesn't get saddle sore like the rest of us. 'Tis some arcane philosophical problem that's making him squirm on his bench, not a bruised ass."

Peter and Guy got a chuckle out of this. Rainulf smiled to be polite and swiftly tossed the brandy down his throat.

Guy nudged Peter and both stared fixedly at something beyond Rainulf's shoulder. Thorne followed their line of sight, and after a moment he looked pointedly at Rainulf, his expression an odd blend of amusement and respect. "Well, Magister. You've got excellent taste, after all. What I'd thought to be a common pebble has polished up into quite a gem."

Rainulf turned to find Martine standing with another luxuriously gowned woman at the sink near the stairwell. When he realized the second woman was Corliss, the empty brandy cup slipped from his fingers and rolled onto the floor. He leaned over to pick it up, never taking his eyes off the young woman in the gleaming purple kirtle.

Her raven hair was caught up in a snood of glittering golden mesh, effectively disguising its short length; a circlet of gold filigree held the snood in place. The purple gown was laced tightly up the back in the Parisian style. It conformed mercilessly to her graceful curves, curves he rarely had had the opportunity to admire. The kirtle's snug, low-cut bodice revealed much of her pale shoulders and upper chest, and accentuated her high, firm breasts. From there his gaze was drawn to the jeweled sash looped low around hips that flared from an exquisitely narrow waist.

She was so thoroughly and unquestionably feminine. Not for the first time, he found himself awed at her ability to pass so well for a male.

Martine washed her hands first. Because Rainulf's gaze was trained on Corliss, he saw her intent observation of everything his sister did—the way she flipped the long sleeves of her tunic over her arms to get them out of the way, accepted the soap from a waiting page, and turned the brass spigot. For just a moment there, when water began to run from the faucet, Corliss lost her composure. Her eyes widened and a grin of delight broke out on her face. Indoor plumbing, courtesy of a rooftop cistern, was one of the more extraordinary innovations in this immense, newly built castle.

Corliss wrapped her own trailing sleeves around her arms, took the soap from Martine, and turned on the water, as casually as if she'd done it a hundred times. As she leaned over the sink, her bosom strained against its silken confinement, the milky upper slopes of her breasts swelling above the heavy gold braid that edged the gown's neckline. Rainulf's hand tightened reflexively around the little brandy cup; his loins stirred. Perhaps bringing Corliss to Blackburn hadn't been such a good idea after all.

"Who is she?" Peter asked quietly.

Not a good idea at all. Without wresting his gaze from Corliss, Rainulf opened his mouth to answer, but Thorne beat him to it. "She's Corliss of Oxford. She arrived with Rainulf."

Guy turned to Peter. "She looks exactly like Lady Magdalen."

A stricken expression crossed Peter's face. "I've asked you not to speak of her," he said hoarsely.

Thorne leaned toward Rainulf and said quietly, " 'Twas a great tragedy. They were betrothed since infancy, and he loved her to distraction. In March she died of smallpox."

"Oh, God." It seemed Cuxham hadn't been the only place in England affected by that cursed disease last spring. Rainulf recalled his grief on hearing of Corliss's death, yet he'd barely known her. How much more devastated must Peter have been—must still be—to have lost the woman he'd loved all his life.

Thorne shook his head. "He hasn't been the same since."

Peter *had* seemed preoccupied. . . . Nay, not preoccupied, Rainulf decided, regarding him thoughtfully. Haunted. Peter's jaw clenched, and he quickly swallowed the contents of his cup. But then he returned his attention to Corliss, and the pain left his eyes.

Rainulf's gaze sought out the young woman who had so captivated the grief-stricken knight. Corliss accepted a towel from a second page. As she dried her hands, she discreetly inspected her surroundings. Rainulf tore his eyes from her to follow her line of sight, trying to see the great hall of Castle Blackburn as if for the first time. It was a magnificent hall, round like the keep that surrounded it, handsomely plastered and wainscotted, and with a high, vaulted ceiling. A gallery, onto which many of the upstairs chambers opened, completely encircled the massive room. The floors were covered not with rushes, but with a scattering of colorful Saracen carpets, gifts from Queen Eleanor when she made Thorne a baron.

But the most remarkable aspect of the hall was its many tall, arched windows. It wasn't their number or size that made Corliss's mouth fall open, he was sure, but the fact that they were glazed—something she had undoubtedly never seen outside of a cathedral. Each one was fitted with a panel composed of dozens of panes of sea-green glass set into lead. The panels could be opened, and in fact, they all were, revealing a brilliant orange-gold sunset and allowing the summer evening's warm breezes to circulate through the hall.

The table at which Rainulf and his companions sat was situated before a massive fireplace, larger even than that in his Oxford town house; the servants' tables were arranged around the edge of the hall. Corliss's attention was drawn first to the enormous hearth, in which a low fire flickered, and then to Rainulf. She met his gaze, her expression one of both amazement and amusement. With ingenuous deliberation, she made her laughing brown eyes go wide, just for the briefest moment, before Martine spoke to her and she turned away. Rainulf smiled, pleased by her disclosure of her amazement to him and him alone, warmed by the intimacy of it.

"She came with you, Rainulf?"

He turned to face Peter, sensing an undercurrent of disappointment beneath the civil question. "Aye." He wished he didn't know where this was leading.

Peter leaned forward and lowered his voice. "Is she your mis—"

"Nay!" Rainulf said, a bit too sharply. "I'm offering her protection from someone who would do her harm. She's naught to me but ... a friend."

"A friend," said Thorne, with a glimmer in those blue Saxon eyes. "Of course."

Rainulf had taken Thorne and Martine aside when he returned from his ride and explained the situation, but asked them not to discuss the details with others. For this reason, only his sister and brother by marriage knew of Corliss's humble origins and their living arrangement. But despite his protestations to the contrary, they both apparently still thought of her as his lover.

Rainulf looked back at Corliss chatting with his sister and the squires and ladies' maids gathering around the sink. He heard her throaty laughter as she made conversation with those highborn attendants, and felt both pride and a certain measure of vague discomfort at the ease with which she handled herself.

"Is she marriageable?" Peter asked.

Marriageable! Rainulf stared at the handsome young knight who, judging from his sincere expression, was completely serious. "She has no property."

"I have no need of property. Thorne's granted me a choice holding. Has she a husband somewhere?"

Rainulf heard himself say, "She's widowed."

"And not promised to anyone?"

Waving over the boy with the jug, Rainulf mumbled, "Nay. She's ..." He grimaced and shook his head as the page filled his cup with brandy. "Nay."

Martine and Corliss and the rest of the ladies approached the table, the squires behind. Peter smiled and tossed back his sandy mane as he rose, his gaze fixed on Corliss. The men all stood as the ladies took their seats.

Martine introduced "Lady Corliss" to the knights and motioned for her to sit next to Rainulf. He saw the relief in Corliss's smile as she walked over to him, and felt gratified that she viewed his nearness as a source of comfort in this strange place.

Her silken gown rustled as she settled down beside him, keeping her back straight and her chin raised, just as he had shown her. A warm, evocative scent rose from her and enveloped him like an enchanted mist. There was something darkly exotic about the scent, something compelling and enigmatic that reminded him of the East—of fragrant blossoms that opened only at night, of aromatic spice markets, and hot, swirling windstorms.

Martine, seated across the table from him, met his gaze and smiled in a self-satisfied way, then cocked her eyebrows as if to say, *Well? What do you think of my handiwork?* She'd dressed and adorned Corliss just for him, he realized. The intoxicating perfume rising from Corliss's warm skin was one of Martine's obscure herbal concoctions. The sapphires encircling her slender throat, the tiny gold rings flashing on her tapered fingers, catching his eye again and again, were all part of Martine's vision.

Smiling politely, Rainulf nodded and raised his cup toward your sister, acknowledging the skill with which she had transformed his—how had Thorne put it?— smooth little pebble into a precious gem.

Peter cleared his throat. "My lady?"

Corliss, seemingly oblivious to the knight, thanked the page who poured her wine and took a sip.

"My lady? Lady Corliss."

She lowered her goblet slowly, her expression of surprise giving way to a gracious smile. "I'm sorry, Sir Peter. I didn't realize you were speaking to me."

He returned the smile. "Of course I was speaking to you. You might as well be the only person at this table, for your beauty is so blinding that I can barely see the others."

Rainulf gulped down his brandy and gestured grimly for another.

Corliss watched Rainulf hand the two books to his sister and then slowly circle the table and return to his seat next to her. She smiled and pretended interest as Martine exclaimed over the gifts, all the while keeping a close watch on Rainulf out of the corner of her eye.

He was drunk. Very drunk. He'd barely nibbled at his supper, and now his almond-spice cake sat untouched before him while he poured himself yet another goblet of wine. She'd often seen men drink to excess, but never Rainulf Fairfax. Once, he'd told her how much he hated the unbalanced feeling that came with drunkenness, and she'd gotten the impression it almost frightened him. Yet he'd spent this entire meal getting steadily—and, it seemed, deliberately—intoxicated.

He was the only person at the table who was truly in his cups, but she seemed to be the only one who recognized his condition. Conversation had been lively during the meal, and no one seemed to notice Rainulf's silence, or the increasing lack of focus in his eyes. All his movements were slow and deliberate, as if it was important to him to seem his normal, cool-headed, unflappable self. He'd fooled the others.

But not me. Perhaps it was because she sat right next to him, and could see the slight unsteadiness in his careful gestures. Or perhaps it was simply that she'd come to know him so well—too well to be taken in by his feigned sobriety.

"My lady? Did you hear me?"

She started, and met Sir Peter's intent gaze. "Aye . . ." She grinned sheepishly. "Nay."

He smiled compassionately. "You're fatigued from your journey. I understand. I had asked you if you'd care to join me for some hawking tomorrow afternoon."

"Hawking?" She saw Rainulf's knuckles turn white as he gripped his goblet, then brought it to his mouth and emptied it swiftly. "I'm afraid I've never . . . I don't know how—"

"Oh, I'll show you everything you need to know. And the baron can supply you with a gauntlet and a suitable bird. What say you, Thorne? Have you a tame little falcon for my lady to hunt with?"

Corliss saw the Saxon's amused gaze flick toward Rainulf before turning to her. "I've got a lovely little merlin who'll serve you well, my lady. Meek as a newborn pup—till she lands her prey, of course. Then she shows her true colors. Falcons need meat like they need to breathe."

Thorne popped the last bit of his cake into his mouth and dusted off his hands, his azure eyes trained on Rainulf. "No creature can keep its true needs in check forever. One can go years pretending they don't exist. But nature despises pretense, and eventually the desire to satisfy them becomes . . . overpowering. Impossible to resist."

Rainulf glowered at him. Thorne grinned and said to Corliss, "The merlin's name is Guinevere, after Arthur's queen. I'll introduce you to her on the morrow."

With a mumbled "Excuse me," Rainulf stood. For a moment he clutched at the tablecloth. His wavering gaze took in the diners and then rested on Corliss. He started to say something, but then seemed to change his mind. Beneath the wine-induced haze in his eyes she thought she saw a hint of uneasiness, even dread.

He hates being drunk. It scares him. She watched him as he took his leave, crossing the great hall with cautious, unhurried steps.

"Do you play chess, Lady Corliss?"

She glanced briefly at Sir Peter, then returned her attention to Rainulf as he made his way to the stairwell. "Nay, I never learned how."

"Then I'd be honored if you'd let me teach you after supper."

"Tonight?" she asked distractedly as Rainulf ducked into the stairwell and disappeared from view.

"Aye. Unless ... That is, if you're too tired from your trip—"

"I am, I'm afraid." She rose, and the men all stood. "More tired than I'd realized. I hate to retire so early, but ..."

"Of course," Peter said. "But you must let me walk you upstairs."

"Nay, don't trouble yourself."

"But it's no—"

"Please. I'll be fine."

"But—"

"What time shall I meet you tomorrow, Sir Peter?"

"Ah." Her ruse worked; he left off arguing and smiled in anticipation. "After the noon meal? At the hawk house?"

"I'll be there." She bid the company a hasty good night and followed Rainulf into the torchlit stairwell.

Halfway up the circular stairs, she came upon him sitting on one of the cold stone steps and leaning against the wall.

"Oh, Rainulf."

He groaned when he saw her.

"Let me help you." She went to lift him under the arms, but he grabbed her hands.

"I'm fine," he said thickly.

"You're not fine. You're drunk."

"Nay, I'm fine. Just don't make me move."

"You can't stay here." She tried to raise him up by the hands, but he resisted her, pulling her down until she sank to her knees on the step beneath him, his long legs flanking her.

"I can damn well stay wherever I want."

She'd never heard him sound so surly. "Come on," she said, struggling to her feet. "I'm taking you to—"

"Stop it!" Releasing her hands, he seized her shoulders and lowered her roughly. "I just ..." He shook his head helplessly. "I can't ..."

She made her voice gentle and tried to rise again. "Rainulf, please."

"No!" He shoved her to her knees so abruptly that one side of her gown slid down her arm. With a seemingly great effort he focused on the crumpled silk beneath his hand, and the shoulder that he had inadvertently exposed.

Very slowly his hand moved up, hot and slightly rough against the bare skin of her upper arm. She shivered as he gripped her naked shoulder. He caressed her, his expression one of mystification, as if he were watching the unfathomable actions of another person. His thumb glided along the shaft of her collarbone, and back again, robbing the breath from her lungs. She felt dizzy, and as he swayed slightly, so did she.

She saw his throat move as he swallowed. Then his expression sobered and he righted her sleeve, smoothing the purple silk carefully over her shoulder. He sighed and closed his eyes, his hands urging her toward him until she was crushed against him, his chin resting on her head. She thought she heard him murmur her name, and something that sounded like "I'm such a fool," as his arms encircled her.

She wrapped her arms around him and pressed her ear to his chest, listening to the erratic thudding of his heart beneath the wool tunic. "Shh ... You're just drunk."

"I was a fool to get drunk," he whispered.

" 'Tis no great sin. Everyone does it once in a while."

"I hate it, though," he mumbled.

"I know." She looked up at him. "But you'll feel better once you're in your own bed. Try closing your eyes while I walk you back to your chamber. I'll bet that'll do the trick."

He shook his head, but she pressed her fingertips to his eyelids and forced him to do as she asked. "There. Keep them closed." This time, when she stood and lifted him under the arms, he rose willingly, leaning on her shoulder as she walked him up the stairs and into his lamplit chamber, closing the door behind them.

"This way." She guided him to his big bed, swept aside the curtains, and helped him to lie down on his back. "Let's get you comfortable." Sitting next to him, she pulled his boots off and set them on the floor, then reached for his belt and hesitated. He had his eyes closed, his face turned away. Biting her lip, she took hold of the silver buckle and began working the thick leather belt through it, but it didn't slide easily, and the buckle was designed in some peculiar way that she couldn't figure out. As she fumbled with it, she became aware of his eyes on her, studying her face as she struggled to undress him, and her cheeks stung.

He managed a small smile and closed a hand over both of hers. "Let me." She slid her hands out of his. He undid the buckle and whipped the belt off, then sat up. "Ohhh ..." He covered his face with his hands.

"I know, Rainulf. I know."

"Help me with my tunic?"

Between the two of them, they managed to get the heavy garment over his head. The shirt came with it, leaving him in naught but his chausses.

"Are you comfortable?" she asked, trying to keep from staring at his bare chest. "Do you need some water?"

He shook his head and groaned. "Oh, God. I just wish ... God, I wish everything would stop moving."

"I know." She tried to rise, but he reached out and took her by the upper arms, pulling her with him as he lay back down.

"Stay," he pleaded, wrapping his arms around her and forcing her to lie next to him. "Just until it stops. Till everything is still."

He held her with her head on his shoulder. Thinking her gold circlet must be digging into him, she pulled it off and tossed it aside, then lay stiffly, wondering what to do with her outside arm.

"Here." He took it and draped it across his stomach, then tightened his arms around her and held her close.

As his breathing slowed and steadied, and his arms around her grew heavy, she began to relax. It was quite wonderful, really, lying there in Rainulf Fairfax's embrace, even if he was dead drunk and only wanted her for a bit of comfort. She was glad to be of comfort, gratified that she could make his world stop spinning long enough for him to get to sleep.

She yawned, thinking she would have to get up and return to her own chamber before she succumbed to the drowsiness that was creeping over her.

Just a few more moments. She closed her eyes and settled against him, feeling the heat from his half-naked body through the thin silk of her gown.

Rainulf stood at St. Mary's high lectern and looked down on the faces of hundreds—no, thousands—of young, black-robed scholars, staring up at him expectantly. No, not scholars, he realized ... birds, little black baby birds, their mouths agape, waiting to be fed.

He wanted to feed them, but he hadn't any food, not the right kind, anyway. They'd trusted him, but they shouldn't have. He was consumed with doubt, and his doubt made him unworthy. He'd deluded them, gathered them here under false pretenses. . . .

He shook his head violently. "I can't," he muttered, his voice dull and distant. "I want to, but I can't. I have nothing for you."

A soft rustling . . . the beating of thousands of tiny wings. He felt their silken feathers brush his skin as the birds flew into the air, gathering around him, their beaks wide open, begging for food. Begging, begging . . .

"Nay!" He lashed out at them, fighting them off as they closed in on him, wanting what he had no right to give. . . .

A whisper: "Shh . . . easy."

His fist connected and one of them cried out. No, it wasn't one of the birds, he realized, growing still as soft hands closed around his wrists. The cry had been that of a woman.

"Rainulf . . . Rainulf, open your eyes."

With a great effort, he slitted his eyes open and saw her in the darkness, hovering over him . . . an angel come to rescue him. Her eyes were huge, her face iridescent in the moonlight. She released his wrists, and he reached up with both trembling hands, taking her face between them. He'd never thought an angel could feel so soft, so real. . . . He stroked her lips, traced the inky brushstroke of an eyebrow. . . .

"It's all right," she whispered, her breath soft on his face. "Nothing's wrong. Go back to sleep."

She touched his eyelids, and they closed. He felt her cool fingers around his wrists again as she gently lowered his arms across his chest. "Sleep."

He sensed her weight easing off him, heard again that delicate, silken rustle as her wings lifted her into the air, felt the lack of her, the emptiness where she had been.

The last thing he heard before unconsciousness re-claimed him was a door softly closing.

Rainulf opened his eyes and squinted at the mid-morning sunlight pouring through the window. He lifted his head and fell back with a groan, squeezing his eyes shut against a blinding spasm of pain. "Damn."

His mouth tasted sour; his stomach roiled. He thought back to last night, concentrating. The last thing he remembered was drinking wine at supper. He must have drunk too much, far too much. This was his first hangover since his university days.

He covered his face with his hands and sniffed, breathing in the scent that clung to them, and—per-plexingly—to his arms and shoulders and chest ... night-opening flowers and Oriental spices ... sweet-ness and sensuality and the wisdom of the ages ...

Corliss.

A longing unfurled within him, tainted with uneasi-ness. How had he come to have Corliss's perfume on him? He sat up slowly, wincing, and looked down at himself, bare-chested atop rumpled bed coverings. Reaching behind him for a pillow, he brought it to his nose and inhaled the exotic fragrance with which it was imbued. Corliss's fragrance.

The longing intensified, gathering in his loins and taking shape as a rigid, aching need. With a moan he lay back down and rested a hand on his throbbing groin, feeling a demand so sudden and intense as to be painful. Surrendering to that pain, he untied his chausses to relieve it—an indulgence he generally dis-dained, but could not resist in the face of this over-powering need. He closed his eyes and imagined that it was Corliss's hot, tight body closing around him, coaxing the pain from him and replacing it with pleasure.

Relief came quickly, but it brought little real solace. He still felt empty, and so needful.

And he still wondered how Corliss's maddeningly arousing scent had permeated his bed, and him.

He washed and dressed, his movements careful in deference to his queasy stomach and pulsing head. Voices from outside drew him to the window. Shielding his eyes, he peered down into the garden that took up a good part of the bailey to the east of the keep—Martine's precisely laid-out, geometrically designed herb garden.

His sister was there, and next to her, Corliss kneeling over a row of something Rainulf couldn't hope to identify. Martine pulled weeds while Corliss drew on a wax tablet. Both women wore aprons over their kirtles, and wide-brimmed straw hats such as villeins wore in the fields. Despite his body's miseries, he smiled. No one would think that these two hardworking, humbly dressed women were a baroness and her houseguest.

Martine looked up and saw him, then grinned and nudged her companion. Corliss lifted her head and followed Martine's pointing hand. She met his gaze and held it for a moment, her expression inscrutable. Rainulf raised his hand, then froze, staring at a dark spot on Corliss's jaw—a bruise. She must have seen his dismay, because she reached up to touch the purpling blemish, then looked away quickly.

Too quickly.

Rainulf gripped the windowsill, appalled. Had *he* given her that bruise? No ... it was impossible. He could never hurt her.

He scoured his memory, straining to remember anything about last night, anything after all that drinking. Had she really been in his bed? Was it possible he had simply imagined the perfume? Closing his eyes, he conjured up a vague recollection of seizing her and pulling her down, forcing her to lie with him. He could still feel the liquid-smooth whisper of silk against his naked skin, the soft pressure of her breasts on his chest, the heat of her cheek against his shoulder.

He turned and looked toward the bed. Something glimmered on the floor beneath it, half-hidden by the edge of the quilt. Crossing to it, he crouched and picked it up; it was the golden circlet that Corliss had worn last night.

God, no. What had he done? He struggled to remember as he returned to the window. Corliss glanced back up at him and then lowered her head over her tablet. Had he tried to force himself on her? Was that how she'd gotten hurt? If so, he hadn't been successful; he was certain of that. After eleven years of abstinence, if he had bedded a woman—particularly Corliss—he would surely remember, regardless of how much wine he had drunk.

But had he tried?

Never in his life had he taken an unwilling woman, or attempted to. The idea disgusted him and, in truth, he'd never had the need. As a young scholar in Paris, they'd come to him—even wellborn girls betrothed to others. Their coy flirtations quickly metamorphosed into heated whispers and secret meetings. He never lied to them, never pretended to feelings that didn't exist. Yet still they would press his hands to their breasts, unlace their kirtles, and raise their skirts. He'd been young and unfettered by vows, and what they offered, he took.

But he'd always waited until they gave their bodies freely; he never pushed the matter. He'd never had to. Then.

Had he changed so much? Was he now capable of such shameful behavior—toward Corliss? He thought of himself as a good man, a principled man. Disgustedly, he shook his head. He thought of himself as better than other men, holier, more in command of his animal nature. As usual, the sin of pride weighed heavily on him. In truth, he was just a man, with a man's weaknesses. Just how weak had he been last night? *Damn*, if he could only remember!

He closed the window's glass panels and leaned his forehead against them. He must keep his distance from her. He must. His desire for her had grown too unruly. He mustn't think about her as a woman, mustn't indulge his body's carnal needs while imagining that it was she who touched him, she who took him inside her.

Even if he hadn't tried to take advantage of her last night, he feared he was capable of doing so—a chilling prospect. She was ever on his mind, ever stirring up thoughts and desires best left dormant.

He was worn-out, used up. All he wanted in life was to be appointed Chancellor of Oxford and then to live out the rest of his years in a kind of numb, unthinking repose. Until Corliss came along, he'd never questioned that goal. But she'd touched his heart, made him itch for things he'd given up wanting long ago, made him question his well-laid plans. And that was not a good thing.

He'd spend the day at St. Dunstan's. And perhaps tomorrow as well. Let Peter go hawking with Corliss. Let him flatter her and charm her and court her. He didn't care. He couldn't afford to.

Chapter 11

Corliss watched Rainulf back away from the window, his eyes trained on her, and then turn and disappear. When she lowered her gaze, she found Martine staring at the bruise on her jaw. "How did that happen?"

Her expression carefully neutral, Corliss scratched another daisylike flower onto her sketch of the foul-smelling plant Martine called feverfew and praised as a strengthener of wombs. Corliss had promised to ink it onto parchment for the young baroness's new herbarium of curatives for female disorders. Taking a deep breath, she said, "I'm clumsy, that's all."

Martine sat utterly still for a long moment. Very quietly, she said, "Please tell me Rainulf didn't do that to you."

Corliss looked up at her; Martine was ashen. "He was having a nightmare," she explained quickly. "He didn't know what he was doing. He would never hurt me on purpose."

His sister expelled a long sigh. "Thank God. He's the last man on earth I'd think capable of striking a woman, but for a moment there . . ." Clearly relieved, she stretched and rubbed her back, then slid a little weed out of the dark, crumbly earth, shook the soil from its roots, and tossed it into her basket. "I could give him some anise to chew before bedtime. 'Tis said to be very effective in warding off nightmares. Does he get them very often?"

Corliss moved on to the leaves, which she drew with painstaking care, trying to get their jagged edges just right. "I wouldn't know."

Two more weeds joined the mound in the basket. "Does he toss and turn in his sleep?"

Corliss's stylus slipped and she ruined one of the leaves. "Um . . . I have my own bedchamber. We don't . . . It's not like that between us."

Smiling, the other woman patted Corliss's arm. "You needn't keep up appearances with me. I just want Rainulf to be happy. I'm delighted that he's found you."

Corliss tried to rub the mistake out of the wax. "No, you don't understand. Rainulf and I aren't . . . We don't sleep together."

Martine's eyebrows—dramatically dark, like her brother's—rose sharply, and she smiled. "You slept with him last night, did you not?"

"Only for a couple of hours."

Martine chuckled.

"No, I mean . . . That is, he just needed me for a while, and then I went back to my . . ."

Laughing, Martine took her hand and squeezed. "You needn't explain. I'm not judging you, Corliss. You're obviously good for him. From the moment I first saw him yesterday, 'twas clear how much he's changed since you came into his life. He's more content, more—"

"I'm not his mistress!" The words tumbled from Corliss's mouth as she stared at the wax tablet in her lap. "We are not lovers. We're just friends, nothing more. I don't want to be chained to any man, and Rainulf wants to be Chancellor of Oxford, and that means . . . that means he's got to remain celibate. And even if he didn't, he wouldn't want—" She took a deep breath. "He'd pick someone else, someone more . . ." She shrugged and bit her lip, painfully aware of Martine's sad, knowing gaze on her.

"I see. I'm sorry. I didn't mean ..." She put her arm around Corliss and said softly, "I didn't mean to be so thoughtless. I was just so pleased to think he'd finally found someone—and someone so wonderful. He does seem happier, though. I can't help but think it must have something to do with you."

Corliss shrugged, remembering Father Gregory's words: *It's your influence, you know. Somehow you've managed to crack that armor of his.*

Martine abruptly squeezed her eyes shut and massaged the small of her back with both hands.

"Are you all right, Martine? Are you sure you should be out here, working like this?"

"I'm fine. My back's been troubling me, that's all. It woke me up in the middle of the night, and I couldn't get back to sleep. 'Twasn't just the aching. I kept thinking I had to get all these weeds pulled before the baby came. It sounds silly, I know."

"Not at all. When are you due?"

Martine smiled. "Any day now."

" 'Twill be a big one, from the looks of you."

The expectant mother patted her unwieldy belly and grinned. "And from the looks of the father, too, I should think. The midwife told me she doesn't even have to see this babe to know it will be a giant." Another back pain seized Martine, and this time a little startled breath escaped her.

"I'm taking you inside," Corliss said. "You've overdone it."

"Perhaps you're right," Martine conceded, her voice strangely weak.

Corliss rose and helped Martine to her feet. "Are you all right?"

Martine smiled and stretched her back. "Yes. I feel much ..."

Both women stilled at a soft, damp sound, like something wet trickling onto the earth. Corliss glanced around, thinking perhaps the watering pot had gotten kicked over.

Lifting her tunic, Martine bent over to examine a dark, moist spot on the soil beneath her. "Oh." A look of alarm crossed her features, and she pressed both hands to her bulging stomach and leaned over. "Oh."

"Oh!" Corliss put an arm around her new friend and looked around wildly. Shielding her eyes, she made out Thorne and Rainulf talking at the gate to the outer bailey. She waved her arm free. "Oh! Oh!"

Still gripping her stomach, Martine laughed. " 'Oh?' Is that all we two learned women can think of to say at a time like this?"

Corliss laughed, too, more from nerves, she knew, than any other reason. When she looked back toward the two men, she saw them running full-speed in their direction. By the time they arrived, Corliss and Martine were laughing so hard, they had to hold on to each other to keep from falling down.

Thorne and Rainulf exchanged a look of utter bewilderment. "What's wrong?" asked Rainulf. "We thought perhaps . . ."

"Martine's in labor," Corliss managed.

Thorne turned white. "Oh!"

The women burst out laughing, much to Thorne and Rainulf's evident puzzlement. Regaining his composure, Thorne swept Martine up in his massive arms. She groaned and clutched at his tunic. "Thorne! I think the baby's coming!"

"Yes, I know. I'll send Peter for the midwife . . ."

"No, I think"—she broke off, her body stiffening, her teeth clenched—"I think it's coming *now*."

"Oh, my God," Corliss moaned, suddenly sobered. "She's been in labor since last night and didn't realize—"

"Can you help her?" Thorne asked. "Do you know anything about—"

"Me? Nay, I ... I ..." Corliss grabbed Martine's hand and squeezed it tight, "But I won't leave your side."

"We've got to find someone who can help."

"Felda," Martine rasped. "Go fetch Felda, too."

"Get her maid," Thorne commanded as he wheeled around and carried his wife toward the keep. "Get Felda." A whimper escaped Martine, and he added, over his shoulder, "Fast!"

"You did it, Martine!" Corliss held the baby—an enormous boy—to her chest for a moment and then placed him into the arms of his pale and trembling mother.

"*You* did it," Martine corrected, with a look of affection that filled Corliss with pride and gladness. "And you, too, Felda," she added quickly.

Felda shook her head. "I had nothin' to do with it, milady. 'Twas Lady Corliss saved that baby. The midwife couldn't of done no better, even if she *had* gotten here in time."

Martine, recovering from her trial with remarkable speed, pried the little mouth open and cleared it out, then briskly rubbed the bluish infant's feet. "His collarbone is broken, but 'twill heal on its own." She massaged his back. "Come now, you troublesome little man. Have you nothing to say after this ordeal?"

Opening his mouth wide, the baby let loose with a loud and lusty howl.

The door flew open and Thorne burst into the room, his eyes, wide with wonder, riveted on his son. Rainulf, who'd been standing vigil outside the bedchamber door with him, froze in amazement, then beamed. Slumping against the doorframe, he crossed himself. Behind him, servants anxiously craned their necks to see into the room.

"Milord! Master Fairfax!" Felda hastily yanked the bedclothes over Martine as Thorne crossed the room in two swift strides; Rainulf stepped into the room and closed the door. "Go away! Wait till I've had a chance to get them both cleaned up—"

"I've waited long enough," Thorne declared. Sitting on the edge of the bed, he gathered his wife and child in his arms, rocking them and murmuring things—in *French,* Corliss noted with surprise—that she couldn't make out. How touching, she mused, that he would think to comfort his wife in her native language, when he'd made such a point of banning it from his barony.

Rainulf leaned back against the wall as if he could no longer support his weight. He looked drained, but relieved. Catching Corliss's eye, he smiled. A sweet tide of warmth spread through her, and she smiled back ... until Rainulf's gaze lowered to her bruised jaw. His smile faded, and hers followed suit.

"I need to bathe that baby," Felda announced.

"In due time," said Thorne, as he counted his son's fingers and toes. The babe's skin had turned a healthy pink, Corliss noted with relief. He blinked his puffy eyes open and grimaced, making him look like a small, angry man.

When Thorne had completed his inspection, Felda wrapped the infant in a length of linen. "Don't want him to catch cold within minutes of being born."

"Wulfric's much too robust to get sick," Martine said.

Corliss grinned. "A good Saxon name. Your inspiration, Thorne?"

He nodded. " 'Twas my father's name."

Martine untied her shift to expose a breast, seemingly indifferent to Rainulf's presence, although he averted his gaze. She gently tickled Wulfric's cheek with a fingertip. He instinctively turned toward it, mouth wide open, head shifting back and forth as he searched for the nipple. Thorne chuckled as his son latched on and began suckling with an expression of dreamy contentment, his eyes rolling up before they closed completely. "The boy knows what he wants," he said, covering his wife's bare shoulder and breast with a shawl.

Turning her back on the intimate tableau, Corliss helped Felda to arrange the soap and clean cloths and swaddling clothes next to the little, carved wooden bathtub.

A knock came, followed by Peter's urgent voice: "I've got the midwife!"

"Bring her in," Thorne said.

Peter guided a small, elderly woman into the chamber. When he saw the baby at Martine's breast, he grinned delightedly and excused himself, closing the door behind him.

"Milady!" squawked the midwife. "What are you doing? You ought to let the wet nurse do that. It'll only make it harder for your milk to dry up."

Martine sighed. "I don't intend for my milk to dry up, Hazel. I'm going to nurse him myself. I told you that."

"Aye, but I naturally thought you'd change your mind. The idea! A baroness givin' suck to her babe like a cow in the field. It ain't natural."

Martine exchanged a wry smile with Thorne as the old woman opened her satchel and began laying out tools and flasks and mysterious packets on a chest. "Did the babe come easy?" Hazel asked.

"Hardly," Martine replied. "Wulfric's got his father's shoulders, and they got stuck inside me. Corliss reached in and freed them. He broke a collarbone, but if it weren't for her, I think we both would have died."

"Christ," Thorne whispered as his face drained of color.

Rainulf stared at Corliss as if she had just sprouted wings and a halo.

"Tight swaddling will set that collarbone," Hazel said.

Martine cradled the infant tightly. "Nay! No swaddling."

"Oh, for God's sake," the midwife growled. "I'll just swaddle the one arm, then, to keep it still so the collarbone heals."

Martine nodded grudgingly.

Rainulf still hadn't taken his eyes off her. *It's as if he's never seen me before,* Corliss thought.

"Now, milady . . ." Hazel poured something that looked like wine into a cup and stirred a bit of whitish powder into it. "You realize you oughtn't to have any more babes. They're all bound to be just as brutish as that one, and you've obviously got too tight a womb. This here birthwort will help to bring away your afterbirth. Once it's out, I can pour a handful of barley into it, and you'll be barren as a stone."

"Absolutely not!" Martine exclaimed.

"Martine," Thorne began gently, "shouldn't you consider it? I mean, not the barley, but something that might actually work?"

Hazel sputtered indignantly. "It works! Perhaps not every time, but often enough."

"Is there something that *will* work every time?" Thorne asked, ignoring Martine's furious glare.

"Aye. The most effective method is to cut the testicles from a weasel—leaving the weasel alive—and wrap them in the skin of a goose, tying them up tight. If milady wears that around her neck day and night, she's guaranteed not to conceive."

Thorne just stared at the midwife while a slow smile crept across Martine's face. "You know," she said, "I do believe that one *might* work."

Thorne shot her a baleful look. She leaned forward carefully—so as not to disturb the nursing babe—and kissed him soundly. "I love you, Thorne Falconer. I intend to fill this castle with enormous baby boys who look just like you, and there's nothing you can do to stop me."

"But, Martine," he pleaded, "you could ... you could die. And it would be my fault for letting it happen. I wouldn't be able to live with myself, knowing I'd sired a babe too big for you to give birth to." He lowered his voice, but Corliss was close enough to hear. "We don't have to rely on Hazel's methods. I want to be certain this never happens to you again. I'll do anything—do you understand?—*anything,* make any sacrifice—"

"Well, I won't!" she declared, loudly enough for everyone to hear. "I'm your wife, in more than just name. That means sharing your bed and giving you children."

"But the danger—"

"Is far less than it might seem." She grinned and looked in Corliss's direction. "Especially if we make sure Corliss comes visiting when the babies are due."

Thorne met Corliss's gaze. "This is the second time I've come close to losing Martine," he said, his voice rough with emotion. His eyes shimmered with unshed tears. "I'm forever in your debt."

There was a heavy moment of silence. Rainulf and Thorne and Martine were all looking at her. "I hardly know what to say," Corliss murmured.

"Well, I do!" Hazel thrust the cup of dissolved birthwort at Martine, then turned to scowl at the onlookers. "Everyone out! Everyone but Felda. We've got to get milady and this babe tidied up."

Thorne didn't move. "I'm staying."

An expression of outrage crossed the midwife's face. "I beg your pardon, milord, but you are not! I've never heard of such a thing. You get out of here right now. Go!" She swatted at him with her bony little hand. "Shoo! Go!"

Corliss and Rainulf watched from the doorway as Thorne rose slowly, towering over the birdlike woman, who prodded him ineffectually in the chest. "I'm not

going anywhere," he said quietly. "Tell me what I can
do to help."

"You can get out, that's what you can do!"

"It's no use, Hazel," said Felda. "If Thorne Falconer don't want to do something, he don't do it.
You'd best give him a job so he keeps out of your
way."

Hazel grunted and rolled her eyes, then uncovered
the baby and tied a piece of string around his umbili-
cal cord. "Soon as I've cut young Master Wulfric loose
from his mum, you can help Felda bathe him."

The midwife produced a knife from the pouch on
her belt. Rainulf closed the door and guided Corliss
into the stairwell.

You're alone with her now, he thought. *Ask her. Just
ask her, for God's sake.*

She began descending the stairs, but he said,
"Wait!" and she turned around. As he looked down
on her, his gaze lit once again on her bruised jaw. He
backed up a step, and when he spoke, his tone was
formal, wary. "I don't remember much of last night,
but I'm deeply sorry if . . . if I did anything—"

"You needn't apologize."

He paused. "What did I do? Tell me the truth."

Her brows drew together.

"To you," he said softly. "What did I do to you,
Corliss?"

"To me?"

"You were in my bed, I know that, but I don't know
anything else. Except that I hit you. Did I . . ." His
hands curled into fists. "Damn it, Corliss, just tell me
what I did!"

Her eyes slowly widened as she stared at him. "You
think . . ." She surveyed his face, and the anguish he
knew must show on it. "Oh, Rainulf . . ." She smiled
sadly.

They stared at each other. Rainulf didn't know what
to say, what to think. She came to stand on the step

below his. Taking his fists in her hands, she forced his fingers open and caressed his palms soothingly.

She looked up at him. "You had a nightmare last night. You started throwing punches, and my face got in the way—that's all. You could never hurt me, Rainulf. You could never . . . try to force yourself on me, if that's what you think happened. Drunk or not."

He squeezed her hands. "Thank God."

"You should know that. And you would, if you only knew yourself better. Father Gregory was right. I once told him that you were a mystery to me, and he said you were a mystery to yourself as well."

She released one of his hands to reach up and lay her cool palm against his cheek. He closed his eyes, savoring her touch. "If you'd just listen to your instincts," she gently berated, "instead of making everything so damn complicated, you wouldn't jump to such asinine conclusions."

When he opened his eyes, she was grinning at him. As usual, her good humor was infectious, and he found himself smiling back.

"You scrutinize everything," she said, "question everything, dig and dig, searching for answers. Your torment is self-induced. You can make it stop. You can. Don't turn all that doubt in on yourself. Save it for the lecture hall, where it belongs. Where *you* belong."

"Do I?"

"How can you question it? When I watch you up there, engrossed in your *disputatio,* it's as if you come alive, as if you're doing what you were born to do." She took his face between her hands. "Try accepting who you are. Everyone has the right to that much."

Rainulf couldn't think of anything to say, nothing to match her guileless eloquence, at any rate. Instead he encircled her with his arms and drew her close, burying his face in her fragrant hair. They held each other for a long time without speaking, a healing, silent embrace. She felt so warm beneath the thin wool of her kirtle, so human. God, how he needed her.

He stiffened. He couldn't afford to need her. What was happening to him? What was he letting happen?

Corliss looked up at him, questioning him with her eyes. When he avoided her gaze, she released him. She chewed her lip for a moment, and then smiled enigmatically. "You'll get used to it."

"To what?"

"Being in your skin. Feeling what you feel and"—she shrugged—"not fighting it."

"I'm too old to get used to anything new. And some things"—*like you, like how I want you and need you*—"ought to be fought."

She held his gaze for a moment. "Perhaps. Perhaps not." Turning, she continued down the stairs, and he followed her to the great hall, where the rest of the household was finishing its noon meal. She began walking toward the high table, but he stilled her with a hand on her shoulder.

"Thorne's not the only one who's in your debt, Corliss. I am, too. Forever. Anything you need, anything you want, you need but ask me, and it shall be yours. I couldn't have borne Martine's death. She's all the family I've got."

"What of your brother in Rouen, the baron?"

"Etienne?" Rainulf's face lost expression. "I doubt I'll ever see him again. That's for the best. He and I are ... We're very different. Martine was always ... close to my heart. She was always special."

He searched her eyes, struggling to come up with the right words. "I don't know what to say. I don't know how to thank you."

"You're letting me live in your home," she pointed out. "You're keeping me safe from Roger Foliot. That's thanks enough."

"There will never be thanks enough."

"There you are!" Peter said, joining them. "You

must be hungry, my lady. Come sit." His expression
brightened. "Or perhaps you'd prefer to take some
bread and cheese with you while we go hawking."

"Ah . . ." She glanced quickly at Rainulf. "I'm sorry,
Sir Peter. I'd quite forgotten about the hawking."

"Little surprise," he said. "It's been such a trying
morning for you. I hope you haven't changed your
mind, though. A bit of fresh air will serve you well."

"Yes, I suppose it will," she murmured.

"Would you care to join us?" Peter asked Rainulf
blandly.

Rainulf shook his head, knowing that it was duty,
not desire to make the afternoon a threesome, that
had prompted the invitation. "Nay, I think I'll go to
St. Dunstan's, as I had planned." He ducked into the
stairwell, adding, "I'll be back in time for supper."

It was late afternoon when Corliss returned from
hawking with Peter. She washed quickly and exchanged her dusty kirtle for an emerald brocade tunic
suitable for supper.

Rainulf had been right; Peter *was* good company.
He was quick-witted and charming and an excellent
conversationalist. It impressed her that he spoke little
of himself, trying instead to draw her out with questions, mostly about her family and background. She
deflected them as smoothly as she could, bearing in
mind Rainulf's advice to offer as little as possible
about herself until Roger Foliot was no longer a
threat.

Although she knew Peter fancied her, he didn't attempt any liberties or say anything inappropriate. She
was grateful for his chivalric reserve, for although she
liked him, there was no question of any kind of romantic involvement. For one thing, her feelings for
Rainulf, ill advised though they were, prevented her
from being seriously attracted to another man.

Even had that not been the case, such an attraction

would be pointless. She and Peter were almost as far apart in rank as she and Rainulf. If the attentive young knight knew that "Lady Corliss of Oxford" was actually the daughter of a Cuxham villein, he surely wouldn't waste any time courting her. More likely he'd toss her onto the straw in an empty stable stall, throw her skirts up, and be done with it. For, despite his affability, he was, she reminded herself, a highborn Norman. With the exception of Rainulf Fairfax, they were all alike. They used women like her for sexual release, saving their lofty affections for ladies of their own rank.

Felda came to lace her up and dress her hair. "Milady and the baby are asleep," she said. "I finally talked milord into going downstairs for something to eat." She shook her head as she settled a jeweled circlet onto Corliss's veiled head. "I never thought to see a baron bathe his own baby. You wouldn't believe how gentle he was. I'll remember it to my dying day."

Felda pronounced Corliss "magnificent," pinched her cheeks, and left. Corliss wished she didn't have to go down to supper alone, but she finally got her courage up and slowly descended the stairs. As she neared the great hall, she heard men talking, and paused to listen.

Rainulf, Peter, and Guy were congratulating Thorne on Wulfric's birth.

"A son," Thorne said proudly. "And all boy!"

"Ah, you checked, did you?" Rainulf asked, sounding amused and a good deal more relaxed than the last time she spoke to him.

Thorne chuckled. "Aye, and it's the size of your thumb!"

There was a moment of silence. Corliss grinned at the mental image of Rainulf and the two knights examining their thumbs. Presently there came a chorus of whistles and exclamations of awe. Corliss cleared her throat and stepped out of the stairwell, whereupon the men rushed to hide their hands behind their backs.

Thorne coughed. "My lady."

"Gentlemen."

Peter quickly recovered his composure and took Corliss by the arm. "Would you do me the honor of sitting next to me at supper, my lady?"

She glanced at Rainulf and found him frowning. For a moment, he seemed about to speak, and she thought—hoped—he might ask her to sit with *him*. But then he schooled his expression and—almost reluctantly, it seemed—turned away.

"Aye, Sir Peter," she said, forcing a tactful smile, "I'd be happy to."

Chapter 12

"**W**e'd like you to be godmother to Wulfric," said Martine, sitting up in bed with the baby asleep in her arms. Thorne, sitting by her side, reached over to caress Wulfric's thick shock of gold hair and wipe away the trickle of milk that escaped from his half-open mouth.

"Me?"

"If it weren't for you, there would be no baby to baptize tomorrow." Martine smiled toward her brother, standing near the bedchamber door. "Rainulf will be his godfather."

"I'm ... I'm honored," Corliss said. "Truly."

Father John, the barony chaplain, cleared his throat. "There is something I'm obliged to mention before you agree." He glanced uneasily between Corliss and Rainulf. "The sacrament of baptism spiritually binds the godparents not only to the child, but to each other. Under canon law, lifting up the same child from the font is an impediment to marriage."

"We didn't realize ..." Thorne began, his brow furrowed.

"Ah," Father John said. "Then perhaps you ought to think about choosing another godmother."

A great silence descended on the chamber. Presently Rainulf cleared his throat. "She can serve as godmother," he said tightly. Drawing in a breath, he added, "We can both serve. There's no problem."

Thorne and Martine exchanged a look. A great sadness welled up within Corliss, a sadness reflected in Rainulf's expression of grim resignation.

"He's right," Corliss said in a monotone. "There's no reason we can't both serve as godparents. Thank you for asking me. I gladly accept."

Rainulf received the naked infant and held him above the big marble font, nodding to Corliss, who took hold of the feet. The afternoon sun streaming in through the stained-glass window overhead bathed her face in multicolored light. The sight transfixed him for a long, breathless moment.

A hand closed over his arm. "Immerse the child," Father John whispered.

Together, he and Corliss dipped a squalling Wulfric into the water, then lifted him up. Father John anointed the babe's forehead with sacred chrism and tied a white cloth around it, then took him into his arms.

Corliss smiled at Rainulf, and after a moment's hesitation, he smiled back.

So this is how it's to be. I'm to continue on as if I don't ache with wanting her, as if it doesn't hurt just to look upon her.

We're to act as if we don't care.

So be it. If she can do it, so can I.

Corliss lay in bed, gazing at the light from beneath the door to Rainulf's chamber. Tomorrow they would begin their return journey to Oxford. She looked forward to the trip with a fair measure of anticipation, for it meant they'd have two days alone together.

She'd missed him during their visit to Blackburn. In truth, she'd seen him only at supper, for he spent his days at St. Dunstan's and his evenings closeted in his chamber reading books borrowed from the priory's library. When she awoke during the night—as now— she would see the light beneath his door, no matter how late it was. Sometimes, if she lay very still and held her breath, she fancied she could hear the soft whisper of pages being turned ... the creak of his chair.

She'd had little opportunity to talk to him, and none to ask him the question that had obsessed her for the past fortnight, ever since their arrival at Blackburn. It was a question she couldn't ask just anybody, only a trusted confidant, someone who wouldn't laugh at her ignorance or look askance at her for asking such things.

Only Rainulf. He was the only one she could have asked, except they hadn't been alone together for two weeks, and it wasn't a question one blurted out over roast stag at supper.

She studied the pale strip of lamplight beneath his door—the only light in her pitch-black chamber, it being well past midnight.

She could ask it now. She could get up and throw a wrapper over her shift and knock on the door of his chamber. They'd be alone. No one to overhear her foolish question or laugh at her ignorance or think her immoral for contemplating such matters.

Biting her lip, she stared at the ribbon of golden light.

She could.

Rainulf thought he heard something as he turned a page of the *Decretum*—two soft thumps. He listened for a moment, heard nothing more, and returned his attention to the volume of canon law on the desk in front of him. The prohibition against godparents marrying had come as news to him, and he sought—for the sake of curiosity only—to confirm it in print. Not that he doubted Father John's knowledge, and not that it mattered. It didn't. Not to him personally, at any rate—

There it was again, a little louder. He turned toward the door to the chamber adjoining his. Corliss?

Saving his place with a piece of straw—a habit acquired during his university days—he donned a shirt over his chausses and opened the door.

He forgot to breathe when he saw her standing there in a silken shift and wrapper, her sleep-tousled hair curling around her face—the very picture of seductive innocence. She had her lower lip caught between those perfect white teeth; when she released it, the lip was reddened and swollen. He did breathe then, a sharp inhalation that filled his senses with that exotic, maddening perfume of hers.

A jolt of sexual longing shook him, and he turned away abruptly, wondering what she was doing here in his chamber in the middle of the night. To cover his awkwardness, he sat back down and picked up his book. "Couldn't you sleep?" he said, his voice rougher than he would have liked.

"There's something I've been wanting to ask you about."

He hesitated, uncomfortably aware of her breasts and hips beneath the thin silk.

She took a step back. "I suppose this isn't a good—"

"Nay. Come in." He laid the book aside. "Have a seat."

He followed her gaze as she looked around the chamber, realizing belatedly that his bed was the only place left to sit, since he'd taken the one chair. "You can sit here," he offered, rising.

"That's all right." She drew aside the curtain and sat on the edge of the big bed. "I'm comfortable here."

He had often—too often—envisioned her on his bed in her nightclothes ... or less. During the past fortnight he had struggled to keep from entertaining such thoughts, immersing himself in monastic life and exhausting himself with endless nights of reading while the rest of the household lay sleeping. He'd been successful, for the most part—at least during his waking hours. At night, she still came to him in his dreams ... dreams in which they surrendered to each other, heart and soul and flesh ... dreams from which he awoke shaking and sweating and moaning her name.

It was getting harder and harder to keep his desire for her in perspective. When she'd first come to Oxford, it had been easier; he'd been long used to self-denial. *You were proud of it, you sanctimonious bastard. Proud and complacent and self-righteous. Better than everyone else because you could resist the human needs that held them captive.*

When had it started to change? *When you started to change. ... When Corliss changed you. When she made you smile. When she made you want. When she made you care.*

Whatever it was she'd wanted to ask him was evidently difficult for her. She fingered her wrapper nervously as though working up her courage. In the uneasy silence, he found himself reflecting, as he often did lately, on how much simpler his life would be if he'd never met her. As it was, all he wanted anymore was to be with her. To talk to her. To touch her. God help him, to make love to her. The need for restraint, although he hated it more than ever, hadn't changed; he still wanted the chancellorship, didn't he? But the effort it took to exercise that restraint had increased a hundredfold.

He watched her run her hand over the quilt. She regarded him thoughtfully for a moment and then looked at the carpeted floor. "What I wanted to ask you is a little embarrassing."

"You needn't be embarrassed with me."

She took a deep breath. "It has to do with the story Thorne told when we first arrived. The story about the Rhineland widow. What was her name ... ?"

"Sigfreda." He wasn't sure he liked where this might lead.

"That's right. I've been thinking about it a lot, and there's a part of it that I just don't understand. The part where she ... screamed."

No, he was definitely sure he didn't like where this was going. "What don't you understand about it?" he asked carefully.

She met his gaze for a moment and then looked away again. "Why she did it. Why she screamed."

"You don't know?" She shook her head. He wished he had a brandy. " 'Twas exactly as Thorne said. She was ... enjoying herself." *Very much.*

"Enjoying herself."

Rainulf nodded.

"I still don't understand."

Oh, for pity's sake. "Climaxing," he said shortly.

Her eyes grew wide as wagon wheels, then narrowed. "Women don't ..." Her expression became indignant. "You're teasing me. I trusted you to tell me the truth."

"*Teasing* you! Have you never—" He bit back the question, since it was evident that she never had. "Don't you know that women can ... achieve that kind of pleasure, too?"

She cast him a skeptical look. "Nay. I've never heard of such a thing. And I've certainly never ..." A hot blush spread upward along her throat, staining her face pink.

This revelation surprised Rainulf. After all, she was so earthy, so comfortable with herself. And she was hardly inexperienced. She'd been married at sixteen. *To an old man,* he reminded himself. The mistress to another old man. Men who clearly had never bothered to satisfy her. What fools they had been, to have such a woman in their beds—so young and beautiful and passionate—and use her so uncaringly. How often had he imagined Corliss writhing in ecstasy beneath him, crying out as she dug her fingers into his back. . . . He adjusted his long shirt to hide his sudden, fierce erection.

Her eyes searched his. "You're telling me the truth, aren't you?"

"Of course."

"What does it feel like?"

He licked his dry lips. "Corliss, I'm sorry. I can't discuss this with you."

"But—"

"Ask Martine about it. She's a woman. And you two seem to get along so well."

"Aye, but I've only known her a short time, and . . . I've always been able to ask you everything."

"Ask Martine," he repeated.

"I'm asking you. Tell me what it feels like. I just want to know. I feel so ignorant, so foolish, not having even known such a thing was possible."

"Corliss . . . Nay. I can't. Besides, I really don't think it can be described. Perhaps someday you'll remarry and have a husband who cares enough to show you—"

"I'll never remarry! I'll never know what other women know, I'll never feel what they feel." Her voice quavered; her eyes glistened.

"God, Corliss, don't cry . . ."

"I never cry!" She raised her chin defiantly. That was true, Rainulf realized. Although generally free with her emotions, he'd never seen her shed a tear— evidently a point of pride with her. "And I certainly wouldn't cry over this. I just want to know what it's like for other women, women who live normal lives and have husbands who love them. I just want you to tell me what it is they feel—"

"I don't know what it feels like for a woman."

"What does it feel like for a man?"

"I told you. It can't be described. I can't help you."

She studied him in silence for a moment. "I think

you can," she said quietly. "You just won't. You're afraid."

He bolted up out of his seat and strode to her chamber door. "I can't and I won't." He held the door open. "I think you should go back to bed, Corliss."

She stood, but made no move to leave. "Are you—" she took a deep breath. "Are you sorry you have to put up with my ceaseless questions and my ..." She met his gaze squarely. "Do you wish I'd never come to Oxford?"

He looked away, rubbing his eyes, trying to obliterate a torrent of images—her breasts through sheer linen, her hips encased in snug chausses, a thin ribbon of steaming flesh viewed through a doorway. They were images that tormented him, stirring up unwanted feelings, complicating his well-ordered life.

Did he wish she'd never come to Oxford? "Sometimes, yes. Frequently."

He heard her rapid footsteps, felt the door yanked out of his hand, flinched at the reverberation as she slammed it closed. He opened his eyes on the empty chamber, feeling a sudden, ungovernable sense of loss.

Without thinking, he wheeled on the door and slammed his fist into it, hard. Pain sucked the breath from his lungs. *"Damn!"*

Lurching to the washstand, he plunged his hand into the ewer, letting the cold water numb it. "Damn." He closed his eyes and filled his lungs with air, letting it out slowly. Then again, and again.

He remembered the things she'd done and said in the stairwell after Wulfric's birth, recalled the cool pressure of her palm against his cheek, and her artless wisdom: *Just be in your skin ... feel what you feel ... Don't fight it.*

Withdrawing his hand from the water, he dried it off, then flexed his fingers thoughtfully.

He returned to the door and hesitated, questioning

the wisdom of this. *You scrutinize everything . . . question everything. Just listen to your instinct.*

His instinct told him to turn the handle of the door, and he did.

Chapter 13

Corliss heard the door open and turned toward the sound. The bed curtains enclosed her. A brief shaft of lamplight glowed through the filmy linen, then winked out as the door closed, plunging the chamber once more into absolute darkness.

She held her breath, but heard nothing for several long moments. Presently there came a soft footfall, and another. She turned to face the wall, pulling the quilt up around her as he approached the bed.

Go away. Just go away. If he spoke one more word to her, she feared she would burst into tears, and she didn't want to cry. She hated to cry.

There came a whispery rustle as the curtains parted. For a breathless interval nothing happened, and then she felt the quilt shift behind her as he turned it down. She sensed his weight on the mattress, and thought insanely that he was going to get under the covers with her, but of course, he didn't. He sat, then waited, as if letting her get used to his being there.

Presently she felt the first soft suggestion of his fingers on her hair. He tucked the unruly waves behind her exposed ear; then lightly touched her face, as if searching for something. *Tears,* she realized. He wanted to know whether she'd been crying, despite her proud insistence that she never did. She was glad she'd managed to keep the tears at bay.

His hand slipped under the quilt to caress her shoulder, and then her back, massaging her slowly through

the sleek silk in an obvious effort to comfort her. It
was comforting, she realized. His touch told her, more
effectively than words, that nothing all that dreadful
had happened between them, that he still cared for
her, that he had always cared for her. What surprised
her was that he chose this way to reveal his feelings,
rather than the tiresome and endless *words* on which
he relied overly much. Was it possible that he'd taken
to heart her admonition to save his complicated analy-
ses for the lecture hall?

He closed his hand over her shoulder and urged her
onto her back. She looked up at him, but all she could
make out was an indistinct form that might have been
slightly darker than the blackness surrounding it. His
hand glided lower beneath the quilt, along her bare
arm, leaving a hot trail of sensation in its wake.

Her heart accelerated as his fingertips moved from
her wrist to her hip. He paused, resting his hand on
her thigh, its warmth nearly scorching her through the
silken shift. His fingers tightened, gathering the silk
and pulling it up. He slowly raised her shift until her
legs were bare beneath the quilt.

She swallowed hard, but her voice emerged as an
unsteady whisper. "Rainulf?"

"Shh."

When she felt his light touch on her bare thigh, she
bit her lip so hard it hurt. He smoothed his hand upward, over the ridge of hipbone and then, slowly,
across her lower belly until it brushed the patch of
hair there.

She clutched the linen sheeting, her heart hammering, her mind a storm of emotions. What was he
doing, touching her like this? What was he—

He was *showing her*, she realized as he softly caressed her, his touch so feathery, so insubstantial, that
she might have been imagining it. He was showing her
that which she'd begged him to tell her about, but
which he'd said could not be described.

Oh, my God. Oh, my God. He burrowed a finger through the hair and gently stroked the tight cleft of her sex. No one had ever touched her there, and at first she was too astounded by the raw intimacy of it to feel much. At first. Gradually, as she relaxed, she found her senses focused exclusively on his mesmerizing touch and her body's strange reaction to it.

His fingertip barely grazed her, yet suffused her with a thrilling heat, a delicious buzz of sensation. The feeling grew and grew as he stroked her, very slowly, very patiently. Presently he brought his other fingers into play, caressing her until her heart pounded painfully in her chest and her breathing accelerated.

She closed her eyes and pictured a tightly closed flower bud slowly swelling, opening.... That's what she felt like, that's what his touch did to her. When he slipped a finger between the petals, she gasped at the sudden charge of pleasure. This soft, hidden part of her had become so sensitized that every delicate touch made her quiver.

He moved a finger lower, to the mouth of her sex, drawing its moisture up....

Corliss's breathing grew ragged as he explored the slippery heat between her legs. It was almost too intense, too much to bear. She had the sense of something welling up, building to a fever pitch. Her heart raced wildly; her fingernails bit into her palms through the linen sheet. An element of alarm mingled with the pleasure. She had never traveled the path on which he led her, and didn't know what to expect at its end.

He deepened the caress, massaging her slick, aching flesh until she moaned. The reaction embarrassed her; even though he couldn't see her in the dark, she turned her head toward the wall, fighting the urge to move her hips. She thought of the young Rhineland widow and her screams.

Sorcerer's hands. The widow said he had sorcerer's

hands.... It was true. He was using them to cast a
spell over her, a spell both marvelous and frightening.

He paused, backing off a bit. Her hips rose, hungry
for his touch. He obliged her, then lifted his fingers
again; again she thrust upward, aware this time that
he was teasing her deliberately, *trying* to make her
move At this point, she had no choice, no conscious
control over her body. She rocked her hips in rhythm
to his caress, as if she were a puppet and his sorcerer's
hands were pulling the strings.

She felt herself approaching a dark threshold at the
end of the path. It beckoned with irresistibly seductive
force, even as it made her heart tighten with fear of
the unknown. It was as if she were about to tumble
off the edge of the world.

His quickening fingers coaxed her swiftly toward
that threshold. No longer could she still her writhing
body or silence the low moans that escaped from her.

The dark abyss beckoned. Yet even as she approached the edge, she felt a lacking, an emptiness, a
need deep inside her.

Him. She needed *him....*

And then she felt him, felt a long finger enter her,
sliding deep inside. *He knew it. He knew this was what
I needed.*

He pressed down with the heel of his hand; she
cried out, arching her back, as she felt contractions,
like pulsing waves, plunging her over the edge of that
mysterious void. A delicious frenzy overcame her,
pummeling her from the inside as he continued stroking her. Her heart stopped. She couldn't breathe,
couldn't think as the rapturous seizure crested, rocking
her with convulsive pleasure.

The movement of his hand gentled as the spasms
gradually subsided. She kept her eyes closed, as if this
had all been an astonishing dream that would vaporize
if she opened them. To her surprise, he was breathing
as rapidly as she was.

When he began to withdraw his finger, her body clenched it involuntarily. She heard his sharp intake of breath as he stilled his hand, then eased it away slowly. A flurry of little tremors coursed through her. She brought her hands up to cover her face, finding it damp with perspiration.

He smoothed her hair off her forehead, his hand unsteady. She uncovered her face and looked at him, finding that she could make out his image, now that her eyes had gotten used to the lack of light. His eyes glittered in the dark as they locked with hers. She knew that look; all women were born knowing it. It was a look akin to that of the hungry wolf—a look universal to the male animal, a look as old as the ages, as primal as breathing. He wanted her.

He wrenched his gaze from hers and took a deep breath, letting it out shakily. Aye, she had no doubt he wanted her ... but he was not going to take her. He wasn't just any male animal; he was Rainulf Fairfax. And this wasn't lovemaking; she'd known that all along. It had been more in the nature of a ... friendly demonstration. At least, that was obviously how he had intended it, even if he now had to battle his natural response to her.

She wondered about that response, wondered what his reaction would be if she were to reach for him and pull him down on top of her. She wanted him with a desperation that stunned her. She wanted to make love to him, wanted them to join their bodies and their souls, wanted to spend the rest of her life in his arms.

Martine was right. I'm in love with him. What do I do now?

Nothing. To tempt Rainulf into making love to her would be unfair to him. The chancellorship was all he wanted in life. Toward that end, he'd made a commitment to celibacy. For her to undermine that commitment by seducing him—and that's what she'd be doing, for he'd never meant to share her bed tonight—would be inexcusable.

She'd best accept tonight as he had intended it—a kind of gift from him to her, a favor.

She cleared her throat. "Is that what you made happen to that woman in the Rhineland?"

"Aye."

"More than once?"

She saw him smile slowly. "Quite a few times, as I recall."

"No wonder the ladies of Paris went into mourning when you took your vows."

He chuckled and tucked the quilt up around her, then stroked her cheek. She felt the tension in him, and knew he wasn't nearly as calm and unaffected as he wanted her to think. "Good night, Corliss."

"Good night."

He rose and pulled the bed curtains closed. She heard his footsteps retreating, saw the fleeting shaft of lamplight as he opened and closed his chamber door. And then all was quiet and dark once more.

Rainulf and Corliss set out from Blackburn at dawn. They'd ridden perhaps a hundred yards from the castle when the distant rumble of hoofbeats from behind made them rein in their mounts.

What's this? thought Rainulf as he and Corliss looked back over their shoulders. Thorne and Martine still stood on the drawbridge, where they'd said goodbye. On the path, advancing at a gallop, was a lone horseman.

Peter

He drew up his mount, nodded in a cursory way to Rainulf, then reached over to take Corliss's hand. "I didn't realize you were leaving so early. I wanted to . . ." He glanced uneasily at Rainulf.

"I'll wait up the road a bit," Rainulf said tersely, nudging his horse into a walk.

Of course Peter would want to say a private farewell to Corliss. They'd been inseparable, and from all accounts, she'd affected a remarkable change in him. Gone was the haunted creature he'd been when they'd arrived, replaced by the old Peter—the charming, easygoing fellow women had always found irresistible.

A little ember of jealousy glowed red-hot in Rainulf's stomach. He wondered how Corliss felt about Peter's attentions. She'd be flattered, certainly. Peter was young, handsome, and of noble blood. He was the perfect knight, a skilled and loyal soldier whose prowess with his fists had become legendary. Young knights and mercenaries from all over England journeyed to Blackburn to challenge him, hoping in vain to best him and thereby steal his fame. Rainulf himself had sparred with him during his last visit, and had found it a punishing experience, although Peter seemed impressed; he claimed Rainulf had fought better and lasted longer than anyone in recent memory. The praise had taken some of the sting out of his bruised and battered flesh.

"Whoa." Rainulf patted his bay stallion on the neck and glanced back down the road. Corliss and Peter had dismounted. From this distance, they looked like two young men, Corliss having returned to her male disguise, although her saddlebags bulged with the kirtles and tunics Martine had had altered for her. Peter took both her hands in his and spoke to her while she stared at the ground. Then he reached down and lifted her chin, lowering his face to hers.

The little ember burst into flame as Rainulf watched her accept the kiss. When the couple drew apart, Corliss turned to look in his direction. He abruptly looked away, yanking on the reins and kicking his mount into a trot. He didn't stop until he reached the main road that led north. By then, Corliss and Peter were a quarter mile away, and he could barely see them.

Self-doubt—Rainulf's special curse—curled its claws

around him. What kind of a man *was* he? How could he just look on as Peter kissed her, given what had happened between them last night?

Nothing happened between us. He had satisfied her curiosity about the mysteries of the flesh, nothing more. *She'd* known it was nothing more. It was nothing. Nothing.

Nothing? It had been the first time he'd touched a woman so intimately in eleven years. And it had been . . .

He expelled a shuddering sigh. It had been more than he'd wanted it to be, more than he'd intended. He closed his eyes, reliving the breathless excitement that had gripped him as he caressed her, guiding her toward a fulfillment she'd never known. How he'd missed the magic of a woman's body . . . the hot, hidden places that felt like wet satin to the touch . . . the challenge of coaxing that mysterious flesh into revealing its secrets . . . the thrill of driving a woman senseless with pleasure.

It had gratified him to be the first man to make Corliss lose herself so completely. He could still picture her at the end, her head thrown back, her eyes half-closed, moaning and writhing. He could still feel her, slick and tight around his finger. He'd wondered how it would feel to be buried deep inside that pulsing heat. Then, as how, such speculation aroused him painfully.

He'd been hard as a steel rod as he touched her, and perilously close to orgasm. When she climaxed, it was all he could do to keep from whipping the quilt aside and ramming himself into her. But even then, even in the grip of such excruciating arousal, he'd known better than that. Had he surrendered to his aching hunger, had he crossed that line, they could never have gone back to the way it was before. Corliss was not like the women he knew in Paris; she was not someone he could enjoy briefly and then set aside. But anything more was out of the question.

The effort of will it had taken for him to get up and walk away from her last night had been profound. Alone in his chamber, he'd leaned back against the door and untied his chausses with trembling hands. Cursing himself, he closed his fist around his tortured flesh; release came almost instantly. The ache in his heart had persisted, however; he felt it still.

He watched Corliss ride toward him, turning to wave to Peter, on horseback, who gazed after her. What would the enamored young knight think if he knew what had transpired between Rainulf and Corliss in her darkened chamber?

She joined him, and they wordlessly proceeded north along the main road. The rhythm of his horse's gait and his stubborn memories of last night conspired to keep him in a state of high arousal most of the morning; he was grateful for his concealing tunic.

At noon they spread a blanket in a clearing in the woods through which they had ridden. They ate their cheese and bread in near silence, and then Corliss lay on her back and squinted up at the forest canopy above them. Flickers of sunlight danced on the translucent skin of her face. A very singular face, a face like no other he had ever seen. *God, she's exquisite.*

"Looks like diamonds," she murmured.

He lay down next to her and shielded his eyes to study the sun glittering through the leaves, something he hadn't done since he was a boy. That part of him—the part that looked at the world with childlike wonder—had lain dormant until she'd come to Oxford. His memories of life before Corliss were shadowy and vague, like a poorly recalled dream. Now, colors and scents and sounds were sharper, details more vivid, everything more . . . real, more *there*. She'd awakened so much in him, changed him so immeasurably.

"You're right," he said softly. "It does look like diamonds."

"Peter asked me to marry him."

Rainulf turned his head to look at her; she continued to stare up at the sky. "This morning," she added softly, "while he was saying good-bye."

Deeply shaken, Rainulf sat up with his elbows on his knees and rested his head in his hands. For a long time, neither of them moved or spoke.

I've lost her. Christ, I've lost her. the knowledge devastated him. He felt as though his insides had been pulled out, leaving him a hollow shell. After a while, he was able to think clearly enough to gather his thoughts and formulate a response. When he realized what it would be—what it had to be—his melancholy only deepened.

"It's a good marriage," he said tonelessly, feeling as though he were listening to another man's voice. "A very good marriage."

He heard her shift behind him as she sat up. "I turned him down."

Thank God! He wheeled around to face her. He wanted to laugh and throw his arms around her. He wanted to tear off her clothes and claim her, body and soul, whisper lover's words, promises. . . .

Promises he couldn't keep. "Why?"

"Oh, Rainulf." Her eyes were sad. "There are so many reasons. Peter is ... Well, he's very troubled, but he doesn't realize it. He's got me all confused with his Lady Magdalen."

"I wondered whether he'd told you about her."

"It took him a while. He doesn't like to talk about her. He's never properly mourned her. It's as if he doesn't want to admit to himself that she"s really gone. He wants *me* to be her, but I can't. 'Twould be unfair to both of us for me to try to replace her."

"He'll get over her eventually," Rainulf said. "And

then he'll learn to appreciate you for who you really are."

"Rainulf, if Peter ever found out who I really am, he'd be shocked to the core. He'd probably hate me for deceiving him. He thinks I'm ... I don't know. Some sort of Saxon nobility, I suppose. A far cry from the truth."

"You *are* nobility," he said with conviction. "You're the most noble and gentle woman I've ever known. The most accomplished, the most ..." He shook his head in frustration. "For God's sake, Corliss, he's obviously smitten with you. And he's a good man. Your background would make no difference to him. The woman you've become is so ... unique. You defy easy categories. That's why you can pass so well for whatever you set your mind to."

"Then there's the most important reason," she said, rising and strolling away from him to yank a handful of berries from a bush. "I hate marriage. I hate being bound to a man. You know that."

"I think you should reconsider," he said, despising the words even as they left his mouth. "You need protection from Roger Foliot, and marriage is the best way to get it."

"Is that really what you want?"

"I want you to be safe."

"I want to be *free*." She turned to face him, the berries crushed in her hand. "I'm tired of being a whore, a *safe* whore. I've been a whore since I was sixteen."

"You were a married woman part of that time."

She flung the berries away and squatted to wipe her hands on the grass. "I was just as much Sully's whore as Father's Osred's. The Church may have blessed the union, but it was no different. I bartered my body for protection, and lost my freedom in the process. It wasn't worth it." She met his gaze, her eyes fiery. "I'll never do that again. Never!"

"Marriage doesn't have to mean losing your freedom," he said. "There are men who value their wives as equals. Look at Abelard and Héloïse."

She straightened up, tossing her head with a smirk. "How many men are that enlightened?"

"I am."

The smirk faded.

"And there are others," he hastily added.

Her eyebrows shot up. "Name one."

He groped quickly for a name. "Brother Matthew."

She laughed bitingly. "I don't suppose you know of any who aren't celibate."

"What about Thorne?"

"Or married?"

He tried to think of someone else, but couldn't.

"You can forget about getting rid of me through marriage," she said. "Though, if you want, I'll move out of your house."

He jumped up. "Nay!"

"But last night . . ." She bit her lip and crossed her arms, staring at the ground. "Last night, when I asked you if you wished I'd never come to Oxford, you said—"

"Last night never happened," he said, quietly but firmly. He took a deep breath and added, "Any of it."

There was a long pause as she continued to look down; then she nodded.

"We'll return to Oxford and all will be as it was before. Nothing will have changed."

She closed her eyes and nodded again. "I understand."

They stood in silence for a moment, and then she looked up. The light had left her eyes. "He said he's going to write to me."

"Peter?"

She nodded and began gathering up the remains of their meal. "He thinks he can change my mind."

"Can he?" He nearly choked on the words.

"Nay. But he's going to try."

"What reason did you give for turning him down?"

She stood and shook the blanket out, then handed him one end. Together they folded it. "I told him I wasn't in love with him."

Had he just imagined the emphasis on the word *him*?

She stuffed the folded blanket into a saddlebag while he stowed away the food.

"He's going to write to you, too," she said as she mounted up.

"To me?" He settled into his saddle. "Why?"

"To ask your permission to press his suit, since I have no family. And to enlist your aid in wearing me down."

"Wearing you down?"

"Getting me to say yes."

"Doesn't he care that you don't love him?"

"He says he loves *me,* and can't live without me. He says if one's love is strong enough, nothing else matters, nothing else has any meaning—that love is all that's really important in life." She flicked the reins and guided her mount toward the path. "Imagine that."

Chapter 14

"What's tonight's *disputatio* about?" Corliss asked as she and Rainulf left his house and began walking up St. John Street. The August evening was warm, the sky rusty with the setting sun.

"I'm arguing against the notion of an all-powerful God."

The air left her lungs in a startled little laugh. "Do you never worry about what people think?"

He smiled indulgently and began to say something, but stopped short, squinting at the alley across the street. "Did you see that?"

"Nay," she lied. She *had* noticed the shadowy movement, but it was probably just Rad, who continued to materialize from time to time on the edge of her vision. She'd hoped her two-week absence from Oxford would cure him of the habit of following her around, but during the past few weeks she'd seen him at least half a dozen times. Twice she'd cornered him and pleaded with him to stop, but he'd stubbornly insisted that she needed his protection. The last thing she wanted was for Rainulf to run him to ground again; he refused to believe that the hulking, pock-marked peddler was harmless.

Rainulf took a step toward the darkened alley, but Corliss held him back. He looked down at her hand on his arm, and she dropped it. Since returning from Blackburn, they never touched, even casually, as if by avoiding physical contact they could pretend that all

was as it had been—that he had never come to her chamber and touched her as lovers touched each other.

" 'Twas just a pig foraging for garbage," she said.

He shook his head. " 'Twas a man."

"Come. We'll be late getting to St. Mary's. You'll have less time to spout your damnable heresy."

"It's not heresy," he answered automatically.

She turned so he couldn't see her smile, and continued walking. "The Church fathers might disagree."

"Some would." She heard his footsteps as he came up behind her. "Others understand my method of academic argument."

"You're saying there are men of the cloth who would justify an attack on the Church's teachings?"

"Not an attack," he said, falling in beside her as she strode quickly up St. John Street. "An argument, for academic purposes only. It's the Aristotelian method. One argues both sides of the issue to reach a solution. In arguing the case against God's omnipotence, we can actually affirm it."

She shrugged elaborately as they crossed Grope Lane. "Why engage in tiresome arguments about something you know you're going to end up affirming anyway?"

"Since when do you find *disputatio* tiresome?" he asked with a smile. "You come to almost all my lectures, and you absorb my teachings like a sea sponge. You obviously enjoy the mental exercise."

"Aye," she admitted. "I'm just baiting you for sport."

He rolled his eyes, then narrowed them on her. "Not just for sport. You brought up all that heresy business to lure me away from that alley, didn't you? You know I can't resist an argument."

She laughed. " 'Tis what makes you such a brilliant teacher. You were born to argue."

" 'Brilliant' may be overstating things a bit."

Progress! There was a time when he would have insisted that he was completely unworthy to teach; now, he was simply not quite "brilliant."

"If you're not brilliant," she challenged, "then how, in one short summer, did you manage to get me speaking French like a royal princess?"

"You've got a facility for languages."

"But what of the rest of it? How many Oxfordshire peasants know how to calculate the velocity of a body in motion, for God's sake?"

"You have a very quick mind." They turned onto Shidyerd, and he nodded to a group of scholars. "The credit lies with you, not me."

"I think not. All this new knowledge I've gained is knowledge you've given me. I've learned an amazing amount from you."

He shrugged. "An amazing amount of the sorts of things one can learn simply by opening a book. Those things are easy to teach."

"Easy for *you.* I don't think I could do it."

"Don't underrate yourself. I've learned a great deal from you."

She snorted. "Such as?"

He smiled enigmatically. "Various things. Important things. More important than fiddling with numbers and perfecting one's accent." He fell silent for a while, and then said, "Living with you has ... it's changed me. For the better. And ... and I've enjoyed your company."

She looked up at him; he wouldn't meet her gaze. "What are you trying to say, Rainulf?"

"I received a letter from Peter today."

She groaned. Peter had written to her twice since she left Blackburn, begging her to marry him. Her responses to both letters had been the same—that although she cared for him, her affection was as that of a sister for a brother, and she must therefore decline his proposal.

Rainulf's expression, like his voice, was strained. "He has a manor of his own, and a much better income than I would have thought."

"We've discussed this already, Rainulf. Please don't do this. I can't bear your trying to talk me into marrying anoth—" *Careful.* "Into . . . into marrying—"

"I don't enjoy it very much, either," he said gruffly. "But it's for your own good. Just think about it."

"I *have* thought about it."

"You've dismissed it out of hand."

"Hardly. I have excellent reasons, and I've shared them with you."

She sensed that he was relaxing fractionally, as if secretly relieved by her continued refusal to consider Peter's suit.

"He's a good man," he said, but with little enthusiasm.

"Aye. He's a wonderful man, and he'll make some woman a wonderful husband someday, but that woman won't be me."

There was a pause. "He claims," Rainulf said slowly, "to be madly in love with you. He makes quite a case for it."

"He was madly in love with his lady Magdalen. I just look like her."

"He insists it's you he loves, and that he'd do everything in his power to make you happy."

"My definition of happiness is freedom. A man's love is the worst enemy of a woman's freedom."

Except yours, she silently amended. Were Rainulf Fairfax ever to love a woman, whether wife or mistress, she would still be free. Corliss knew that now. But most men weren't like Rainulf.

They crossed High Street in silence. On the steps of St. Mary's, he paused and regarded her pensively. A swarm of scholars hollered greetings as they streamed into the church, elbowing each other aside

for the best benches. "I just want you to be safe. If
anything were to happen to you . . ."

She indicated her masculine garb. "I'm safe dressed
like this." She thought about, but didn't mention, the
dagger secreted in her boot. "And free as well. I've
never felt so liberated."

He smiled wryly. "Chausses don't make you free,
Corliss. Or safe. Being male carries risks of its own.
'Tis a false sense of liberty you feel."

She smiled, too. "I'll take any kind of liberty I
can get."

Rainulf and Corliss left St. Mary's that night amid
a throng of departing scholars. She'd found the unor-
thodox *disputatio* engrossing, and not in the least heretical. Rainulf was truly the most gifted teacher in
Oxford; no wonder his students idolized him.

"Good night, Master Fairfax!" called one as he
sprinted down the church steps, cappa flapping.

"Another triumph, Magister!" cried another. "Join
us at the Nightingale for a pint?"

"Not tonight, boys."

"Master Fairfax." They turned to find Thomas com-
ing up behind them, followed, as always, by Brad.
"There's something I don't understand. Why is it that
God can't move the heavens with rec . . . rec—"

"Rectilinear motion." Rainulf nodded toward her.
"Corliss?"

"Because a vacuum would remain," she said. Rainulf smiled, and she felt the glow of pride that always
accompanied his approval.

"What's wrong with that?" Thomas asked.

"It's never even been established that such a thing
as a vacuum can exist," she said. "And even if it did,
its nature might preclude—"

"Perhaps," Rainulf interrupted, clearly sensing a
long debate in the making, "we can pursue these *ques-
tiones* at my house, over a pitcher of ale."

The boys readily took him up on the invitation, but Corliss hesitated. She cocked her head toward Victor, waiting for her with his followers across the street. "I've been asked to come to a meeting at St. Frideswide's."

"Nay!"

Corliss gasped indignantly. In truth, she wasn't particularly eager to attend the meeting—a strategy session regarding tavern prices—in part because of the late hour and in part because Victor's fanaticism was beginning to wear thin with her. But Rainulf's arrogance in forbidding her to go wore even thinner. Drawing herself up, she said tightly, "I'm going," and strode swiftly away.

Behind her, she heard Rainulf tell the young men to wait. He caught up with her and grabbed her arm. She shook him off. "Who do you think you are," she fumed, "ordering me about as if I were—"

"You're right."

She snapped her mouth shut.

" 'Twas a rash reaction," he conceded. "Born of concern for you. I worry about you associating with Victor and that crowd, and it's so late. You'd have to walk home alone in the dark."

"Victor lives on the East End, so I can walk home with him. I'll be safe."

Rainulf frowned uncertainly.

"He's a former mercenary," she reminded him. "If anyone can protect me, Victor can. I'll be fine."

Rainulf raked his fingers through his hair. "All right. But come home as soon as you can. I'll wait up for you."

Corliss sat in the back of the church and yawned all through the meeting, wishing she hadn't felt obliged to attend just to make a point with Rainulf. She paid little attention to the issues that were discussed and the action that was decided on. Instead, she pondered the question of what sort of decorations to paint around Rainulf's fireplace that would complement the dancing monkeys encircling the windows.

Lions, perhaps ... noble golden beasts, like the magister himself. She had just finished illuminating another signature of Chancellor Becket's Bible, and would have time before starting the next one to sketch the lions onto the whitewashed wall. She pictured a row of them, one after the other, each gripping in its mouth the tail of his brother in front. One after the other they would march around the fireplace ... marching ... marching. ...

A hand jiggled her shoulder. "Corliss? Wake up." She groaned.

"Was it that boring?" Victor asked.

"Yes."

He grinned and shook his head. "Come on. I'll walk with you as far as the magister's house."

The moon was full, bathing the narrow streets in a dusky half-light. Conversation during the walk was decidedly one-sided, with Victor discoursing at length on the justification of force to attain his ends, and Corliss pretending to listen. As they approached the corner of St. John Street, she thought she heard footsteps from behind. Heavy footsteps.

Must be Rad. She toyed with the idea of confronting him. It would be unwise to do so in the presence of Victor who, at any rate, was too preoccupied with his oration to even notice that they were being followed.

The footsteps quickened. What was this? Rad never tried to catch up with her, preferring to skulk in the shadows. She turned to look back at him just as he raised a massive club and brought it down on Victor's head.

She watched in speechless horror as the blow shuddered through Victor. He didn't make a sound, merely collapsed bonelessly, like a rag doll tossed onto the ground. A scream welled up inside her, but her throat wouldn't work. She couldn't feel her legs or arms.

Rainulf's calm voice came to her as clearly as it had during their fighting lesson in the stable yard: *Don't panic. Get away if you can.*

She turned to run as the hulking brute with the club advanced on her. Was it Rad? He was big like Rad, but he wore a sacklike mask over his head.

A dull burst of pain exploded in her lower back, hurling her sideways into the street. She landed hard, the air whooshing out of her lungs on impact. When she tried to draw a breath, she found she couldn't. Panic found a foothold, and raced through her.

Victor still lay facedown on the road, unconscious. Struggling for air, Corliss watched as his assailant tossed the club away and yanked Victor's purse from his belt, pocketing it. Then he searched his victim's boot, withdrawing something that gleamed maliciously in the moonlight.

A dagger. Victor's dagger. "A taste of your own steel," the masked man growled. "That's what you're needin', you goddamn troublemaker."

Exerting an enormous effort, Corliss managed to suck in a breath. The air seared her lungs, and she choked on it. *At least I'm breathing.*

The big man pressed a knee into Victor's back, grabbed a handful of black hair, and yanked his head up. Victor groaned and blinked; a ribbon of blood ran from his mouth.

"What do you say?" His attacker held Victor's own blade in front of his eyes. "Should I open up your throat quicklike or make it last a bit?"

"Burnell," Victor rasped, "you bastard!"

"Guilty." He tore the mask off. "Including the bastard part. I reckon that's something we have in common, eh?"

My dagger! The brutal tavern keeper had his back to her. If she was very quiet . . .

Corliss reached down into her own boot, closed her fingers around the hilt of her dagger, and slid it out. Clutching the weapon in her fist, she crept stealthily toward the two men.

Burnell pressed the blade against Victor's throat and chuckled harshly. "Do y' suppose I'll get extra time in purgatory for killin' the son of a priest?"

Victor bared his teeth. "You'll roast in hell where you belong, you son of a bitch!"

"I'll see you there, then."

As Corliss approached Burnell, her nostrils flared at his ripe, greasy odor: stale sweat and rancid meat. Coming up behind the big man, she grabbed him by the neck of his tunic and held her dagger to his throat. "Drop it."

Burnell froze; Victor grinned.

"Now!"

Burnell eased the blade away from Victor's throat and let go of his hair. . . .

Then he grabbed Corliss's wrist, raised her hand to his mouth, and bit it, hard. Corliss yelped. The dagger fell from her fingers. She grappled for it, but Burnell got it first.

No!

Corliss and Victor both struggled to rise, but Burnell, laughing, was already on his feet, a dagger in each mammoth fist. He kicked Victor in the head. The young scholar flopped onto his back and groaned, then went limp.

Burnell wheeled on Corliss and kicked her in the stomach. She went down like a sack of rocks, gasping in pain.

Looking up, she saw his dark form looming over her, saw teeth and steel glinting in the light of the full moon. "You and him and them others been costin' me money," he growled, fumbling with the pouch on her belt. "You owe me some silver." He tried to tear the pouch off, but it wouldn't budge, so he jammed his fingers inside and felt around. "What the hell's this?" he demanded as he fumbled with her little reliquary, which was all that the pouch contained. "Where's your money?"

"I left it home," she managed. It was the truth, but he clearly didn't believe her. He knelt close to her, overwhelming her with his sickening smell. Gripping both daggers in one hand and pressing them to her throat, he shoved the other under the hem of her tunic and groped along the waist-cord of her chausses for a hidden purse.

The feel of his hand beneath her tunic filled her with revulsion . . . and fear. If he searched her thoroughly, he might detect the lack of more than a purse. She tried to writhe away, and he flicked the blades at her throat; she felt a stinging pain, followed by a hot trickle down her neck.

"Next time I'll slice you open." He ran his hand over her belly. . . .

And back again.

And paused.

Desperately she tried to skitter back, but that only brought his meaty palm directly between her legs. His eyes widened and then narrowed. "What have we here?" He grabbed her hard, and she cried out. "More to the point, what *don't* we have?"

His low, sinister laughter made her insides spin around slowly. Snatching his hand out from under her tunic, he ran it over her chest, frowning in puzzlement at its flatness. Keeping one blade at her throat, he used the other to slash open her tunic. A second pass slit her shirt down the front. A third tore into the linen bindings around her chest—and her skin as well.

She screamed in pain and tried to push his hand away. He raised it and slammed the hilt of the dagger into her forehead.

Bursts of light filled her vision and a blessed numbness overtook her . . . but not completely. She felt him push aside the shreds of linen, heard his awful chuckle as she lay exposed beneath him. Through slitted eyes she saw him shove one dagger into the sheath on his belt and hurl the other into the hard-packed earth, where it stuck, quivering.

Then she felt his hands on her.

No! No! She thrashed fiercely and he chuckled. "You're a live one, are you?"

He grabbed her under her arms and pulled her between two buildings. *For privacy?* She struggled, but couldn't dislodge his firm grip.

The space between the stone walls was very narrow, and black as hell. He dropped her; she landed with a thud. She tried to rise, but he was there, on top of her, pawing her, groping.

No! God, no!

He grabbed her knees. She focused all her strength on keeping her legs together, but he wrenched them apart and knelt between them. By what little moonlight penetrated the dark passage, she saw him untie his braies.

Don't panic! Again she heard Rainulf's voice of cool reason: *Go for the nose ... use the heel of your hand.*

She cocked her wrist and whipped it down. It connected with a soft crunch, and he howled.

"Fuckin' bitch!" He slapped her hard across the face. "I'll teach you." Breathing harshly, he lifted her tunic and fumbled with the cord that secured her chausses.

Or you can break a finger, Rainulf had instructed. *Here's how ...*

Reaching down, she grabbed one of his hands, located the little finger, and snapped it sharply. His roar of pain filled the alleyway. Yet she was too confined to escape. She couldn't move, couldn't maneuver in a space that was no wider than her opponent. Squeezing out between Burnell and the wall was impossible, so while he cradled his hand, moaning, she retreated quickly. . . .

Only to find another wall at her back. On three sides of her there was stone; on the fourth, Burnell. *Oh, God, no* . . . She scrambled to her feet.

With a bellow of rage, he rose and charged her.

She ducked, grabbing him around his thick waist; she felt the wide leather belt, the sheath . . . *the dagger!* Her hand closed around the weapon's hilt a split second before his would have. She yanked it out and rose. *What now? Where do I strike?* Taking advantage of her moment of indecision, Burnell seized her wrist and twisted. She felt her fingers open. *No, no* . . .

With a guttural cry of triumph, he took possession of the dagger and pointed its tip at her bare chest. "You're a plucky little wench, I'll give you that. You think you're invincible, don't you?"

Ah, you're invincible now, are you? Rainulf had said. Right before she'd . . .

Yes. Do it.

She hooked her leg around Burnell's, and they went down together, limbs tangled, grunting. They grappled savagely in the dark, confined space. She groped for the dagger. Burnell wrested it away and rolled on top of her as she flailed at him.

And then he cried out, a long, harrowing shriek that echoed and echoed off the stone walls.

What. . . ?

He rose over her, quivering. She heard a wet, strangled gurgle and saw the dagger sticking out of his throat.

Jesus!

Eyes wild, he grabbed the weapon with both hands and yanked it free. Something warm and wet pulsed onto her. He collapsed on her, jerking as the blood pumped out of him, soaking her.

"No!" she pushed against him. But it was no use.

His twitching body pinned her down; his garbled cries filled her ears. She tasted his blood in her mouth.

She closed her eyes and raised her voice in a long, hoarse scream.

Suddenly she felt his weight lift off her. She opened her eyes, and he wasn't there anymore.

Rainulf. He stood over her, stricken with horror. "Corliss! Oh, God!" He crouched, touching her gingerly. "You're hurt! What did he—"

His voice caught in her throat as his hands traveled from her face to her chest, encountering her shredded garments and bare skin, soaked with blood. His fingers brushed one of the dagger cuts and she winced.

"Oh, Jesus," he rasped, gathering her in his arms. "Corliss. Oh, God."

A sound from behind made them both turn to see Burnell lurching out of the alley with his hands clutching his throat, his braies around his ankles. Rainulf stiffened, his face contorting with hatred. A dark, unsteady figure—Victor, clearly still dazed—lunged at Burnell, but he managed to throw him off and stumble away.

Victor started after the wounded tavern keeper, but Rainulf yelled, "Let the bastard go, Victor! He's done for."

"Oh, no," Victor moaned, staggering into the alley. "Corliss?"

"She's hurt," Rainulf managed. "Badly, I think."

"She?" Victor peered down at her, his eyes widening in the dark.

Corliss pulled the two halves of her shirt together with trembling hands. "It's not that bad."

Victor looked stunned, whether from the blows Burnell had dealt him, or the revelation of her true sex, she couldn't say.

Rainulf glared at him. "This is your fault, damn you."

For a moment, Corliss thought Victor was going to

argue with him, but after a moment's hesitation, he closed his eyes and nodded.

"Do some good for once," Rainulf ground out. "Go fetch a surgeon."

"Which one?" Victor asked.

"Will Geary," Rainulf said as he lifted Corliss in his arms and stood. "He's got a shop on Pennyfarthing Street. Bring him back to my house. And for God's sake, *hurry*!"

Chapter 15

As Rainulf carried Corliss back to the house, she began to shiver in his arms. "Everything's all right," he soothed. Insipid words; nothing was all right. Corliss was hurt. He didn't know how badly, and he dreaded finding out.

At his front door, he called, "Thomas! Brad!" Two sets of footsteps pounded down the stairs, and the door swung open. Rainulf muscled them aside and bounded up the steps with Corliss, ignoring their horrified gasps and offers of help. They'd told him the screams he'd heard must have been student horseplay; thank God he'd gone to investigate.

"Magister!" Thomas exclaimed as they followed him, stumbling over their feet and each other as they clambered up the stairs. "What happened?"

"Burnell attacked her."

He heard them hesitate on the stairs, and could sense their bewilderment. *Her?* Rainulf winced inwardly, wishing he'd had more presence of mind than to slip up this way, not once, but twice. But could he hope for presence of mind when the woman he loved had been . . .

The woman he loved.

God help him.

In the well-lit main hall, he paused to look down at her. "Corliss. Oh, Corliss." She was covered with blood, *covered* with it, especially her upper body. The remnants of her shredded clothes were saturated with it, although it seemed to have stopped flowing; it stained her face, matted her hair.

Please, God, let her be all right, he prayed, with more pure, simple faith than he had felt in years.

He strode into her chamber, shouting commands over his shoulder, which the young men hurried to obey: "Unfold that blanket on her bed. Bring me a bowl of water and some clean cloths. And a brazier. She needs warmth."

Wrapping her in the blanket, he lay down beside her and enfolded her in his arms. Her trembling had grown into a convulsive shuddering that racked her body, as if a great hand shook her in its grip. "There now, it's all right," he murmured inanely as he stroked her hair, her face. He kissed her forehead, her eyelids, her temple, holding her as tightly as he could.

She freed her hands to grip his tunic. "It's not that bad," she whispered shakily. "It's not—"

"Shh, it's all right." He kissed her cheek, her hair. "It's all right. Rest."

He glanced up to find Thomas and Brad exchanging a look, their expressions a mixture of astonishment and concern.

"Go outside," Rainulf told them. "Watch for Victor and the surgeon."

A pointless assignment, but one they eagerly accepted, colliding with each other in their haste to get downstairs. When they were gone, Rainulf gently drew back from Corliss. She clutched at him with palsied hands.

"I'm not going anywhere," he assured her as he dipped a cloth in the water and wrung it out. "Just lie back. Yes, like that."

He carefully dabbed her face with the wet cloth, breathing a sign of relief to find it uninjured, except for a knot on the side of her forehead. For the second time since he'd met her, he silently thanked God that her face—that extraordinary, singular face—had been spared.

Rinsing out the cloth, he bathed her throat, blotting cautiously when he discovered the nick at its base, already scabbing over. He swore under his breath, imagining the fear that must have consumed her to be at the mercy of that animal. "He had a knife?"

"Victor's dagger," she rasped. "And mine."

"Yours? You've been carrying ..." Obviously she had. He grimaced and shook his head.

Her eyes clouded with anguish, and she squeezed them shut. "You were right. I was a fool to buy that dagger." Her voice quavered so badly, he could scarcely understand her. "I-I didn't know what to do with it. And-and he took it away from me, just as you said he would. Oh, Rainulf, I'm sorry." Her quaking worsened. "I'm sorry."

"Shh ..."

She shook her head violently, her eyes glassy. "It's all my fault. I should have listened to you. I shouldn't have had anything to do with Victor. I shouldn't have gone out at night. I shouldn't have bought that—"

"Nonsense." He took her face between his hands and forced her to look at him. "None of this is your fault. You're not to blame. What happened was no one's fault but Burnell's. He's a monster." Or *was* a monster. Chances were good that even now he lay dead on some dark side street.

Rainulf dipped the cloth in the bowl again, parted her torn clothes slightly, and pressed it to her bloody chest. She sucked in a breath. "Easy," he said. "I'll be careful."

As delicately as he could, he wiped the blood off her skin, revealing a long, shallow cut running halfway down her chest. He hissed a low oath.

"He kn-knew I was a w-woman," Corliss said. "He wanted to ... he tried to ..."

"But he didn't. Did he?"

She shook her head. "Nay, you came just in time. I fought him, but he was too strong for me. I broke his nose and his finger, though."

He took her in his arms. "Good for you. You did well. I'm proud of you."

Was that the only cut on her chest, he wondered, or were there others? How badly had the son of a bitch hurt her? "I need to get this tunic off you." He unbuckled her belt and threw it on the floor, then eased her out of the ruined wool garment and tossed that aside as well. Her bleached linen shirt, once snow white, had turned the brownish red of drying blood. He left it on out of deference to her modesty, but ripped it open the rest of the way, pulling out and discarding the shredded strips of linen that had bound her breasts.

He pushed aside the bloodied halves of the shirt, exposing more of her chest. Taking up the wet cloth, he cleaned the blood off, relieved to find no more wounds. He rinsed the cloth out again and passed it under her shirt at her waist, smoothing it up her side and over a breast. She shivered and threw an arm across her eyes.

"Did he cut you here?" She shook her head. "Anywhere else?" he asked as he tended to the other side.

"Nay."

Thank God, thought Rainulf, realizing her injuries were far less than he'd supposed. Most of the blood must have been Burnell's.

"But . . ." Corliss began.

"Aye?"

She turned her face away. "He-he touched me," she whispered brokenly. "He t-touched—"

"Oh, Corliss." He dropped the cloth in the bowl and wrapped her in his arms, breathing against her hair, "It's over. It's over. He can't hurt you anymore. He's probably dead by now." That was Rainulf's only consolation, the only thing that kept him calm and sane in the face of what had happened to Corliss. His rage toward Burnell was pure and savage; the bastard *deserved* to pay for his brutality with his life. Was it un-Christian to take satisfaction in his death? He felt a moment of guilt—a stab of self-doubt: *What kind of man am I to rejoice in the death of another?* And then Corliss's voice came to him: *Save your doubt for the lecture hall, where it belongs. Don't turn it in on yourself.*

How right she'd been. How wise she was. Wiser in many respects than he.

He threaded his fingers through Corliss's hair and kissed the glossy black waves. Her trembling had abated, but not gone away entirely. He rubbed her arms and back, murmuring a litany of comforting words. It would have killed him, he realized, had anything happened to her. She'd gotten inside him, become a part of him. How had that happened?

He heard voices from the street, and then the door opening; footsteps on the stairs. "Will's here."

He sat up and pulled the two sides of her shirt together.

"Stay here with me," she pleaded.

He smoothed her hair off her face. "Of course."

The leather curtain parted, and Will hurried into the chamber, bag in hand; Rainulf had a fleeting glimpse of Thomas, Brad, and Victor in the main hall. "They told me someone was hurt," Will said. "Corliss? What happened, boy?"

Corliss glanced uneasily toward Rainulf. Taking a deep breath, he said, "Can I trust you to keep your counsel about something, Will? Something important?"

"Of course."

"The young woman who disappeared from Cuxham—Father Osred's housekeeper, Constance ..."

Will nodded. Rainulf took Corliss's hand.

The surgeon blinked. His eyes grew round. His mouth opened, then shut, then opened again. And then he laughed in astonishment. "Well! I'd just about decided you preferred boys, and here you've been hiding your mistress in your own home, dressed as a—"

"She's not my mistress," Rainulf hastily corrected, squeezing Corliss's hand. "I took her in to protect her."

"From Pigot?" Will asked.

"Is that his name?" asked Corliss. "The madman who finds runaways for Sir Roger?"

Will walked around the big bed, sitting on the opposite side from Rainulf. "That's what they call him. No one knows his real name." He shook his head. "Every man, woman, and child in Cuxham trembles at the mention of him."

"Is he really mad?" Rainulf asked.

The surgeon moved aside the oil lamp on the night table, set his bag down and opened it. "Quite. So you'd best tread carefully, both of you." His gaze took in Corliss's chausses, and he smiled. "Although I see you have been. Very clever, young lady."

"Thank you."

Will scrutinized Corliss's face, lightly touching the lump on her forehead. "Have you any marjoram in the house?"

"I think so."

"Mix it with honey and use it as a poultice on this— and any other lumps and bruises you may have sustained."

Corliss nodded. Her trembling had let up, but she was parchment pale, and her eyes were pools of sadness.

"Is this the only cut?" Will asked, indicating the small gash on her throat.

"Nay." She parted her shirt just enough for the surgeon to see the long dagger wound that marred her chest.

He frowned. "Vicious bastard." He grinned sheepishly at Corliss. "Pardon the language. I don't quite think of you as a woman yet."

"That's all right," Corliss mumbled. Rainulf didn't like the lack of spark in her eyes, the apathy in her expression. It was so unlike her. Even under the most trying of circumstances—even when she'd been ravaged by smallpox—she'd retained her ... sense of herself, her love of life, her irrepressible humor. But now ...

Rainulf shook his head. She was just a shell that looked like Corliss, but didn't have Corliss inside it. There was more of Corliss in *him* right now than there seemed to be in her.

"This will sting," Will warned her before cleaning her wounds with something from a small flask. She gripped Rainulf's hand painfully as the surgeon sponged on the fluid, apologizing all the while. "These are really naught but scratches," he assured her. "Although I've no doubt they hurt. They should heal quickly, without scarring. Don't bother bandaging them—just keep them clean. I'll leave this salve for them." He placed a small jar on the night table. "That's all I can do."

Will packed up his things, then patted Corliss's cheek. "Be careful out there. I've seen this Pigot's handiwork."

"So have I," she said quietly.

They exchanged a grim look, and then Will rose.

"What do I owe you, Will?" Rainulf asked, taking out his purse.

The surgeon waved his hand in dismissal as he crossed the chamber. "Don't be an idiot, Rainulf. I wouldn't take your silver."

"You have a right to payment for your services," Rainulf persisted. "I insist."

Will whipped aside the leather curtain; the three young scholars, seated at the table, turned to look. "You can pay me by taking good care of Corliss." He directed one last look toward the woman on the bed. Rainulf saw the frank interest in his gaze and felt a little knife thrust of jealousy. Did every man who met her fall in love with her?

"I will," Rainulf assured his friend stonily. "Rest assured of that."

Will nodded, and Rainulf thought he detected a glimmer of amusement in his eyes. He *knew* Rainulf was jealous.

"Send for me again if you need me," Will said. "I'll come at a moment's notice." He grinned as he disappeared into the stairwell. "Anything for Corliss!"

Rainulf swore Victor, Thomas, and Brad to secrecy, then sent them home. Returning to the bedchamber, he found Corliss staring at the ceiling, expressionless.

He sat on the edge of the bed. "Are you all right?"

She mumbled something shakily that sounded like "He touched me."

Rainulf leaned closer. "Who? Will?"

She sat up and looked down at herself with an expression of revulsion. "Burnell." Wrapping her arms around herself, she closed her eyes tight. "I can feel his hands on me. Everywhere he touched me, I can feel his hands."

Rainulf encircled her with his arms. "He's gone, Corliss. He's dead."

"I can smell him," she choked. "I can smell him on me. And his blood ... I'll never get it off." Staring in horror at her bloody arms and chest, she began to shake again.

He held her tightly. "You can wash it off, Corliss. All of it, the blood, the smell ... and then he'll be gone. You can wash him off with soap and water." She shook her head, but he was insistent. "Yes. I'll heat up some water for a bath. 'Twill work. You'll see."

He put the kettle on and dragged the bathtub into her chamber, next to the brazier for warmth.

"Will they talk about me?" she asked, sitting on the edge of the bed. "Victor and Thomas and Brad. Will they tell people I'm a woman?"

"I made them promise not to."

She nodded slowly. "Will it work?"

He sighed. "I trust them. But . . ." He raked a hand through his hair.

"But?"

He sat next to her and took her hand; it felt as lifeless as she looked. "I wish I could say with certainty that no one will ever find out. But in my experience, secrets are the most fragile of commodities. The truth is far stronger, far more stubborn. Sooner or later, it will assert itself."

"So people *will* find out who I am."

"Not necessarily that you're Constance of Cuxham. But I'm fairly certain your true sex will become public knowledge eventually."

She was silent for a long moment. "Then I should leave here."

"Nay!" He turned to face her.

"But what of the chancellorship? The bishop will never appoint you if he knows you're living with a woman. And if he finds out after you accept it, he'll probably remove you from office. You'll be disciplined, and your reputation—"

He closed his hands over her shoulders. "Let me worry about my reputation. You need my protection— now, more than ever."

"But if the price for my protection is the chancellorship—"

"This is not the time for you to leave here, Corliss," he said fiercely, "not after what's happened. Not when you're hurt, and with this Pigot still looking for you." He gripped her shoulders hard and gave them a little shake. "Promise me you'll do nothing rash. Promise me you'll stay."

She lowered her head, biting her lip. "I can't stay

if my presence jeopardizes everything you've been working for."

"Right now it jeopardizes nothing. No one knows."

"But they will. You said so yourself."

"God, Corliss, you're exasperating. And you're scaring me. I can see you taking it into your head to leave, just for the sake of the damned chancellorship."

"I won't leave . . ."

"Thank God."

"Until I have to."

"Corliss . . ."

"Right now, a handful of people know I'm a woman. If anyone else figures it out, I'm going to go away—before the bishop finds out."

"Why can't you just let *me* decide what's best for me?"

"Because you're too kindhearted. If you heard people talking about me, you'd probably just ignore it, for my sake."

"No, I wouldn't."

"You'd ask me to leave if I become a liability to you?"

"Aye." Would he? Could he find it in his heart to order her from his home? Perhaps; he wouldn't be ordering her out of his life, after all. It wasn't as if he'd never see her again—as long as she stayed in Oxford. She'd probably want to, having established such a dazzling reputation on Catte Street. Everyone in the book business admired her work. The Becket Bible was almost finished, and then she'd have her choice of lucrative commissions. He could find her an apartment, some suitable place where she could work and live. He might be able to do it.

"Really?" she asked, perhaps sensing his uncertainty.

He adopted a resolute expression. "Absolutely. When the time comes, I'll ask you to leave."

She said nothing for a moment. Her face was pale

and drawn; her eyes glistened. "Good," she said hoarsely, looking away.

"Corliss . . ."

"I think the water's probably hot by now," she said. He tried to turn her to face him, but she wrested out of his grasp and started for the main hall. "I'll get it."

"Nay, I will. You rest."

Rainulf filled the wooden tub and left her, pulling the curtain closed behind him. Then he poured himself a brandy in the main hall. He heard the water being displaced as she got in the tub, and turned automatically toward the sound. Through a narrow gap in the curtain, he saw a flicker of pale flesh as she sat in the tub. The sight reminded him of that time he'd seen her bathing at Blackburn Castle, and it made him ache in the same way; it made him long to touch and hold and possess that which he had only ever seen in brief, tantalizing glimpses.

He exchanged his bloodstained shirt for a fresh one; then nursed the brandy for some time, letting his thoughts float where they would. He mused on the chancellorship, wondering how it would feel to give up teaching for the sterile, dispassionate arena of administration. He thought about Corliss, and how she had forced him to feel what he hadn't felt in years, as well as some things—like his love for her—that he'd never felt. She'd made him human again. She'd awakened him, as if he'd been a hibernating creature and she'd reached into his hole and dragged him, growling and clawing, out into the sunlight.

A soft sound from the bedchamber drew his attention, and he stilled, straining to hear. An indrawn breath . . . and another . . . and another, this time with a slight hitch.

He stood, set down his cup, and crossed to the leather curtain. "Corliss?"

She didn't answer, but he could hear muffled gasps; not gasps, but sobs being choked back.

"Corliss. Are you all right?" Foolish question, not deserving of an answer; none was forthcoming.

"I'm coming in, Corliss." He paused, then drew aside the curtain.

She sat facing away from him in the big wooden tub, her arms wrapped tightly around her updrawn knees, her bare back shaking, although little sound came from her. He had the sense that she was trying to contain her sobs, but having a hard time of it.

He circled the tub and knelt in front of her. She lowered her head to her knees, her fine-boned shoulders convulsing with the strain it took to keep from crying out loud. He wove his fingers through her damp hair, stroking her scalp. Her nudity—although he could see little of her in the dim lamplight, tightly enfolded as she was—enhanced her aura of vulnerability. The effort it cost her to fight her tears broke his heart.

"Let it out, Corliss," he softly urged. "Go ahead. Cry."

She shook her head.

"Yes." He gently rubbed her wet shoulders and back. "Come on." Leaning over, her kissed her on the top of her head. That simple gesture of affection seemed to push her over the edge, robbing her of her hard-fought control. She cried in earnest, shaking with her sobs, tears streaming down her reddened face.

"That's right," he soothed, holding her as best he could. "That's right. 'Twill make you feel better. Everything's all right."

She shook her head.

"Yes, it is."

"N-nay," she choked out. "I'm a f-fool."

"No you're not. I told you—you didn't bring this on yourself. None of this is your fault. You know that in your heart. Don't torment yourself this way." He murmured reassurances to her for some time, until her tears diminished and her breathing steadied.

They'd switched positions, he realized. Always in the past, she'd been the one trying to cheer him up, to encourage him to accept what he knew in his heart and stop analyzing things. Now it was the other way around. He didn't seem to be doing a very good job of it, though. She may have stopped crying, but she looked miserable, devastated. Still curled into a tight ball, she rubbed her face, her breath catching as she struggled to regain her composure.

"Here." He rose and fetched the towel she'd laid out to dry herself off with. Standing behind her, he unfolded the large square of linen and held it open. "Stand up."

She hesitated; then, apparently realizing the towel would shield her from his view, she stood. He wrapped the big cloth around her and supported her as she stepped out of the tub. Taking her in his arms, he rubbed her through the linen. "How do you feel?"

She shrugged.

He sighed and held her close, feeling her trembling heat through the thin, damp cloth. Something inside him unfurled, warming him from within. It was something he'd never felt before: part protectiveness and part desire. He wanted to shelter her. He also wanted to join his body with hers. As he held her, the two urges merged into something unique and strangely powerful.

So this is what it feels like to love a woman.

He left the chamber to give her some privacy, returning once she'd changed into her nightgown—one of the silk shifts Martine had given her. While he emptied and removed the bathtub, she sat on the edge of her bed, hands curled limply in her lap, eyes vacant.

Kneeling at her feet, Rainulf enclosed her hands in his, rubbing her palms with his thumbs. She still gazed at nothing, lost in her melancholy. He felt so helpless, so useless, so terrified to see her this way.

"I don't know what to do, what to say to ease your

sadness," he whispered. "You're so much better at this than I am."

She bit her lip; tears welled in her eyes. He lowered his head to her lap and wrapped his arms around her waist. "Nay, don't cry. I didn't mean to make you cry again." He felt her fingers in his hair and felt a flutter of optimism. She wasn't completely closed off from him; he *was* doing some good.

He raised his head and found her looking at him. Forcing a smile, he reached up and stroked her cheek. She closed her eyes.

His gaze followed the curve of her throat to the nick at its base. The long scratch down her chest was hidden by her silk shift, which laced down the front. "Did you put on the salve Will left?"

She shook her head. "I forgot," she said, her voice rusty from crying.

Rainulf got up and fetched the little jar. "Lie down."

She scooted back on the bed and lay with her head on the pillow. Sitting beside her, he opened the jar and dipped a finger into the amber-colored balm. She closed her eyes, tilting her chin up to give him access to her throat, and he dabbed the salve gingerly on the little cut.

He hesitated for just a moment before untying the cord that laced her shift closed. She opened her eyes and looked at him, but he avoided her gaze. Drawing the cord through the eyelets carefully, to avoid irritating her wound, he slowly unlaced the gown almost to the waist. He pushed aside the silk, then dipped up some more salve. Starting at the top of the shallow cut, he applied the soothing medication with as gentle a touch as he could manage.

Her breathing quickened as he slowly worked his way down the shallow cut; so did his. When he was done, he cleared his throat. "Does it still hurt?"

"Nay." She hadn't looked away from him this whole time. "The one on my neck does a little."

Bending down, he softly pressed his lips to one side of the little wound. He felt her pulse speed up just beneath the hot satin skin, felt her throat move as she swallowed. The sensation was unexpectedly erotic; he felt a heaviness in his lower body, felt his chausses stretch as he grew hard.

He kissed her throat again and again, all over—whispering-soft kisses, his lips barely grazing the creamy flesh. Taking her head gently between his hands and tilting it, he touched his lips to the underside of her jaw, which was indescribably, unbearably soft; and then to the edge of the jaw itself, bestowing a path of soft kisses along the graceful curve of bone beneath smooth-stretched skin. When his mouth passed lightly over her ear, she took in a startled little breath. Closing his lips over her delicate earlobe, he touched his tongue to it, and heard her sigh.

He tangled his hands in her hair, half-dried by the warm night air into unruly curls. Hers skimmed upward from his elbows, braced on either side of her, to his shoulders, which she gripped ever more tightly in response to his gentle attentions.

Kissing her cheek, he tasted salt. Without thinking, he licked her dried tears. Instinct had taken over; his analytical mind had shut down. He'd never felt so unencumbered, so free of restraint, so driven. The heat that consumed him wasn't limited to his stiff and aching member; his entire body felt as if it were on the verge of a crisis of pleasure. He vibrated with a power and energy that went beyond lust, that promised limitless possibilities.

Corliss's eyelids were puffy; he pressed his lips to them, and then to the tip of her nose, pink and shiny. His mouth hovered over hers now, and for the first time, he looked her directly in the eyes. Her pupils were enormous black pools encircled with flecks of bronze and copper and gold. She met his gaze unwaveringly, but with a sharp little glimmer of wonder, a spark that shot between them like heat lightning. He felt the same wonder, the same ecstatic incredulity. They smiled into each other's eyes, two beings with the same thought, the same desire, the same driving need to merge their bodies into one; Rainulf had never experienced such intimacy with anyone.

He looked at her lips, blood flushed and swollen from crying; his own lips tingled with the need to touch them. The prospect of kissing her, after all these months of wanting to, imagining it, craving it, filled him with a drunken excitement that made his senses whirl. She watched him intently, her breath coming faster, as he lowered his mouth on hers. The moment before contact, she closed her eyes, and so did he.

Her lips were warm satin beneath his, and they tasted of her tears. He kissed her lightly at first, barely brushing her lips with his, reveling in her soft sighs of capitulation and pleasure—wordless promises of things to come. Her hands roamed over his shoulders through his linen shirt, meeting behind his neck to bring him closer. He deepened the kiss, devouring her mouth, greedy for that which he'd imagined so vividly and waited for so long. Flicking his tongue across her lips, he darted it between them until it found her own.

She gasped. He opened his eyes and saw her bewildered expression.

Had she never felt a man's tongue in her mouth before? Clearly not. Just as she'd never been properly bedded; just as she'd never been well and thoroughly kissed. Despite her sexual experience, there was an untapped innocence about Corliss. The same could be said of him, of course, after eleven years of abstinence. If Corliss had much to learn, so did he; they must teach each other.

He kissed her again, at first chastely, murmuring reassurances, then lightly stroking the seam of her lips with the tip of his tongue. She quivered. "Let me in," he breathed. Another light caress of the tongue, and another ... Her lips parted tremulously, and his tongue slipped between them ... to meet hers.

Yes ... She held him by the back of the head as she explored this new pleasure. A hum of satisfaction coursed through him. He settled against her, one leg resting between hers, his erection hard against her soft stomach. She pressed her hands to the small of his back to urge him closer.

He thrust against her just once, then held himself still, sucking in a breath. *It's too soon. ... You're too close.*

Breaking the kiss, he shifted his weight and moved down, lowering his mouth to her collarbone. He touched it with his lips, and she shivered. Easing aside the silk, he trailed kisses along the delicate ridge, and back again. He lay next to her and kissed a slow path adjacent to the thin red line etched down the center of her chest, breathing in the sweetness of her skin mingled with the herbal salve.

He felt her silk-clad breast against the side of his face, felt her nipple stiffen as his cheek grazed it. Arousal flared within him, and he tightened his arms around her. When he felt her hands in his hair, he heard a low, shuddering groan, and realized it had come from him.

Chapter 16

Overwhelmed with sensation, Corliss closed her eyes. She felt the soft flax of his hair between her fingers, felt the heat of his breath through the thin silk covering her breast. Her melancholy, so bleak and suffocating, had evaporated almost completely, like nighttime fog burned off by the hot morning sun.

Again she felt, through the sleek fabric, the pressure of his cheek—scratchy with the slight growth of beard that always darkened it in the evening. This time, she knew, the contact was deliberate. He nuzzled her, gently rubbing his prickly jaw on her tender flesh. The friction against her nipple sparked little thrills of pleasure that coursed throughout her, coming together between her legs like streaks of lightning converting at a single white-hot target point.

She felt a shivery heat and realized he was kissing her breast through the shift. Her heart pumped so hard, it hurt. She arched her back. His lips brushed her nipple, and she gasped. Impatiently sweeping aside the silk, he closed his mouth over the tight little bud.

So hot. So hot and wet. She moaned softly as Rainulf gently tugged on her supersensitive nipple, caressing it with his tongue. He threw a long leg over hers and let the hard length of his erection rest against her thigh. For a timeless, dreamy interlude, they lay together like that, Rainulf suckling while she spiraled slowly upward, into a state of breathless arousal.

She felt the dampness between her legs, the little

pulses of pleasure, and was astounded. The last time she'd felt like this was when he'd come to her that night at Blackburn and slipped his hand beneath her quilt. That she could experience the same kind of physical passion without that kind of touch was a revelation.

When he finally moved, it was to slide his hot, rough hand beneath the silk and close it over her other breast. He squeezed her gently, fondling her nipple until she thought she'd scream.

She writhed as his mouth and hand worked their dark sorcery; he tensed his hips, pressing himself against her thigh. Her own hips moved without her willing it. He answered her unspoken need by smoothing his hand downward from her breast until it found the white-hot need between her legs.

Oh, God, she thought as he caressed her through the damp silk, *I'm going to go mad from pleasure.*

He pulled her shift up and glided his hand between her legs. The first light probing of his fingers galvanized her. She moaned unself-consciously, clutching at his hair as he explored her wet recesses. It was torment—sweet, unbearable torment.

"Rainulf . . . Rainulf . . ."

He raised his head and met her gaze. His eyes glittered with the same wolflike hunger she'd seen one time before, when he'd gotten up and walked away from her after giving her such incredible pleasure. This time, she knew, he would not walk away. This time he would find what he wanted—what they both wanted.

He sat beside her and whipped his shirt off over his head, then untied his chausses and kicked them off.

God, he's magnificent! She sat up, staring openly as he kneeled before her, gathering her shift in his clutched hands. From wide, sinuous shoulders, his torso was carved in a graceful contour, sloping dramatically toward narrow hips. He was the epitome of masculine strength and beauty.

Rainulf pulled the nightgown over her head and smiled. For a few hushed moments, they just looked at each other, naked together for the first time.

Rainulf's lean body vibrated with immense strength held in reserve. His arms and legs, banded with muscle, might have been those of a stonecutter. His flat belly was strikingly ridged; on one side of his lower abdomen, just beneath the taut surface, a single vein snaked from hipbone to pubic hair. Her gaze was drawn to the straining organ rising from that hair. It gleamed silkily in the lamplight, a tiny teardrop at the tip. *So . . . arousal makes him wet, too.* It seemed she had much to learn about men, after all.

Rainulf reached out almost tentatively and trailed his fingertips over her face, her throat, her shoulders, breasts, belly, and hips. "God, you're so beautiful," he whispered. "I can't believe how beautiful you are."

"So are you." She ran her fingers through the impossibly soft fur that blanketed his solid chest, following it down to the dense tangle between his legs. He sucked in a breath when her hand brushed his rampant sex. She lightly touched it, and he gripped her shoulders hard. Drawing her hand up its taut length, she smoothed the hot little droplet with her fingertips.

He growled low in his throat. "Corliss . . ." She glided her moist fingers down the quivering shaft, and up again. He groaned and grabbed her wrist, then seized her by the back of the head and took her mouth in a hard, searing kiss, his beard abrading the tender skin around her lips. The rhythmic invasion of his tongue felt so frankly sexual that she moved her body against him; he grabbed her hips and thrust hard against her belly. She wrapped her arms around him— flinching when his chest hair came in contact with her dagger wound.

He backed away sharply. "Corliss! God, I'm such an ass. What am I doing?"

"What I want you to do." She tried to embrace him, but he held her at arm's length.

"I can't. 'Twill hurt you."

She laughed incredulously and grabbed him around the neck, pulling him down on top of her as she fell backward onto the bed. "If you don't, *I'll* hurt *you*!"

He chuckled as he lowered himself carefully, holding himself up on his elbows to keep his weight off her. It so gratified her to hear his easy laughter; to see the way he looked at her with such longing; and to feel him hot and hard and ready between her legs. She was ready, too; she throbbed with need. He nudged her wet opening. She closed her hands over his shoulders and arched against him, begging him wordlessly to fill her. *Now.*

"Nay," he whispered, poised to enter her but making no move to do so. Beneath her hands, the hard muscles of his shoulders quivered with strain. His face was darkly flushed and the little vein on his forehead pulsed.

"Rainulf ... Oh, God ..." Frustration swelled in her throat, tears stung her eyes. Had he changed his mind? After all those years of celibacy, had he decided, at the last moment, that he couldn't do this?

He shook his head. "Corliss, I can't—"

"*No!*"

"—without telling you—"

"Don't do this!" The tears spilled out; her chest shook. "God, Rainulf, don't stop now."

"*Stop?*" An astonished huff of laughter escaped him. "I couldn't stop now. I just need you to know that I love you." His voice caught. To her astonishment, his eyes shimmered wetly. "I love you, Corliss. I'm in love with you."

He flexed his hips. She felt the broad, wet tip of him inch into her, just enough to stretch her open.

"Oh, God ..." She laughed and cried as he paused and then pressed in again—a delicious, almost painful intrusion, sharply pleasurable. "I love you, too." Taking his face between her hands, she kissed him. "I love you." And again. "I love you. I've always loved you."

Rainulf watched the tears spill down her cheeks: hers and his, mingling together. *She loves me! Corliss loves me!*

She threw her head back, her eyes half-closed in ecstasy, smiling that guilessly joyful smile of hers. He should have known that she'd approach lovemaking as she did the rest of life: eagerly and uninhibitedly, with an awe-inspiring sense of wonder.

And she loved him! She loved him!

Painfully aroused, he longed to drive himself into her with one fierce stab, but she was so extremely tight that he worried about hurting her. Instead, he gritted his teeth against that urge and pushed in slowly, again and again, easing farther and farther into her as she stretched around his unyielding thickness.

Her hips trembled, her breath came in frantic little pants. Just seeing her like this—half-delirious with pleasure as her climax approached—nearly stripped him of his resolve to go slowly. That resolve vanished altogether when she reached around him to slide her hands from the small of his back to his buttocks, pressing down hard—a wordless but eloquent entreaty, and one that he couldn't resist.

Bracing himself on one forearm, he reached beneath her and tilted her hips up. He withdrew to the tip, then thrust forcefully, sheathing himself completely within her. They groaned in unison. God, it was incredible, being buried deep inside her—even better than he'd imagined it would be, better than all his exaggerated memories of women from his past. He did feel virginal. This might as well have been the first time he'd ever lain with a woman. It felt extraordinary—the slick, tight heat and maddening pressure, compelling him all too swiftly toward completion.

Pulling almost all the way out, he sank in again to the hilt.

"Oh, God . . ." She grew rigid, clutching his back.

With his next thrust, she cried out—a raw, womanly cry of fulfillment—as her body convulsed, rocking beneath him. From deep within her, a succession of spasms gripped him, like a slippery hand stroking, pulling, squeezing. . . .

Not yet . . . not yet . . . Gripping her hair in his fists, he tried to hold still, to make it last, but her ecstatic cries and movements, and the rhythmic contractions pumping him from within, undid him. His body took over—tightening, arching, ramming deep, deep inside her. Pleasure gathered, drew up, erupted, shooting into her with astonishing force, wracking him with its power.

For a few endless moments, he couldn't think or see or hear. His blood ceased to flow; his lungs ceased to breathe. He came with luxurious intensity, as if his entire body were coming, filling her with his essence, his seed, his love.

When his ears stopped ringing and his body stopped quaking, he became aware of hands on his shoulders, pushing. He opened his eyes to find himself lying heavy and sated atop Corliss, his head limp in the crook of her neck, his face buried in her fragrant hair. She was trying to push him off her. . . .

Her cut! He was hurting her. "Oh, God." He levered himself up, taking his weight on his arms. "Corliss, I'm sor—"

Pressing her fingertips to his mouth, she smiled. "Shh." She caressed his beard-roughened cheek and jaw and chin.

"I wish I'd shaved for you," he said.

"Nay, I like it." She grinned and bit her lip. "I like the way it scratches me." She stretched like a cat, then pressed down again on his buttocks. "And I love feeling you inside me. I want you to stay inside me forever."

"I'd give anything if that were possible."

For a moment, he sobered, as the reality of their situation intruded on his bliss. They were lovers now, he and Corliss. Lovers, and in more than a physical sense. He loved her. He needed her, wanted her.

He also needed and wanted the chancellorship, to which he would be appointed within the next few weeks. A man with a mistress might teach, if he were willing to forsake higher administrative posts, but he could not hold the position of Chancellor of Oxford. And any attempt to keep a *secret* lover—in or out of his home—was pointless, of course. He'd seen colleagues ruined more than once over a woman they were convinced would never be discovered.

Her hand lightly stroking his furrowed brow drew him out of his dark ruminations. "You mustn't be sad," she gently scolded.

He expelled a long, troubled sigh, and rested his forehead against hers. "But what are we—"

"Shh." She caressed his hair, his neck and shoulders. "We're going to love each other. For as long as it lasts."

"But I want it to last forever."

"So do I. I wish it could." She did, desperately. But the unalterable truth was that it couldn't. It was a painful truth, unbearably painful, and one that she couldn't bear to contemplate right now, with his arms around her, his body inside hers. "Promise me," she said, "that you won't think of these things while we're together. We only have until the end of the summer. Let's spend that time making each other happy." Smiling, she wrapped her legs around his waist. "Let's spend it making love."

He smiled, too. "Vixen. You've always been adept at changing the subject." Slipping an arm beneath her, he scooped her up—still intimately connected to him, with her legs encircling him—and sat back on his heels. She laughed delightedly, never having conceived that a man and a woman could be joined in such a position.

Gripping her hips, he drove into her, quick and fierce. "I want to feel you come again," he whispered hoarsely. His erection had waned, of course, but he was still mostly hard, and the friction of his thrusts against her slippery-wet sex was incredibly stimulating. Closing her eyes, she held on to his shoulders and arched her back, matching his vigorous strokes with her own.

"God, you're beautiful," he rasped. "So beautiful."

They connected with increasing urgency, the bed ropes creaking in time to their ragged gasps. He moaned, and she realized he'd grown fully erect again. His shoulders felt slippery beneath her hands, like rain-slicked rocks. Opening her eyes, she saw that he was wet with perspiration. So was she; he could barely keep a grip on her hips. He had his head thrown back, his expression one of excruciating pleasure, the cords on his neck standing out in sharp relief.

"Oh ... oh, God ..." With a guttural growl, he shuddered, his fingers digging into her hips. He rammed her down hard on his pulsing organ. She felt the hot jetting of his seed inside her, and then her own climax was upon her, exploding from their joined flesh and rolling throughout her, shaking her senseless.

Oh, yes, she thought as the tremors diminished and he eased her down to lie next to him, their bodies, breathless and soaking wet, still joined, his arms gathering her to him, his kisses all over her face hot and sweet and a little rough, a little unbearably, heartbreakingly scratchy ... *I want him to stay inside me forever. Forever and ever ...*

Rainulf awoke, blinking at the brilliant sunrise that glowed through the closed, saffron bed curtains. After being awake most of the night, he wanted nothing more than to roll over and go back to sleep, but it was far too bright.

He turned his head and smiled. Corliss lay on her back beneath the sheet, her face and arms golden in the diffuse yellow light. Like a child, she slept in awkward elegance, one arm thrown over her head, her legs at impossible angles. Her breathing was slow and steady, lips slightly parted, showing the edges of her perfect teeth. Across her forehead lay a wriggly lock of hair, enhancing the image of sensual dishevelment. She smelled warm and sleepy and deliciously sexual.

Last night had been a feast of passion after eleven years of famine. Rainulf had been as indefatigable as a randy youth, eager to do everything he'd denied himself for so long. He'd taken her from behind; he'd taken her against the wall. The variety of positions had amazed Corliss, but she'd been eager to learn, eager to please. She *had* pleased him, profoundly. There was no pretense about her, no pointless effort to act the blushing lady even in the throes of passion, as had been the case with too many of his youthful conquests. He'd come to think of them as willing vessels, whereas Corliss was much more an eager participant—wonderfully uninhibited, not bothering to temper her reactions or stifle her cries of pleasure.

The only thing he'd done last night that had shocked her—truly shocked her—was when he lowered his mouth to the damp, intoxicating nest of curls between her thighs. Speechless at first, she shoved him away. He went slowly then, persuading her with gentle entreaties and the skillful coaxing of his lips and tongue (funny the things one never forgets how to do!) into giving this strange new pleasure a chance. Gradually her murmurs of distaste were replaced by sighs of gratification; her resistance mellowed, her legs opened, her fingers clutched his hair. . . . Her ecstasy became his ecstasy, his satisfaction. Afterward, she turned the tables on him, stunning him by pleasuring him with her mouth as he had pleasured her. He'd roused to her for the fifth time, but finished inside her, making slow, dreamy love, as if they had all the time in the world, as if they truly could be united in sensual bliss forever.

Remembering last night made the blood rush fast and hot to his groin. Reaching beneath the sheet, he touched his distended flesh gingerly. After last night's excesses, it felt as raw as if it had been sanded, yet still it throbbed with the need to reclaim its territory, to penetrate, to possess.

Reclining next to the sleeping Corliss, he reached out and gradually lowered his hand over the sheet covering her chest. He barely grazed the finely woven linen, which tickled his palm and fingertips. Slowly— so slowly—he smoothed his hand over the subtle rise of one breast and then the other, feeling their warmth and softness through the sheet. It was strangely mesmerizing to touch her this way, while she slept unaware. As he softly stroked her, her nipples began to stiffen.

He trailed his hand down over the gentle slope of her belly, feeling the drum-tight flesh and the tiny, oddly seductive indentation of her navel. From there, he let his hand drift down between her parted legs, caressing her with aching gentleness until she grew hot and damp through the thin sheet. His touch was airy as a feather, and she slept through this as well, although her breathing quickened.

She moved slightly, snuggling into the feather mattress and arching her hips, just once. With careful movements he rolled on top of her, entering her in one long, smooth stroke. Her only acknowledgment of this was a contented exhalation. She was still asleep! Holding himself stiff-armed above her, he thrust very slowly, too sore in any case to do otherwise.

Her eyelids fluttered. "Rainulf ..." He liked the

way she said his name, all sleepy-gruff, like the growl of a kitten. Her eyes crinkled with pleasure when she realized he was inside her. She bent her knees and raised her hips, meeting his languid strokes.

He touched her where they were joined, and she writhed, transported. "Yes ..." she breathed. "Yes ... yes ..."

He teased her sensitive flesh, backing off occasionally to add an element of frustration to her escalating arousal, wanting to drive her half-mad with desire before granting her release. It worked; she thrashed beneath him, fairly whimpering with her need.

A door opened. Footsteps thudded on the stairs.

They froze.

"Luella!" Corliss whispered.

Rainulf groaned deep in his throat. God, he was on the verge of climax! So was Corliss. He tried to lie still, but his body betrayed him, the muscles of his buttocks tensing and releasing and tensing again.

"Father Rainulf!" the housekeeper hollered from the main hall. "Are you home, Father?"

He couldn't stop, not now. Cupping Corliss's small bottom, he thrust again, and again—slowly, so as not to make the bed ropes complain—as he forced his groans back down into his chest. The woman in his arms trembled violently. She stilled, her body taut and shivering, her nails sinking into his back.

"Corliss?" Luella called. Rainulf heard the leather curtain being swept aside, heard the old woman's heavy footsteps as she entered the chamber. She was in the room with them, separated only by the bed curtains!

Corliss opened her mouth in a wordless scream. She felt her internal contractions squeeze him, and then his own body convulsed suddenly, fiercely, discharging a torrent of seed deep into her heat.

As his orgasm waned, he slumped down, taking his weight on his elbows, and drew in a long, calming breath. Shuddering, they held each other as Luella slowly shuffled out of the chamber and reclosed the curtain.

"Do you think she heard us?" Corliss whispered.

"I don't know." She frowned. He recalled what she'd told him last night, about leaving here if anyone else discovered her true sex, and quickly amended his answer: "Nay. She didn't hear. These curtains are heavy."

Corliss glanced at the curtains, as if to verify that assessment. He held his breath until she nodded, her lower lip between her teeth.

Luella's footsteps slowly descended the stairs. The door opened and closed. Her voice rose from the street as she greeted a neighbor, telling him she was going marketing.

Rainulf drew himself slowly out of Corliss, and she flinched. "You're sore, too," he said, sitting up.

She sat facing him. "A little. 'Twas worth it." She smiled, but her eyes were sad.

He lightly stroked her face with his fingertips. "What is it?"

"I should leave now, you know. I should move out of here and get my own—"

"Nay! Luella doesn't know, she doesn't! And if we're discreet, she needn't—"

"I know that."

"Then why leave? You said you'd stay until people started suspecting—"

"That was before. Before we ..." She looked around at the mammoth bed, with its rumpled sheets and scattered pillows. "Before this." She shook her head miserably. "It was dangerous enough before, but now ..."

"How can you speak of the danger to me, when Pigot is still lurking out there, searching for you? You need my protection."

"My male disguise is my protection."

"You still believe that after last night?" He raked his fingers through his hair in frustration. "You have a bad habit of believing what you want to believe, Corliss. You're in grave danger. You must stay here until I can find safe accommodations for you elsewhere." He took her face in his hands and forced her to look at him. "You said we had until the end of the summer. I'm holding you to that. I'll be damned if I'll give you up yet."

He started to say more, but she cut him off. "I'll stay until you're formally appointed chancellor, as long as no one finds out about me before then. But after that, I—" Her voice quavered. "I'll have to cut myself off from you entirely. No horrid little secret meetings—I'd hate that, and there'd be the risk of discovery. A clean break. It's the only way."

He squeezed his eyes closed against the grim immutability of her words. Drawing her into his arms, he rasped, "We aren't supposed to be talking about this, remember? We're just going to love each other. That's all. No talking."

An hour later, as Corliss sat down to share a breakfast of bread and watered ale with Rainulf, there came a furious pounding on the door. She flinched. *What now?*

"Master Fairfax! Master Fairfax! Come quickly!"

"That's Thomas." Rainulf sprinted down the stairs, and Corliss followed, her heart rattling in her chest. Downstairs they found Thomas and Brad, breathless and overwrought.

"It's Victor!"

"The townsmen came and dragged him out of bed! They've beaten him half to death!"

"Damn."

Corliss ran as fast as she could to keep up with Rainulf and the two scholars as they raced down St. John Street and up Grope Lane. A group of townsmen, their voices raised in fury, stood in a loose circle around something on the ground. Corliss smelled death.

"What goes here?" Rainulf demanded loudly.

The circle parted, revealing, beneath a swarm of flies, Burnell's rank, gray-faced corpse supine in a pool of dried blood. Two men held Victor by the arms—held him up, for he was bloodied and battered, and doubtless couldn't have stood on his own. Corliss recognized him only from his long, dark hair and the green tunic beneath his torn cappa, which she knew to be his. His striking features were obscured by cuts and bruises. Around his neck he wore a noose at the end of a rope, which a third man held wound around his fist.

To Corliss's amazement, Victor half bowed when he saw Rainulf, and even managed a grim smile. "Good morning, Magister. Care to get in a few licks before they stretch my neck?"

One of the men holding him rammed a fist into his lower back. He doubled over, grunting.

Rainulf shouldered the men aside and stepped into the circle. "Where's the sheriff?"

The man holding the rope—massive, red faced, and slightly familiar looking—jabbed a finger toward Rainulf, growling in Anglicized French, "Piss on the sheriff! Piss on Victor of Aeskirche! And piss on you! Piss on all of you!" He screamed at the handful of black-robed scholars gathering at a distance, who responded with obscene gestures and a few choice epithets.

Rainulf nodded toward the noose around Victor's neck. "You're going to hang him just like that?"

The man with the rope pointed to the corpse. Corliss felt a tickle of wrongness in the back of her mind. Something was different about Burnell—out of place—although she couldn't put her finger on it. "He killed my brother—*just like that*!" the big man spat out.

"He killed Pyt's brother!" someone cried out. "He deserves to die!"

"Bloodthirsty, murderin' bastard!" another voice screamed. "Shit-eating spawn of a whoring priest!"

"I've never eaten shit," Victor informed this man, who blinked at this news.

Pyt yanked on the rope, almost jerking Victor out of the grip of the men holding him. "Last night this whoreson jumped my brother and slit his throat in cold blood."

Corliss stepped forward. "Nay!" Rainulf seized her arm and yanked her back, hard. She looked at him. He met her gaze for only the briefest moment, his eyes flashing a sharp warning. She understood the warning perfectly: This crowd was primed for a hanging; it could be hers as easily as Victor's. She didn't want to hang, but nor did she want to see Victor take the blame for something he didn't do. If anyone was responsible for Burnell's death, it was she, although she doubted these men would care that it was in self-defense.

Rainulf folded his arms and addressed Burnell's brother in calm, authoritative tones. "What makes you think Victor was responsible for this?"

Before Pyt could answer, Victor made a raspy, pained sound that Corliss realized was laughter of sorts. "Now, honestly, Magister. Can you think of a more likely candidate?"

The red-faced brute punched Victor in the stomach, then brought forth a dagger, which he handed to Rainulf. Corliss moved closer to inspect it as the magister turned it over in his hands. Carved into the bone hilt was the initial *V.*

"We found this on St. John Street, at the end of a trail of blood," said Pyt. "Everyone knows it's Victor's. He's waved it around often enough—usually at Burnell."

"Did anyone bother to question Victor?" Rainulf inquired. "What does *he* say?"

That was smart, thought Corliss. Get the accused's story before he starts speculating—offering alternatives.

The brute grunted dismissively. "He didn't have much to say. Claims he didn't do it, but wouldn't say who did. Don't take one of you"—he sneered—"*fine gentlemen of learning* to figure out he's lying."

"Oh, God," Corliss moaned. Victor was protecting her! He could have named her, but instead he'd taken this savage beating and let them drape a noose around his neck. She couldn't let him do this! She had to stop this! Victor must have sensed her panicky determination; he caught her eye and shook his head fractionally.

"Hang the bastard!" someone yelled, and others quickly took up the chant: "Hang him! Hang him! Hang him!"

As they started dragging Victor away, the audience of scholars began gathering rocks and sticks, and closing in; some had daggers, and one even produced a sword from beneath his cappa. "Wait!" Rainulf ordered them, and they paused. He grabbed Pyt by the arm and swung him around. "You've no right to hang him without a trial."

Pyt drew himself up and seized Rainulf by the front of his tunic, screaming, "He had no right to do what he done to my brother!" He pointed to the corpse. "Look at him!"

Corliss did look at him. Burnell's filmy eyes were half-open; his flesh, drained of life, was a sickly noncolor. His coarse tunic was stiff with dried blood; the braies that encased his legs were spattered with it.

Blinking, she focused harder. The braies . . . She gasped. The braies!

She plucked at Rainulf's sleeve.

"Not now, Corliss," he ground out, pulling away.

"Rainulf, look at him!" she whispered, pointing to the lifeless body. "Don't you see?"

"What are you—"

Grabbing his arm, she whispered into his ear, "His braies! Somebody pulled them up."

Rainulf absorbed this for a moment; she saw enlightenment dawn in his eyes. "Who found the body?" he demanded.

The men looked at each other. "Marley found him.... Where's Marley?"

A rotund fellow stepped forward. "It was me," he said with an odd mixture of sheepishness and defiance. "I was driving my cart past here at dawn, and I seen him lyin' there, dead."

"What did you do?" Rainulf asked. "Tell me everything you did, as you did it."

Marley gaped. "I went and got Pyt and brung him back, so's he could see what they done to his brother."

"You didn't touch the body first?" Rainulf asked.

The fat carter crossed himself as he regarded the corpse with an expression of distaste. "Nay. I kept clear of it."

Rainulf turned toward Pyt. "Did *you* touch the body? Did you change anything about it?"

Corliss understood Rainulf's strategy: If he were to announce outright that Burnell had had his braies down last night, everyone would wonder how he'd known. It might come out that he—and she—had been there when Burnell took his dagger in the throat. Rainulf had to tease the information forth as if he were just fishing for facts in general, not one fact in particular.

"I don't see what you're gettin' at," Pyt said, "and I don't know as it's any of your business if I did touch him."

"Perhaps not," Rainulf conceded, "but the sheriff might consider it his business. He wouldn't like it if the body was disturbed before he had a chance to look it over. Now, think again." He spoke to Pyt, but looked significantly toward Victor, who frowned in puzzlement. "Did you move anything on the body, adjust anything . . . ?"

"His braies!" Victor exclaimed.

Rainulf expelled an audible sigh of relief; Corliss closed her eyes briefly, breathing a prayer of thanks.

"They were down around his ankles last night!" Victor said. "That's how I saw him last, stumbling away with his pants down."

A murmur bubbled through the crowd.

"Did you pull up his braies?" Rainulf asked Pyt.

"N-nay! I done nothin'!"

Pyt was lying, of course. Corliss could tell from Rainulf's skeptical expression that he knew this, but rather than confronting him, he focused his stern gaze on the carter. "It must have been you, then. The sheriff won't be pleased about this. You'll be lucky if you get off with a flogging."

"It wasn't me!" the fat man wailed. "I didn't do it! 'Twas Pyt!"

"You squealing pig," Pyt snarled, making a fist. "You lying son of a—"

"It's the truth!" Marley claimed, backing away from the enraged brute. "I swear it on my mother's soul. I saw him pull Burnell's braies up. I saw it with my own eyes!"

"What if I did?" said Pyt, wheeling on Rainulf. "I was just trying to set him straight, trying to give the man some dignity. Where's the harm in that?"

"The harm," Rainulf explained, loudly enough for everyone to hear, "lies in the fact that evidence has been altered. Burnell's having his pants down might indicate that last night's altercation was of an entirely different nature than what you're all assuming."

There were mumbles of bewilderment.

"I would recommend shorter words," Victor suggested dryly. He earned another fist in the stomach for this bit of insolence, but it looked to Corliss like a rather half-hearted punch compared to the others.

"In other words," Rainulf continued, "if it's true that Victor jumped Burnell and cut his throat, why did Burnell have his braies down? Is it possible that Burnell was in the middle of doing something he shouldn't have been, and Victor just happened on the scene?"

Pyt made a show of looking affronted. "If you're trying to say my brother was in the habit of peein' in the street—"

"That wasn't what I was implying," Rainulf said.

Pyt considered this for a moment, then managed a look of almost believable outrage. "Burnell was a married man!"

Snickering broke out in the crowd; men cleared their throats. The scholars were less discreet, hooting and offering loud and ribald observations on the character of the deceased. So much for Burnell having been "a married man."

"Your brother," Rainulf told Pyt, "had a reputation for viciousness. My guess is that he was trying to force himself on some unwilling woman—and that it wouldn't have been the first time."

Several of the men exchanged glances—glances that spoke volumes. Rainulf saw this and nodded slowly. "Nay . . . 'twouldn't have been the first time. Probably some of your own wives and sisters and daughters have fallen prey to Burnell, and not even told you."

Pyt looked furious. "Now, wait a minute—"

"Shut up, Pyt!" someone said. "Let the man talk."

"Here's a hypothesis," Rainulf said. The crowd muttered in confusion. "An idea," he said, "a possible explanation of what happened last night. Burnell attacked a woman. She defended herself. He ended up with his own dagger in his throat." A current of murmurs swept through the crowd. "Victor came upon the scene as Burnell was running away. He let the

attacker go in order to aid the victim, who begged
him not to speak of what had happened."

Victor chuckled. He looked impressed. "Excellent
hypothesis, Magister."

One of the men holding Victor asked him, "Is that
what happened? Take us to this woman. Prove it!"

"The idea," Victor explained slowly, "is that I can't
take you to her without violating her confidence.
Which I'm far too much of a gentleman to do." He
grinned. "Have I got it right, Master Fairfax?"

Rainulf, clearly unamused, said, "That's one possible scenario. And it seems a much more likely one—
given the braies around Burnell's ankles—than Victor's having committed coldblooded murder. The truth
is, you don't know what happened. I say let Victor
go, and let the sheriff do his job."

He reached for the rope, but Pyt held it out of his
reach. "Nay! You talk real smooth, Magister, and
maybe you can dupe some of these sorry curs, but you
can't dupe me. I'm on to you. You'll say anything to
protect one of your little pets."

Victor laughed. "Is that what I am now, Magister?
How touching."

Pyt backhanded Victor across the face and began
dragging him by the rope. "No more talk! It's time
for a hanging."

Rainulf stepped forward as several men closed in
on Pyt, knocking him aside and whipping the noose
from around Victor's neck.

"Give it up, Pyt," one of them said.

"Fairfax is right," said another as he shoved Victor
toward Rainulf, who grabbed him and held him up.
"We don't know what happened. We could be hanging
an innocent man."

"*Innocent?*" Pyt screamed as his friends led him
away to the raucous cheering of the scholars. "Victor
of Aeskirche was *born* guilty!"

"Good point," muttered Victor as he fainted dead
away.

Chapter 17

"I thought about you all through tonight's *disputatio*," Rainulf said, tossing a coin to a scholar with his cap out at the corner of Grope and St. John. Lowering his voice, he added, "About what I want to do to you when we get home."

Heat suffused Corliss. She smiled. "I *thought* you seemed a little distracted."

"Distracted?" He chuckled. "I was hard as a rock beneath my cappa the whole time. We definitely aren't having enough sex."

Corliss laughed, knowing this for the jest it was. Since the night before last, when they'd first shared a bed, they'd tupped like a pair of rabbits. Not a private moment went by that they didn't seize the opportunity, coupling with the fatalistic intensity of lovers who know they have but a limited time together.

When they weren't making love, they were doing what they could to ease the rapidly growing friction between the scholars and the townspeople. Victor's beating and near hanging had incensed his fellow students, even those moderates who had formerly eschewed his militant ways. They were up in arms now, vowing revenge. Several shops on High Street and Brewers Lane had been vandalized, and a handful of locals—including Burnell's brother, Pyt—had been beaten, though not severely.

Ironically, the man who had been instrumental in stoking these tensions—Victor of Aeskirche—seemed to be the only scholar in Oxford not espousing retribution. Although he hadn't left his rooms since his own beating, he'd issued two open letters to the academic community, pleading for tolerance and conciliation. He argued that the matter had gone too far, endangering innocent people—Corliss knew he meant her, not him—and publicly apologized for his part in bringing these troubles about.

Corliss used her influence with Victor's followers to try to persuade them to back off, but with limited success. Meanwhile, Rainulf played the role of mediator, meeting with groups on both sides to argue the points of the opposing faction, since no one would agree to convene face-to-face.

Throughout all of this, Corliss was never without an escort, usually Rainulf. As he reminded her regularly, Pigot was still presumably looking for her; she mustn't be alone for a moment. In truth, she didn't mind the protection, since it meant she had Rainulf's company on a nearly constant basis. Every moment she was with him, she felt an intoxicating buzz of sensual awareness. The way he looked at her, all hunger and heat ... his whispered words of love and yearning ... his stolen caresses in dark corners.... These things conspired to keep her ever in a state of breathless wanting. God, how she wanted him.

"It's late," Rainulf said. Then he added suggestively, "Luella will be gone when we get home."

"Oh?" Corliss said coyly. " 'Twill be quiet, then. Perhaps I can get started on this." She patted her satchel, which contained the last signature of the Becket Bible. But for these final pages, the illumination was complete. It merely remained for Mistress Clark to put the signatures in order and send them to the bookbinder.

"I'll give you something else to get started on," Rainulf said. "And we'll see if we can both finish at the same time."

Corliss yawned elaborately, hiding her grin behind her hand. "Mistress Clark nailed a 'For Sale' sign on the door of her shop this morning."

"Vixen!" His laugh was more of a growl. He greeted some passing scholars. "Aye, I saw the sign. I seem to recall she wants to raise sheep or some such."

"Goats and chickens," Corliss corrected. "Now she'll be able to. I don't know how much she's asking for the shop, but I'm sure it's a small fortune—it's the biggest one on Catte Street. And, of course, Chancellor Becket's paying her forty pounds for that Bible." She shook her head wistfully. "Forty pounds."

"There's a lot of money to be made in books. Especially in this city."

"Don't I know it," Corliss said. "A person could make a fortune, if they went about it the right way."

"Are you saying people like Enid Clark go about it the wrong way? She seems to have done well enough."

"She could do better. That shop of hers is enormous, and she only uses a small part of it. She's got two empty rooms downstairs, and I don't think she uses her cellar at all. If I had a shop that size, I wouldn't limit myself to just copying manuscripts and hiring out the rest. I'd do everything all in the one shop, from start to finish. I'd hire writers, parchmenters, scribes, illuminators, and bookbinders, and have them work together. 'Twould be much more efficient. One could make dozens of books in the time it takes to make three or four by this piecemeal method. Oh! And I wouldn't just take commissions. I'd turn part of it into a used-book shop, the best in Oxford. I'd live above the shop."

"An ambitious plan. There's no shop of its kind in Oxford—nor in Paris, that I know of."

She grinned, fully warmed to her topic. "I'd have a sign over the shop: Corliss of Oxford, *Venditrix Librorum.*"

"What would you do, exactly?"

"Well, I'd run things. And I'd illuminate books, of course. I'd save the fanciest illustrations for myself."

"Of course."

She glanced at him, suddenly self-conscious. "You're smiling at me. You think I'm a daydreaming idiot."

"I think you're delightful. So full of enthusiasm. I also think you're very perversely skilled at changing the subject, when all I really want is to seduce you. Does it amuse you to torment me?"

She shrugged. "It passes the time."

His smile became a grin—a decidedly wolfish grin. Pausing, he closed a hand around the back of her head and whispered in her ear, "I've got a better way to pass the time. When we get home, I'm going to strip those chausses off you and give you this." He stood close enough that she could feel, against her hip, the solid ridge beneath his layers of clothes. Her body reacted instantly, flooding with liquid heat.

She grinned. "I've got just the place to put it."

"I'll bet you do."

"It may be a little too tight."

"I'll manage."

"And wet."

He groaned. "Come on. Let's go home."

"Wouldn't you rather stop for a pint ... ?" she asked ingenuously.

"Nay!" Looking around quickly—St. John Street had grown dark and empty—he grabbed her hand and pulled. "Let's go home."

She giggled. "What's your hurry?"

Another furtive glance, and then he drew her hand through the front opening of his cappa, pressing it between his legs. He was enormous; even through his woolen tunic, she felt him throb. "Does this answer your question?"

"Oh, my." She stroked him firmly, and he caught his breath. "That's quite impressive, but I really do need to work on this book for Mistress Clark. A pity."

She turned and continued walking up the street. "I imagine you'll be terribly frustrated."

He fell into step next to her. "I *imagine* I'll throw you on the floor as soon as we get home, and—"

"Not if I get there first and lock you out!" Laughing, she sprinted ahead, running as fast as she could toward the big stone house. He called her name, but she didn't slow her pace. As she neared the front door, she head him behind her, racing to catch up, and felt an exhilarating little thrill of panic. She wrested the door open, darted inside, and slammed it, panting and giggling in the vestibule at the bottom of the stairwell, dark except for a faint wash of light from above.

She wondered about that light for a moment, trying to remember having lit any lamps before they left. But then the door shook; the handle jiggled. "Corliss!"

Breathless, she dropped her satchel and leaned with all her weight against the quaking door as she groped for the bolt, grinning to think of the look on his face if she *did* lock him out. Just as she thought she'd be able to slide the bolt home, the door jerked open.

Muscling his way inside, he seized her shoulders and shoved her back against the door, kicking it shut. She made as if to push him away, but he grabbed her wrists, pinning them over her head as he crushed her against the slab of oak. His kissed her hard and rubbed against her, groaning into her mouth.

She trembled with anticipation. When he released her wrists, her legs gave out. Rainulf caught her around the waist as she slid to the wooden floor. With strong, determined hands, he turned her around, guiding her onto her hands and knees. He knelt behind her, his cappa enclosing both of them, and gripped her hips, thrusting against her.

She'd never been so wet, so ready. "Now," she moaned, pulling at the drawstring around her waist. "Oh, God, *now!*"

He chuckled deep in his throat. "Are you sure? What about your work?"

Corliss grabbed his hand and brought it beneath her loosened chausses, to the slippery heat between her legs. They both gasped. He tugged the woolen hose down over her hips. She felt his fingers graze her bare flesh as he hurriedly untied his own chausses. Then she felt the hot, satin length of him brush her lightly as he positioned himself. . . .

A floorboard groaned overhead. Startled, they both looked up the stairs, their breath coming in harsh gasps.

Rainulf lowered his mouth to her ear. "Did you light those—"

"Nay."

There came another footstep from above, and another, and then the intruder began descending the stairs. Fear gripped Corliss with a paralyzing fist. Her heart thudded in her chest.

"Rainulf?" called a familiar voice. "Corliss?"

"Peter?" she whispered. Relief came and went in the space of a heartbeat. "Oh, my God!" She yanked her chausses up, fumbling with the waist-cord.

"Jesus!" Rainulf hissed as he pulled up his own chausses.

"I thought I heard you come in," Peter said as he came within view, "but you didn't come upstairs, so I wasn't . . ." His voice trailed off as his gaze took in the two of them, on the floor of the semidark vestibule, frantically righting their clothes. His smile faded. He looked at Corliss; she looked away. He looked at Rainulf. "You son of a bitch," he said quietly.

Rainulf rose to his feet. "Peter . . ."

"What kind of a man are you?" Peter's hands curled into fists at his side.

Corliss stood. "Peter, listen to me. I know how this looks. I know you must hate both of us right now, but—"

"Not you," he said in a low, strained voice. "I could never hate you. You're not to blame." He regarded Rainulf with a venomous glare, his fists quivering. "*He* is."

Rainulf held his palms up appeasingly. "Peter, let's talk about this."

Peter laughed harshly. "You're very good at talking, Rainulf. Very ... skillful, very persuasive." He glanced wretchedly at Corliss, smoothing down her tunic and finger combing her hair. "You used that skill to take advantage of Corliss. You violated the woman I'm going to marry."

"Peter, please," Corliss said, "I can't marry you."

"I still want you," he said. "This was *his* fault, not yours. I still love you."

"Peter, for God's sake," Rainulf said, "listen to her. She doesn't want to marry you."

Peter took a step toward him, brandishing the fists whose destructive power had become famous throughout England. "Shut up."

Rainulf stood his ground. "She tried to tell you, but you wouldn't—"

"*Shut up!*" The young knight leaped across the vestibule, grabbed Rainulf by the tunic, and hurled him against the wall. Hauling back, he drove his fist into Rainulf's stomach with the force of a battering ram.

"Peter, stop it!" Corliss begged.

"I don't want to fight you, Peter," Rainulf rasped as he struggled upright.

"I'm sure you don't."

Rainulf shook his head. "Not because you'll win. Because you're my friend."

"Our friendship is over." Peter aimed a punch at Rainulf's head. Rainulf dodged it. Howling as his fist hit the stone wall, Peter balled up his other hand and whipped it across Rainulf's face.

"Stop it!" Corliss screamed.

Rainulf's head wobbled; blood trickled from his

nose and stained his lips. "Damn it, Peter." He shook his head wearily, but didn't move from where he stood, there being no room for maneuvering in the tiny vestibule. "Don't do this." He took another powerful blow to the stomach, but blocked one intended for his ribs.

Corliss grabbed Peter's right arm as he swung it again. "It's not his fault, Peter! Stop this!"

Rainulf shook his head, saying hoarsely, "Go upstairs, Corliss."

"Nay!"

Peter wrested his arm free and swung again, connecting with the side of Rainulf's face. Grimacing, Rainulf swore under his breath as he massaged his jaw.

"Damn you!" Peter screamed. "What's the matter with you? Fight back!"

Rainulf shook his head slowly. "Nay. I won't fight you."

"Fight me!" Peter's face was a mask of anguish; his voice quavered. "Goddamn you, Rainulf, I know you can fight! What are you going to do? Just stand there and let me beat you to death?"

"You wouldn't do that," Rainulf said quietly.

"Don't be so sure." Peter's voice broke; his eyes shone in the dim half-light. "You've compromised my betrothed. I love her, and you—"

"You loved Magdalen."

Peter shoved Rainulf roughly. "Don't speak of Magdalen!"

"You loved Magdalen," Rainulf repeated calmly as he wiped his bloody mouth and chin with the back of his hand, "and she died."

"Shut up!"

"I'm sorry, Peter. Truly I am. But—"

"Shut up," Peter choked out.

"If you want me to shut up," Rainulf said, "you *will* have to beat me to death. There are things you need to face, things you need to accept. Corliss isn't Magdalen. You don't know what to do with your love for Magdalen, so you're trying to give it to Corliss, but it's not fair to either of you." He examined the blood on his hand and added wryly, "Or me."

"You're wrong," Peter insisted. "It's Corliss I love."

"Why? What do you love about her?"

The young knight looked slightly taken aback. "Her ... her beauty, her learning. Her—"

"Do you love the way she bites her lower lip when she's nervous about something?" Before Peter could formulate an answer, he went on: "Do you love the way you can see right through her skin, like it was the thinnest, softest parchment? Do you love the way she can't stop asking questions? The way she finds the damnedest things funny? The way she turns everything inside out and shows you the way things really are, not the way you think you want them to be, not the way you always thought they were, but the way they really are?"

Now it was Rainulf who appeared to struggle for composure. Corliss could barely hear him when he said, in an unsteady whisper, "She turned *me* inside out, Peter. She showed me"—he cupped his hands, as if cradling an invisible, fluttering bird—"my own heart, my own soul. I'd never seen it before." He looked up, his expression one of helpless awe. "I love her, Peter. I love her with my entire being." Through a wavering film of tears, Corliss saw him meet her gaze. "I'll always love her. She's a part of me."

Peter turned and looked at her. Her chin trembled and her throat felt as if it were swollen closed, but she managed to say, "I'm sorry, Peter."

He closed his eyes, as if in great pain. "Nay, I'm sorry. I ..." He looked toward Rainulf and shook his head. "Look what I did to you."

Rainulf shrugged magnanimously. "There was a demon inside you. It needed to come out, and I happened to be in its way." He smiled and clapped his friend on the back, as if he'd just met him on the street and not been soundly beaten by him. "And now you need a brandy. You, too, Corliss." Guiding them up the stairs, he muttered, "I think I need two."

"Did you have many mistresses before taking your vows?"

Rainulf rose up on an elbow to look at Corliss lying on her stomach in the middle of the big, tousled bed, plucking grapes and popping them into her mouth. The grapes shared a platter with a wheel of cheese, a half-eaten squire's loaf, some sweet wafers, and a pot of honey—a late supper of sorts, shared by two naked and sated lovers. Her inquiry about mistresses represented a shift in the conversation, for they'd been talking about Peter's visit earlier that evening.

"There were many women who gave themselves to me," he said. "I never thought of them as mistresses. In truth, I rarely slept with a woman more than two or three times."

"Why not?" She dipped a grape in the honey pot and touched the tip of her tongue to it experimentally; the sight stirred his loins.

"Because they weren't you."

She rolled her eyes as she took the grape into her mouth. Chuckling, he moved closer, breathing in the exotic perfume that Martine had given her, and which she'd applied that evening just for him.

Earlier, when it had come time for Peter to return to where he was staying, the prior's lodge at St. Frideswide's, Rainulf had walked him downstairs and chatted in the street for a while. When he returned to Corliss's chamber, he'd found her sitting in her night shift on the edge of the bed, brushing her hair . . . and smelling of hot, musky Oriental perfume. Dropping to his knees, he'd taken her hard and fast, right there, tearing her shift in the process.

He reached over to lightly skim his fingertips from her upper back to her small, shapely bottom.

"I'm your first mistress?" she asked disbelievingly.

He frowned slightly as he caressed her. "You're my first lover ... my first *true* lover. For some reason I don't think of you as a mistress, exactly."

She seemed to ponder this. He watched her insert a finger in the honey and close her lips over it. Heat swelled in his lower body; he stiffened, rose. She saw this and smiled, sucking lazily on her glistening finger, licking it like a cat as she watched him out of the corner of her eye.

He cleared his throat. "What made you ask that, about how many mistresses I'd had?"

Her cheeks pinkened beguilingly, and she avoided his gaze. "I was just wondering where you learned ... all those things."

He smiled and drew looping patterns on her taut buttocks with his fingertips. "What things?"

"Those things that ... we do. The things you do to me. You know. The positions, and ... well, like before, with the honey, when you dripped it on my, um ... and licked it off. Who taught you that?"

He let his hand glide over her sweet curves and down between her thighs to where she was moist from recent lovemaking ... and residual honey. "I'm self-taught," he murmured as he investigated her sticky-sweet folds. "You're very inspiring."

She emitted a soft, feminine growl as his curious fingertips stroked and explored. Her legs parted. Presently that delectable bottom began to move, just slightly, in rhythm with his caress. He waited until she went still, her expression almost surprised as she clutched the sheet reflexively.

Now. He was on top of her—and inside her—in less time than it took her to draw an astonished breath. As she cried out, he plunged deep, savoring the sweet violence of her release. He slid his hands beneath her, one cradling a breast, the other her honeyed sex, until her passion renewed itself. He went slower then, grinding sinuously against her until she moaned his name and clawed at the sheets. With a strangled cry that echoed her own, he erupted inside her, his arms locked around her as she thrashed beneath him.

As their passion ebbed and their breathing steadied, he kissed her hair, the back of her neck, her shoulders. He felt his erection shrinking, and sighed in resignation, hating that feeling of loss whenever they uncoupled.

What would it be like, he wondered, when he left her completely—or rather, when she left him? How would it feel to watch her walking away from his house for the last time?

"Christ," he whispered.

"What's wrong?"

"Nothing." *Everything.* She couldn't leave him. He couldn't lose her. He really couldn't.

It wouldn't just hurt. It would empty him out.

It wouldn't just drive him mad. It would plunge him into nothingness. His own bleak, personal hell.

He'd thought that, when the time came, he'd find a way to deal with it, to cope with the loss of her. But now he realized, with sudden, startling clarity, that he would never be able to deal with it. She had joined herself to him in such a real and critical way that he couldn't do without her. He needed her as he needed his heart, his lungs. The loss of her would destroy him; worse, it would destroy *them,* the incredible, singular *them* that lived and breathed and loved as one.

This revelation of her indispensability filled him with awe, this awe producing a kind of astonished chuckle that shuddered through him.

She giggled. "I feel you throbbing inside me when you laugh. What's so funny?"

He raised himself up on his elbows and plucked strands of hair off her sweat-slicked cheek. "Not funny, just ... sort of overwhelming. I've had an epiphany and I don't know what to do with it."

"I beg your pardon?"

He chuckled again, the movement causing him to slide out of her. With a pointless groan of complaint, he rolled to the side and gathered her up, entwining his arms and legs with hers. He loved the way she felt after sex, all warm and damp and limp. She lightly kissed his bruised cheekbone. He trailed a fingertip over the half-healed scar on her chest.

"So," she murmured, "these women in Paris, these women who weren't mistresses but gave themselves to you anyway. . . ."

He laughed. "Are you still thinking about them?"

"You're laughing an awful lot tonight," she noted.

"It's a bad habit I've acquired from you," he mumbled into her hair. "So, what more do you want to know about the ladies who weren't mistresses?"

She hesitated. "After you slept with these women, and it was all over, did you remain friends?"

"For the most part, we were never friends to begin with. I barely knew most of them. It wasn't like it is with you and me."

She snuggled against him contentedly, clearly pleased that he considered her a friend. "So you just said 'Good-bye, and oh, yes, thank you for having sex with me?' "

He laughed again; it *was* becoming habitual. "I generally thought up something a bit more elegant to say. And I usually bought them a gift of some sort."

"A gift . . ."

"A parting gift. A jeweled girdle, a brooch, perhaps a book if she could read. There was one who liked to hunt, so I gave her a litter of deerhound pups."

Corliss grew still. In the ensuing silence, it occurred to him that she was wondering whether he'd give *her* a parting gift when the time came. He felt the tension in her, and knew this prospect displeased her, inasmuch as it would reduce her to just another of his faceless non-mistresses. An absurd notion, of course, yet this talk of gifts did give him an idea. . . .

He smiled to himself. A very good idea, actually.

She looked at him. "You're laughing at me. You think my ceaseless questions are ridiculous."

"I love your ceaseless questions."

"I only ask you about these women because such affairs are so foreign to me. The idea of giving oneself to men one hardly knows, and then getting dogs in return . . ." She shook her head against his chest. "You must think me hopelessly unsophisticated, but it strikes me as very strange. Then again, I've never even been to Paris. I'm just a simple Oxfordshire peasant."

He tightened his arms around her. "There's nothing simple about you, my love."

She fell silent for a moment. Although she didn't look at him, he felt her face heat up; was she blushing?

"Call me that again?" she asked.

"My love," he said softly. He kissed the top of her head. "My love." He kissed the hotly flushed edge of her ear. "My love . . . my love . . ."

He kissed every part of her he could reach, and then he laid her on her back and kissed the rest— slow, sweet, hot, endless kisses that tasted of night-opening flowers and sweaty lovemaking and honey— whispering, over and over, "My love . . . my love . . . my love . . ."

Pigot stood in the shadows of his St. John Street alleyway, watching the windows of Corliss's chamber until they went dark some time after midnight.

Corliss indeed . . . It was Constance of Cuxham up there, spreading her legs for the magister in exchange for a roof and four walls—in which she'd hidden from Pigot all damned summer. It was Constance of Cuxham, whoring still because she knew no other way.

It was Constance of Cuxham, after all, who had trotted alongside Rainulf Fairfax for four months, right out there in the open for all the world—himself included—to see. It was Constance of Cuxham, in her tunic and chausses, who laughed at everyone—at *him*, most especially—for not seeing through her deception.

And it was Constance of Cuxham who would pay for that deception with the very female charms she seemed so eager to deny. He'd start, as always, with the face: those wide, childish eyes; and that lovely mouth, with its quick tongue. The tongue would go first, he decided. That way she couldn't scream when he did the rest of it. He'd found that constant screaming in his ear gave him a headache.

This ceaseless waiting gave him a headache, too. How frustrating, to have discovered her disguise—to have located his prize!—yet be denied the capture simply because she was always with someone, usually Fairfax. One lesson he'd learned during his years of finding runaways for Roger Foliot: wait till they were alone. That way, there'd be no bothersome witnesses to deal with. But he'd never had to wait as long as this, and it was beginning to wear on him. His knife hand itched with the need to slice, to excise.

With a heavy sigh, he left the alley and began walking home. On the way, he passed a whore with yellow hair. She reminded him of Fabienne, the first woman he'd punished with his knives, so long ago. Fabienne, who had scorned him when he was young and easily stung. She had laughed at his face, had compared him to a spotted toad. But he'd taught her a lesson in humility. His clever steel had transformed her from a beauty into a monster, and then he was the one who'd laughed. It made him hard just to think about what he'd done to her.

He considered offering the wench with yellow hair tuppence for her services. Then, when she took him to whatever private place she'd set aside for her whoring, he could, among other things, appease his itchy knife hand. . . .

No. That was messy, risky. And ultimately unsatisfying, for she wasn't the woman he wanted, merely a convenient substitute. He'd have Constance of Cuxham herself soon enough. Until then, he should do nothing to distract himself from his goal of apprehending her. He must return to the alley on St. John Street before dawn and follow her every move.

The moment she was alone, he'd pounce.

Chapter 18

Felice lit up when Corliss walked into Mistress Clark's establishment on Catte Street, accompanied by Thomas and Brad. The young girl seemed to barely notice the two scholars, who busied themselves by perusing the pattern books and exemplars lying about; she gazed at Corliss, grinning in delight.

"Is your mother in?" Corliss asked her.

"Nay!" barked a voice from behind. Corliss turned to find Bertram glaring at her as he nailed a board across the largest of the shop's big front windows.

This wasn't the only storefront being boarded up that morning. All along Catte Street—and all over Oxford—merchants were securing their businesses and fleeing, a response to the unrest rapidly sweeping through the city. During the past few days, scholars had advanced from beating the occasional townsman to looting and burning shops. The locals had retaliated by arming themselves, attacking with clubs and knives anyone foolish enough to go out alone wearing a cappa. The situation reminded Corliss of a cauldron of water hanging over a fire. The water grows hotter and hotter, until at last the pot can contain it no longer.

The streets through which Thomas and Brad had escorted her—at the request of Rainulf, who was occupied with trying to quell the impending riot—were filled with chaos. It seemed to Corliss as if everybody in Oxford—scholar and townsman alike—was running somewhere, weapon in hand. Most of them were screaming. Fights broke out at regular intervals. The pot was boiling over.

Bertram drove a nail into the board with one angry whack of the hammer, his gaze never leaving Corliss. "Mistress Clark ain't in. You'd best be on your way."

"I've got the last signature with me," Corliss said, dumping her satchel on a desk and withdrawing the gathering of pages. "I need to give it to her and get my money."

"You finished it already?" Felice asked. "You've only had it three days."

" 'Twas naught but capitals and paragraph marks. Those don't take long."

Felice smiled shyly. "Only because you're so good at it. Mama says you're the most talented illuminator she's ever—"

"Your mama," Bertram interrupted, "is too kind by far."

" 'Tis the truth and you know it!" Felice snapped. "You're just jealous because all you can do is copy—"

"I am not!"

Corliss left the two to their bickering—and Thomas and Brad to their snooping—and carried the signature through the leather-curtained doorway into the back room. The completed pages of Master Becket's Bible were arranged on the long worktable in neat stacks, ready to be sewn. She studied the stacks to determine their order, then inserted her signature where it belonged.

Hearing the leather curtain open and close, she turned. Felice, her eyes huge in the semidark chamber, stood twisting her hands in the skirt of her kirtle. "Mama found a buyer for the shop. We're leaving Oxford as soon as Master Becket has his Bible. A fortnight from now at the latest."

"Where are you going?"

"Up around Wolvercot," Felice replied miserably. "To raise goats and chickens."

"Yes, well ..." Corliss shrugged. "I hope you'll be very happy."

"I'll be wretched." Felice crossed to her, her big eyes glimmering. "Heartbroken," she whispered hoarsely.

Corliss took a step back and felt the table behind her legs. "Ah. I'm sorry to hear that."

"Don't you want to know why?" Felice asked in a tremulous voice.

Corliss shook her head. She suspected she knew the source of this heartbreak and had no desire to hear the sentiments voiced.

Felice closed in on her, yet still Corliss had to strain to hear her when she spoke: "Because you won't be there."

"Uh ..." Corliss tried to sidestep along the edge of the table, but Felice clutched the front of her tunic.

"I can't stand this," she choked out as her arms encircled Corliss's waist. "I might never see you again. It's unendurable."

"Felice ..." Corliss tried to pry the young girl's arms from around her, but she held on tight.

"I love you!" Felice blurted out.

"No, you don't," Corliss said gently.

"I do! I'll wither up and die without you."

"You barely know me, Felice. You don't love me. You love the person you think I am—some man I can never be." Felice had needed someone to fall in love with, Corliss realized, just as Peter had. But they'd both fallen in love with someone who didn't even exist—an imagined, idealized lover with Corliss's face.

Felice sniffed. "You sound like Mama. She wants me to marry Bertram."

"Perhaps you should. He loves you."

"But I love *you*!"

Before Corliss could react, Felice locked her hands

around the back of her neck and kissed her on the mouth.

"Mmph!" Corliss wrested free, pushing Felice away. The girl lost her footing and slipped, pulling Corliss down with her. They landed on the floor, Corliss on top.

"Marry me," Felice pleaded, gripping Corliss around the back of the head and tugging her down for another kiss.

"Stop this!" Corliss grabbed Felice's hands and pinned them to the floor.

"Please," Felice begged. "Oh, please . . ."

The leather curtain flew aside and Bertram charged into the room. "What the devil—!"

"Oh, hell," Corliss moaned as Bertram seized her and hauled her off Felice. Enraged, he flung her roughly across the room. She thudded against the wall.

Bertram advanced on her, hands in fists. "You'll pay for this!"

Felice scrambled to her feet. "Bertram! What are you going to—

"He tried to force himself on you. I'm going to kill him."

If Corliss had expected Felice to beseech Bertram on her behalf, she was soon to be disappointed, for the girl merely blinked like a young owl . . . before smiling in a very feminine and self-satisfied way. "Really? You'd really kill him? For me?"

Oh, that's just fine, thought Corliss as Bertram puffed himself up, trying his best to look the avenging champion. "I would and I will," he said. "You just watch me." Corliss tried to run past Bertram, but he grabbed her and slammed her back against the wall. "Not so fast."

"Corliss?" Thomas swept aside the curtain and stepped into the room, followed by Brad. "Oh, here you are."

"It's about time," she said. *My protectors!*

Thomas frowned as he took in the scene. "What's going on?"

"He was attacking Felice," Bertram said.

Thomas and Brad exchanged a look. "That's not possible," Thomas said with a lopsided grin.

"Why not?"

Brad couldn't suppress a gust of laughter. "It's just not."

Bertram turned his back on Corliss to argue the point. Taking advantage of the distraction, she darted between the men and through the doorway to the front room. Without stopping, she grabbed her satchel and ran outside.

"Come back here!" Bertram screamed as he pursued her through the unruly throng hurrying to and fro along Catte Street. She hadn't gotten far when she felt him grab her by the back of the tunic and swing her around.

The punch—a swift blow to the stomach—dropped her like a stone. She rolled into a ball, her arms clamped around her middle, fighting the urge to vomit.

Bertram grabbed the neck of her tunic, made a fist, and hauled back, aiming for her face. She kicked him hard in both shins before he could connect. His feet flew out from under him, sending him sprawling. As she clambered to her feet, so did he.

"Leave her alone!" someone yelled. *Thomas.* He wrapped his arms around Bertram, immobilizing him. Corliss saw that a crowd had gathered.

"Don't hurt her!" Brad pulled her erect. "Are you all right, Corliss?"

Some of the bystanders looked at her strangely. Through her haze of pain and nausea, a warning bell tolled. *Her.* They were saying *her.* She shook her head frantically as Thomas and Brad helped her to her feet.

"You're *not* all right?" Brad looking helplessly toward Thomas. "Master Fairfax told us to look after her, and—"

"Shut up!" she croaked, holding her stomach. "For God's sake . . ."

"Well, I'll be damned." Bertram's astonished gaze inspected her from head to toe.

Behind him, a breathless Felice gaped at Corliss. "Nay . . ."

"Aye," Bertram said quietly. "I can see it now. The softness around the face . . . she's a woman, all right." A slow smile spread across his face, the cause of which was obvious: His rival was no rival after all.

"Nay," Felice repeated.

The spectators whispered and gasped. Corliss heard the same words over and over: ". . . a woman . . . men's clothes . . ." How long, she wondered, would it take for them to connect her to Rainulf? Would Bishop Fresney find out she'd been living with him? Would Rainulf be ruined?

Thomas and Brad groaned softly when they realized what they'd done.

Felice's chin trembled as she stared at Corliss. She shook her head slowly, her eyes glassy. Bertram embraced her and she collapsed in his arms, sobbing. "There there," he murmured, smiling slightly—clearly relishing this opportunity to comfort the girl who had spurned him up till now. "Come along." He guided her back toward the shop, and they disappeared in the crowd.

Thomas looked stricken. "Corliss, I . . ." He shook his head. "I'm sorry, I . . ."

"Me, too," Brad offered.

The spectators still gawked and commented. There was some laughter, but mostly just expressions of surprise and bewilderment.

They knew now. Dozens of people knew. By nightfall, all of Oxford would know. The truth had asserted itself, just as Rainulf had warned her it would.

It was over. Just like that, it was all over.

"What do we do now?" Thomas asked her. "What should we—"

"Take me to Rainulf," she said woodenly. "I have to talk to Rainulf."

Thomas and Brad guided her through the mayhem of Catte Street to the corner of High, where an enormous, black-robed horde had assembled around one tall figure on the steps of St. Mary's: Rainulf.

". . . settle our differences like civilized men," he was intoning.

"What's civilized about *them*?" a voice called out. "After what they did to Victor, we should burn down the whole damned city!"

Rainulf gestured to someone who came to stand alongside him: Victor of Aeskirche. Corliss hadn't seen him in the five days since Pyt and his friends had dragged him from his bed, beaten him, and thrown a noose around his neck. The sight of his once handsome face, still bruised and swollen, prompted a flurry of indignant exclamations from the assembled scholars.

"No one," Victor said loudly, "knows better than I what was done to me." He paused meaningfully, his piercing gaze sweeping the crowd; he was nearly as good at this as Rainulf, if a bit more dramatic. "And no one knows better than I how well I deserved it."

A chorus of denials greeted this statement. "You deserved nothing of the kind!" someone yelled. "They're savages!"

"And we're not?" Rainulf demanded, scanning the audience. His gaze lit on Corliss, and for a fleeting moment he focused only on her, his eyes smiling their secret smile, as the hundred or so scholars faded into a dark, shadowy mass; and then he wrested his attention from her and continued his impassioned plea for restraint and reconciliation.

What will I say to him? How can I tell him it's all over, just like that? Her disguise was a disguise no longer. She had to leave him. And not just his home, she realized suddenly; she would have to leave Oxford. This was Rainulf's city. As chancellor, he would all but own it. She could never escape him, never hope to forget him—or at least learn to live without him—if she stayed here. And her continuing presence in the community could hurt Rainulf. If she left now, it was possible that the bishop would never even find out she'd lived with him. Even if he did, he'd most likely forgive Rainulf a brief transgression; a continuing relationship with a woman would never be tolerated, though. The man she loved would be destroyed.

Saying good-bye to him would be agonizing. Would he make it even harder by trying to talk her into staying, or would he grit his teeth and send her on her way? Would he kiss her good-bye? Would he call her "my love" one more time? She hoped he would know better than to give her some trinket, as he had his Parisian conquests—some parting gift intended to soften the pain.

The pain can't be softened. 'Tis unendurable. I can't bear this.

How would she ever be able to walk away from him? How could she say good-bye?

I can't. Not to his face.

"We've answered rage with rage," Rainulf was saying. "Violence with violence. Fear with fear. We should know better than that—all of us! We live in one of the greatest centers of learning in the world, during the most enlightened time in the history of man. . . ."

As he spoke, the students gradually quieted. They ceased their restless fidgeting, their interruptions, and lapsed into a rapt silence. Rainulf spoke calmly, but with fervor and conviction. He talked of the need to abort the cycle of violence that threatened to destroy the city of Oxford, and with it, the great university that might someday flourish here.

Rainulf was in his element—not just competent, but

brilliant. He shone like the sun, radiating light and wisdom and strength. Corliss basked in his glow, absorbing him as he spoke—every nuance of his deep, commanding voice; every feature of his face; the way the sun glinted off his hair; the way he gestured with his hands; and the way he stood and moved. . . .

I'm memorizing him, she realized. *I'm searing him onto my mind, burning his image into my very soul. That way he'll always be with me.*

"I've been talking to representatives of the townsmen," Rainulf announced to his engrossed audience. "And, for the most part, they want peaceful relations with the academic community. It seems they're even willing to compromise on the matters that spawned this whole mess in the first place. I'm going to meet with them now, on their turf—St. Martin's Church. Victor will come with me, and I urge the rest of you to do the same, as a gesture of support. Put away your weapons and come with me. Let's see if talk can cure what violence could not."

Rainulf caught her eye as he descended the steps, waving to her and her companions to join him.

"Let's go with him," Thomas urged as the crowd began following their magister toward St. Martin's.

"Nay," said Corliss, "I want to go home. You go on ahead."

Brad shook his head. "We can't do that. We promised Master Fairfax we'd look after you."

Corliss shot him a look. He had the grace to blush in acknowledgment of the inept job he and Thomas had done "looking after" her.

"Then walk me home," she said. "After that, you two can go wherever you want. I'll be safe at home."

Alone in the big stone house—Luella, like many others, had chosen to leave Oxford until things cooled down—Corliss packed up as many of her clothes, tools, and supplies as would fit in her satchel. She retrieved her saltcellar of coins from beneath the bed and emptied it into her purse, which she stowed in the bottom of the satchel. Pushing aside the saffron curtains, she gazed at the huge featherbed heaped high with pillows, burning hot, sweet memories into her soul alongside images of Rainulf.

She brought her precious *Biblia Pauperum* to her big desk in the main hall and set it down in the middle, running her fingers for the last time over its delicately embroidered cover. Her only parchment was a large scrap with a hole in it, on which she had tested pigments, scribbled ideas, and sketched out preliminary versions of monkeys and angels and fanciful borders. There was a relatively clean area on the back, surrounded by a procession of little lions, each holding in its mouth the tail of the one in front—practice for the fireplace decoration. She sharpened a quill, dipped it in the inkhorn, and bit her lip.

My love, she wrote in the lion-encircled space, *By now, you will know what has happened. You will know that I can remain here no longer. I must leave not just your home, but this city. By the time you read this, I will be far from Oxford, and I doubt that I shall ever return.*

Moisture welled in her eyes; the words swam on the page. *Forgive me for not having the courage to say good-bye to you in person. I'm weak, and I love you so much—*

A tear dropped onto the wet ink, which ran in a little rivulet down the page. Wiping her eyes, she dipped her pen and wrote *Please keep my* Biblia Pauperum. *Look at it from time to time and think of me. And I will always carry with me your little reliquary containing the hair of St. Nicaise. I was right—it did bring me good luck. It brought me you.*

Another tear marred her words. Reinking her quill, she wrote *I will love you forever. Corliss.*

* * *

Closing the door behind her, Corliss looked up at Rainulf's big stone house for the last time. She'd grown to love this house, and this city, and him far more than she would ever have dreamed. And leaving was more inexpressibly painful than she could have imagined.

Don't think about it. Just go.

But where? As she walked up St. John Street, her satchel over her shoulder, she set her mind to the problem of her destination. London was the only English city besides Oxford where she'd have any hope of finding work as an illuminator. There were opportunities on the Continent—Paris, Bologna, Salerno—but the prospect of traveling so far on her own was daunting to a young woman who'd never been farther than twelve miles from the village of her birth.

On her own. Only then did it dawn on her that she was walking the streets of Oxford alone for the first time in weeks. Rainulf wouldn't like her taking such a chance, what with Pigot on her trail. *She* didn't much like it, either, but she didn't know that she had any real choice.

The streets were chaotic and crowded, and she was still dressed as a male; that should help her to blend in until she could ... Until she could what? Where was she going? She needed to find transportation to London as soon as possible. Perhaps she could find one of the merchants fleeing eastward from the city, and pay him to take her as far as he was going.

Lost in these ruminations, she turned north onto Shidyerd. As she did so, she noticed out of the corner of her eye a dark form ducking into a doorway. She kept walking, prickles of foreboding tightening her scalp.

She wove her way through the riotous noise and activity of Shidyerd, alert and wary.

There he is again. This time she turned quickly, catching a glimpse of him before he disappeared between two shops. She saw the hulking body, the cowl drawn down low, and a glimpse of his grotesquely spotted face.

Rad. It was just Rad.

She willed calmness upon herself as she continued walking. It was just Rad, after all, just harmless Rad—but wearing an expression she'd never seen on him before. There was something in his eyes—something grim and resolute—that she couldn't help but find unnerving.

She walked faster, threading through the roiling crowd until she came to the corner of High Street. Which way should she go? Was Rad still following her?

Not wanting to linger too long in any one spot, she made a quick decision and turned left. Someone bumped into her. She gasped, but it was just an excited young boy not looking where he was running. "The troubles are over!" he was yelling. "Everyone lay down your weapons!"

She saw Rad again, on the edge of her vision. He was closer now. As she picked up her pace, so did he. He gained on her swiftly, looking fiercely determined. A student got in his way; he pushed the young man aside without a glance, and began running.

Oh, God! Corliss ran, too. "Get out of my way!" she rasped as she struggled through a sea of black robes. "Get out of my—"

A hand closed over her arm from behind, seizing her in a viselike grip. "Where are you off to in such a hurry?"

Don't panic.

Corliss wheeled toward the voice, swinging her satchel. It hit his face with a *whump*. He released her arm and fell backward.

As she turned to flee, she saw his thicket of coppery hair gleaming in the noon sun. . . .

What—? She turned, gaping at the man she had

felled as he gained his feet, dusting off his tunic. "Will?" She released a shaky breath, her legs like water. "Oh, God, Will, I thought . . ."

She looked behind her, but couldn't see Rad; a herd of scholars was crossing the street between them. "I didn't know it was you. I . . . I'm sorry! Look—I can't stay here. I have to go."

The surgeon fell in step with her as she quickly walked west along High Street. "Where *are* you off to in such a hurry?" he asked with smile.

"I was being followed." She glanced over her shoulder, but all she could see was a solid wall of black cappas. "A peddler. I think he may be Sir Roger's bloodhound. The one they call Pigot."

"*Pigot's* following you?" Will's expression sobered. "You oughtn't to be on the streets by yourself, especially in the midst of all this bedlam."

There was much cheering and whooping on High Street. Scholars coming from the direction of St. Martin's called out news about lowered rents and a reduction in the price of ale. Each announcement was greeted by a roar of approval.

"I know, but I have to leave Oxford. Thomas and Brad let it slip to all of Catte Street that I'm a woman. Rainulf will be ruined if I stay here. I'm going to try to get to London if I can."

He brightened. "I'm on my way to Wallingford to see some patients. That's on the way to London. I'd be happy to escort you that far, if you'd like."

Relief flooded Corliss. "Would you? I'd be so grateful."

"Of course. I'd be glad to have the company."

Will had two mounts stabled behind his shop, so that was where they headed. They negotiated the teeming streets as quickly as they could, mindful that Rad—or rather, Pigot—might be trying to follow.

The front of Will's place of business, like the rest of the storefronts on Pennyfarthing, was boarded up.

He unlocked the door and let them in, then relocked it. The only light came from the open back door and a large side window that looked out onto an alley.

"I've never been in a surgical shop," Corliss said as she inspected it curiously: the sawdust-covered floor, the big oak table with the leather shackles dangling from iron rings, the open cupboard lined with mysterious flasks and rolls of bandages, the coffins stacked against the back wall. She shivered. "How can you bear it? I mean, all the pain and death."

He closed and latched the back door, then the window shutters, muffling the street noise and plunging the shop into a dim twilight. When he turned to face her, she could barely see him, although she thought he smiled. "One gets used to pain." He set his bag down on a small table next to the larger one fitted with restraints. "And death."

With the sunlight blocked out, Corliss felt chilly, although it was a warm day. She watched the surgeon light a lantern and lift it up to a hook over the big oak table. It swung back and forth as he hung it, casting his pale, densely freckled face alternately in light and shadow.

The bright light revealed a detail about the table that she hadn't noticed before: a channel carved all around its edge, which tilted toward a hole at the foot. Will reached beneath the table for a bucket, which he positioned carefully under the hole. Corliss noticed dark spots in the sawdust, and realized it was blood.

She took a step back. "Are we leaving soon?"

The surgeon didn't answer her or even look in her direction. Instead, he opened his bag and brought out a small, curved knife. Corliss saw the white flash of steel as he laid it on the table. He reached back into the bag and brought forth another blade, this one straight and pointed. He set it next to the other, taking care, it seemed, to line them up neatly. More instruments emerged from the bag—cutting tools of all shapes and sizes—which he arranged painstakingly on the little table.

Corliss's heart beat so fast that it shook her entire body from head to toe. She heard herself breathe, and wondered if Will did, too. "I want to leave now."

Will set his empty bag in a corner, pulled off his tunic, and hung it up. He plucked a bloodstained leather apron off the hook next to it and tied it over his shirt and chausses.

Corliss backed up to the door and tried the handle with trembling fingers; pointless, of course, since it was locked. She swallowed hard, her mouth dry as ashes. "I said I want to leave now."

He walked toward her, saying softly, "I'm quite sure you do."

Chapter 19

Rainulf flung open his front door and bounded up the stairs, grinning. "Corliss?"

Thomas and Brad followed behind him, their arms loaded with fresh bread, savory meat pasties, hot dumplings, and sweet puddings—provisions for a celebratory feast. The delicacies were gifts from merchants who'd reopened their shops on learning that Rainulf Fairfax had gotten matters in hand, his mediation having resulted in a truce between the scholars and the townsmen.

The two young scholars had been shocked when Rainulf had invited them back to the house. They'd assumed he'd be furious at them for exposing Corliss's true sex; his sanguine acceptance of their blunder clearly confused them.

"Corliss!" Rainulf called from the main hall. He wanted to celebrate his victory with her—wrap his arms around her and kiss her. He wanted to brag like a little boy, whispering "I did it!" for her ears only.

He tore aside the leather curtain and inspected the bedchamber, empty and preternaturally neat—no clothes tossed over chair backs, as was her habit; no comb and brush on the washstand.

No Corliss.

He went back into the main hall and looked around, ignoring the two scholars as they fetched the ale and laid dinner out on the table. Her desk was unnaturally tidy, too. Approaching it, he saw her *Biblia Pauperum*, and on top of it, a sheet of parchment covered with scribbled drawings. A closer look revealed writing in the middle—he recognized her elegantly simple hand—enclosed within a procession of tiny lions.

He smiled as he lifted the sheet, grinning when he read the words *My love.* But his grin faded as he read on.

Rainulf felt the blood drain from his face.

"Magister?"

"What's wrong?"

A great emptiness engulfed him; he felt dizzy.

"Sit down, Magister."

Someone eased him into the chair, Corliss's chair. He held on to the edge of her desk and read the note again. . . . *By the time you read this, I will be far from Oxford, and I doubt that I shall ever return.*

He muttered an oath and dropped his head into his hands. Someone picked up the sheet of parchment and read it. The two young men passed it wordlessly between each other.

A cup was thrust into his hand. "Drink."

It looked like brandy. He drank. Its heat stung his eyes, but he couldn't taste it.

He felt a hand on his shoulder. "Magister, I'm—"

"Don't." He shrugged off the hand. Thomas and Brad retreated to the table. They picked at their food and sipped their ale in pensive silence.

The note lay on the desk, and he picked it up. Corliss had pointed out to him once that parchment felt soft on what had once been the sheep's fur side, smooth on the flesh side; and if you closed your eyes and really concentrated, you could feel the very ink on the page. Running his fingers lightly over the sheet in his hand, he found that this was true. He closed his eyes and brought it to his nose, inhaling the traces of an enigmatic scent which lingered there—her scent.

A knock came from downstairs. Someone went down to answer it. He heard a murmured conversation. Two sets of footsteps ascended the stairs, and then came Peter's voice behind him. "Rainulf?"

"Peter."

"I came here to say good-bye. I'm leaving for Blackburn."

Rainulf nodded without turning around.

Peter pulled a chair up next to the desk and sat down. He had the brandy jug in his hand, and he refilled Rainulf's cup. "They told me about Corliss. Will you be all right?"

Rainulf caressed the dried trails on the note: tears mixed with ink. "As soon as I find her."

Peter looked at the note; he looked at Rainulf's face. "Are you sure you should?"

"How can you ask that?"

The knight hesitated, as if trying to find the proper words. "She left for a reason, Rainulf—a good reason. She left for you. And, although 'twas clearly hard for her, she wanted to break things off cleanly. Wouldn't it be better to let her do that than to go after her and—"

"God, this has all gotten so . . ." Rainulf shook his head helplessly and swallowed the contents of his cup. "You don't understand. Neither did she. I must find her. I *will* find her. She probably went to London. She could illuminate books there."

Peter sighed heavily, then took the note from Rainulf and examined it. "How long has she been gone?"

"I'm not sure. It could be a few minutes or a few hours. She could be miles away by now, on one of several different roads."

Peter nodded. "If you set out for London in the morning, you can be there by—"

"Nay—I'm leaving now." He started to rise, but Peter grabbed his arm and lowered him to his seat.

"That's pointless," Peter said. "You said yourself you have no idea what road she might have taken. 'Twill be easier to find her once she gets to London than en route. You can go to the quarter where the books are made and see if she's asked for work." Peter tilted the jug over Rainulf's cup again. "Wait till the morning to leave for London."

"Let me go, Will."

Will smiled as he slowly walked toward her. "Let you go? After all the trouble I went through to get you?" He chuckled and shook his head. "I hardly think that's likely, do you?"

Corliss eyed the largest of the knives laid out on the little table. If she could get to it before he could . . .

She pushed away from the door, but he grabbed her by her tunic and shoved her against it, hard. "Save your energy, my dear. You'll need all your reserves to get through what I've got in store for you."

"It was you all along—not Rad. *You're* Pigot."

He backhanded her swiftly across the face, catching her before she could fall. "My name," he said in a menacing whisper as his fingers dug into her shoulders, "is William Geary. The name Pigot is an insult, and if you call me that again, I'll kill you."

He leaned in close until he was nose-to-nose with her, his breath hot on her face. She'd never noticed how colorless his eyes were, like frozen lakes. In truth, it was hard to see beyond all those freckles, so dark and numerous that it almost looked as if he'd been splattered with red ink—or blood.

"Does my face disgust you?" he asked quietly.

She couldn't stop quaking, but she strove to keep her voice steady. "Nay."

"Liar!" He shook her; her head rattled against the door. "Just wait till I get you strapped down." Corliss followed his gaze to the big table—and the orderly array of surgical instruments next to it.

Scream. Sucking in a great lungful of air, Corliss shrieked, "Help! Somebody help me!"

Will smiled indulgently. "Go ahead. But all you'll

earn for your efforts is a sore throat." He cocked his head toward the boarded-up front window, through which could be heard the sounds of celebration, including a great many voices raised in a ribald drinking song. "No one will hear you. I can do anything I want to you—*anything*—and no one will come to your aid."

Was it possible he could be reasoned with? "Will . . . think about it. I've done nothing to hurt you. Why would you want to—"

"*Because you're a lying whore!*" he screamed in her face. Abruptly he calmed, his voice lowering in a murmur. "I know how to punish lying whores. And *your* punishments shall be especially . . . exquisite, given the merry chase you've led me. You laughed at me, you and—"

"No, I didn't. I didn't even know you were Pi—" She swallowed hard. "I . . . I had no idea you were Sir Roger's . . ." His what? Was there a name for a creature like him? "I thought you were just his surgeon."

"I'm both. Since I travel a great deal, I found I was in a good position to locate runaways—for a price, of course. And, too, I have a natural aptitude for the work. No one ever suspects me—until it's too late."

She certainly hadn't; and neither had Rainulf. "You even came to us, to warn us. You told us Sir Roger had sent someone after me."

He smiled sardonically. "I thought that was particularly clever. I wanted to find out from Fairfax himself whether you were his mistress. He denied it, of course, the lying mongrel."

"But I wasn't—"

"*No more lies!*" He closed his eyes; when they opened, he was eerily serene again. "I also wanted to light a fire under him, scare him a little. When people feel threatened, they often get clumsy and give themselves away. It didn't work, of course. But at least he didn't see through me. I take it he suspected that simple-minded freak of a peddler. I should thank the drooling idiot for hounding you the way he did. Quite the perfect distraction."

"Rad was trying to protect me."

He snorted. "Yes, I'm quite aware of that. He saw me today, you know. I was so excited to find you alone at last that I got sloppy and trailed you too openly. Your Guardian Peddler, witless though he is, appeared to have caught on that I was after you. He tried to get to you first, but he's slow and clumsy. I, on the other hand, strike like a snake. And once I've got my prey, I *never* let go." His frigid gaze crawled over her, assessing her with unnatural interest. "Although I do rather enjoy toying with my kill."

"You're mad."

"Absolutely. So you'd best tread carefully with me. I suggest you stop fighting me and accept whatever punishments I see fit to mete out." He moved closer. She felt his erection beneath the leather apron, and flinched.

"Nay!" She tried to push him away, but he lowered his hands to her upper arms, pinioning them to her sides. In desperation, she whipped one leg up, knee bent, but he was standing too close, and his apron provided a sort of armor against that kind of attack.

"Typical whore's trick," he growled.

She lifted her leg again, this time bringing her heel down sharply on his instep. He howled, his hands loosening from around her arms. She tried to flee, but he grabbed her. He seized her head and slammed it against the door. Pain reverberated in her skull. White light obliterated her vision and then dissolved, leaving a numbing nothingness. . . .

Consciousness returned as a twist of discomfort around her left wrist. Something tightened around it, biting into her skin. She heard the snap of leather being buckled.

No . . . no! She opened her eyes, then squeezed

them shut against the light of the overhead lantern. She lay on her back. When she tried to sit up, she discovered that her feet and left hand were bound to the corners of the table.

Will stood to the side. She fisted her right hand and aimed for his face. He seized her wrist, his grip painfully tight. With a gentle *tsk,* he stretched this arm above her head and swiftly encircled it with a leather strap. She tried to resist him, but he was strong, and snickered at her feeble efforts. The restraint pinched. He buckled it, then gave it a tug as if to test it.

Seemingly satisfied, he turned to the smaller table and pondered the assortment of knives. With a malevolent smile, he chose the little curved one and held it up; his icy eyes reflected its gleam.

Panic flooded her like a dam breaking. She thrashed violently, yanking at the bindings. He ignored her completely, running his thumb slowly along the edge of the rounded blade.

Don't panic. Don't panic. She forced herself to lie still, although her heart thundered in her ears and she couldn't seem to get enough air. A thought occurred to her. "I have money—lots of it. I'll give it to you if you let me go."

He leaned over her, his face blocking out the harsh lantern light. "I'll take it anyway. And you don't seem to understand, my dear. I have no intention of letting you go. You've led me a merry chase all summer, and I deserve a better reward than mere money now that it's over. I deserve to avenge myself on that pretty face of yours."

"I can't think that will make Sir Roger happy."

"Nay, but he'll pay me the rest of what he owes me anyway. He always does, the fat, spineless swine. And then—after I've got the other pound—I'll arrange a conveniently plausible death for you. Perhaps a suicide, like Hildreth's."

Corliss remembered the fragile girl who'd drowned

herself—or had she?—rather than go through life mutilated beyond recognition. "*You* killed Hildreth?"

He shrugged casually. "She could have identified me."

"Without her tongue?"

"She could read and write—not well, but well enough." He tapped the curved knife against her forehead. "So can you—in three different languages, if I'm not mistaken. Rest assured, you *will* die. But not"—he trailed the edge of the blade delicately down her nose, over her lips, and along her throat—"until I've taken my own particular form of pleasure with you."

So that's how it's to be. She was condemned to death—but only after unspeakable tortures. Swiftly assessing her predicament, she came to a grim but pragmatic conclusion: If death was inevitable, she'd rather it came before this maniac had done his worst to her than after. But bound as she was, there was nothing she could do to hasten her own death—or was there?

Closing her eyes briefly, she transmitted a silent prayer of forgiveness for her act of de facto suicide. And then she swallowed hard and said, "You're a vicious, murdering bastard, Pigot."

His face darkened with fury. "Don't call me—"

"What? *Pigot?* Because it reminds you what an ugly son of a bitch you are?"

He grimaced, pressing the curved blade against her throat. "You're trying my—"

"Pigot—that's what we called this grotesque little dog we had when I was a child. You should have seen it—speckled all over, just like you. People would laugh every time they saw—" She sucked in a gasp as the blade cut through her skin. She felt blood trickle down her neck, onto the table.

He was hoarse with rage. "I told you I'd kill you if you called me that."

Steeling herself, she said, "Do it, then. What's the

matter, *Pigot*? Don't have the nerve to finish what you start?"

He stood there frozen for a moment, the blade just piercing her throat, and then he began to chuckle.

Oh, no . . .

"You're good," he said, grinning as he backed off. He wiped the bloody knife on his apron. "Damned good. Most of them are blubbering and begging by this point, but you're still trying to control the situation, trying to get your own way, trying to trick me. You're really quite spirited, aren't you?"

His smile vaporized. "I hate that in a woman. Luckily, I've discovered that spirit, like any poisonous lump, can be excised." He drew the tip of the knife around each of her eye sockets, just lightly enough so that he didn't break the skin. She shivered all over. "One simply has to know where to cut." He circled her nose, and then each of her ears in turn, with the razor-sharp blade. "Often it's a matter of trial and error. It can take quite a while. But I'm a patient man. What about you? Are you patient?"

She drew in a deep, steadying breath. "Bugger yourself!"

He clucked softly and touched the blade to her lips. "That's quite a tongue you've got there. I shall have to do something about that tongue of yours."

Will began to slip the blade between her lips. She wrestled her head to the side. He grabbed her by the hair and yanked it back. She pressed her lips closed, clenched her teeth. The blade slid into her mouth. He twisted his wrist and it pried her teeth open, flirted with her tongue. She tasted steel, and couldn't stifle the whimper that rose from her.

A crash of splintering wood made both of them start. Will withdrew the blade and turned toward the sound. The shutters covering the alley window were shattered, and a large rock lay on the floor. As they watched, a cowled head appeared.

Rad. He'd followed them, after all! He punched through the remaining slats of wood and scrambled through the window with surprising agility. His horrified gaze took in the big table, the restraints. He met her eyes, his expression grim.

Will laid down the curved blade and picked up the big knife. "You've made a very grave mistake, peddler."

He had, Corliss realized; Will could kill Rad as easily as he would butcher a sheep. "Leave, Rad," she implored. "Find Rainulf. Tell him Pigot's got me—"

"Shut up!" Will cracked her across the forehead with the handle of the knife. Through the burst of red-hot pain, she heard Rad's roar of anger, and the sounds of a scuffle.

It was over quickly. When she refocused her gaze, Rad was stumbling backward, the knife in his gut.

"No!" She yanked ineffectually at the bindings.

Facing Rad, Will grabbed him by his cowl and pulled out the knife; Rad winced and sank to his knees in the debris from the shutter. Holding the blade to Rad's throat, Will said, "I told you you'd made a grave mistake."

"Stop it!" Corliss screamed. "Don't!"

Will spun around. "You shut up!"

Behind him, Rad grabbed the rock, hefting it in both hands. As Will turned toward him, he slammed it into the surgeon's midsection.

Will fell, whacking his head on the table and hitting the floor with a grunt. Rad doubled over, clutching his bleeding stomach. Shaking his head, Will groped in the sawdust for his knife. Corliss knew Rad didn't have a chance. No match for Will to begin with, he was further weakened by his injury.

"Leave, Rad!" she screamed. "Go!"

Rad nodded as he struggled to stand up. "I'll g-get—"

"Just go!"

He clambered out the window, leaving it smeared

with blood. Will, one hand cradling his head, the other clutching the knife, rose unsteadily to his feet. "Damn." He lurched to the window and peered out. Rad's retreating footfalls were soon absorbed by the boisterous street noise.

Will, his breathing labored, stood with his back to her for a few moments. "Can't stay here now," he muttered. "Got to get you to Cuxham. *Damn!* I hate to do this in broad daylight."

He hurled the knife across the shop. It stuck in one of the coffins. Crossing the room, he yanked it out, then ran his hand thoughtfully over the wooden box. To her surprise, he began to chuckle. "But I've got just the way to get you there without drawing attention."

"No more," said Rainulf as Thomas tried to pour him another brandy. "I've no desire to end up drunk."

"A sound came from downstairs—a thump against the front door.

"No more visitors," Rainulf muttered.

"I'll send him away," offered Brad, sprinting downstairs. Rainulf heard the door open, then a startled exclamation in English. "Magister!" Brad called up the stairs. "I think you should come down here!"

Thomas followed Rainulf down the narrow staircase to the street. At first he thought the tattered mass on the ground was a bundle of rags—but then he noticed the blood, and a cowled head. Kneeling, he pulled back the cowl and saw the familiar, hideously pockmarked face. "Rad?"

The peddler opened his eyes and met Rainulf's gaze. A strange look passed over his face. He muttered something unintelligible.

"What's he saying?" Thomas asked.

"I've no idea, but I don't like this. This cur used to follow Corliss around. For all I know, he's ..." Captured her? Cut her up? Then what was he doing here? He was mad, that's what—and clearly hurt.

Rad seemed agitated. He tried to sit up, but grimaced and collapsed again.

Rainulf shook him. "What happened? Where's Corliss?" Rad's eyes opened at the mention of her name. "I'll kill you if you've hurt her." He shook him harder. "Rad! Rad!"

"P-Pigot," the peddler gasped.

"What's that?" asked Brad. "Pigot?"

Rad nodded furiously, and then his eyes rolled up and he slumped heavily to the ground. His chest still rose and fell, shakily; he wasn't dead quite yet.

Brad regarded the unconscious peddler with a furrowed brow. "Was he saying that's what *his* name is? Pigot?"

"I think so," Rainulf said. "Why?"

"It's a Saxon name," explained the young scholar. "Means speckled."

Rainulf pointed to Rad's ravaged face. "I think he qualifies."

"I suppose," Brad said. "But usually that's what they call you if you're covered with freckles."

Freckles . . . A face materialized in Rainulf's mind—milk white and showered with hundreds of bright red freckles. He saw the pale, knowing eyes, the thin smile. . . .

"Like that surgeon," Brad offered. "What's his—"

"Will Geary." Rainulf stood, raking his fingers through his hair.

Was it possible? He recalled the first time he'd seen Will, standing in the doorway of Burnell's Tavern, his surgical bag in his hand. *It's my fault you got involved in this mess in the first place,* Will had told him later. *I'm the one who sent you to Cuxham.* That was true. If it weren't for Will, he would never even have known the little village existed.

Rainulf had always found it vaguely troubling that

Will sold his services to the likes of Roger Foliot—a
man who thought nothing of smashing a boy's legs
with a mallet. *So I set the legs,* Will had told him over
a tankard of ale, *and then I ate my fill of stag and
turnips and went on my way . . .*

He sends for me, when he needs me.

"Sweet Jesus . . ."

"Magister?" Thomas began. "What's the—"

"You and Brad stay here," Rainulf commanded.
"Tend to Rad."

"Where are you going?"

"Pennyfarthing Street. If I'm not back by nightfall,
send for the sheriff."

Corliss caught fleeting glimpses of Will through the
back door as he harnessed two horses to a cart. Reen-
tering the shop, he substituted his tunic for the leather
apron, then lifted one of the coffins and brought it
out back, laying it on the bed of the cart.

No . . .

"Will, don't do this," she said as he snatched a roll
of bandages from the cupboard.

"Oh, it's 'Will' again, is it?" He tore a strip of linen
from the roll and stuffed it into her mouth, then
wound a second strip around her head to hold it in
place, and tied it off.

Unlatching the leather restraints from her hands, he
tied them behind her with another length of bandage,
then released her feet.

"Let's go." He pulled her off the table and dragged
her by her tunic toward the back door.

As she staggered along behind him, she raised her
bound hands to the back of her belt, shifting it to the
side until the little pouch, which had hung in front,
was within reach. Loosening its drawstring with quivering fingers, she fumbled inside it for the little
reliquary.

"Come *on*!" He jerked her toward the back door,

not noticing when she let the small silver box drop from her fingers into the sawdust.

He hauled her into the cart and shoved her into the coffin, grinning when she began to kick and thrash. "Get used to it. 'Twill be your permanent home soon." He lowered the lid, and everything went black. Presently she heard hammering all around the edge of the lid, as he nailed it shut.

The sense of confinement overwhelmed her; the gag felt suffocating. Alone and bound in the dark confines of the narrow box, she broke out in a sweat. When she heard the horses' hoofbeats and felt the cart move, rumbling and rocking over the rutted ground, she began to tremble uncontrollably.

Rainulf entered the surgical shop through the back door, which stood open. With a sense of dread he approached the big oaken table, lit by an overhead lantern, a sinister array of surgical tools laid out next to it. One of them was a small, curved knife, its blade stained crimson. There were drops of blood on the table itself, where a head would have been. He closed his eyes, straining for composure.

It might not be Corliss's blood. She might never have set foot in this place.

Turning around, he scanned the rest of the shop, seeing nothing of importance ... until his gaze lit on something glimmering in the sawdust near the open doorway. He didn't recognize it until he was kneeling over it; he crossed himself before he lifted it.

Rainulf's chest grew tight as he cradled the little reliquary in his hand. *She wanted me to know she'd been here.* He closed his fist around the tiny silver box, his gaze on that monstrous, bloodstained table with its dangling leather straps. *And that she's still alive.*

Chapter 20

Corliss was drenched in sweat by the time the cart rattled to a halt. She felt Will jump to the ground; heard a series of creaks as he pried open the lid of the coffin.

The bright afternoon sun made her eyes snap shut. He grabbed her by her tunic and yanked her up, hauling her unceremoniously out of the coffin and off the cart.

"Stand up!"

Her legs wobbled beneath her. She felt a sharp prick of pain beneath her chin and opened her eyes to find his big knife poised there.

"Walk!" He shifted the knife to her back and prodded her with it in the direction of the building looming over them: an L-shaped stone hall over an undercroft, the whole roofed in thatch. Sir Roger Foliot's manor house, and the grandest structure in Cuxham. While she'd lived in this village, she'd stood in awe of it. Yet now, as Will hurried her up the exterior staircase to the raised hall, glancing furtively over his shoulder, it struck her as small and humble—if undeniably menacing.

Once inside the hall, she struggled to orient herself in the dim light from the narrow windows. The long part of the *L* was the main hall, separated from the short section by a partition of newer stone, fitted with a heavy door. Sir Roger's solar lay beyond that door. When he'd had the partition built, shortly after inheriting this manor from his sire, there'd been much speculation as to why he should feel the need to keep his sleeping quarters so private. The bruised faces and harrowing tales of his bed partners had provided all the answer needed.

Hugh Hest, Sir Roger's reeve and husband to her friend Ella, looked up from the high table at the opposite end of the hall from the solar. He swore under his breath as he took in Will, with his knife, and her, bound and gagged. Setting down his stylus—for he'd been writing on a wax tablet—he rose slowly.

"Rent time?" asked Will with oily calm.

Hugh nodded. Only then did Corliss notice the vast array of goods spread out on the table: baskets of eggs, stacks of hides, cheeses, dried meats, bunches of candles, half a dozen dead fowl, and numerous linen-wrapped bundles containing God knew what. Against the walls were heaped huge sacks of grain, malt, and flour.

Will jerked his head toward the door to the solar. "Is he in there?"

"Sir Roger? Nay, he's down at the mill, talking to—"

"Do you have the key to that door?" Pigot demanded.

Corliss implored Hugh with her eyes. *Don't do this. . . . Don't go along with him. You're a decent man.*

Hugh hesitated. Will brought the blade to her scarred throat and pressed; she winced. "I said, do you have the—"

"Aye!" Hugh produced a key ring and circled the table. "Just don't hurt her."

Will chuckled as he dragged Corliss by her sleeve to the door of the solar. Opening it, he thrust her inside. She stumbled and fell in the rushes.

"Lock it!" Will ordered Hugh. She heard the snick of the key in the lock, and then Will's muffled voice through the heavy door: "Fetch Sir Roger and bring him back here. Hurry!"

Corliss's gaze immediately flew to the chamber's single shuttered window, but her spirits plummeted when she found it to be a two-light, like those in the main hall: a pointed arch bisected by a stone midshaft, both openings far too narrow for her to fit through, even if she were willing to break a leg on landing. There were no other doors or openings to be seen.

With her hands bound behind her, the simple act of standing became an awkward maneuver. Once on her feet, she gave the dim chamber a quick inspection, finding it surprisingly ornate, given the rustic surroundings. Scarlet brocade curtains enclosed the mammoth bed. Gilt crosses shared wall space with tapestries depicting scenes of the basest sensual depravity. She'd seen obscene artwork before—the scholars of Oxford maintained a lively clandestine commerce in the stuff—but never anything as perverted as this.

An illuminated book lay open on a chest, and she approached it with a certain sordid curiosity. One whole page was taken up with an intricately detailed painting featuring naked men and women being tortured in most brutal and imaginative ways by horned demons. She noticed the writhing flames, and realized that this was a particularly graphic illustration of the torments of hell.

Something *thunked* against the window shutters.

Corliss approached the window slowly, prepared for anything. There was a pause, and then came a second *thunk,* as of something small striking the wooden slats. Turning her back to the window, she managed to push one of the shutters open. When she turned back around and looked through, she spied Hugh Hest on the lawn below, his arm in throwing position. He saw her, and a look of relief swept across his face. He dropped the pebble he'd been holding and wrested a key from the ring on his belt. Holding it up, he pantomimed throwing it.

The key to the solar? He *was* a decent man! She

nodded furiously—*Yes! Yes!*—and backed away from the window. He threw the key, which soared in a perfect arc to land in the rushes at her feet. When she looked through the window again, he'd turned and was heading away from her—toward the mill ... and Roger Foliot. He would be helpful only up to a point, she realized—the point at which he himself would be at risk. But any help was better than no help at all, and she was immensely grateful for it.

Squatting down, she probed blindly in the rushes until she located the key, which she slipped into her pouch, still hanging on the back of her belt. Then she rose and conducted a swift, behind-the-back search of the contents of Sir Roger's chests and cupboards until, at last, she found what she'd been looking for: his razor.

Cutting through the linen bandages securing her wrists was harder than she'd thought it would be: her fingers had no mobility, and her thumbs were all but useless. But after long minutes of desperate sawing, the bindings came loose, and her hands were free! Sliding the razor beneath the gag, she sliced it off and tossed it aside, rubbing her stiff and aching jaw.

She moved her pouch to the front of her belt, slipped the razor into it, and retrieved the key. Biting her lip, she approached the door, crossed herself, and gingerly inserted the key in the lock. The metallic click sounded very loud in her ears, but when she heard nothing from the other side of the door, she slowly— oh, so slowly—opened it.

When it was open wide enough for her to poke her head through, she did. Will stood at the high table, his back to her, idly inspecting the various bundles. Would he hear her if she left the solar? Glancing down at the rushes, she saw that they looked fresh; most likely they'd crackle underfoot. She didn't dare try to walk through them.

Will pressed his big knife to one of the bundles and

sliced it open; dried beans spilled out, rattling loudly
as they flowed over the table and onto the floor. He
chuckled and took the knife to a second bundle. Corliss held her breath. When the blade pierced the linen,
she left the solar, closing the door behind her; the
waterfall of beans covered the noise she made. He
would see her, however, were she to make a dash for
the door—and then he'd slice *her* open.

A mountain of huge sacks was piled next to her
against the wall. Will slit open another bundle; as its
contents exploded noisily, she took four steps toward
the sacks. He sighed and scratched his neck with the
tip of the big knife, turning toward her as he did. Her
heart seized up as she slid down behind the nearest
sack. *Please, God, don't let him see me.*

Evidently he hadn't, for he merely sighed again and
began pacing the main hall, tapping the knife against
his thigh as he waited for Hugh to return with Sir
Roger.

"Short hair and chausses?" gasped Roger Foliot as
he heaved his obese form up the outer staircase of his
house, his yapping dog held tightly in his arms. Hugh
had never seen him move so fast. The prospect of
finally getting his hands on Constance had lit a fire
under the randy old pig. Hugh hoped with all his heart
that she had managed to escape. The notion of her
subjected to Sir Roger's depraved lust filled him with
revulsion. And God knew what Ella would do if she
thought he'd delivered her friend into Sir Roger's
hands—probably exile him permanently from her bed.

"Aye," Hugh replied as he followed Sir Roger up
the stairs. "I take it she disguised herself as a male to
avoid capture."

The fat knight chuckled. "She was always a clever
bitch." Detinée yelped. "Not you, my dear. And you
say her face is intact."

"So it seems."

At the top of the stairs, Sir Roger turned and lowered his voice. "You see? Pigot spared her face, after all. He did as I told him because he fears and respects—"

"For God's sake," Hugh whispered, "don't call the man Pigot to his face."

"I'm not afraid of him."

You would be if you had any sense. Sir Roger strode into the hall, Hugh behind him, and looked around, scratching Detinée on the head. Presently, Will Geary emerged from the shadows, holding that huge, bloody knife of his.

"So," Sir Roger began, "you've brought her back."

"I have," the surgeon replied. "You owe me a pound sterling."

"You'll get your money," said the knight as he crossed to the solar. "But first I have to see her. Got to make sure I'm getting what I pay for." He inserted his own key in the lock and frowned. "It's unlocked. What's this, Hugh? I thought you said you locked her in."

"I did," Hugh said carefully. "I can't imagine . . ." He shrugged, secretly overjoyed. *She did it! She got out!*

Roger Foliot opened the door and stepped into the solar, Hugh right behind; Geary waited outside. "Constance?" He turned around in the big chamber, frowning. The little dog leapt from his arms and darted under the bed. It's master's eyes grew wide. "Is that where you've hidden yourself?" Hugh watched in disgust as Sir Roger got down on his hands and knees and peered under the bed. "Shit!" He glared at Hugh, his face a deep, livid purple. "Where is she?"

"I . . ."

"Help me up, damn you!"

Groaning, Hugh took the plump hands offered to him and hauled Sir Roger up. As soon as he'd gained his feet, he pushed Hugh aside to confront the surgeon, standing in the doorway wearing an expression of crazed bewilderment.

Uh-oh, thought Hugh, taking in Geary's frigid eyes and the white-knuckled grip with which he held his knife.

The fat knight planted his hands on his hips and thrust out his massive chest. "All right. Where is she?"

Geary's piercing gaze scanned the room; a muscle jumped in his jaw.

"I said where is she?" Sir Roger demanded.

The answer was menacingly soft: "I don't know."

"Rubbish! You've spirited her away. You want her for yourself, after all. Well, she's not yours—she's mine! Bought and paid for. So hand her over."

"Not quite bought and paid for," Geary said quietly through a clenched jaw. "You still owe me a pound."

"Hah!" Sir Roger turned to Hugh, his expression one of amused outrage. "Will you listen to the man? He thinks I owe him money!" Turning, he indicated the empty solar with a sweep of his huge arm. "For what? I don't see anything here worth paying for, do you?"

"You'll fetch her back," Geary said. "She can't have gotten far. And even if you don't, you still owe me. I brought her back. Your reeve will attest to that."

Sir Roger shook his head. "Oh, no, Pigot. I don't pay until I've got her. *You've* got to go fetch her back."

"What did you call—"

"*You'll* fetch her back ... *Pigot.* And you'll return her to me, with her face whole, or I'll—"

"You'll what?" the surgeon growled as he grabbed Sir Roger by the hair and circled behind him, the big knife at his throat. "You'll *what*, you fat, whining bag of entrails?"

Sir Roger's face grew chalk white. His eyes, half buried in folds of fat, sought out Hugh's. "Help me, Hugh. Get this maniac off me. *Please!*"

A strange sense of tranquility overtook Hugh. He spread his hands wide, allowing himself a small smile. "I don't seem to have a weapon handy, Sir Roger. I'm afraid I can't help you."

"Then *talk* to him, for God's sake!"

"Can't really think of anything to say. Sorry."

Geary snickered and pressed the knife further into the fleshy throat. "For nine years I've sold my services to you, you great, worthless, maggoty bucket of lard. I've put up with you for one reason and one reason only—money. If there's no money to be had from you, your existence no longer serves a purpose." His fist tightened around the handle of the knife.

"No!" wailed Sir Roger, furiously crossing himself. "I need to make confession! I can't die without absolution! I'll go to hell!"

"Most likely." The knife became a blur as Geary whipped it across the fat throat. Hugh closed his eyes. He heard a strangled groan, felt hot droplets spatter him. The floor shook; something landed heavily in the rushes.

When he opened his eyes he found Sir Roger facedown at his feet—and Will Geary's chilly gaze boring into him. "Help me to find her."

Hugh backed up a step into the main hall.

Geary walked toward him, wiping the knife absently on his tunic—strange, considering how fastidious he'd always seemed. Clearly he was even less in control than usual. "I've got to find the bitch and make her suffer. On top of everything else, she's cost me a pound sterling. Damn!"

Wheeling around, he kicked the nearest object— one of the giant sacks of grain heaped against the wall. A gasp emerged from behind the sack.

Oh, no ...

The mad surgeon grinned. "What have we here?" He grabbed the sack and flung it aside, revealing Constance huddled against the wall. Snickering, he reached for her. "Now we're going to have a little fun."

Her foot shot out with lightning speed, ramming him in the stomach. He toppled over, sucking great lungfuls of air, as she darted to her feet. She ran, but he grabbed her leg, and down she went. She kicked and clawed, but he stilled her with a knife to the chest.

"Stand up," he demanded breathlessly.

She did.

"I promised," he said, "that I would punish you exquisitely, and I always keep my promises." He turned her toward the corner staircase that led to the undercroft and urged her forward with the knife. "We'll have more privacy downstairs," he said. "Move!"

Not knowing what else to do, Hugh uttered a quick and heartfelt prayer for guidance as the two disappeared in the stairwell. In the silence following their departure, he thought he heard hoofbeats in the distance.

Corliss concentrated on taking deep breaths as she descended the narrow, winding stairwell. *Keep your head ... keep your head ...*

If Will had been insane before, he was doubly so now. She felt the tip of the knife quiver as it propelled her down the stairs. She shivered as she entered the chilly undercroft—a vaulted cellar lit only by a handful of arrow slits set high in walls of moist rock. On the west side, hazy slices of sunlight streamed through the slits to play over the barrels, baskets, and chests lining the walls of the musty chamber.

Will prodded her forward until she faced a wall fitted with hand and leg irons, then chucked his knife into the earthen floor and reached for her. "No!" She turned abruptly, but he seized both hands and swiftly shackled them above her head.

He retrieved something from a corner—a huge mallet. The handle was almost as long as a man, and the head—which had the dull, heavy gleam of lead—was adorned with a spike. Corliss had seen farmers use such a tool for driving stakes and the like, but she suspected Will's intent to be a good deal less benign. He tested the mallet's weight in his hand, then brought his face very close to hers. His pupils were so small that his eyes looked blindingly silver.

"The first time I met Roger Foliot," he said, "he brought me down here and had me watch while he used this to crush a young man's legs. And all I could think was, if *I'd* been charged with punishing a runaway, I wouldn't have stopped with just the legs. Punishment needn't be so crudely simple. It can be elevated to an art, if one truly has the soul of an artist. Of course, art takes dedication and perseverance . . . and a certain measure of natural talent. All of which I have in abundance."

He smiled and stepped back, taking practice swings with the mallet. "The legs first, just to give you a taste. Then the rest."

Rainulf's mount was in a lather by the time he reined the poor beast in and dismounted in front of Roger Foliot's manor house. A man appeared at the top of the staircase leading to the upper hall. Although a stranger to Rainulf, he appeared to recognize him. He gazed heavenward and executed a frantic sign of the cross. "They're inside," he called out. "Downstairs. This way."

Rainulf raced up the outer stairs and through the main hall to a winding staircase in the corner.

"Here!" The man handed him a dagger. "It's all I've got, but you're welcome to it."

Rainulf took the dagger and descended the stairs silently, hoping to take advantage of the element of surprise. He paused at the bottom and heard Will Geary's voice: "Shall we begin?"

As he stepped out into the undercroft, Rainulf thought *Let him have his back turned!*

He didn't. Will blinked at him, his expression of astonishment turning into amusement as he took in the dagger—a pitiful weapon with which to defend oneself against a mallet of the size he wielded. Rainulf's heart lurched when he saw Corliss against the wall, her hands in irons. She met his gaze, her mouth forming his name.

Rainulf, she pleaded silently, *Go ... please! He'll kill you! Don't make me watch him kill you.*

"Move away from her," Rainulf told Will.

"Or what?"

"Or this." Corliss saw Rainulf shift his grip on the dagger and throw it, aiming for Will's chest. Perhaps madness imparted superior reflexes, for his opponent moved as the blade approached, taking it in the upper left arm, where it stuck. He screamed and yanked it out, then began to laugh uproariously. "Congratulations—you've unarmed yourself. And done yourself a disservice in the process, for pain only makes me angrier."

Will tossed the dagger into a corner and wrapped both fists around the handle of the mallet, swinging it in wide arcs as he edged toward Rainulf. "What about it, Magister? Shall we see what pain does to *you*?" He charged, aiming the weapon at Rainulf's head. Corliss screamed. Rainulf ducked and struck out with a foot, catching Will in the leg.

An enraged bellow filled the undercroft as Will toppled to the ground. The mallet rolled away, and he reached for it as he rose. Rainulf, on his feet, kicked it away and grabbed Will by the tunic, landing him a hard punch to the head.

Will staggered, but recovered quickly, hunkering down low and ramming his fists into Rainulf's stomach. Rainulf countered with blows of his own.

Corliss shut her eyes, listening to the brutal sounds

of fists against flesh ... the grunts of pain. *I can't bear this.* ... When she looked again, Rainulf and Will were circling each other, bloodied and wary.

Will glanced toward the mallet lying a couple of yards away. Rainulf saw this and dove for it, but Will was closer and got to it first. Seizing it, he spun around to face Corliss, brandishing the weapon.

"Nay!" Rainulf grabbed the head of the mallet. Will wrenched it away and slammed it into Rainulf's midsection. He doubled over, gasping, then straightened and lunged for the mallet again, but Will sidestepped him easily.

"The only way you can stop me," Will said as he took up position in front of Corliss and prepared to swing again, "is by killing me, and I don't believe you've got the stomach for that."

Rainulf pressed a hand to his middle and rasped, "I killed on Crusade." And tormented himself about it for years afterward, Corliss knew.

"That was a long time ago, Magister." Will grinned, as if at a child who'd overestimated his own abilities. Turning toward Corliss, he hauled back with the massive weapon, aiming for her legs. "You've forgotten how."

Rainulf moved with breathtaking speed. This time he seized not the mallet, but Will's head, closing his hands around it and twisting sharply. The mallet fell from Will's hands. He grew rigid, and looked startled for a moment; then his eyes closed and he went slack. "It's not the kind of thing one forgets," Rainulf said grimly as Will slumped to the floor, limp and—Corliss quickly realized—lifeless.

A flood of almost painful relief consumed Corliss; her eyes filled with tears. She wanted to say something, but couldn't wrest words from her throat.

Rainulf took her face in his hands and rested his forehead against hers. "Oh, God ... Corliss." Working quickly, he freed her hands from their shackles.

Her legs were trembling. She didn't know whether she was laughing or crying; tears streamed down her face.

"Come." Wrapping an arm around her, he guided her up the curved stairwell. Hugh Hest crossed himself and fell to his knees when he saw them.

"Let's get out of here," Rainulf said. They stumbled down the outer stairs and made their way to the middle of the lawn before their legs gave out simultaneously. Sinking to their knees, they held each other tight, Rainulf murmuring reassurances and words of love until at last she stopped shaking.

"Do you think you can ride?" he asked, drawing back and threading his fingers through her hair.

She nodded as she used her sleeve to wipe the blood from his face.

"Let's go home, then."

Fresh tears stung her eyes. *Home.* It sounded so wonderful . . . and so impossible. Summoning all her reserves of strength, she said, "I . . . I can't. I can't go back with you, Rainulf."

He gripped her shoulders hard. "Corliss . . ."

She caressed his cheek with her palm. "I can't. I left once. I don't think I can do it again."

"You don't have to leave."

"I can't stay in Oxford. 'Twould be too painful."

A hint of a smile played around his lips. "Would it be less painful if you had your own shop?"

She shook her head. "I can't afford my own shop yet, and besides—"

"I bought Mistress Clark's shop for you," he said.

Corliss stared at him, dumbfounded. "Why did you do that?"

He shrugged. "Oxford can use another bookshop. Especially one as ambitious as what you have in—"

"Oh, my God." She rose to her feet, her hands fisted at her sides. "You did it, didn't you?"

"Did what?"

"Bought me a gift, as if I were one of your . . . your . . ."

"Ladies who aren't mistresses?

"Aye!"

He stood and reached for her, but she pulled away. "Believe me, Corliss, I never bought one of them her own business."

She turned her back to him. "Am I supposed to be flattered? Rainulf, why did you have to—"

"I thought you'd be pleased." He paused. "I even hired someone to paint a sign to go over the front door—'Corliss Fairfax, *Venditrix Librorum.*'"

She slowly turned to face him. "Corliss what?"

He tilted her chin up and kissed her lightly. "Fairfax. It's not a parting gift, you little idiot. It's a wedding gift." His smile widened . . . and then faded. "That is . . . if you'll have me."

"If I'll . . ."

"I know I've been more trouble than I'm worth. I'll try to be easier to deal with, though. I've resolved to take your advice and keep my doubt in the lecture hall, where it belongs."

"Now *you're* being an idiot," she chided gently. "How could I possibly not want to marry you? But . . ."

He grinned and wrapped his arms around her. "Then you'll—"

"Rainulf . . . please. You know I can't." His crestfallen expression took her by surprise. How could he not understand? What was he thinking of? "It's completely impossible."

"Why? The chancellorship?"

"For one thing."

"I've done a lot of thinking about the chancellorship the past few days. And about teaching. And about you." He kissed her forehead. "I've tried to just . . . live in my skin, as you put it. To just be myself and feel what I feel, want what I want. I discovered that what I want, more than anything, is you."

He closed his mouth over hers and kissed her, a long, sweet, ardent kiss full of hope and promise.

"And," he added when they drew apart, "to teach. You were right about that. I decided Bishop Chesney will just have to find another chancellor to create his grand university."

"No one else is qualified—you know that."

He shrugged carelessly. "Then Oxford will just have to remain a humble little *studium generale* until he finds someone who is."

"I'm pleased," she said. "You were born to teach. But there's still the matter of Wulfric's baptism. Father John said we were spiritually bound when we lifted him from the font. The Church won't let us marry."

He chuckled and pressed his lips against her eyelids. "You and I were spiritually bound from the moment we met." He kissed her nose. "From the beginning of time." He brought his mouth to hers, murmuring, "We'll be bound to each other always and forever. I hardly think that should be an impediment to marriage."

"Aye, but the Church—"

"The Church," he said, "makes her rules, and from time to time the thoughtful man must think of ways to circumvent them. I've already put Father Gregory to work arranging a dispensation for us."

"Is that possible?"

He smiled indulgently. "If I can get out of my vows, anything is possible."

"You've thought of everything, haven't you?"

"I've always been thorough."

"I know." She allowed herself a wicked grin. "Quite exceptionally thorough at times."

He kissed her again, deeply, his hand gliding down her throat to her chest. She felt his frustration as he tried to caress her through her tunic and the strip of linen wound tightly around her breasts. Breaking the kiss, he growled, "Damn those bindings of yours. And those chausses and tunics. The first thing I'm going to do when we get back to Oxford is order a dozen kirtles made up for you. Silk kirtles," he murmured. "Thin ones that rustle when you walk."

"That's the *first* thing you're going to do?" She asked playfully as she stroked his shoulders, his back, his hips . . . pressing him to her as she moved languidly against him.

"Perhaps the second," he amended with a smile. "You've turned into quite the tease, my love."

She had to ask: "Please . . . say that ag—"

"My love," he whispered against her lips. "My love," he breathed into her ear. "My love." He kissed her temple, her hair, and then her mouth again, with great passion and heartbreaking tenderness. "My love . . . from the beginning of time until the end. Always and forever. You'll always be my love. Always."

Epilogue

Rad the Peddler stood half-hidden behind a pillar in the shadowy nave of St. Mary's Church. Outside, an enormous crowd of townspeople, their hands filled with seeds, waited in the bright September sunshine. Rad had never heard so many people make so little noise; their silence made him feel warm and shivery at the same time. They were quiet out of respect, he knew. They were quiet because Oxford's Master of Schools, Rainulf Fairfax, was getting married.

The bride and groom had already exchanged vows on the church steps. Now they were inside. They knelt on the altar, their backs to the hundreds of black-robed scholars who'd gathered to witness their union, as Father Gregory celebrated the nuptial mass.

Masses had always perplexed Rad. Ordinarily he avoided churches entirely, but he was happy to be here today—happy and proud. Master Fairfax had wanted him here, had asked him to come! He'd even tried to get Rad to stand up with him, alongside the Saxon baron. But he couldn't have. He never quite knew what to do in church. And there'd be all those people, looking at him. . . .

No, he was happier where he was, in back where he wouldn't draw attention. He could see everything he needed to see. He could see *her*.

She looked like an angel, in glimmery silks and veils, emeralds sparkling as she moved. She didn't look like a boy anymore, that was for sure. Of course, he'd always known she was a woman, right from the very start. She had a woman's silvery light shimmering around her. How could anyone ever have been fooled?

She belonged to Master Fairfax now. Rad didn't have to watch out for her anymore. Master Fairfax would take care of her. He was smart. He'd figure out a way to do it so she didn't know he was doing it.

A baby cried. A woman in the front row—the Saxon's young baroness—hefted the squalling child onto her shoulder so he could look around. Rad smiled as he watched the infant's curious little eyes survey the sea of black robes. He liked babies. He'd rather watch a baby than listen to mass any day.

The couple rose for the kiss of peace. Master Fairfax, tall and elegant in a long, ceremonial black tunic, received the kiss from Father Gregory and turned to Corliss, lifting her veils. They smiled at each other. Rad thought maybe she was crying; he wasn't sure, because then the kiss began, and it didn't stop for a long time.

The scholars laughed and cheered as their magister and his bride walked hand in hand down the aisle, smiling as if they'd never stop. Rad tried to hide in the shadows as they passed through the nave, but they saw him anyway. They both embraced him.

She kissed him on the cheek.

When they reached the steps of the church, the townspeople roared happily and showered them with their seeds. Master Fairfax pulled her into his arms. They kissed as the seeds rained down on them, twinkling like gold dust in the sunshine. Her silver light was glorious against the bright blue sky.

Rad stood mesmerized by the sight ... the sparkle of gold, the glow of silver, the kiss. It looked like everything good and beautiful in the world.

It looked like Heaven.

Dear Reader,

The reader response to my first medieval romance, *Falcon's Fire,* has been so gratifying! Many of the people who wrote told me how taken they were with Rainulf and how eagerly they were awaiting his story. I hope *Heaven's Fire* has been worth the wait. It was a joy to write. I adore Corliss, and of course I've been madly in love with Rainulf since he first introduced himself to me on the deck of the *Lady's Slipper* so very long ago.

In my next medieval, *The Black Dragon,* I step even further back in time, to the year 1067 A.D. and the aftermath of the Norman Conquest of England. Young Faithe of Hauekleah, widowed by the conquering Normans, is horrified to learn that they've given her hand in marriage, and therefore her estate, to one of their own: the notorious Luke de Périgueux, a Norman soldier known as the Black Dragon for his ruthlessness against her people. She could refuse the marriage, but that would mean losing her ancestral farmstead, an even worse prospect than giving herself to some Norman devil. *The Black Dragon,* a Beauty and the Beast tale set in a turbulent and earthy time, will be a 1997 release from Topaz.

One of the most exciting things about being a romance writer is hearing from my readers. Please write and let me know what you think of *Heaven's Fire.* If you include a stamped, self-addressed business-size envelope, I can add you to the mailing list for my newsletter. Write to me at P.O. Box 26207, Rochester, NY 14626. My E-mail address is P.RYAN10@GENIE.GEIS.COM.

Pat Ryan

Don't miss Patricia Ryan's next
romance, *The Black Dragon*,
coming soon from Topaz.

*The Cambridgeshire manor
of Hauekleah, 1067* A.D.

"Milady! Milady!"

Faithe looked up from the daisies she was tying together to see young Edyth burst through the open doorway of Hauekleah Hall, red-faced and breathless. Ewes' milk spilled from her two full buckets, soaking into the fresh rushes.

"Edyth!" Faithe scolded. "Slow down. You're getting the new rushes all—"

"There's two Normans headin' up the road," the dairymaid gasped. "One of 'em must be him—the Black Dragon."

Silence fell over the great hall as the house servants turned apprehensive gazes on their young mistress. Faithe's fingers grew cold, and she realized she had stopped breathing. She set down the daisy garland and rose from her bench, summoning all the composure at her disposal.

"His name," Faithe said quietly, "is Luke de Périgueux."

Edyth blinked. "But Master Orrik, he says they call him the Black—"

"His name is Luke de Périgueux," Faithe repeated,

her gaze sweeping every member of her raptly attentive audience, "and as he's to be your new master"— she drew in a steadying breath—"and my lord husband, you are to address him with respect or suffer the consequences. Am I understood?"

Faithe's *famuli,* unused to such threats or admonishments—for Faithe rarely found them necessary— exchanged uneasy glances.

"Am I understood?" Her words were softly spoken but clear.

There came a chorus of murmured assents, accompanied by the occasional pitying look. They viewed her as a martyr, she realized, first widowed by the Normans, then forced to choose between marriage to one of their own or the loss of her ancestral home.

Faithe smoothed her kirtle, hearing the crackle of parchment in the pocket of her skirt. The letter from Lord Alberic, one of King William's new tenants-inchief and the earl to whom she now owed allegiance, had been treacherously courteous in that manner the Normans seemed to have perfected. He'd told her little about the husband he'd chosen for her, only that his name was Luke de Périgueux and that he was famous for his soldiering skills, skills used against her people . . . her husband.

Know, my lady, his lordship—or, more likely, his lordship's clerk—had written, *that you would be fully within your rights to refuse this marriage. In such an event, I will endeavor to dispose of the estate by other means.* In other words, she could marry the notorious Luke de Périgueux and remain at Hauekleah, or refuse to marry him and let the Normans seize it, in which case she'd no doubt spend the rest of her days languishing in a convent somewhere. Worse, the sprawling farmstead that had been her family's for over eight hundred years would fall into the hands of strangers, *enemy* strangers.

Better to give myself to some Norman devil and keep

Hauekleah, she'd decided. Her grandmother, Hlynn, had done much the same, entering into a loveless marriage to a Danish warrior chief rather than relinquish Hauekleah to the Northmen. Finding farm life tiresome, Thorgeirr had stayed but a single summer, long enough to build a new manor house and plant the seed of Faithe's father in Hlynn's belly, and then moved on. Although it was rumored that he lived for many more years, Hlynn never saw him again, and counted herself lucky.

Perhaps, Faithe told herself as she stepped out into the warm spring afternoon, she would be as fortunate. Her new husband, used to the ways of the sword and the crossbow, might be so bored here that he'd leave her in peace and she'd have Hauekleah all to herself again.

All eyes were upon her as she walked slowly through the entry gate that provided passage through the stone wall surrounding Hauekleah Hall, a wall that had stood since Roman times. Shielding her eyes against the sun, she squinted down the dirt path that connected her manor, and the village it encompassed, to the great market towns and thoroughfares to the west.

Two men on horseback rode toward her on that path, one tall in the saddle, the other slumped over. Faithe's mouth felt chalky. She wiped her damp palms on her plain wool kirtle. Field workers abandoned their plows and livestock and ran to join her house staff in what felt like a defensive phalanx around her. As always, their loyalty and affection moved her immeasurably. If for their sakes only, she could never abandon Hauekleah to the Normans.

As the riders drew closer, she saw that the upright man gripped a sword in one hand and the reins of both mounts in the other. The insensible one swayed in his saddle. The fellow with the sword dropped the reins and grasped the other man's tunic to keep him from falling. Leaning over, he whispered something into his companion's ear and gently patted his shoulder.

"He's hurt." Faithe stepped forward.

Nyle Plowman grabbed her arm. "Nay, milady . . ."

"That man's hurt." Faithe shook Nyle off and approached the two men, wondering which one was Luke de Périgueux. They were sizable men, both of them, with hair as black as ink. The injured man—she saw the blood now, soaking his tunic and one leg of his chausses—had his hair shorn in the Norman style, while the other wore his unusually long and bound in back.

Faithe's servants followed her, some of the burlier men flanking her protectively. The man with the sword pointed it at them as they approached. Faithe hesitated, along with the others. It wasn't the weapon that gave her pause, for although he was armed, he was but one man, and they were many; it was the way he looked at them.

Some of his hair had come loose and hung over his broad forehead, enhancing his feral image. His eyes were deep-set and fierce against oddly swarthy skin. Black stubble darkened his grimly set jaw. He didn't look like any Norman soldier Faithe had ever seen. He looked untamed . . . as menacing s a beast with its fangs bared.

Faithe's gaze traveled to the ornate pin holding his mantle closed—a golden disk inset with black stone in the shape of . . . a dragon. A black dragon. *Merciful God.*

"That's him," someone whispered.

Faithe stifled a sudden urge to cross herself. So this was the man to whom she would be wed within a matter of days, this dark, savage creature with murder in his eyes and a quivering broadsword in his hand.

Forcing her fear beneath the surface, Faithe stepped forward, her escorts at her sides.

"Stop right there," de Périgueux ordered in French-accented English as he thrust the weapon toward them. "I'll have none of your Saxon tricks."

Faithe clutched her skirt in both fists. "We mean you no harm."

"Tell that to my brother. We were ambushed in the woods not a mile back."

"Ambushed!"

He scanned the faces behind her. "Where's your mistress? My brother needs help. He's badly wounded."

Faithe lifted her chin, consciously ignoring his sword which was aimed directly at her. "I'm Faithe of Hauekleah. I'll tend to your brother."

His intense eyes pinned her with a look of astonishment. He surveyed her from head to toe, taking in the unbound hair that hung loose over her breasts, the humble kirtle she'd shortened for field work, and the patched slippers soiled from that morning's gardening. As usual, she'd gotten too caught up in the day's chores to bother much with her grooming, and as a result she looked more like an untidy adolescent than the chatelaine of an estate like Hauekleah.

Even when she did bother to dress in her finest silks and adorn herself with jewels, Faithe looked far younger than her four-and-twenty years. She'd learned to counteract her youthful appearance with displays of unflinching confidence, even when they had to be feigned. Therefore, when Luke de Périgueux's attention returned to her face, she steadfastly met his eyes.

He held her gaze. She saw his throat move as he swallowed, his penetrating eyes darkening from brown to black. So ... it unnerved even the infamous Black Dragon to come face to face with his betrothed.

Faithe nodded toward his sword, still aimed at her throat, and said quietly, "If you'll lower that, my lord, I shall see to your brother."

WE NEED YOUR HELP
To continue to bring you quality romance
that meets your personal expectations,
we at TOPAZ books want to hear from you.
Help us by filling out this questionnaire, and in exchange
we will give you a **free gift** as a token of our gratitude.

- Is this the first TOPAZ book you've purchased? (circle one)

    YES   NO

    The title and author of this book is: _____

- If this was not the first TOPAZ book you've purchased, how many have you bought in the past year?

    a: 0 - 5   b 6 - 10   c: more than 10   d: more than 20

- How many romances in total did you buy in the past year?

    a: 0 - 5   b: 6 - 10   c: more than 10   d: more than 20 ____

- How would you rate your overall satisfaction with this book?

    a: Excellent   b: Good   c: Fair   d: Poor

- What was the main reason you bought this book?

    a: It is a TOPAZ novel, and I know that TOPAZ stands
       for quality romance fiction
    b: I liked the cover
    c: The story-line intrigued me
    d: I love this author
    e: I really liked the setting
    f: I love the cover models
    g: Other: _____

- Where did you buy this TOPAZ novel?

    a: Bookstore   b: Airport   c: Warehouse Club
    d: Department Store   e: Supermarket   f: Drugstore
    g: Other: _____

- Did you pay the full cover price for this TOPAZ novel? (circle one)

    YES   NO

    If you did not, what price did you pay? _____

- Who are your favorite TOPAZ authors? (Please list)

- How did you first hear about TOPAZ books?

    a: I saw the books in a bookstore
    b: I saw the TOPAZ Man on TV or at a signing
    c: A friend told me about TOPAZ
    d: I saw an advertisement in_____magazine
    e: Other: _____

- What type of romance do you generally prefer?

    a: Historical   b: Contemporary
    c: Romantic Suspense   d: Paranormal (time travel,
       futuristic, vampires, ghosts, warlocks, etc.)
    d: Regency   e: Other: _____

- What historical settings do you prefer?

    a: England   b: Regency England   c: Scotland
    e: Ireland   f: America   g: Western Americana
    h: American Indian   i: Other: _____

- What type of story do you prefer?

  a: Very sexy   b: Sweet, less explicit
  c: Light and humorous   d: More emotionally intense
  e: Dealing with darker issues   f: Other

- What kind of covers do you prefer?

  a: Illustrating both hero and heroine   b: Hero alone
  c: No people (art only)   d: Other_____

- What other genres do you like to read (circle all that apply)

  Mystery   Medical Thrillers   Science Fiction
  Suspense   Fantasy   Self-help
  Classics   General Fiction   Legal Thrillers
  Historical Fiction

- Who is your favorite author, and why?_____
  _____

- What magazines do you like to read? (circle all that apply)

  a: *People*   b: *Time/Newsweek*
  c: *Entertainment Weekly*   d: *Romantic Times*
  e: *Star*   f: *National Enquirer*
  g: *Cosmopolitan*   h: *Woman's Day*
  i: *Ladies' Home Journal*   j: *Redbook*
  k: Other:_____

- In which region of the United States do you reside?

  a: Northeast   b: Midatlantic   c: South
  d: Midwest   e: Mountain   f: Southwest
  g: Pacific Coast

- What is your age group/sex?   a: Female   b: Male

  a: under 18   b: 19-25   c: 26-30   d: 31-35   e: 36-40
  f: 41-45   g: 46-50   h: 51-55   i: 56-60   j: Over 60

- What is your marital status?

  a: Married   b: Single   c: No longer married

- What is your current level of education?

  a: High school   b: College Degree
  c: Graduate Degree   d: Other: _____

- Do you receive the TOPAZ *Romantic Liaisons* newsletter, a quarterly newsletter with the latest information on Topaz books and authors?

  YES   NO

  If not, would you like to?   YES   NO

  Fill in the address where you would like your free gift to be sent:

  Name: _____
  Address: _____
  City:_____Zip Code: _____

  You should receive your free gift in 6 to 8 weeks.
  Please send the completed survey to:

  Penguin USA•Mass Market
  Dept. TS
  375 Hudson St.
  New York, NY 10014